About the

Michael B Jones grew up in Lancashire before going on to study in Leeds and Bremen. After a ten-year career in Germany, working in jobs as diverse as washing up in hotel kitchens, parading around supermarkets dressed as a costume character, and being a senior manager within the corporate sector (which was much less fun!), he moved to London.

With a view to meeting some new people, and on the advice of a friend, Michael went along to a gay and lesbian Country and Western dancing club called Renegade Ranch, as one does. This was with some reticence, not being a huge fan of the musical genre at that time. Pleasantly surprised with the welcoming and attitude-free approach, however, he persevered with the dance steps (and the music) and shortly afterwards met his now long-term partner there along with many, many good friends.

Michael still enjoys going to two wonderful, long-running clubs - Lines and Bears in London and Prairie Dogs in Manchester - and spends his time living between these two cities. Same Again Please is his first novel.

Same Again Please

MICHAEL B JONES

MBJ

First published in Great Britain in 2010 by Michael B Jones

A CIP catalogue record for this book is available from the British Library

ISBN 978-0-9565552-0-5

Edited by Nick Stellmacher in London
Cover design by Maya Jones in Blackrod

Michael B Jones
24 Russell Chambers
Bury Place
London
WC1A 2JU

www.michaelbjones.co.uk

Printed and bound in Great Britain by CPI Anthony Rowe Ltd, Chippenham, Wiltshire

For Christopher

Acknowledgements

There are many people I want to thank for helping me to write Same Again Please. Marcel Wiel for encouraging me to start it. Christopher Tynes for helping me to keep going, and to actually finish it. My mum Rita for her assistance and candour, and for telling me that I should prune down some of the more 'intimate' scenes. Janette Coogan for her review and her insistence that I should spice things back up – sorry mum.

Other friends I would like to thank for advice, support and invaluable, honest feedback are: Caroline Wilson, Susan Rogers, Brent Payne & Terry Riley, John Manning, Steve Johnson & David Carr, Nancy Kitson, Christopher Cox, Edgar Rolf-McGregor & Roman Dubowski, Patrick Alexander, The Phils (Gledhill & Oliver) and Jules Baxter.

Thanks also to my brother Martin, his partner Karen and my nephew Luke, who all managed to smile sanely and appear genuinely interested, enquiring on my frequent visits about how the novel was progressing.

I'd especially like to thank my wonderful (and ruthless) editor Nick Stellmacher for all his professional insight and skilful guidance. Huge thanks also to my niece Maya Jones for her creativity for the cover illustration and design.

Most of all I'd like to thank my partner Isao Tanahara who has patiently endured my rambling on about 'The Book' on a scale I could never have done, had things been the other way round. For years he has listened with patience, affection and loving support as I said the words 'I'm almost finished with the final draft' - only to find that what I actually meant was 'I'm just starting on the next draft, and what do you think about this or that?' There's absolutely no way I could have written this without him. *Arigato and totemo aishiteru!*

Chapter 1

Clare gripped her seat as the plane made its perilous descent through the low clouds. It landed with a sharp jolt and then skidded before making a hook to the left and slowly crawling back to the main terminal. Clare's head still felt fuzzy from all the champagne she'd drunk - one of the business class perks she had long become accustomed to. She decided to check the damage. Fishing around in her Gucci handbag she located the compact, the small silver one that Jack had given her for Christmas last year. It was nestled amongst the nicotine patches, nicotine chewing gum and other long-haul flight essentials of the twenty-first century. She flicked it open and was unimpressed with what she saw. This wasn't quite how she had planned to look for her second date. The flight had been a long one, and the incessant talking from the man in the next seat, the drinks and the dry air had all taken their toll. Although Clare had mildly enjoyed the flirtatious chatter with him at times, she certainly had no desire to 'stay in touch'.

Real sleep had escaped her and she had had to make do with a couple of hours of alcohol-induced semi-consciousness. She felt as if she'd been forced into a body vice for the duration of the flight, with her head clamped at ninety degrees to her shoulders and her legs twisted into a figure of eight. Her back ached and her buttocks were numb. She felt genuine pity for the passengers sitting behind her in economy, especially those souls unfortunate enough to have been trapped in the dreaded 'middle seats'. They would just be coming to the end of a gruelling eleven-hour physical and psychological battle with their neighbours for that most coveted of prizes – the armrest.

Clare scowled as she continued her self-appraisal in the small mirror. One glance at her hair confirmed the worst. It looked as if it had been through a combine harvester. Entering the arrivals hall looking like this was out of the question. In an attempt to restore her hair to its former glory she worked with her travel brush and teased a few strands, but it was useless. She still appeared to be wearing a small bale of hay on her head.

It was two weeks to the day since Clare had first met Luke in Japan and she couldn't wait to see him again. She'd recently been there quite regularly on business and had just arrived again for a short trip. Before flying home last time, they'd agreed that Luke would pick her up from the airport tonight. He was then going to drive them to her hotel so that she could freshen up in time for a late dinner at a local restaurant. Annoyingly, she had been unable to speak to him from London because his phone didn't seem to be working whenever she tried to call.

In a final effort to look half-decent she daubed the sponge from the compact with the fine particles of the all-concealing powder and then smoothed it onto her face. The flattering effects of the 'instant lift' applied earlier that day had completely disappeared, leaving a deep wrinkle across her forehead. It was perfectly horizontal and not dissimilar to a scar from a machete wound. Clare found to her horror that she could actually press the edge of the sponge into the wrinkle itself. She then ran her black eyeliner pencil around what she thought were her eyes, and applied a fresh coat of red lipstick. Doing so, she spotted a small fishbone wedged firmly between her front teeth, probably from the mullet she'd eaten yesterday. She tried to ease it out with a wooden toothpick, but succeeded only in lodging it higher up towards her gum. She tried pulling it, but the bone snapped, leaving half of it poking out behind her teeth. Oh fuck it. She'd have to floss the remnants later in the hotel, rather than make further removal attempts on the plane. She snapped the compact shut.

'You look great,' boomed American John as she started to get up.

'Thanks,' said Clare, brushing off her short skirt. 'But I don't feel it.'

'Say, perhaps we can get together for dinner sometime while you're in Osaka,' he suggested.

Clare was appalled at the idea.

'Here's my card,' he said, thrusting it into her hand. 'Call me when you're free. It's the number for my secretary in our Osaka office.'

That'll be never, she thought, dropping the card into her handbag.

'We'll see,' she replied, 'but I've got a very tight schedule. It was nice meeting you.'

And with that she pushed herself forward and tried to squeeze past a woman who was wrestling with cases and bags in the overhead locker. Clare had learned to travel light and carried only a small, but smart, travel case. She breathed in deeply and just about managed the transition from size fourteen to size six and back to fourteen again, while the woman almost tried to hoist herself into the locker in search of her duty-free gin, which had gone astray.

As Clare approached the exit she smiled at the minuscule stewardess, who was standing by the door to thank her for her custom. After saying goodbye she climbed down the stairs from the plane. Apparently there was a problem with their boarding bridge and they would now need to take a transit bus to complete their journey. The heat and humidity, unusual for April, hit her as she boarded the bus to join in what appeared to be a game of Twister. The bus was filled to capacity and Clare reeled from the lack of both oxygen and air-conditioning. It was like a sauna, and a nasty looking damp patch started to appear on her close-fitting blouse, just below her left breast.

Shit, she thought. This was all she needed for her grand entrance. Thankfully it was only a short ride, during which she had to endure having her nose and mouth stuck like a leech to a less than hygienic sleeveless armpit and something rammed against her crotch. Still, it was better than the Northern Line.

Running into the building, Clare already had her cigarette packet poised. She was gasping. She knew the routine and headed straight towards the smoking area, where she promptly lit a cigarette and took a deep, luxurious drag. Satisfied with the hit, she exhaled, piping half a cigarette's worth of smoke through her nostrils. She stared through the glass panel and watched the steady stream of passengers scuttling past, casting scornful looks at her. Perhaps they thought that Clare and her fellow inmates had been sectioned and were being incinerated for suspected swine flu. Grinding her cigarette into the overfilled ashtray, she left the room in a cloud of smoke and rushed to passport control.

Would he have flowers? What would he say to her? Clare could hardly contain her excitement – but she had to! – more damp patches were out of the question. OK, she mused, so she'd only had a few drinks with Luke in a downtown bar. They hadn't had sex. All right, she thought, wrestling with the facts, so they hadn't even kissed properly – unless you counted the parting 'granny kiss' on her cheek. But he had been impressed with her job, and they'd polished off three bottles of champagne together – which she'd paid for. What's £360 between friends? She was sure he'd fancied her, and began to gain more confidence as she charged towards the Nothing to Declare gate. Unfortunately, her passage was blocked by someone resembling a female sumo wrestler dressed in a tight military-style outfit. Sumo's not inconsiderable ballast was contrasted by her short-cropped hair, looking as if it had been ripped out from the roots rather than conventionally cut with scissors.

'Christ,' muttered Clare.

She could do without this, though thankfully there was just the one small bag for Sumo to rummage around in. After scrunching her new designer two-piece in every conceivable way, Sumo proudly produced a small bottle. She slowly opened her cavernous mouth to speak, revealing a single blackened stub on her top gum and a few teeth at odd intervals on the bottom.

'And what are these?' questioned Sumo victoriously, thrusting the bottle under Clare's nose.

'They're just sleeping tablets.'

Sumo stared at Clare, narrowing her eyes.

'Try one if you don't believe me,' said Clare, becoming irritated.

Sumo unscrewed the bottle and tried to insert her forefinger to ease a tablet out. Failing miserably she shook one onto the palm of her hand instead, eyeing it suspiciously.

'Trust me, they're not very exciting – just prescription drugs.'

'Why do you need sleeping tablets?'

'Why don't you go to the dentist?' retorted Clare quietly.

'What did you say?' asked Sumo.

'I said why don't you go and check your list. These tablets are harmless and I think I'm allowed to bring my medication into the country. Here's my prescription.'

Sumo read it, looked at Clare's passport and then handed the bottle back to her before waving her off.

At last she was in Arrivals. It was packed with important-looking suits holding placards:

'Mr Moffitt', 'Señorita Garcia', 'Herr Schultz'.

She scoured the entire area with the precision of an astronomical telescope, but there was no placard for 'Miss Clare Houghton' - and there was no sign of Luke. He hadn't come. Unable to bear the disappointment she lit another cigarette, not giving a damn whether or not she was risking capital punishment. She switched her phone on. After a few moments it beeped. Thank goodness, she thought, breathing out. This'll be a text message from him.

'Hope you have a great trip and don't do anything I wouldn't do :o) see you when you get back love Jack.'

Much as she loved her friend Jack, his wasn't the text that

she wanted to read right now. But there were no other text messages. There weren't any voicemails or missed calls either. Clare tried calling his phone again. Still nothing. What was wrong with the damned thing? He must have got caught up somewhere. Or maybe he'd got the wrong flight? These were her first thoughts. She came to the conclusion that he'd probably left a message for her at the hotel. Of course, that's it. Clinging to this shred of hope, Clare went outside to find a taxi.

Forty minutes later and she was checking into the Osaka Metropol. It was Clare's favourite hotel. Besides the air miles, hotel rewards and supermarket points that she would earn from her stay, the panoramic views from the top floors were amazing. She loved looking down through the windows to watch the mayhem on the streets below, while she was tucked away high above in her ivory tower.

'Good evening Liu, *konbanwa,*' she cooed in her best Japanese, reaching the familiar check-in desk after being whisked through the over-enthusiastic revolving doors. Clare had wanted to do something different after finishing university, before starting her career proper, and had decided to teach English in Japan for a few months. She'd stayed for almost two years.

'Miss Houghton! Good evening to you too. It is a pleasure to welcome you back again,' the receptionist responded with a polite smile, accompanied by a deep bow.

Clare wasn't really in the mood for bowing or other social niceties. She wanted news from Luke. She couldn't hold back any longer.

'Are there any messages for me?' she burst out.

'I'll just go and check,' said Liu, surprised.

There had to be something, surely.

'I'm sorry, Miss Houghton,' he said returning, 'there are no messages for you.'

Clare felt as if she'd been punched in the stomach. This just wasn't fair. How could he?

'All right, thanks Liu,' she said bravely. Not able to give up completely, she added, 'I'm expecting an important call from a man called Luke…something.' Clare then realised that she had no idea what his surname was. 'Please contact me immediately when he calls.'

'Yes, Miss Houghton,' he said with another bow.

Realising that there wasn't anything else she could do, Clare decided to get on with the matter of checking in.

'I have a double room booked for two nights. Smoking.'

'Certainly, Miss Houghton,' he replied, tapping away at his keyboard. 'I'm afraid we don't seem to have your reservation, when did you book?'

Clare could feel her face reddening as her temper started to flare. Could anything else go wrong today? 'Last week, through Peak Travel,' she barked.

'Yes, Miss Houghton,' said Liu quietly, taking a wise step backwards. 'I'll see what I can do.'

Clare lit a cigarette and rapped her purple fingernails on the marble desk.

'We are very busy this week and only have one double room left on the executive floor, but it is a no smoking room. Is that OK?'

'NO, Liu, it isn't. Please can you look again?'

Liu furrowed his brow in concentration as he scoured the screen. Clare knew she was being a bitch and did feel sorry for him, but she needed her smoking room, now more than ever.

'So, I have found a smoking room but it is a single and on the first floor,' he said a few moments later, sounding quite pleased with himself.

Clare winced. She hated being practically at ground level.

'OK I'll take it.' Frankly, she'd have taken a smoking cat basket if need be.

Armed with her plastic key Clare made her way towards the lift, followed by an eager bellboy. She'd tried to explain that she could manage on her own, but eventually gave up trying to prise her bag from his iron grip.

'Thank you,' she said, turning to the loitering bellboy on reaching the room. 'Oh, all right,' she added, handing him a tip.

She slammed the door shut and threw herself down on the bed. Where was he? Why hadn't he come to meet her at the airport? After considering a range of other possible reasons and excuses that she could have pacified herself with, she finally faced up to the more probable truth. He just didn't fancy her. He wasn't going to call. She had been looking forward to seeing him again so much, but she was determined not to cry. So she'd been let down again. What's new? Her last boyfriend, Richard, had popped out from their home to buy some milk one evening and had never come back. She would have called the police had it not been for the brief note she'd found later, neatly folded underneath the kettle. It was such a bolt out of the blue. No reasons. No explanations. That was the last she had heard from him. Another four years of her life wasted!

Clare felt filthy after the long plane journey. She undressed and padded over towards the bathroom. Just as she was putting a foot inside, she caught an unwelcome reflection of herself in the mirror attached to the back of the door. Why can't hotel rooms have bathrooms with tinted mirrors and soft lighting, she thought? Detesting the bright overhead beam, Clare put her hands around the small, illuminated paunch. She couldn't believe that after all her recent trips to the gym, the electronic body patches and a weekly 'green-tea-only' detox it was still there.

After a long hot and cold shower Clare began to feel marginally better as she dried her shoulder-length, chestnut-coloured hair. She glanced at her watch. It was almost midnight local time, but she thought she would console herself with a nightcap in the bar before going to bed. She re-applied her make-up with a keener eye than she had had on the plane, and put on her new outfit. She looked at herself critically in the horrid mirror, in various postures and from several angles. Her magic hairdryer and revitalising products had worked

8

wonders, turning the prickly hay back into a soft, flowing sheen. The skirt was a bit short for her size of thigh, but as she was tall she thought she could just about get away with it. The low-cut top hugged her breasts and if she left the top button unfastened on her jacket, her paunch would be disguised. This was what she was planning to wear for her meeting in the morning.

Smoothing out the creases in her skirt with a few swift strokes, Clare decided to have a quick coffee and another cigarette before going downstairs to the bar. She liked the little cans of coffee that were available in Japan, a small supply of which were kept constantly hot in drinks vending machines. There was a vending machine on each floor of the hotel, so she popped outside to buy a can. On returning to her room Clare took a sip of the strong, sweet liquid and then lit a cigarette. Although she felt a sense of excitement about being back again, it was darkly overshadowed by the intense disappointment of being let down – or simply ditched – by Luke. She picked up the phone and called Jack for some sympathy.

Chapter 2

'Hello,' answered Jack. 'Clare! You got there safely I take it?' He listened as she reeled off the tales of the flight, the irritating chain of events that ensued on arrival and, of course, how Luke had stood her up.

'He didn't come to the airport? Oh no, how awful. What, nothing at the hotel either? I'm sure there must be a good reason. Yes, you're right, he's a bastard. I know it has. But you need to try and put him out of your mind for now. You must be exhausted and you've got to get some rest and psyche yourself up for your big meeting in the morning. That's my girl. OK. I will. See you on Friday.'

Jack hung up and strolled over to the fridge. There was still some chardonnay left from last night so he poured himself a large glass and sat down at the breakfast bar. He did feel sorry for Clare. It just never seemed to work out for her with the men she wanted, and she deserved better. They'd been close friends since studying together in London in the late nineties.

It was mid-afternoon and already getting a bit cooler, despite having been a lovely, warm spring day. He got up and took his glass through to the lounge and out onto the roof terrace, where he'd been catching a few rays earlier on. He watched the sun as it started to disappear behind the treetops and leant against the railing. Mrs Petrovski, one of Jack's neighbours, was digging in her window boxes.

'Good afternoon, Mrs Petrovski! Your geraniums are looking wonderful.'

She waved back at him with her trowel from across the

road. Jack adored the view from the terrace, which was remarkably quiet considering the flat was just off Gower Street. He loved living in Bloomsbury. Soho was only a short walk away and Covent Garden, where he worked, was literally around the corner. He'd made a wise choice when deciding what to do with the inheritance that his grandfather had left him and had bought his home. The flat was a well proportioned maisonette, which occupied the top two floors of a Georgian end-of-terrace. The living room, open-plan kitchen and washroom were on the third floor, with the main bedroom, second bedroom and bathroom on the top floor above. Clare had lived there with him during university, but she had her own place now in Finsbury Park.

Closing the patio doors behind him, Jack went back inside and refilled his glass. After taking a mouthful of wine he decided it was time he got ready – Brian would be here soon. He turned his stereo on and went upstairs to change. He took off his t-shirt and studied himself briefly in the mirror, before putting on a black shirt, singing along with the music. After pulling on his jeans he tweaked a few strands of his short dark hair with some gel.

'You'll do,' he said, looking in the mirror again before going back downstairs.

The doorbell to number nineteen rang. Jack pressed the door release button on the intercom.

'Hi man,' said Brian, brushing past to go through to the kitchen after Jack had let him in.

Jack followed him and they sat down at the breakfast bar.

'Wine?'

'Cheers, just what I need after the day I've had. I'm knackered. It's taken me hours to fit some shelves I made for a woman in Shoreditch.'

Brian had his own furniture-making business in Hackney, where he also lived. Jack poured him a glass from a fresh bottle.

'Well you chose the right day to have off, didn't you, you lucky bastard? What have you been up to?' asked Brian.

'Not a lot, really. Got up about ten, had a stroll around Russell Square, ate lunch in my favourite Italian restaurant, Amici's, and then chilled out on the terrace for a couple of hours.'

'So you didn't pull then?'

'How many times do I have to tell you? I don't go to Russell Square to pull,' replied Jack, pretending to be bored with Brian's predictable comments. 'I just love it there in the mornings before the lunch and tourist crowd take over, the oak trees, the squirrels, the café.'

Central London waking up had always thrilled Jack and gave him a sense of anticipation as to what the day ahead would bring.

'Sure you do,' said Brian dryly. 'And I watch porn films because the storylines are always so interesting. I know what people like you do in places like that.'

'What do you mean people like me?'

'You know, queers.'

'Get stuffed.'

This was their usual banter. Brian and Jack had been best friends for years, despite one being straight and the other gay. Jack had never tried it on with Brian. Well, not since he came out to him one night at a party when they were eighteen and in their first year of university. They'd both had far too much to drink and Jack had groped Brian's ass, with both hands, in a dark corner. Leading up to the grope they had been embraced in a manly hug after slurring how much they liked each other – as mates – and how you can't beat a proper friendship between two blokes. Jack hadn't consciously meant anything by it, but conceded that holding your mate's ass during a hug was perhaps an excessive expression of affection, particularly for a heterosexual man.

And that's how Brian found out that Jack was gay. Brian just took it in his stride. He'd been through it all before with his brother, George. George was now an actor and had been living in New York for the last five years.

'Clare called,' said Jack, lighting a cigarette.

'Oh yeah, did she get there OK?'

'Yes she did, but that new guy Luke that was supposed to meet her off the plane didn't show up, surprise surprise. She was so upset. I wish she could meet someone decent. She's really stressed out with her job and she desperately needs to get laid, the poor cow.'

'That's a shame. But our Clare can sometimes be a bit abrasive, though,' said Brian, topping up his glass. 'I can imagine it putting some guys off.'

'Oh come off it. She's good-looking, rich, successful, and she's got great tits and a huge house in Finsbury Park,' said Jack.

'And she thinks that she's a size too big, as she's told us more than once,' said Brian.

'Lots of men like a fuller figure. Anyway, she's only a fourteen and size isn't everything.'

'That's not what you usually say.'

'Ha fucking ha. Right, get that wine down your neck and let's be off.'

Brian stood up and put his jacket on.

'Soho OK?' asked Jack, casting a look at Brian's jeans. 'Bit tight for you, aren't they?'

'They're new. Don't they look alright?'

'They look great – though they don't leave much to the imagination. I'll have to keep a close eye on you. Don't want you attracting the wrong kind tonight, do we now?'

'Let's go,' Brian laughed, pushing Jack through the door.

It was quite cold now as they strolled down Shaftsbury Avenue towards Cambridge Circus, which marked one of the corners of the gay square mile and the beginning of Old Compton Street.

'Where do you fancy first?' asked Brian.

'Do you mind if we have a quick one in Spartacus?'

Spartacus was Jack's favourite bar.

'Sure, great. We won't be able to stay too long though. We're meeting Rachel later for a drink.'

'Are we?' said Jack.

'She called me yesterday, said she's got some news.'

Brian and Rachel had slept with each other once, about eight years before. It was all thanks to Clare. She had invited her new friend Rachel, who she had met at the gym, to her sister's wedding reception. Jack and Brian were going too. Clare could tell immediately that Brian and Rachel fancied each other. But Clare knew that Rachel, like her, was looking for someone she could have a relationship with. She also knew that Brian wasn't yet at the nesting stage of his life, to put it mildly. Not wanting Rachel to get hurt, Clare shared her insider knowledge with Rachel in the hope that it would put her off doing anything stupid. It did put her off, but not enough to stop her from sleeping with him – that very night.

If they had been more 'in tune' on the commitment side Rachel would definitely have wanted to see Brian again. Brian *had* wanted to see Rachel again on a no-strings-attached basis - and she might have done it, had she not been asked out by someone called Edward. She chose Edward over Brian, and Brian actually respected her more for it. It was probably a good decision, because two years later Rachel married Edward and now had Brian as one of her best friends instead.

The bar was quiet for a Wednesday evening and they managed to get seats next to the window.

'A bottle of chardonnay please,' Jack said to the young Italian barman.

'So how are you getting on with that bloke from your office?' asked Brian, sitting down.

'It's impossible. I think my gaydar is telling me that he's interested in me and he's always friendly whenever I have to speak to him or bump into him making coffee in the kitchen. I think he's gorgeous, but something's holding me back from making the first move. Besides, he's the trendy new A&R guy and I'm a mere clerk,' he joked, refilling Brian's glass and then his own.

Jack worked in the accounts department of an independent record label called Spring Records.

'What's A&R?'

'Artists and repertoire, he's responsible for discovering our new talent and then nurturing them into the megastars of tomorrow.'

'Well, my advice is to be careful mate. I've told you before, don't shit where you eat.'

'Oh, that's rich, coming from you.'

Brian had recently done an excellent job making a bespoke bed for Doris Elliot, a famous photographer. Not only had he made and installed the bed - he had tested it to rigorous standards.

'That was different,' defended Brian, smiling and taking a quick mouthful of wine.

'It was at work, wasn't it?'

'Yes, but she came on to me.'

'Ah, I see. And why is that different?'

'We both knew the score, which is not the same thing as you and your bloke.'

'Well I'll never bloody know what he wants if I don't do something to find out, will I?' exclaimed Jack.

Jack had been single for just under a year now, though he had had a few one-night stands. He'd been with his last partner, Nathan, for about six months before they'd decided to call it a day. Nathan had been offered a job he really wanted up in Edinburgh, and they'd agreed that long-distance relationships rarely work out. It had all been very amicable and they were still in touch.

'Did you ever see her again?'

'No, you're all right.'

'So you just exploited her?'

'Well what would you have done? The woman knelt up on the bed in her knickers and bra just after I'd finished assembling it, saying that there's a nice tip in it for me if she's satisfied with the suspension.'

'Is that a new sideline that you're running then?'

'Oh, fuck off. I've got my bills to pay as well, you know. You'd have done the same thing if it had been Mr A&R up on the bed.'

They started laughing, causing a few heads in the bar to turn towards them.

'Oh, there you go,' chirped Brian, 'one for you over there. He's looking at us now.'

'Where?'

'Behind you, at the bar.'

Jack stole a surreptitious glance into the mirrored wall over by the entrance door.

'The one with the ripped jeans and tattoos?' asked Jack hopefully.

'No, the one next to him with the grey perm.'

Jack couldn't see the man in the mirror because his view was blocked by a bottle of vodka. He wasn't sure he wanted to, but curiosity got the better of him and he turned around.

Their admirer was perched on a barstool and squeezed into a pair of black leather trousers that were so tight they made Olivia Newton-John look like she was wearing slacks in Grease. He smiled at Jack, who quickly turned away.

'Well, thanks a lot, mate. Now I've got that tired old Pancake Ass smiling at me,' he cursed.

'I thought you liked leather, don't you?'

'You're so funny.'

'Well, it looks like you're in there,' grinned Brian, glancing behind Jack. 'Your friend's on his way over here.'

'Shit.'

Pancake Ass minced towards them.

'Hello! My name's Brian and this is my friend Jack.'

'A pleasure to meet you both. I'm Donald. Have you got a light by any chance?' he asked, waving a cigarette, seemingly mesmerised by Brian's hazel eyes.

'You can't smoke in bars anymore – it's been banned for years now,' said Jack.

'Yes I know dear, but it's still my favourite conversation starter,' said Donald, as he swivelled around on one heel to go.

'Oh, don't go. Jack was just saying how he'd like to get to know you better.'

'He was? I'll just get my drink.'

'And what the fuck was that all about?' asked an irate Jack, once Donald was at the other side of the room and out of earshot.

'It's just a bit of fun. Besides, I want to see how you're going to get out of it,' said Brian under his breath, as Pancake Ass returned.

'So, what do you two boys do when you're not around here?' asked Donald, polishing off his gin and tonic.

'I'm a furniture designer and maker.'

'And I'm in the music business.'

Although he wasn't in the least bit interested in Donald, Jack still did what he always did when he met someone new – which was never to admit to working in an accounts department in your opening line. To do so inevitably resulted in as little interest as if he had said that he worked in a soap factory.

'How exciting,' said Donald, leaning over the bar to catch the barman's attention.

'Same again please, Enrico. Boys?'

'Not for us, thanks. We've still got this,' said Brian, refilling their glasses from the bottle.

'And are you two an item?' Donald asked Jack, continuing with his assessment of this surprising development to his evening.

'Yes,' said Jack quickly, before Brian could get a word in. 'We've been together for about two years now, haven't we, hon?' he added jovially, grasping Brian's thighs, causing him to choke on his wine.

'He's only kidding,' blurted Brian. 'I'm actually straight, but I come here with Jack when he's on the pull.'

Donald looked at Brian's short blond hair and eyed his biceps.

'Is that so?' he drooled.

Jack leant over towards Donald and whispered, but just loud enough for Brian to hear.

'It's all part of the game. Brian pretends that we're not together when we go out and that he's 'straight'. I've then got to pick up a guy and take him back to the flat. Brian comes back after about half an hour and catches us at it, pretending to be shocked. We're then supposed to beg him to 'give it a try' and promise not to tell his 'girlfriend'. After a while he gives up, strips off and joins in. Don't you, darling?'

'What a load of crap,' spluttered Brian. 'Don't believe a word he says.'

Donald drained his gin and tonic, supposing that Jack was probably only having a laugh, but half-hoping that he wasn't.

'Look at the time!' shouted Brian, bringing Donald back down to earth with a crash. 'We're going to have to leave you, I'm afraid.'

'What a pity. I was just going to ask if you could perhaps help me with a wardrobe that I need making.'

'Well…I don't know. I'm a bit busy at the moment, he answered, hoping Donald wouldn't pursue it.

'Oh I'm sure you can squeeze it in, Bri,' chipped in Jack.

'That really would be marvellous, if you were able to. And if you could pop round to my house with your portfolio sometime soon to talk about it, that would be even better. Here's my card. Do you have one?'

'Thanks,' said Brian, taking it cautiously. 'I'm sorry, I don't seem to have any with me,' he lied, pretending to look in his jacket pocket.

'Don't worry,' said Jack, coming to the rescue. 'I've got the new one that you gave me last week right here in my wallet,' he added, taking it out and handing it triumphantly to Donald.

'Splendid.'

'OK, come on, handsome,' said Jack to Brian, standing up.
'Well, it was lovely meeting you Donald.'

'Er, yes, bye Donald,' stammered Brian, wanting to throttle Jack.

'I'll be in touch about that wardrobe!'

Donald climbed back up onto his barstool.

'Same again please, Enrico – there's a dear.'

Chapter 3

Clare hadn't slept at all well in the confines of the small bed that she had been given, and she had only picked at her breakfast. She hadn't been able to resist checking one last time for any messages at reception, but there was nothing. Fuck him then.

She left the hotel at eight-thirty and was now studying her notes carefully in a taxi. She was preparing for her meeting with Mrs Suzuki, President of a national chain of top-end women's clothes stores called Just for You. The street was jammed solid and Clare was getting worried about being late. It was a very important meeting. Clare worked as Head of International Sales for a company called Destiny, based in London, which owned the ladies-wear designer label of the same name.

Today was the day that Clare hoped Mrs Suzuki was going to sign up for the exclusive distributorship of Destiny product in Japan. Mrs Suzuki just had to say yes. Clare had worked incredibly hard on this deal and had been up night after night with her nose glued to her laptop, developing business plans and profit projections. It had, after all, been her idea. She'd made a strong case to persuade her boss, Grace, who was Destiny's Chief Executive, into supporting investment in the Japanese market. Both her annual bonus and her head were potential casualties if she didn't pull it off.

The car hadn't moved for a full four minutes and it was now almost nine o'clock.

'*Sumimasen, sumimasen*,' she said, furiously patting the

driver's left shoulder to get his attention. 'Is there no other way to go? It's only another three blocks.'

The driver just shrugged, clearly displeased with the unfamiliar physical contact from a passenger.

'OK, then STOP!' she yelled.

After she had thrust two 1,000 yen bills at him, the taxi door automatically opened and she quickly climbed out. Clare stood on the pavement and lit a cigarette, taking a drag that was so deep she almost burnt her lips. Stabbing at her phone and striding at a furious pace, she put a call through to Just for You's offices, explaining that she was on her way. It was considered highly disrespectful to be late for a business meeting in Japan, especially if it was you doing the selling.

'Fuck,' said Clare, seeing that it was now twenty past nine, as she sped past reception and got into the lift which would take her up to the familiar eleventh floor. This was where Mrs Suzuki conducted most of her business and where they'd met a number of times before.

Clare knocked gently on the meeting room door.

'Enter.'

As Clare went in she saw Mrs Suzuki sitting at her usual place, facing inwards at the centre of the enormous table, with three suits on either side of her. She always positioned herself there for morning meetings so as to make sure that she was backlit by the sun rising behind her, which presented her in the most favourable way. For Clare this usually meant being half-blinded by the strong sun and made her feel as if every line and wrinkle had a dedicated spotlight blazing down on it.

Mrs Suzuki stood up. She had an immaculate, short black bob and she was sporting a crisp, black trouser suit that looked as if it had cost thousands.

'Good Morning, Mrs President,' said Clare deferentially, commencing her obligatory bow, at about a sixty degree angle.

'Welcome, Miss Houghton,' replied Mrs Suzuki curtly, also bowing to the same level.

Shit, thought Clare, she's angry. Now she would have to

bow further as a mark of respect, reflecting their relative seniorities. Breathing in, Clare descended to the full ninety degrees. She was extremely conscious of her paunch and the fragile button that was being tested to its limits in this most uncomfortable of postures. She was sure this was her punishment for being late. Feeling her blood returning to its natural equilibrium on her ascent, Clare started her apology.

'Please excuse my lateness, but the traffic from....'

'Can we get on?' interrupted Mrs Suzuki firmly, sitting down again. 'Allow me to introduce my lawyer, Lance Rubenstein of Rosenberg & Hoffmann, New York,' she said, gesturing to the tall, distinguished looking gentleman to her right.

'Miss Houghton,' said Lance, rising to shake Clare's hand, presenting her with his business card.

Clare held the card with both hands as if it was the original Magna Carta and stared at it for a few seconds. It didn't do in Japan to just put a newly presented card down on the table, or even worse, straight into your pocket.

'My eldest son Takeshi,' continued Mrs Suzuki.

The handsome young man seated to the right of Lance rose and bowed. Unsure of the degree of bow required for the son of the Senior One, Clare offered him a half smile as she went down. The wizened man at the end of the table to Mrs Suzuki's far right looked about ninety-five and wasn't introduced. He hadn't taken his beady eyes off Clare since she'd arrived.

Turning to the three gentlemen sitting on her left, Mrs Suzuki continued with the introductions.

'And these are my Financial, Operations and Merchandising Directors, Tanahara-san, Hayashi-san and Katsumoto-san.'

The men stood up and then all starting bowing simultaneously in different directions and at varying degrees. Completely thrown, and with her back still aching from the flight, Clare opted for deep nods directed at each of them individually, accompanied by a swaying motion that made her feel dizzy. Exhausted, she sat down and distributed her business cards to the men.

'Miss Houghton,' began Lance. 'As you know my client is keen to move forward with the concept of selling Destiny merchandise throughout her stores. We have worked through the draft contract and agree to most of it in principle.'

But... thought Clare.

'But Mrs Suzuki would feel more comfortable if we could incorporate a twelve-month trial period without having to commit to the minimum order that you suggest. Could that work for you?'

Was he kidding? Grace would have her hide if she agreed to anything of the kind! The whole point of the deal was to get two million pounds worth of stock as a minimum initial order, with payment up-front.

'Mr Rubenstein,' started Clare.

'Lance, please.'

'Lance, when we first began these talks it was clear that both Just for You and Destiny want the same thing. We want a strategic partnership that will offer the Japanese lady the opportunity to enjoy exclusive, high-quality merchandise that is only available in your stores. We want a collaboration of vision, retail expertise and capital to make our investments yield sustained, long-term revenue and profit streams for both organisations. I truly believe (she lied) that the idea of toe-dipping into the market will be detrimental to achieving those objectives.'

Clare didn't really have a choice but to play tough. Either she got the agreement for the initial minimum order or she needn't go back to the office next week.

'Mrs Suzuki,' said Clare, turning to face her. 'We have made many concessions to our standard agreement for you and we are offering you substantial reductions on our wholesale prices. We have also pledged to develop specific merchandise for the Japanese market.'

Clare reached into her bag for the samples that had been

sent directly to her hotel. It was time to deliver the punchline of the sales pitch.

'Let's not forget why we are all here.'

Mrs Suzuki lit a cigarette and then squashed it out again after two wasp-like drags.

Holding up a white silk blouse, Clare continued.

'When your customer buys this blouse in one of your stores, she is not just buying a blouse. Oh no. It's much more than that. She's buying her Destiny.'

Clare paused for effect, focusing her gaze on the garment, wondering if she hadn't gone just a little over-the-top.

Mrs Suzuki lit another cigarette and then extinguished it before walking around the table to stand next to her. Clare always found her unsettling at such close proximity, mainly because of their height differences. She stooped slightly, trying to make eye contact. Mrs Suzuki rubbed the bottom of the blouse between her thumb and forefinger.

'Isn't the quality amazing?' said Clare enthusiastically.

Mrs Suzuki suddenly screwed up her face and then returned to her seat. Not knowing quite what the problem was Clare looked across to Lance for some sort of signal, but none was forthcoming. Mrs Suzuki lit yet another cigarette as she leant back to say something to the Wizened One. Clare was fascinated by the ashtray, which was brimming with cigarettes that all seemed largely unsmoked. She contemplated her own ashtrays at home with barely anything in them but ash – she usually smoked half the filter as well.

She could just about hear what Mrs Suzuki was saying.

'There's an old Chinese proverb that says that the fish always starts to smell from the head first. That woman's got an oral hygiene problem and this deal stinks too.'

The Wizened One nodded his agreement. Clare was mortified. Her Japanese wasn't perfect, but she'd got the general gist. Just managing to maintain her composure her tongue brushed against something sharp behind her front teeth. Oh shit! She'd forgotten to floss last night at the hotel and the bloody fishbone was still stuck between her teeth after two days, probably with half a pound of festering mullet attached to it. Concluding that she must reek like a plate of *sashimi* that had gone off a week ago, she prepared herself for the worst.

Mrs Suzuki whispered something to Lance and then sat back.

'Er… my client has... erm... decided, that she needs some more time to think it over. She is concerned that perhaps there is not such a good strategic fit after all,' said Lance, looking a little embarrassed.

I've fucked it up, thought Clare.

'Thank you for taking the time to come and see us,' he said smiling, but with finality. He reached across to shake her hand.

So that was that, surmised Clare. She was dismissed. Knowing better than to protest, she stood up and thanked them all for their time, bowed again and left the room. Despair filled her head. What was she going to do?

*

'Cheers,' slurped Clare, knocking back her fourth glass of *sake*. Although it was still only just gone ten in the morning Clare had decided that she needed a drink and had found a small bar that was still open a short walk away in downtown Doyama. She'd been able to pick up some dental floss and mouthwash on her way and had finally managed to remove the offending bone from between her teeth. The strong rice-wine was beginning to kick in and she was starting to relax a little. She could hardly believe that she'd been in Japan for a little over twelve hours and already things had turned out so devastatingly. She was going to have to think things through and try to work out a way to get the negotiations with Mrs Suzuki back on track within the next twenty-four hours, before her return to London. She was due on the lunchtime flight back home tomorrow.

Lighting a cigarette Clare looked at her watch. Ten-thirty. She nodded at the barman, signalling that she wanted another drink. He looked as if he'd had a long night, but still managed a smile as he obliged.

'What am I doing?' she suddenly said out loud. She was supposed to be having lunch at the *Tsunami*, one of the finest whale-meat restaurants in the city. She should be drinking champagne with Mrs Suzuki, toasting their future working relationship together. Not sitting alone with a barman in a dead end back-street bar, drunk on cheap *sake*.

Well, not entirely alone, confirmed the stiletto heels clicking into the bar from the right.

'Absinthe on the rocks,' said the red-haired woman to the barman in a Canadian accent as she eased herself onto the barstool next to Clare. 'Make it a large one.'

There is hope then, thought Clare. The day she starts drinking over-proof spirits before lunchtime is the day to check into the Betty Ford Clinic.

'Cheers, darling. This helps me to unwind,' she said, holding up her glass.

Unwind? Clare decided that there must have been enough absinthe in that glass to tranquilise a small horse.

'You just finished as well, doll?' asked the woman.

'Finished? Finished what?' answered Clare, glancing down at her new friend's boot-clad legs. 'No, I er, I just came out of a business meeting actually. My name's Clare, by the way.'

'I'm Marleen. You're new, aren't you?'

'New?'

'Don't worry. It can be a bit slow to begin with, but once you make the right contacts it'll pick up. The western girls fly out here thinking it works the same way as back home, but it don't, sweetie.'

Clare shot a glance at the barman for help and pointed at her glass for another drink.

'Let me get that for you, honey, you can't have made much last night dressed like that.'

'No, really, there's no need,' protested Clare. And anyway, what did she mean 'dressed like that'? The two-piece had cost her a small fortune – probably more than Marleen's entire wardrobe put together.

She studied Marleen's face for a moment, though it was half-hidden behind the masses of red curly hair that flowed down to her waist. Not the most attractive face she had ever seen, though it was difficult to tell with all the make-up and the low lighting of the bar. She noticed a small L-shaped scar just above her left eyebrow.

'Well I've had a bitch of a night,' announced Marleen loudly, shattering Clare's trance.

'Have you?' asked Clare politely, not sure if she wanted to know the details.

'I'll say. If I see another Japanese ass that wants caning, biting, spanking or whipping in the next few days I swear I'll beat it so hard it'll drop off.'

'What do you mean?'

'You know, S&M, bondage, domination. That's what I do. And I'm fucking good at it,' touted Marleen, taking another swig of absinthe.

'And men actually pay you for that?' asked Clare.

'Pay? Oh they pay all right – and top dollar for me, darling,' guffawed Marleen, shaking back her red mane, for a mad moment resembling Bonnie Langford, pre-pantomime.

'Candy, you're gonna have to wise up a bit if you're gonna make it over here. Jesus, what do you normally do, Little Bo Peep?'

'My name's CLARE, and no offence, but I'm a business woman, an accountant actually.'

Marleen pouted back and paused.

'Well I suppose that explains the costume. So tell me then, Miss Accountant, what's a grand lady like you doing in a dive like this, in the middle of Japan, drinking *sake* for breakfast?'

'Breakfast?' laughed Clare, 'I've been awake for hours. I've just had a horrible morning, that's all.'

'Well, are you gonna tell me about it?'

'Oh it's not really very interesting, just disappointing.'

'C'mon, I'm all ears,' encouraged Marleen, offering Clare a cigarette.

Clare gave in and told Marleen the whole story, except the part about being stood up by Luke. She couldn't bear the humiliation of sharing that with a complete stranger.

'So you lost out on the deal just because you forgot to clean your teeth and your breath smelled like a cat's butt-hole?'

Clare resented the analogy, though she feared it wasn't too far from the mark.

'Well there was nothing else. I know I was late, but that doesn't usually result in expulsion.'

'Jeez, that's a tough one. Maybe she was jealous of your fine looks? Or maybe she's got the hots for you?' suggested Marleen, trying to cheer Clare up a bit.

'I really doubt that. She's happily married with four children,' laughed Clare.

'Well it had to be something, didn't it?'

'But I'm sure it wasn't that. Look, Marleen, we've both had quite a lot to drink and thanks for listening, but I don't think that this is going to sort out my mess. I'm going to have to go.'

'Suit yourself. Good luck, Candy,' slurred Marleen, before ordering another drink.

Her brain was obviously addled by absinthe, thought Clare, but her heart seemed to be in the right place.

'Thanks for listening. Take it easy,' shouted Clare over her shoulder as she turned to walk out of the bar.

It was boiling hot now as she stumbled out onto the road to hail a cab. Luckily she didn't have to wait long, and within twenty minutes she was back at the hotel. She struggled to stand up straight as she approached the reception desk to collect her key from Liu. It was hard to believe that it was only about three hours since she'd left the hotel earlier.

'Miss Houghton,' he said gaily. 'Back already? I hope you had a successful morning.'

'Hmm,' grunted Clare.

'I have a surprise for you. There has been a cancellation and you have a new room.'

'Really?' said Clare, perking up.

'Yes, The Carlton Suite is free now and we have upgraded you for the inconvenience. Your bags have already been moved.'

'Oh Liu, that's marvellous.' At last something had turned out well. A suite! Perhaps this marked a change in her fortunes.

Clare resisted the wrenching temptation to ask, yet again, if any messages had been left for her. It wasn't easy, but deep down she knew that there wouldn't be any. It was time to move on. Instead she took the lift straight up to the top floor and eagerly swiped the key card through the lock. She'd never stayed in one of the real suites before. It was huge. An expansive lounge with exquisite furniture lay before her as she entered the room. The bedroom was tastefully furnished with a four-poster as its centrepiece, and the ensuite bathroom even had a Jacuzzi bath.

Clare thought it was fantastic. Sitting down on the bed, she suddenly realised how tired she was. Not surprising, really, considering the vast amounts of alcohol she'd consumed over the last two days, with minimal sleep.

'But what am I going to do?' she cried out loud, quickly remembering her other, more pressing problem.

Whatever she *was* going to do, she desperately needed to get a few hours sleep first to try to get over her jetlag. Although she felt exhausted, Clare decided to take a little something to help her sleep better. She reached for her handbag and prodded around for her sleeping tablets, thankful that Sumo hadn't confiscated them at the airport. She hardly ever took them, but always had some on hand for emergencies. Today was an emergency. As she opened the bottle something else dropped out of her bag. She picked it up.

'That boring claptrap,' she said, reading the business card that the man on the plane had given her yesterday. 'John Goldschmied.'

Clare was about to tear up the card when she noticed something else in the bottom right hand corner. 'Rosenberg & Hoffmann,' she said slowly. 'Now where have I seen that before? Of course!'

Clare opened her purse and took out the business cards that she had collected that morning. 'Lance Rubenstein, Rosenberg & Hoffmann, Mrs Suzuki's law firm,' she read, having found the one she was looking for. It was a long shot, but Clare didn't currently have any viable alternative. She picked up the telephone from the bedside table and carefully dialled John's number.

'John Goldschmied's ahffice,' answered a cutesy voice in a New Jersey drawl.

'Oh hello, this is Clare Houghton. Can I speak to John please?'

'I'm afraid he's in a meeting at this time. Can I take your number and ask him to call you?'

'No, this is important. Just tell him that it's Clare Houghton.'

'I'm sorry, miss, but he said to hold all... '

'TELL HIM it's a family emergency!' yelled Clare.

'Hold the line.'

Clare lit a cigarette and waited impatiently.

'John Goldschmied.'

'John, darling, it's me.'

'What? Who is this? My secretary said it was an emergency. Has someone died?'

'Of course not, it's me, Clare Houghton. We met on the plane yesterday.'

There was a pause.

'Oh right, yeah.'

'I'm sorry for dragging you out of your meeting, but I've got some good news! I've managed to juggle things around and was wondering if you'd like to have dinner with me tonight before I fly back to London tomorrow. We had such fun on the plane, didn't we, and we did say that we'd try and hook up?'

John reflected on this. He didn't remember their parting being quite that promising. In fact he had got the distinct feeling that he had been written off.

'Well, I'm sorry, but I've already got plans actually.'

'Oh John, come on. I was a little... tired yesterday. I know a fabulous *sushi* restaurant that we can go to and really spend some time getting to know each other.'

John gave in.

'Well, I suppose I could reschedule. What time?'

'Let's say eight-ish?'

'OK, leave the details with my secretary. See you later.'

And with that he went back to his meeting.

'Leave the details with my secretary,' repeated Clare. 'The cheek of it! Who does he think he is?' The cutesy voice came back on the line.

Clare briskly gave Cutesy the name and address of the venue and then hung up. Physically feeling the weight lifting from her shoulders, Clare picked up the sleeping tablet and washed it down with some mineral water, before lying flat out on the bed. She wasn't quite sure how she was going to play things, but play them she would.

Chapter 4

Rachel had been waiting in Oasis for about half an hour. She was on her third latte and was leafing through a magazine when Brian and Jack arrived.

'Sorry we're late,' said Brian apologetically. 'It's his fault,' he added, laughing again and pointing at Jack accusingly, 'tried to fix me up with an old queen.'

'Oh right, so it wasn't you who started it in the first place?'

'I was just being a mate and you got cold feet.'

They both stopped laughing and looked at Rachel.

'Are you OK?' frowned Brian.

'Of course, well, sort of.'

Rachel lived in Blackheath with her husband, but their marriage had been going downhill for some time.

'Still no better then?' asked Jack.

'Not a bit,' replied Rachel. 'Actually it's worse. Well, it is in terms of my marriage, I've met someone else!'

'What?' spluttered Jack.

'I know. I'm terrible, aren't I? It's not very straightforward either.'

'Can I just get the drinks in before you say one more word?' pleaded Jack. 'Wine OK, Brian? Rachel, what do you want?'

'Cheers, Jack,' said Brian.

'I'll have a glass with you two if you're getting a bottle,' said Rachel.

'And remember, not another word before I get back,' said Jack eagerly, hastening off to the bar.

'So what's going on?' asked Brian, ignoring him.

'I did love Edward once, you know, truly I did. I can still clearly remember the first day we met, shortly after our quick roll in the hay at that wedding reception,' she said, nodding at Brian, with a smile.

Brian grinned sheepishly. He was glad that things had turned out the way they had and that they'd had the chance to become good friends instead.

'You know, he actually went down on one knee to ask me out on a date. It was so sweet,' she said fondly. 'And then, for my birthday about a month after that, he bought me a beautiful gold necklace. It was perfect. Somehow he'd known just what to buy me. He used to be such a romantic.'

'I always thought you two had it made. I mean, all relationships have their ups and downs, don't they?'

'Oh and you'd know, wouldn't you? You've never been with anyone for longer than their next period!'

Rachel's joke was true enough. Brian had still never had a long-term relationship. He'd had many short affairs, but had no intention of settling down until he felt it was absolutely right. Besides, he quite enjoyed being single and was happy only having to worry about himself when deciding what to do or where to go.

'Very funny,' he smirked. 'Does Edward know?'

'What, about my affair? I doubt it very much. He spends all his time at the office. He wouldn't even notice if I dyed my auburn locks blue. We just seem to have drifted so far apart that there's now an ocean between us. He's become like part of the furniture, an occasional chair on which I don't even want to sit occasionally. The sad truth is, I just don't feel attracted to him anymore. It's gone. It's over.'

'Oh,' groaned Jack, banging the bottle and glasses down on the table. 'How can they charge the prices they do in here and then only have one member of staff behind the bar when it's as busy as this! It's outrageous. So, what did I miss?'

Brian poured the drinks while Jack played with a cigarette. He wanted to go outside, but was putting it off because it was freezing cold. Besides, he didn't want to miss anything else.

'When are you going to stop that filthy habit?' asked Rachel. 'If Brian can do it then so can you.'

Brian had given up smoking with the help of acupuncture two years ago on his thirtieth birthday.

'Yes, yes, yes, all right. I'm working on it. So who are you fucking then?'

'That's all you're interested in, isn't it? Sex and scandal. There is more to life you know.'

'Is there?'

'Yes, there is. Look, I'm having an affair, but I can't tell you who with. Not yet anyway.'

'No worries. When you're ready to talk you know we're here for you,' said Brian giving her a hug.

'I bet you've told Clare,' said Jack with disappointment.

Rachel rolled her eyes and laughed.

'I haven't actually, so don't worry, you're not missing out. Besides, Clare's far too busy with work at the moment. When does she get back? She did tell me, but I've been too preoccupied with my own stuff and I've forgotten.'

'Friday,' said Jack, 'the same day that you're coming over to mine for dinner,' he added drily.

'Oh no, I'm sorry Jack, my head's all over the place. I'm afraid I can't make it then.'

'Why, where are you going? Off for a sly weekend fuck with lover boy?'

'You have such a way with words. Actually, I'm off to Berlin again on Friday. I'm interpreting for two designers at a Berlin fashion show and I'll be working over there for about two weeks.'

Rachel was a freelance interpreter and got most of her assignments through an agency called Tongue Twisters.

'Wow, that sounds exciting, and there'll be all those models. I wish I was going. I hope you get to keep some of the dresses,' said Jack.

Rachel laughed.

'Me too, I'm really looking forward to it.'

They chatted away for another half hour, enjoying the company and finishing off the wine.

'Anyway, guys, I'm going to have to make a move. I've got an early start tomorrow. It was great to see you both again. Sorry to be so secretive about things. Just bear with me for the time being.' Rachel got up and gave each of them a kiss. 'See you soon.'

'Take care, Rachel,' said Brian. 'Have a good trip.'

'Yeah, have fun, you adulteress.'

Rachel shook her head and smiled before turning to go.

'Well, what was that all about?' said Jack excitedly after Rachel had left the bar. 'I wonder who she's sleeping with. It must be someone we know.'

Chapter 5

'Christ, what's going on?' shouted Clare, waking up with a start as her travel alarm clock viciously broke her dreams. She lay there for a moment after terminating the buzzing with her fist, not quite sure where she was. She'd been running gracefully, naked, through a field of golden buttercups. A tall handsome man was in pursuit. She was laughing. He was naked. He caught up with her and they both fell down into the scented, soft green grass. He kissed her breasts passionately. She moaned. His tongue slithered down towards her navel. She let out a gasp. He pulled himself up on top of her. She could feel him pressing against her leg. He rubbed his…Bzzzzzzzzzzzzzzzzzz!

Clare desperately patted the bed to the left of her to see if he was still there, but to her grave disappointment she only found a pillow. So *was* it just a dream? The pill had been stronger than expected and she was having difficulty coming to, feeling as sluggish as if she were waking up from hibernation.

After a long shower, two cans of coffee and three cigarettes, Clare finally concluded that there were no buttercups in the room and remembered that she was meeting John Goldschmied in an hour and a half with the aim of salvaging her career. She took her time getting ready, paying great attention to every detail of her make-up. She pinned her hair up, as she planned to wear her diamond earrings tonight, but let a few strands hang loosely at the sides.

Clare examined herself in the dressing table mirror, which was much more favourable than that ghastly thing in the room she'd had earlier. A touch more rouge was needed. Fortunately she didn't have to worry about what to wear as she only had one other outfit with her besides the two-piece she'd worn earlier. The simple black dress, which came to just above her knees, was perfect. It was low cut and didn't leave much to the imagination. A generous spray of Chanel and she was done.

Clare decided to have a quick drink in the hotel bar to steady her nerves before departing on her quest. It was quite busy, mostly with Western guests, but she found a seat at the bar. Ordering a glass of champagne, Clare noticed the piano player in the far corner of the room and was soothed by the ivory chords as they drifted over to her. Taking a sip of the ice-cold bubbles, she suddenly realised how hungry she was. She hadn't eaten all day. Clare spotted some olives and salted almonds in little glass trays on the bar and greedily helped herself to them.

All very civilised, she mused, taking another sip of champagne. And a far cry from the dive she'd been in this morning with that Marleen. I wonder what she's doing tonight, thought Clare briefly. Remembering that Marleen would probably be horse-whipping some businessman somewhere, she decided not to dwell and that she'd better make tracks. She didn't want to be more than ten minutes late.

Sitting in the taxi it dawned on her that she couldn't quite remember what John looked like, only that he'd been a bulky guy with not much hair. Not that it mattered. She had to do what she had to do in order to get talks back on with Mrs Suzuki. A few minutes later and she was in the brightly-lit suburb of Minami. The flashing, colourful neon signs illuminated the streets that were bustling with diners, drinkers and partygoers.

The car stopped outside *Hai Sushi* and Clare paid the driver. The restaurant was actually on the third floor of the building and Clare had to pass through a *pachinko* hall on the ground floor to get to the elevator at the back of the building. Stepping out of the lift, Clare was greeted by two Japanese girls wearing identical pink outfits. After a spate of bowing, Clare explained that she was meeting John Goldschmied and the girls ushered her over towards the bar area.

Three men were standing there. One of them, a broad-shouldered black guy, smiled at her as she approached. Although she'd been a tad tipsy on the plane, to say the least, she was fairly sure that he wasn't the one – though she wished to God that he could have been. She smiled coyly back, envious of the barmaid flirting outrageously with him.

The other two were white and standing facing the bar with their backs towards her. Both fitted the bill in terms of volume. Suddenly she had a flashback and remembered the horrid turquoise suit that John had been wearing on the plane. The one on the left was wearing such a suit. It had to be him.

'Here goes,' she groaned, preparing herself for the worst.

'John,' she purred, taking up a position next to him. 'I'm so glad you could make it at such short notice.'

He turned towards her.

'Clare!' he replied. 'You look stunning.'

She wished she could say the same. He was so not her type.

'Thanks for trying, John, but I must look really dreadful,' she laughed, fishing for further compliments. 'I've been rushing around all day, haven't had time to sleep a wink and barely managed to get changed before coming here.'

'You look just gorgeous, honey. Lemme get yer' drink.'

'Champagne would be lovely.'

Clare took a cigarette from her packet and John's hand shot across almost instantaneously, flicking open his lighter.

'Allow me, ma'am.'

'Why thank you,' said Clare, inhaling deeply.

'Y'know, I've been working in Japan for years and I never came to this joint before.'

'Really? I suppose it's a bit of an insider place. The food's absolutely delicious.'

'I can't wait, but first here's a toast to you, pretty lady,' he said, raising his glass.

'Cheers, John. So what is it you do here?'

'I'm an attorney.'

'Yes, I remember from the plane. What sort of work do you do?'

'Personally, I'm in corporate litigation, but my firm does a whole bunch of other stuff. How about you? Yer an accountant, right?'

'I am indeed, but my focus is more business development and sales now. I work for a company called Destiny in the UK.'

'And what brings you to these distant shores?'

'A business meeting,' she answered quickly. 'Shall we go and eat? I'm starving.'

Clare didn't want to get into the nitty-gritty just yet – he had to drink much more than a few sips of champagne before she could strike. John agreed and a waiter appeared from nowhere to show them to their seats at the *sushi* belt, carrying their drinks as he led the way. Little plates of local delicacies were being transported slowly around the belt for guests to take off and enjoy. The plates were all different colours, reflecting the different prices of their contents. The extensive menu ranged from simple *sushi*, prawn *tempura* and chicken *teriyaki* for the novice Japanese diner, to raw horsemeat, tuna eyes and chilled crab's eggs for the more adventurous.

'So what takes your fancy, John?' she asked, refilling his glass with more champagne.

'Well, let me see now. I think I'll go for a couple of plates of those deep-fried pork cutlets to start with, and then maybe some of the meatballs. Don't know 'bout you, but I can't stand all that raw fish gunk. Know what I mean?'

Clare knew exactly what he meant. She had half a mind to ask the chef to stick a couple of cheeseburgers with extra ketchup on the conveyor belt. He seemed just the type.

'Raw fish is good for you,' she said reaching for a small plate of *maguro* tuna, which was so fresh she suspected the rest of the fish was still alive, twitching in the kitchen. After the two of them had polished off about fifteen plates each and another bottle of champagne, Clare decided that John was sufficiently inebriated for her to start working on him professionally.

'I can't eat another thing,' she declared.

'Me neither,' said John, patting his bloated belly with both hands.

'John, I can't thank you enough for coming out with me tonight. It's been such fun and you've really helped me to take my mind off things.'

Clare tried to make her voice tremble.

'I've had such a terrible day,' she squeaked, feigning a few sobs. Not quite managing the tears, she pulled out a tissue from her handbag and resorted to smudging her mascara instead.

'Sweetheart, what's wrong?' asked John, appearing genuinely concerned.

'Oh it's nothing, just ignore me.'

'Now come on, you can tell me. I can't have my little lady getting all upset now, can I?'

His little lady? thought Clare, eyeing his wedding ring.

'All right, if you can bear to listen, it's about work.'

Clare went on to tell him about why she was in Japan and the meeting with Mrs Suzuki, omitting the part about the fish bone. She finished off by explaining that the meeting had ended for no apparent reason and that she was sure that it had something to do with her lawyer, Lance Rubenstein.

'I see,' said John with a slur. After a moment's hesitation he added, 'What was that name again? Rubenstein?'

'Yes, Lance Rubenstein of Rosenberg and something.'

'But that's my law firm, Rosenberg & Hoffmann!'

'It is?' said Clare, opening her eyes as wide as possible.

'Sure is and I know Lance too. We don't work in the same field but I know he's working on some big deal out here. He's a really great guy.'

'I thought so as well,' quaked Clare, launching into the second part of her act.

'But it's all gone wrong and I'll lose my job and then my house and….'

As she leant forward, approaching the climax, he put his arms around her.

'There, there, no need to cry, we'll sort something out.'

'But how?'

'I'll speak to Lance tomorrow. I'm sure he can smooth things over with his client. He can be very persuasive, you know.'

Clare lifted her head and treated John to a panda-eyed beam.

'Could you really?'

'Sure, now stop worrying about it and relax.'

'Well, thank you so much! The least I can do is pay for dinner.'

'Absolutely not!' he protested, finishing off the last of the champagne. 'But I insist that you come to a *karaoke* bar with me.'

Clare's jaw dropped. She despised *karaoke*.

'Oh, I couldn't. Just look at me, I'm such a mess and I can't sing at all,' she laughed manically, as her voice shot up an octave just thinking about it.

'I won't take no for an answer,' he said firmly, taking Clare's hand in his as he stood up. 'Now you run along to the bathroom and freshen up that little face of yours and let me get the cheque.'

Mortified, Clare headed towards the ladies. She considered bolting into the lift and disappearing into the night, but knew that this was only wishful thinking. If she wanted John to smooth things over with Lance, then she had to go with him. Luckily the karaoke bar was close, and it was only a short stroll during which Clare had to fend off John's attempts to put his arm around her waist as they walked.

'This is the one,' he said, guiding Clare through a curtained doorway and into a tiny bar. It really was minute, with seating space for only about twelve people on cushioned benches. The benches lined three of the walls with the bar occupying the fourth. *Karaoke* screens were suspended from the ceiling and one of the patrons, a Japanese salary man, was already well into a painful version of My Way.

'Isn't this great?' said John excitedly.

'Different,' said Clare, forcing a smile.

'I need some scotch,' he said as they reached the bar.

'Make that two.'

They sat down with their drinks in the only free seats on the left-hand side of the room and Clare knocked back a large mouthful of her whiskey to dull her senses.

'So what song do you want to sing?' she asked, trying to sound enthusiastic.

'I do quite a good Without You. You know, the Neil Sedaka number.'

'I'd love to hear it. Why don't you have a go?'

Clare wanted to get a couple of songs out of the way, make him feel good about it, and then escape back to her hotel while she was winning. But it wasn't to be. John was on a roll. After his opening number received rapturous applause he insisted on more whiskey and more songs.

She was feeling more than a little drunk and quite sleepy after what seemed like at least three back-to-back, out-of-tune renditions of Unchained Melody.

'Are you OK, doll?'

'I'm getting a bit tired to be honest, John. It's been a long day.'

'Well, I can't have that. Come on, I'll take you back to your hotel.'

'No, you stay and enjoy yourself,' she replied, alarmed at the prospect. 'I'll just hop in a cab and head back.'

'Like hell you will.'

'I beg your pardon?'

'You think I fell for that old routine back there in the restaurant? You must have figured something out before you called me. I might be drunk, but I ain't stupid.'

'Look,' he said, in a gentler voice sitting back down next

to her. You're a special lady and I'd just like to spend a little more time with you, that's all.'

'OK, one more drink,' agreed Clare, annoyed that he'd seen through her act.

'I meant a little more time back at your hotel. Do you want me to speak to Lance or not?'

Although she hadn't reckoned with this, she decided it was all or nothing. If she told him where to get off, the whole evening would have been a complete waste of time and she would be back to square one. If she slept with him, she would feel cheap and used. Or would she? Who was using who? Were they not both using each other? She didn't have much time to deliberate.

'I *meant* back at the hotel, asshole,' she shouted. If she was going to go through with this then she certainly wasn't going to let him think that he was calling the shots.

John grinned, mission accomplished.

'Let's go then.'

Although she was putting on a brave face, Clare was getting very nervous in the taxi. It had been four years since she had last had sex.

Thankfully Liu wasn't at the hotel reception when they arrived back. Clare hurried John into the elevator before anyone had chance to see them, and they zoomed up to the top floor.

'Wow, your room's fantastic. Gee, you must be good for your firm to pay what this place costs,' he said staggering inside.

'Yes, I like it too. Help yourself to some scotch. There's plenty in the mini bar over there. I just need to go to the bathroom.'

Clare locked the bathroom door and took a couple of very deep breaths. This whole thing was getting out of hand. She couldn't possibly have sex with him. She found him repulsive. But he holds the magic key that she needs! Clare splashed some cold water on her face and took another deep breath.

'Pull yourself together,' she said to her reflection. 'This can be over and done with and forgotten in no time, and then you can get on the plane and go home with some hope - as opposed to going home to be told at work to clear your desk.'

When she went back out she found to her horror that John was already undressed and lying on the bed in only his socks and underpants, holding a large glass of whiskey.

'Yours is over there, doll,' he slurred. 'And what's with the clothes? I thought you'd gone to slip into something more comfortable?'

Clare picked up her whiskey, wanting to throw it over his head.

'There's plenty of time for that, tiger. Just relax,' she said sitting down next to him, stroking his right shoulder.

It was time to view the body. In a horizontal position she thought that John resembled a beached walrus, his soft white flesh quivering when he breathed. His Y-fronts were particularly off-putting. Reluctantly she ran her fingers gently over his stomach.

'Oh yeah, that feels good princess,' groaned John, leaning over to get another mouthful of whiskey. 'Just let me get rid of these.'

John wriggled his underpants down to his knees and then hooked in a big toe to fling them off. Clare thought they would probably stick to the wall. Breathing in, she brushed her lips on his stomach for a few moments and then headed south towards his unkempt looking pubic mass.

'Your hair feels good babe. Oh yeah, that's right, just swirl it around a little.'

Clare had a couple of condoms with her that she always carried around in her purse. She hoped they weren't out of date. After she found them, she took the plunge and started to look around in the jungle for his penis. On locating the shrivelled digit she had to stifle a giggle. Back in their university days Jack had taught Clare how to put on a condom, practising with a deodorant canister. A nasal inhaler stick would have sufficed.

As Clare moved her hand towards the dwarfed member she heard a gentle snore. She looked up at his face. His eyes were shut and his mouth was open. Clare could hardly believe her luck. For a brief moment she resented the fact that he had dropped off while she was in full swing, but this thought was quickly dispelled by the enormous relief of not having to go through with it. She eased herself up carefully, not wanting to wake him.

'Cheers, John,' she said thankfully, taking a sip of her whiskey.

She looked at the clock. It was almost midnight and she had to be on her way to the airport by seven. Just as Clare was getting into one side of the enormous bed, it dawned on her that it was in pristine condition. It looked more like a sheet smoothing contest had taken place rather than a night of passion. No, that wouldn't do. John was snoring like a bulldozer, so she didn't need to tiptoe around. She tugged the corners of the sheets from under the mattress and then gave them a good ruffling. Satisfied with her work, she collapsed on the bed and fell exhausted into a deep sleep herself.

During the night, John had managed to move over towards her, and his face was now only two inches away from hers. Clare awoke to the sight of a waxy ear and the foul smell of John's breath that was worse than that of a Moroccan camel. She eyed the clock. It was six forty-five.

'Look at the time, I'm going to be late,' she exclaimed, leaping out of bed.

'Where's the fire?' cried John, waking up with a start. 'Oh my head! There's a war going on in there.'

'I have to fly back this morning. You don't need to get up yet. I can check out and then you can discreetly leave before the maid comes, which is usually about ten-ish.'

Clare quickly got ready to go, not bothering with full make-up for the return flight.

'So how did I do?' asked John, propping himself up on an elbow.

'You were fantastic,' she replied, trying not to be sick.

John was as proud as a peacock and didn't want to admit that he couldn't remember actually doing anything. He just smiled up at her, assuming that he must have had more to drink than he thought.

'Thanks for a great night. I'll speak to Lance when I get into the office. Don't worry, he'll fix things up and get things moving for you. Have you got any headache tablets?'

'I think there are some in the drawer next to you. They think of everything here. Shall I call Lance when I get back to London?'

'No, I'll get him to give your office a call instead.'

She put on her jacket and went over to the bed.

'Thanks, John,' she said, giving him the briefest of pecks on the lips.

'The pleasure was all mine, sweetheart.'

Clare made a face after she'd turned around and walked out of the room. She hoped to God that she would never clap eyes on him again. It had better all have been worth it.

Chapter 6

It was raining as Jack walked to work along Neal Street. His office was on Long Acre, which was about another five minutes away. He'd been working at Spring Records for six years now. It was a relatively small, independent label, though last year had been something of a breakthrough year, with three of the newly signed bands having had top twenty debut singles.

'Morning, Samantha,' he said brightly to the receptionist as he strolled past clutching his coffee and bagel.

'You sound very chirpy today,' she replied, peering over the top of her computer screen.

'It's Thursday, and that means just two days to go 'til the weekend.'

'Doing anything special?'

'Not really, but my friend Clare is coming back from Japan tomorrow night and I'm going to do dinner.'

'That's nice. Nobody ever cooks for me,' she sighed.

Jack went through the door to the open-plan section of the office where his desk was situated.

'Hi, Gloria,' said Jack to his colleague.

Gloria's desk was opposite Jack's and she'd already been at work for two hours.

'Good afternoon,' she said, her Australian accent very clear. 'Did you have a nice day off?'

'Great thanks,' he replied, switching his computer on. 'It's only a quarter to ten.'

'I know, I'm only kidding. It's just that I was here until eight last night working on my blasted royalty schedule. I can't get it to balance and it's doing my head in. Will you have a look at it?'

'Like I have a choice,' said Jack, smiling as he bit into his bagel.

'Oh no, here she comes,' groaned Gloria under her breath.

Their boss, Lisa, swooped over towards them.

'Where's the royalty schedule?' she snapped. 'Your deadline was yesterday.'

'It's almost finished – I just want Jack to have a quick look through it to make sure it balances with his reports,' said Gloria. She knew what was coming next.

'Next month you're going to have to plan your diary better. If you're late with your work, then that makes me late with the management accounts. Do you think that's acceptable?'

Gloria shook her head solemnly.

'Good morning, Jack,' continued Lisa, softening her tone. 'I loved your report on download revenues and I like how you're starting to join up your personal objectives that we agreed on and weave them into a wider strategic context.'

'Thanks, Lisa.'

Lisa turned back to Gloria.

'Make sure I get that schedule before lunchtime,' she hissed, before turning around and strutting back to her own corner office.

'She is being such a bitch to me! Yesterday too. It was all 'Gloria, where's this?' and 'Gloria, what have you done with that?' I wanted to smack her in the mouth. And did you see what she's wearing? How many twenty-nine-year-olds do you know who wear ankle-length tweed skirts? We're supposed to be a trendy record label.'

'I know,' said Jack, 'it's marvellous what you can do with an old pair of curtains, isn't it?'

'It's all right for you though - she likes you,' laughed Gloria. She talks to me like I'm the Whore of Babylon. And it's got worse since I went blonde, you know.'

Jack wasn't listening. The new A&R manager had just walked in.

'Morning,' smiled A&R, revealing a set of perfect white teeth.

Jack was transfixed as A&R went past them, admiring his short, jet black hair and piercing brown eyes.

'I saw that,' said Gloria.

'Saw what?'

'You, lusting after Paolo.'

'Don't be silly.'

'I don't blame you. Did he say he was Spanish or Brazilian?'

'Portuguese, I think,' said Jack, shuffling some papers around his desk.

'You think? Come off it. I bet you can remember every word that he's said to you since he joined us. You were practically salivating on Monday when he had his shirt open, showing off his chest.'

'OK, I admit that he's got something, but he's a bit too 'Latin macho' for my liking,' said Jack, trying to play it cool.

'Yeah, right.'

After about an hour Gloria screwed up ball of paper and threw it at Jack.

'What's that for?' asked Jack, looking up.

'He's coming over,' she whispered.

'What are you on about?'

'Paolo - he's coming over here.'

Jack wasn't happy that Gloria could look directly across to Paolo's desk and observe his every movement and he couldn't.

'Hey, guys,' said Paolo cheerfully, sitting down on Gloria's desk. He was holding a portable CD player.

'Oh, hi Paolo,' said Jack, trying to sound surprised.

'Just listen to this track. I want to see if you guys think that it's as fantastic as I do.'

An infernal screech erupted from the speakers. It sounded like a Sex Pistols track being played backwards.

'Good, no?' asked Paolo enthusiastically.

'It's…,' started Gloria.

'Wow, they're amazing,' cried Jack. 'Where did you find them?'

Paolo glowed proudly.

'Two weeks ago in a pub in Clapham. They're called Revenge. I know we can do something with these guys. They have their, how you say, fingers on the pulse. Punk revival is going to be the next big thing and we can be there first.'

'I think you're right, Paolo. Isn't he?' said Jack, turning to an open-mouthed Gloria. It was only last week that she and Jack had been out to a club with some friends. Somehow her memory of Jack doing a Lady Gaga dance routine wouldn't allow her to seriously imagine him pogoing in a dingy warehouse, being abused and spat on by the lead singer of a punk rock band.

'They're playing again tonight in Camden. Do you two want to come along?'

'I'd love to,' said Gloria, 'but I'm doing my roots.'

'I don't think I've got anything else on' said Jack slowly, checking his diary, though he knew it was empty.

'So you will come?' asked Paolo.

'Sure, why not. Where are they on?'

'The Pitstop at eight o'clock. You know it?'

'Of course, I've been loads of times,' he lied.

'Great! Glad you can make it. See you there.'

Paolo went back to his desk. Gloria decided to wind Jack up.

'Looks like you've got your date, then. What are you going to wear?'

'I know what you're thinking, but you're wrong. I really did think that the music was good.'

'Oh, pleeeease, it was crap and you know it. You just want to get into his knickers, don't you? Though I can't say I blame you. He is pretty tasty. Maybe I will come after all,' she teased.

'You can just stay home with your hair dye and a ready meal for one.'

By six o'clock Jack was back at his flat and getting ready to go out for the evening. He'd grabbed a quick bite to eat and had spiked his hair a little to look more the part. It had pained him to rip his new Abercrombie & Fitch vest, but it had had to be done.

The Pitstop was quite busy when he arrived an hour later and he made his way over to the bar. Paolo was already there, surrounded by a group of his people.

'Hey, Jack, how is it going?' shouted Paolo when he saw him, heartily patting him on the shoulder.

'You want some beer?'

'Love some, thanks.'

Paolo seemed to be quite drunk already.

'Have you been here long?' asked Jack.

'Since about five o'clock. I have to mix with the right contacts, you know. These are some friends from the business. I really want to sign this band.'

They were chatting away for a couple of minutes when suddenly some ear piercing feedback screamed through the sound system as someone spoke into a microphone.

'And now, will you please welcome, Camden's own, Revenge!' shouted a woman from the stage. The group emerged to lukewarm applause from the audience and hearty cheers from Paulo.

An hour and a half later and Jack was beginning to wonder if it had been a mistake to come after all. The music was absolutely dreadful and Paolo had hardly spoken to him again, being far too preoccupied with his other friends. He decided to leave.

'I'm off,' he said, walking over to Paolo.

'You didn't like them?'

'No, they were great, but I've got some phone calls to make at home.'

'Have one more drink, please,' said Paolo, putting his arm around Jack.

The accent did it.

'All right, just the one. Is that tequila you're all drinking?'

'You know, you're a nice guy, Jack,' he said, pouring him a glass.

Jack beamed.

'I have worked for many different labels, but the people at Spring Records are just great. Gloria is a nice girl as well. I think she likes you a lot. I bet she fancies you,' said Paolo.

Here goes, thought Jack.

'Oh, I don't think so. We have a good laugh together and go for drinks, but she knows I'm gay.'

'I knew it,' exclaimed Paolo. All the good-looking men are gay.'

'Well not all of them,' Jack laughed.

'Do you have a boyfriend?'

'Not at the moment,' replied Jack, taking a sip of his tequila. 'How about you?' he dared to ask.

'Listen, I'm really, really sorry but I have to return to my friends now. I need them to help me to promote the band if we sign them to Spring. I'm very pleased you could come tonight.'

'Oh,' said Jack, disappointed that the flirting wasn't going to result in a night of wild Latin sex, but encouraged by the evasive way in which Paolo had dodged his question.

'I'll see you in the office tomorrow?'

'You bet. Bye then.'

Paolo went back to his crowd, and Jack decided to quit while he was ahead and left the club. Back home in Bloomsbury, Jack's answering machine was flashing. There were four messages.

'Jack, it's me, Brian. Are you there?'

'Peeeep.'

'Brian again, come on, pick up the phone. Are you filtering? It's eleven o'clock. Call me when you get in.'

'Peeeep.'

'Hi Jack, Clare here. I'm back tomorrow and land at four so I'll make my way over as planned for dinner. Is it OK if I crash at your place? I can't face the ride back to Finsbury Park afterwards. Love you.'

'Peeeep.'

'For fuck's sake where are you man? It's midnight. Give me a ring when you get back.'

Jack called Brian.

'At last, I've been trying to call you all evening.'

'I can see that - my machine's full. Are you all right?'

'Yeah, yeah, I'm fine, but that Donald called me.'

'Who?'

'You know, the guy we met in the bar the other night. He left a message saying that he wants to talk to me about that wardrobe he mentioned, and to see my portfolio. He said he realises that it'll probably be expensive and would like a quote.'

'Well go and do it then. What have you got to lose, your virginity?'

'Funny. But what if he tries it on?'

'I can just see the headlines. Young Furniture Maker Raped by TOQ.'

'TOQ?'

'Tired Old Queen.'

'Do you think I should go, then?' laughed Brian, seeing the funny side of it.

'Of course you should. I'm sure you'll cope. And you did say work was a bit thin at the moment.'

'Well it is.'

'There you are then. Are you still coming over for dinner tomorrow night? Clare's coming here straight from the airport.'

'Looking forward to it already.'

'Great. Now remember to wear something sexy in the morning, you'll be able to double your price.'

'Fuck off.'

'You'll be fine, trust me.'

'It just feels a bit odd, that's all.'

'Anyway, I had a great night out, thanks for asking.'

'Sorry, mate - how was your night out?'

'I was with A&R and I just know that something is going to happen.'

Chapter 7

Brian was staring at his phone. He'd already started punching in the numbers three times before hanging up again. After another two mugs of coffee and ten laps of the kitchen he finally plucked up the courage to call Donald.

'Hello, Donald. It's me, Brian.'

'Brian! Thank you so much for getting back to me so quickly. I hope I didn't disturb you last night.'

'Er, no, I didn't get in 'til late.'

'I just wanted to ask when you might have time to pop over and talk about my wardrobe.'

'Well, I could come today actually,' replied Brian, thinking he might as well get it over with. 'Where do you live?'

Brian scribbled down the address.

'Is about twelve any good?'

'Perfect,' said Donald. 'I'll make you a spot of lunch, and you can show me your portfolio.'

Brian felt better for having made the call, but felt a bit stupid for his earlier nervousness. It wasn't as if he wasn't used to being around gay men - he just wasn't accustomed to visiting gay men he didn't know very well in their homes. He decided to wear just his normal workshop clothes, so he pulled on his green combat trousers and a white t-shirt. He remembered that he had left his portfolio in his van so, after finishing yet another cup of coffee and eating a piece of toast, he locked his door and set off.

The roads were quite empty for that time in the morning and Brian was enjoying the drive over to Donald's. The sun was shining and he was whistling along to the radio, his mood now much improved. Just before midday Brian turned into Donald's street. He hadn't been to this part of leafy Hampstead before and it looked very grand. The palm trees and exotic shrubbery boasted by many of the front gardens made the street look like it belonged in Los Angeles rather than London.

Brian stopped the van outside number twenty-four. Two tall stone pillars marked the beginning of a long driveway, sealed off from the street by two wrought-iron gates. He tugged at the gates but they wouldn't budge. They were locked. Scratching his head he noticed an intercom attached to a tree next to the left-hand pillar. He walked over and rang the bell. After a few short moments the device crackled and then screeched before Donald's voice came through.

'Brian, is that you? There's a camera just above you on the tree.'

He looked up.

'That's better. Now I can see you. I'm opening the gates for you now, dear.'

The heavy gates started to judder and then slowly swung open. Brian hopped back into the van and drove up the drive towards the house. It resembled a small castle, complete with stone turrets on two corners. Just as he was stepping out of the van he heard a lot of barking and the sound of gravel from the driveway being torn up. Fearing attack from a pack of wolves, he made a hasty retreat back into the van and slammed the door shut.

The pack of wolves turned out to be two black Great Danes hurtling over towards him. They were now snarling fiercely at him through the van window, their jaws salivating.

'Rags, Muffin, stop that!' shouted Donald as he came out of the house. Gone were the tight leather trousers from the bar and in their place were knee length, beige linen shorts complemented by a loose-fitting yellow cotton shirt and a straw hat. Donald patted both Rags and Muffin gently on their backs. The names were unlikely ones for Great Danes, but he had retained them from his last two dogs (which were Pekinese) after they had been squashed in a freak accident involving a wardrobe, a hoist and a banana. It had been a gruesome affair but Donald decided to keep the names for his new dogs in memory of the old. Besides, it would be easier for him to remember when calling out in the park on their walks.

'You naughty boys, scaring poor Brian like that. Sit down and let him get out.'

The dogs dutifully sat and Brian emerged from the van.

'Don't worry, now I've told them who you are they won't bite.'

'Whew. They had me going then for a minute. Bet you feel safe with them in the house,' said Brian, catching his breath.

'I do actually. You can't be too careful these days. And they really are such fun. Let's go in, shall we? Come along boys.'

Brian followed Donald and the dogs inside and was then ushered into the kitchen. Donald opened the patio doors to the garden. It was huge and very well-maintained, complete with statues, garden furniture and a small swimming pool next to an oak tree.

'Can I offer you a drink, Brian? Tea, coffee or perhaps something stronger?'

'Just water, thanks,' replied Brian, his eyes darting around. 'Great place you've got here.'

'Do you like it? I sometimes worry that it's a bit eccentric. Like me really,' he laughed.

'There you go,' said Donald, handing Brian a glass. 'Can I make you a sandwich?'

'No thanks, I'm fine.'

'Well, if you're sure. So tell me Brian, how long have you been making furniture?'

'About ten years now.'

'You must be very good. Is that your portfolio you're holding? I can't wait to see it,' he said with excitement. 'Let's

sit outside on the patio. It'd be a shame to waste the sunshine
– we get so little of it.'

Donald tutted as he sat down on a patio chair.

'Goodness, just look at those roses. Tom's almost pruned
them down to the roots!' He patted the chair next to him.
'Come and sit here and show me your work,' said Donald,
taking a lingering look at Brian's biceps. 'That t-shirt really
suits you. Is that a tattoo I can see under there?' Donald had
now transferred his gaze to Brian's lower back and hint of ass,
which was briefly exposed as he sat down.

Brian blushed and pulled down his t-shirt. His face would
have matched the roses, had there been any of them left.

'Yep, I had it done last year. It's a bull's head.'

'How unusual. You must show me more of it sometime,'
said Donald cheekily.

Brian wanted to change the subject so he offered Donald
his portfolio. Rather than taking the file from him, Donald
moved his chair closer to Brian's so he could see better. Brian
felt even more awkward, sitting so close. Shifting away from
Donald just a little, he gave a commentary on the photographs
as Donald leafed through the pages of his portfolio.

'This is fabulous,' said Donald pointing to a jewellery box.
'And look at this table – is that maple?'

'No, it's ash,' said Brian, pleased that Donald liked his
work. 'It's quite light for ash, though, so it does look a bit like
maple.'

'I need a wardrobe that will fit into an awkward corner in
one of the bedrooms,' declared Donald, closing the folder.
'I've been putting off having it made for the last six months
since the accident, but I should probably be getting on with it
now.'

Donald told Brian the story of how a Polish man-with-a-van
and his friend had been lowering his last wardrobe from the
upstairs landing. The main staircase had been too narrow for
the wardrobe. Donald had recently discovered woodworm in
the antique piece and was sending it off for treatment. As

Donald was taking his breakfast tea outside he'd heard a scream, followed by a horrendous crash and he'd rushed in to see what all the commotion was. The Polish man had slipped on a banana skin and had lost his grip on the hoist. It must have been the one that Donald had left on the table on the landing. He had meant to dispose of it properly, but had been distracted. The wardrobe, which was suspended mid-way between landing and ground level, crashed to the ground. As it did so, the heavy piece fell backwards and came to rest under the staircase. Sadly, it was not just the end of the wardrobe. It was also the end of Rags and Muffin (the Pekinese), who had been curled up asleep in their basket in the same place, peacefully unaware of their impending abrupt and messy end.

'And so, you see, I need a new one,' said Donald. 'I'd like something less gauche this time, in maple. Let's go upstairs and I'll show you where it needs to be.'

As they went up Brian noticed an oriental bamboo screen shielding an area under the stairs.

'Is that where...?'

'I'd rather not talk about it any more. Those poor mites,' cut in a bereft Donald. 'This is the room and that's the corner,' said Donald, entering one of the bedrooms, pointing over towards the corner next to a large sunny window. I'm thinking Shaker, clean straight lines, double-fronted, hanging space for my shirts and trousers, shelves for my smalls and hooks for my hats. Do you think you can do it?'

Brian walked across to the corner and starting measuring up. Scribbling down in his notebook he turned to Donald.

'No worries. I'll do a couple of designs and quotes and get them over to you.'

'That's splendid. How lucky I was bumping into you the other day. How's your friend?'

'Jack's fine. He said to say hello.'

'Oh, he's a dear. Give him my best too when you see him, won't you?'

'Will do. Is next week OK for the designs?'

'There's no rush – just take your time.'

Brian's eye wandered over to a large photograph in a wooden frame on the wall in the hallway as they left the bedroom.

'Who are they?' he asked. The photograph was of two women, posing in swimming costumes by the sea.

'My daughter Jessica and my late wife Latika.'

Brian's mouth hung open in shock as he continued to stare at the photograph. Had he heard right?

'You look surprised,' said Donald, amused.

'No, no, it's just that I thought you were… I mean, with you being in the bar…'

'Jessica's mother was so graceful and beautiful. I met her while I was working in the embassy in Bombay, which of course we call Mumbai now. We were married for thirty-three years. I loved her so much. There's never been anyone else that I've been so close to,' he said tenderly, and with real affection. 'I'm sure she knew deep down about my infrequent encounters with the boys, but it was the one thing that I just couldn't tell her. In a way I think she preferred it that way too. I was always very discreet and careful not to bring any shame on her. She passed away ten years ago. I miss her terribly.'

Brian was stunned into silence – this young goddess on the wall in front of him was Donald's daughter?

'Every time I see my darling daughter I see Latika. I decided to tell Jessica the truth about me a year after her mother had gone. She said she wasn't in the least bit surprised, and promptly invited me to a film premiere after-party that her PR company was organising. 'It'll be stuffed full of queens,' she'd said. I was mortified. I mean, it's not that obvious, is it?'

'Noooo,' coughed Brian, who thought that Donald made Quentin Crisp look butch. Turning his attention back to the photograph of Jessica, he said. 'She really is beautiful – you're very lucky to have her.'

'Yes, she's an angel,' said Donald proudly.

'Right, I'd better make tracks,' said Brian. 'I'll give you a call when I've done the designs.'

'I can't wait to see them,' said Donald, watching Brian stroll towards his van.

Brian could feel Donald's eyes burning a hole in the back of his combats, but he just smiled. He was too busy thinking about the photograph he had seen of Jessica. He had to meet her.

Chapter 8

It was Friday morning and Jack was back in the office. All he could think about was Paolo. He'd been awake the whole night wondering what he should say to him when he saw him again. He still hadn't decided.

'So how was it?' asked Gloria as she put her coffee down on the desk before sitting down.

'How was what?'

'Oh please, how was what? How was your date with Paolo?'

'It wasn't a date. It was a gig. And yes, the band was great. Even better live than recorded,' he said.

'Sure they were. So what happened?'

'Nothing happened. We had a few drinks, chatted, spoke to his friends and listened to the music.'

'So can I have a go then, if it's not sparking between you two?' suggested Gloria mischievously.

Jack couldn't hold back any longer.

'Not so fast, you. He asked me if I had a boyfriend,' he said excitedly, giving up the pretence.

'And you said?'

'No'

'And he said?'

'Nothing.'

'And you said?'

'You?'

'And he said?'

'Nothing.'

'Oh this is ridiculous,' said Gloria. 'Is he gay or not?'

'I don't know yet!'

Gloria looked up.

'Oh God, here she comes again,' she groaned.

Lisa was bounding over towards them with the ferocity of a lioness about to defend her cubs from attack.

'What the hell is this?' she screamed at Gloria waving some papers with her left hand and trying to pick the knicker elastic from between her cheeks with her right.

Jack smirked.

Suspecting that Lisa was probably aware that the paperwork in question was her belated royalty schedule, Gloria refrained from stating the obvious.

'Is something wrong?' she croaked instead.

'You've used the March sales figures instead of the April sales figures and the commission percentage column is picking up last year's royalty rates!' blared Lisa.

'Oh,' said Gloria flatly.

'I've already emailed the schedules through to head office. Now I'm going to have to email again, grovel and make up yet another excuse for why my incompetent team can't get the numbers right!'

That's what you get paid seventy grand a year for, bitch, thought Gloria, twirling a strand of her hair around a pencil.

'Jack, can you fix this please?'

'Yes of course. When do you need it by?'

'Two days ago,' she snarled, glaring at Gloria. 'If you can get it to me by three o'clock you can go home at four.'

'It's a deal,' said Jack cheerfully.

'I don't know how much longer I can stand her,' said Gloria, after Lisa had moved on to the kitchen.

'Oh, don't be silly. You should probably just double-check your spreadsheets when you've finished them.'

'Sorry about the extra work I've given you. So when is Paolo back in?' she asked, trying to lighten her mood.

'He said today,' said Jack, taking a gulp from his glass. 'I'm so nervous about seeing him I don't know what to say.

I've got to stop drinking all this water – I need to pee again. See you in a minute.'

Jack got up to go the toilets, which were at the front of the office, close to the elevator. He had just unzipped his fly when the door opened behind him. In walked Paolo. He strode straight over towards Jack and stood at the urinal right next to him. He unzipped his trousers.

'Hey, Jack, my friend! How did you enjoy yesterday? Was fun, no?'

Jack cringed. He could hardly ever pee if someone was standing next to him. And he had no chance at all if that someone was Paolo.

'I had a great time,' he replied, trying to concentrate on the task in hand.

'I am so glad you liked them. They are gonna make us a lot of money,' said Paolo.

It was almost impossible not to look, and Jack couldn't resist a sly peek through the corner of his eyes. He let out a gasp.

'What did you say? Yes, right, the band. Is the deal in the bag then?'

Paolo turned to face him after he had shaken. Jack was sure that he'd deliberately left a split second for him to see a full frontal before zipping back up and washing his hands.

'Pretty much. Those guys last night were their agents. See you later, my friend. Ah, I almost forgot. Can I put my expenses in your tray? If there's any way you can pay them before Tuesday that would be great.'

'Sure, that's fine, just drop them off.'

'You are a star,' said Paolo patting Jack's shoulders from behind before turning to leave.

After he had gone, Jack breathed a sigh of relief as he finally let go. He couldn't wait to tell Clare all about him when she got back this evening.

Chapter 9

'The flight was awful,' said Clare as she lay on Jack's sofa, exhausted. She was nursing her second glass of wine and happy to be back, both on the ground and in Bloomsbury. 'You're so lucky living here, you know. I really should sell that house in Finsbury Park and compromise with something a bit smaller over here. What do I need five bedrooms for anyway? I'd be next door to work, and we could go out more.'

'I've been telling you that for ages. Now you just relax on there and let me look after you,' said Jack, stirring a pan in the kitchen. 'Brian will be here soon, but Rachel's had to cancel because she's working over in Berlin again. Have you heard the news?'

'What news?' asked Clare, lighting a cigarette.

'Rachel's news.'

'I haven't spoken to her for a while. I've either been in the air, in meetings or in bars with people I'd rather not tell you about.'

'Well, Rachel has met someone else and is having a secret affair. Can you believe it? She hasn't told Edward about it either.'

'Is she really now? Though I told her not to marry him, so I suppose it's not a complete surprise,' said Clare, flicking ash into an ashtray. 'I never thought they were suited. So who is she seeing then?'

'Dunno. That's just it - she wouldn't say. I reckon he must be someone we know then.'

'I'll give her a call and find out what's going on.'

'You don't sound very interested,' said Jack, refreshing Clare's glass and then perching on the arm of the sofa next to her.

'Oh, I know, and I'm sorry. I'm just pissed off that these things never happen to me. Luke never did show up in Japan. No messages, no calls, nothing. I was so excited and looking forward to it. I'm going to be thirty-five in three weeks and still single.'

'Have you tried calling him again since you got back?'

'No. It hurts like hell, but I have managed to find some self-respect and dignity. Fuck him.'

Jack knew that she was upset and that she was just putting on a brave face.

'I've been single again for the last year, remember, and Brian's single too,' he offered. 'So you're not on your own and you've got us as your friends.'

'I know and I love you both very much and I am happy for Rachel, really I am. I suppose I'm just a bit jealous that it always seems to be her that has all the luck with men and not me. I mean, what's wrong with me? Am I too tall, too fat, too ugly, too successful?'

'Come here,' said Jack, putting his arms around her. 'You just haven't met the right guy yet. And you work too hard and don't leave any time for serious partner-hunting.'

'You're right. I do put all my energy into my job.'

Clare told Jack all about her meeting with Mrs Suzuki and her lawyer, Lance. She went on to describe Mrs Suzuki's smoking habits, the annoyingly abrupt end to the proceedings and the drinks she had shared with Marleen afterwards. By the time she got to the part about John and his shortcomings, Jack was laughing, and she'd managed to put the events into some sort of perspective. She had missed him.

'That's too much,' said Jack, wiping an eye. 'And he really had no idea what you'd done?'

'Not a clue. I'll just have to wait and see whether or not he called Lance to put in a good word or whether he's left me high and dry.'

Jack returned to the kitchen to stir the pan. Clare got up and followed him in, peering over his shoulder to see what he was cooking.

'Mmmm, that smells lovely. What is it?'

'It's only chilli con carne. I've been a bit preoccupied today and couldn't concentrate on inspirational menus. Actually, I've sort of met someone at work,' he said cautiously. 'Well, I might have,' he added. Jack didn't want to rub it in that he had met someone while Clare was still licking her wounds about Luke not turning up, but he couldn't resist saying something.

'Have you? Well what's his name then?' she asked valiantly.

Jack told her all about Paolo, the night out, the embarrassing toilet affair - and, of course, his huge cock.

'Lucky you,' she said, thinking briefly about Big Ben, her electronic companion for the last four years.

'To be honest, I don't even know if he's gay, or much about him at all. But he's so hot!'

'So what happens next?' asked Clare, refilling their glasses, making a mental note to buy some new batteries.

'That's where you come in.'

'What?' she spluttered.

'I don't know what to do next - help!'

'Sorry, but with my track record I'm staying out of it. I don't want you blaming me. Though you could, of course, just try the obvious and tell him that you fancy him.'

'But I'll die if he turns me down. I'll have to hide every time I see him at work.'

'Well, that's the risk of mixing business with pleasure. So what are you going to do then?'

Before he could answer, the doorbell rang. Jack went over to the intercom to let Brian in.

'Jack, could we leave my tale about John out of the conversation tonight? I wanted to tell you but I don't want to tell the others. I'm quite embarrassed about it now and can't think what on earth possessed me.'

'I won't say a word,' promised Jack, as he opened the door for Brian.

'Sorry I'm a bit late,' said Brian panting. He'd run from the bus stop. 'Hey Clare, how was Japan?'

'Oh, you know, the usual. No time to do any sightseeing, just work, work and more work. That swine Luke never showed up after all and so I'm still on the market.'

Despite everything Clare couldn't help herself from smiling. Her life hadn't ended and here she was with two of her best friends.

'Yeah, Jack told me. That's a shame,' said Brian, giving her a gentle kiss on the cheek.

'Thanks, Brian. I am so glad to be back home with you guys, and this wine is delicious,' she said, stretching out her legs and curling her toes.

Brian helped himself to a glass too, as Jack and Clare lit cigarettes.

'I thought you two were going to quit smoking. Have you tried yet?'

Both Jack and Clare inhaled deeply. The mere thought of quitting induced instant withdrawal symptoms in both of them.

'I'm going to do it after my birthday,' announced Clare.

Jack coughed.

'That's the first I've heard of it.'

'I've only just decided. More and more people are giving up and I'm getting tired of standing outside bars and restaurants in this country.'

Jack knew what was coming next.

'Well, are you going to do it too?' asked Brian.

'It'll be easier if we do it together,' said Clare.

'I'll see,' said Jack, refusing to be pressured into it at such short notice. 'Can we leave the subject for now? It's Friday night and I *was* in a good mood.'

'Rachel said to say hello,' said Brian. 'She said it's boiling hot in Berlin and that you would love some of the models, Jack.'

'Lucky cow. I've told Clare all about Rachel's mysterious affair by the way. Why do you think she won't she tell us who she's sleeping with?'

'Maybe she's got herself a toy boy,' suggested Clare.

'Maybe she's sleeping with her postman,' joked Jack, 'she told me he was cute.'

Brian wasn't joining in.

'Are you OK?' asked Jack. 'You're not usually this quiet. Hey, how did it all go with Donald by the way?'

'Great. I'm going to do some designs for a wardrobe for him.'

'So you did make it out alive then?' asked Jack.

'I think I'm in love.'

Jack looked at him in disbelief.

'Not with Donald, you moron. With Jessica, his daughter.'

Chapter 10

'Slow down,' shouted Jack at Brian as the van hurtled up Haverstock Hill. 'You'll get us killed.'

Brian and Jack were on their way over to visit Donald. Brian had prepared three different designs and quotes, and Donald had asked Brian if he could deliver them personally on Saturday afternoon. Brian had wanted Jack to see Donald's house, and of course the photograph of Jessica, and so he'd asked Donald if he could bring him along too.

'Have you told Donald you're not gay then?' asked Jack.

'I don't have to, you idiot, he can see that I'm not. He would have guessed that you were only joking when we met him that evening in the bar.'

'How do you work that one out?'

'Because, unlike you, I don't look it,' teased Brian.

'Oh really? Well I can imagine Donald finding a… certain appeal about you. Did you wear those tiny shorts last time?' asked Jack, looking down at Brian's hairy legs. 'They look very gay to me.'

'Funny. But it's obvious that I'm not gay and no, I didn't wear them – and they're not fucking tiny!'

'There are plenty of gay men who look a lot straighter than you,' chuckled Jack.

'I suppose he did try flirting a bit,' admitted Brian. 'Anyway, forget about bloody Donald, it's his daughter I fancy.'

Jack had been as surprised as Brian to discover that Donald was a doting father. Almost as surprised as when he'd heard Brian saying that he was in love – with a photograph.

'You told him that?'

'Not exactly, though I did say she was very beautiful.'

'So what's the plan then?'

'That's the thing. I have absolutely no idea yet. Not a clue.'

'Well she must be something very special, for her to have this effect on you. It's unprecedented,' said Jack, 'you, falling in love like this.'

'Mate, if she looks anything like that photograph in real life, then I've fallen all right. Make sure you ask to go to the bathroom and then you'll see it on the landing upstairs. I want to know what you think.'

'I'm intrigued.'

'Right, this is it, just round here and up on the left.'

'Wow! This looks posh.'

'Wait 'til you see the house.'

Brian told Jack to get out of the van and explained how to do the necessaries with the intercom.

'Look up at that camera once you've pressed the button,' instructed Brian.

After about twenty seconds the intercom started to crackle and squeak.

'Brian, is that you?' shouted Donald into the receiver.

Jack jumped back with a start, holding his ear.

'No, it's Jack. Brian's with me in the van.'

'You're bang on time. I'm opening the gates now, dear.'

'Mind the dogs, they're ferocious bastards,' warned Brian as they drove through, remembering being trapped in the van on his last visit. But there were no dogs this time. Donald was alone as he greeted them at the top of the drive. He was wearing grey overalls tucked into blue wellington boots and a pair of matching blue gardening gloves.

'Hello Brian, dear. Jack, it's lovely to see you again. Come through, come through,' he said, waving a pair of hedge clippers. Donald ushered them into the kitchen. It had just started to rain.

71

'Damn and blast!' he cursed. 'I've been helping Tom with the hedge and was hoping we could finish before the rain. Oh well, never mind,' he added absently.

Brian and Jack stood awkwardly in the kitchen.

'Do sit down,' said Donald, offering them chairs at the breakfast table.

'You've got a great place, Donald. How long have you lived here?' asked Jack.

'Let me see now, it must be twenty-two years. It's a bit big now for just me, but I can't bear to part with it. Will you excuse me a moment?' he said, going through the patio doors into the garden.

It was raining more heavily now.

'Tom! Leave the hedge, you'll get drenched. Sorry about that,' said Donald, coming back into the kitchen, closing the door behind him. 'Oh look at the state of me. I'm just going to pop upstairs to clean up and then we can get on with business. I can't wait to see your designs. Help yourselves to drinks, boys,' he said pointing over to the fridge. 'Glasses are in here,' he added, touching a cupboard on the wall. 'I'll not be a moment.'

Brian went over to the fridge and opened the door.

'What do you fancy?' he asked, taking a look inside. 'Beer, wine, apple juice?'

'I'm not driving so I'll have a beer please.'

Brian opened a bottle of beer for Jack and then poured an apple juice for himself.

'Afternoon.'

Brian and Jack both looked towards the patio doors.

'How do. I'm Tom, Donald's gardener. Are there any more of those beers going spare?' he asked in a thick cockney accent.

'Sure,' said Brian, opening the fridge door to take out another bottle.

Tom took off his dirty boots and left them on the mat, before washing his hands in the kitchen sink.

'Shame about the rain. We wanted to finish the hedge so as we can get on with planting the petunias.'

Jack watched the muscular young man as he dried his hands on a towel next to the sink. Tom stepped out of the overalls he had been wearing over his jeans and t-shirt and dropped them into a laundry basket next to the patio doors.

'Cheers mate! Thirsty work out there,' he said, taking the bottle from Brian with a friendly smile and then drinking half of it in one gulp.

'Cheers. I'm Brian.'

'And I'm Jack.'

They all shook hands.

'Which one of you's the chippy?' asked Tom. 'Donald said you were coming.'

'That'll be me,' replied Brian.

'That's better,' said Donald, sweeping into the kitchen, wearing a Demis Roussos style purple silk kaftan and scandals. He glided over to the fridge and poured himself a glass of wine. 'Mmmm, that's lovely. Nice and dry. I see you've met Tom. Isn't he a dear?'

'I'll come back on Monday if you want. I can finish off that hedge and do the plants,' said Tom.

Jack was picturing the two of them in the small potting shed that he had spotted in the garden through the window. Very cosy, he thought. Just like Mel Gibson and Piper Laurie in the film Tim.

'Could you?' asked Donald. 'That's terribly sweet.'

I'm sure he's all heart, thought Jack, assuming that Tom was being suitably compensated for his services.

'Now, Brian, let's have a look at those designs of yours. Shall we go through to the lounge?'

Brian picked up his rucksack and followed Donald, leaving Jack and Tom in the kitchen. Jack took the opportunity to sneak off to have a peek at the photograph of Jessica, asking Tom for directions to the bathroom.

The lounge was bright and airy with hand-woven Indian rugs dressing the polished oak floor. Donald sat down at a large oval mahogany table and put down his glass. Brian joined him and produced the drawings from his bag.

'I've done three different styles, all in maple,' he explained eagerly. 'This one has a folding door and these two have sliding ones. This one has four shelves, but this one has more hanging space,' continued Brian, showing Donald his designs.

'I'll have this one,' said Donald decisively, pointing to the drawing with the folding door and four shelves. 'When can you start?'

'Straight away. Er, here's the quote,' said Brian, pausing as he handed an envelope to Donald.

Donald tore it open.

'That's fine. I can't wait to see the real thing,' he said, patting Brian's bare leg.

Brian looked at Donald's hand as it lingered on his thigh and suddenly had second thoughts about his decision to wear shorts that day. He didn't want to say anything that might offend him because he still hadn't worked out how best to approach the subject of Jessica. Maybe he should just be upfront about it and tell Donald that he fancied her?

He heaved a sigh of relief as Jack and Tom came into the room. Jack noticed Donald's hand on Brian's leg and raised his eyebrows, nodding at Brian knowingly.

'We've just finished,' said Brian, quickly standing up.

'Your friend's very clever,' Donald said to Jack. 'Have you seen any of his pieces?'

'Just the once, coming out of the shower after he stayed over at my place a couple of years ago,' said Jack with a grin.

Brian glowered at him.

'Only joking. I've seen loads. His order book is full. He'll be very famous one day.'

'Aren't I the lucky one, then?' said Donald. 'Would you boys like to stay for dinner? It'll only be something simple,

I'm afraid. Just some cold cuts and cheeses that I got from Borough market yesterday.'

Brian toyed with the idea of staying. It would give him the chance to ask about Jessica, but he reluctantly decided to leave it for today. He didn't want to do it in front of an audience.

'Sorry,' said Brian. 'I've got another engagement a bit later on, but maybe next time?'

'I'd better get going too,' said Jack.

Donald looked at Tom.

'Oh well never mind, just you and me then?'

'I'm up for it,' said Tom, scratching his balls.

I bet you are, thought Jack, getting ready to leave.

The sound of tyres crunching the gravel driveway caused them all to look up. They heard doors slamming followed by barking and a woman's voice shouting.

'That'll be Jessica,' said Donald.

Brian couldn't believe what he had just heard. She was here?

Within seconds the dogs were tearing around the lounge, barking menacingly as they made a beeline for Jack.

'Stop that, Muffin! Get down, Rags!'

Jack was petrified. He hated dogs and the feeling was usually mutual. The dogs growled and sniffed before obediently sitting down in front of him.

'We've got guests, dear,' said Donald to his daughter as she came in, 'this is Brian and this is his friend Jack.'

'Hello! I'm Jessica,' she said cheerfully, shaking hands with them both.

'Hello,' said Jack, 'good to meet you.'

Brian's mouth had dried up and he could barely utter a word. Forget the photograph. She was twice as stunning in the flesh.

'How was the Heath, dear?' asked Donald.

'I'm exhausted,' she replied, collapsing into a leather

armchair. 'There isn't a patch of Heath left un-trodden by us today. We've been everywhere, haven't we, dogs?'

Brian couldn't take his eyes off her. She had tied her black hair into a ponytail and wasn't wearing any make-up. He just wanted to kiss her lips and lie on top of her on that armchair right there and then. But of course he couldn't.

'Let's at least have some champagne before you boys have to go,' declared Donald. 'I want to celebrate my new wardrobe. Did I tell you, dear?' he continued, turning to Jessica, 'Brian is going to make me a wardrobe – you know, to replace the one that squashed poor Muff...'

He couldn't bring himself to finish the sentence, not wanting to upset Jessica.

'It's all right, Dad, you can say it.'

Although Jessica did miss the two Pekinese, and she wouldn't have wished such a grisly departure from this world on anything, she found she liked the masculine quality of the Danes.

'It was such a coincidence! I only met Brian and Jack in Soho a couple of days ago and Brian turns out to be a master craftsman and here we all are. Jack darling, can you help me with the glasses?'

Jack and Donald went back into the kitchen, while Tom, Brian and Jessica stayed in the lounge. The dogs followed Donald and he opened the patio door to let them outside.

'The garden's looking grand,' said Jessica to Tom, walking over to the window, watching the dogs charging across the lawn. 'Dad says that you're a natural with plants.'

Tom looked pleased with himself.

'Thanks. You've just got to talk to them a bit and look after them and then they grow,' he said. 'A bit like people.'

Despite Tom's profound words of wisdom Brian was still mute, gawping longingly at Jessica. Suddenly he blurted out,

'So how long have you been over here?'

'I beg your pardon?' Jessica said.

'Donald says your mum was from India. When did you move to England?'

'I've been here all my life. I was born here.'

Brian felt stupid. What sort of opening line was that?

'Sorry. I meant… well, I don't really know what I meant… you've definitely got your mother's face, she's beautiful,' he bumbled on, pointing vaguely upwards. 'The picture… upstairs.'

He felt as if he had dug an enormous hole, climbed into it and shovelled the earth back all by himself. What was he saying?

His awkwardness and clumsy attempt at flattery had amused Jessica.

'Thanks. We all miss her.'

Meanwhile, in the kitchen, Jack was holding five glasses and Donald was pulling a bottle of champagne from out of the fridge.

'You do know that Brian's straight, don't you?' said Jack as matter-of-factly as he could. 'I saw your hand on his leg and thought…'

'Oh, don't be silly, of course I know,' interrupted Donald. 'I was only having a little fun, and besides, there's no harm in showing appreciation, is there?'

'There's more. He fancies your daughter.'

'I know that too, dear. Do you think I was born yesterday? Why do you think she's here - by coincidence?'

Donald popped the champagne cork as they returned to the lounge, and he filled the glasses that Jack had handed round.

'Here's to friends, family and my new wardrobe.'

'To friends and family.'

Tom emptied his glass in one go and then turned back to the table to help himself to a refill. Brian finally managed to coordinate eyes, brain and mouth.

'I'm taking part in an exhibition next weekend,' he said, looking at Donald and Jessica. 'It's in Hoxton. If you've got time it would be nice to see you both there.'

Brian leant down and opened his rucksack.

'Here are two tickets. The VIP preview is at eleven o'clock on Saturday morning. It should be a really good exhibition. There'll be loads of artists and designers there, and it's hosted by Doris Elliott. She's quite a well-known photographer.'

'I know Doris,' said Jessica. 'My PR firm has used her a few times. She's brilliant.'

'We'd love to come - wouldn't we darling?' said Donald to Jessica.

'I think I can,' she replied hesitantly, 'but I'll have to check with the office that there's nothing else on that weekend.'

'Splendid, it sounds really exciting,' said Donald, clapping his hands. 'That's a date then.'

Jack could see that Brian was chuffed, and gave him a 'thumbs up' to signal his approval of Jessica when she wasn't looking. Wanting Brian to quit while he was winning, Jack stood up, finishing his champagne.

'Right, we'd better get moving,' he said putting down his glass, 'thanks for the drinks, and nice to see you again, Donald. Jessica, it was a pleasure to meet you, and I hope to see you on Saturday.'

'But I haven't finished yet,' protested Brian.

'Yes you have. I'll drink that - you're driving,' he said, taking Brian's glass and swilling down the rest of Brian's champagne.

'Bye, Tom,' shouted Jack over to Tom, who was now by the window.

Tom turned around, scratching his balls again. He walked back over to Jack and extended his other hand.

'See you, mate. Nice to meet you,' he said with a wink.

'Likewise,' said Jack, shaking it, wondering what all the scratching was about.

'Thank you so much for coming,' said Donald as they all started to move towards the door. 'I can't wait to see more of your work next week.'

'Cheers, Donald,' said Brian, 'see you, Tom.'

Brian looked longingly at Jessica.

'Hope you can come on Saturday – it would really make my day.'

'I'll do my best,' she said with a smile.

Brian was on cloud nine as he and Jack drove off.

'Did you see that? I'm in there!'

Chapter 11

It was a cold and wet Monday morning as Clare came out of Holborn tube station and headed towards her office on Drury Lane. She was dreading going in to work. What if John hadn't spoken to Lance after all as he'd promised, and the deal was still off?

'Good morning, Candice,' said Clare to the receptionist, taking off her wet coat.

'Hi, how was your trip?' Candice asked with a sly smile, looking up from her magazine.

'It was hard work. Why, what are you grinning about?'

'Some flowers have arrived for you. They're in your office,' said Candice in a whisper.

Flowers? Clare was puzzled. She rushed to her office. Surely not from Luke? Well, it's too late for flowers, she thought. On her desk was the biggest bouquet of roses that she had ever seen. They were a blaze of colour and already in a vase. Clare spotted a card tied with a ribbon to one of the stems. Gingerly untying the bow, she picked up the card and read it:

> *Roses are red*
> *Violets are blue*
> *Japan was just great*
> *I can still smell you too*

Although the card was unsigned she knew that the flowers weren't from Luke. They were from John Goldschmied. Was it really necessary to send flowers to the office? That gossip

Candice on reception will be having a field day. And the note - '*I can still smell you too*'. Really! She remembered his underwear. Yuk! Clare tore the card up and threw it into the bin.

She had barely had time to turn on her PC when the door to her office was flung open.

'How's my rising star this morning?'

It was Grace, her boss. Clare tried unsuccessfully to hide the flowers by standing in front of them.

'What lovely blooms! Who are they from?'

'Oh, no-one special,' answered Clare, wanting to avoid specifics.

'Candice signed for them this morning and put them on my desk, naturally assuming they were for me - before we realised they were for you! Well done in Japan,' purred Grace, circling Clare as if she were about to pounce on an injured gazelle. 'It looks like we're almost there.'

This sounded hopeful, but Clare said nothing, waiting for Grace to finish. She might look like a stick insect, but Grace terrified her.

'I got an email last night from Mrs Suzuki's lawyers, Rosenberg & Hoffmann,' said Grace. 'It was from Lance, actually. He wanted to pass on Mrs Suzuki's thanks for your helpful visit. He said there are still a few minor bits and pieces that we need to smooth out, but that we could expect to move forward and hopefully close the full deal soon.'

Clare smiled. John had done it. It had been worth the extra effort and the indignity after all.

'The Suzuki party want to come over and visit some of our stores - and meet some more of our people - in about four weeks,' continued Grace. 'If it goes well, they'll sign the heads of terms while they are here. Isn't Lance great?'

Relieved that she wasn't going to get the chop just yet, Clare relaxed a little.

'That's fantastic. The meeting went really well and they absolutely loved the product.'

'All I can say is, great work Clare. Knowing you I bet you're already thinking ahead about what we should be doing to generate as much leverage as possible from the product launch in Japan, aren't you?'

Nothing could have been further from Clare's mind. She hadn't given it a moment's thought.

'Speak to Simon,' said Grace.

Simon was Head of Marketing.

'Share your ideas with him and see if they chime with what he's visioning for the launch. I have a conference call with the Board on Wednesday afternoon. Clare, how soon do you think you'll be able to get your ideas over to me to have a look at? Just a rough outline will be fine at this stage so that I can keep the Board up to speed. Drop an email to Karen once you've caught up with Simon so that we can fix up a meeting to discuss it.'

Karen was Grace's Personal Assistant.

Great, thought Clare, more things to do.

Just as Grace was about to leave the office, she turned around again.

'Oh, I almost forgot. Just look at these,' she said, waving a bunch of papers clutched in her bejewelled claw.

Grace scattered them on Clare's desk.

'Paul gave them to me.'

Paul was Head of Finance.

'They're this week's stock reports from Germany. He says they're a mess and make no sense. He doesn't think that Waltraut is really up to the job any more.'

Waltraut was the Stock Controller, based in the distribution office in Berlin. Most of Destiny's clothing was made in Eastern Europe, so Berlin was the perfect gateway.

'These are not the first complaints I've had about her either. It's obviously not working out. I've been speaking to Daniel about next steps.'

Daniel was Head of Human Resources.

'Can you just pop over to Berlin with him on Thursday and

sort it out? Paul is drowning in year-end work, but he's comfortable delegating it to you. She's got to go.'

Anything else this week? thought Clare, getting irritated and imagining how far she could stretch Grace's neck before pulling her head off. She hated the word 'just' when used as part of a 'can you just' question. It always made the rest of the request sound incidental, something that required no effort at all.

'Of course. Leave it with me,' she replied.

Then she remembered that Rachel had said that she would be in Berlin this week too. Clare had spoken to her briefly on the phone on Sunday, wanting to fix a date to catch up and, of course, to tell her all about Luke. She hadn't had time to grill Rachel properly about her affair and she was playing her cards very close to her chest. Hopefully they'd be able to meet up over there so that she could wheedle it out of her. She was dying to find out what was going on.

Chapter 12

The plane had landed on time at Tegel airport and Clare was in a taxi with Daniel on their way to the regional office in Schőneberg, in the centre of West Berlin, to resolve the Waltraut situation.

'Are you sure she has no idea that I'm coming too?' asked Daniel.

'No, it'll be a nice surprise for her. I spoke to Stefan yesterday, straight after speaking to Waltraut, and told him to make himself scarce from the office this afternoon.'

Stefan was Waltraut's Assistant Stock Controller.

'I want her to be on her own when I question her about those reports, so that she can't try falling back on anyone else. We're meeting Stefan to fill him in at three fifteen in a café close to the office. What time's your flight back?'

'It's not 'til ten o'clock, so there's plenty of time.'

Clare had made plans to go out later with Rachel, and was staying overnight in a hotel. She couldn't get into the same one as Rachel because it was full, but the one she had found was close by, next to the zoological garden.

'I'm afraid I'm going to have to leave you to your own devices after the meeting, Daniel. I've got some things to do and then I'm meeting up with a friend.'

'No problem,' he said. 'I have some paperwork that I can get on with in the airport lounge.'

The taxi drove them through the leafy districts of Charlottenburg and Wilmersdorf on the way to Schőneberg. Clare sat back and looked through the window. The wide, tree-lined boulevards really did lend themselves to café culture and tables and chairs filled the pavements outside the bars and restaurants. Clare thought that Berlin was one of the most interesting and exciting cities in the whole world.

'Here will be just fine,' said Clare to the driver. She'd spotted Stefan sitting at a table outside the café.

'That will be twenty euros,' said the driver, pulling in.

'There you go, *danke schön*,' said Clare cheerfully. You'd never have guessed she was just about to sack somebody.

'Stefan, how are you?' gushed Clare as she walked over towards him, offering her cheeks for continental kisses. 'Sorry I couldn't tell you that Daniel was coming with me. We didn't want to alarm you.'

'Hello again, Stefan,' said Daniel.

'Hi,' said Stefan, getting nervous. They looked a formidable pair in their black suits. 'Is something wrong?'

'No, no, of course not. You're our number one man in Berlin,' she said, trying to reassure him.

Stefan wasn't reassured. What was going on here?

'Daniel, what would you like to drink?'

'I'll have a cappuccino please.'

'Stefan, anything else?' she asked, looking at his empty cup.

'No, I'm fine, thanks.'

'*Zwei Cappuccinos*,' shouted Clare sharply to the waitress, clicking her fingers, before turning back to face Stefan.

'Stefan, you've been with us for just over twelve months now, haven't you?'

'Yes, and it's flown by. I love working here.'

'I'm so glad to hear that. You see, we will soon have a vacancy in the Stock Controller position.'

'I don't understand,' he said with a frown. 'That's Waltraut's job.'

The waitress brought the cappuccinos over and plonked them down on the table.

'Yes, you're right, Stefan. At this precise moment in time

it is indeed Waltraut's job. But by the end of the day it could be yours – if you're interested?'

'Well, er, I suppose so, yes,' he answered warily, 'but what about Waltraut?'

'What matters most is that we have the right person in that job. The reports this month were embarrassing at worst and rubbish at best. She's lazy and useless. So, if she were to… go, you'd help us out and step into her shoes – at least temporarily?'

'Of course,' replied Stefan, at last getting the drift, attempting a smile.

'Fantastic. Daniel, is there anything else we need from Stefan at this point? If not then we'll go and say hello to Waltraut. Stefan, why don't you go home for the rest of the day? Daniel will call you tomorrow to sort out the arrangements. Daniel, is that OK with you?'

'That should be fine,' said Daniel with a start. He'd been distracted by two chunky guys with beards kissing at the next table and hadn't been listening to a word. He knew Clare would have it covered anyway.

'Paul will be so pleased to finally have someone good holding the reins over here again. Now, is she there?' asked Clare, pointing over to Nollendorfstrasse, where the office was located. The distribution warehouse itself was out in Spandau, but the company had wanted to have a fashionable city centre address too.

'She should be,' said Stefan, feeling a bit like Judas Iscariot.

'Great. Daniel, shall we? Speak soon, Stefan. Ciao.'

Daniel and Clare walked over to Nollendorfstrasse.

'Isn't Berlin just gorgeous at this time of year?' said Clare, striding ahead, clutching her bag.

'Wonderful,' agreed Daniel, wishing that he didn't have to wear a tie in this heat. 'Did you see those two guys next to us, kissing out in the open like that?'

'Oh don't be such a prude. This is Berlin,' laughed Clare.

'Actually, I'm feeling a bit peckish,' she added, patting her stomach. 'Do you mind if I just grab something from here?' she asked, pointing to a Turkish deli on the corner.

'Good idea. I could do with something to eat as well. And anyway, I'm not a prude,' he protested, 'I'm very broad-minded, actually.'

Clare flirted a little with the cute Turkish boy who was serving her and was rewarded with an extra scoop of döner meat in her lamb kebab. They had to walk up the stairs to the office on the third floor because there was no lift. Antje, the receptionist, greeted them as they strode in.

'*Guten Tag* Antje,' said Clare, a little out of breath. 'How are you? We're here to see Waltraut.'

'I'm fine, thanks. I'll just tell her that you're here.'

'No need; she's expecting us so we'll just go through.'

The open plan office was small and Waltraut had a cubicle at the back, next to the only window. Daniel and Clare crept over.

'Hello Waaaaltrauuuut!' cried Clare, peering behind the partition screen. 'Sorry, we're a bit late.'

Waltraut had been eating a large bag of paprika flavoured crisps and reading a self-help book entitled, 'It's not you, it's them'. Snapping the book shut and choking on a mouthful of crisps, Waltraut whipped around, almost twisting her neck in the process.

'But you're two hours early,' she quaked. Waltraut hadn't yet prepared anything for the meeting, and couldn't understand why Daniel was here too. There weren't any new recruitment plans for the warehouse as far as she was aware.

'Are we?' asked Clare with mock surprise. She'd planned to catch her off guard. 'Don't say I told you the wrong time, did I? Silly me! Oh well, it doesn't really matter. Now, I need to talk to you about some paperwork. Shall we go and sit next door where it's a bit more private? And if you could ask Antje to get me a coffee, that would be super. Daniel, would you like anything to drink?'

'Well, I wouldn't mind a peppermint tea, if there is any,' he replied merrily, as if he was at a garden party.

Clare and Daniel went through to the small meeting room and sat down at the table. Clare got out her paperwork and unwrapped the kebabs, handing one to Daniel.

'I'll lead on this. I've spoken to Grace,' said Clare, taking a big bite of lamb döner, red cabbage and pita bread, 'and she's comfortable with the plan.'

Waltraut came into the room and took a seat at the table opposite Clare. She didn't have a good feeling about this meeting. Something was up.

'Antje will bring the drinks over in a few minutes,' she said quietly.

'Oh, thanks Waltraut,' said Clare chewing, reluctant to put down her kebab. Wiping her lips with a serviette she continued.

'Waltraut, I'll cut straight to the chase. Grace and the management team have been... confused with some of your reports recently. They don't seem to... tie up with the control papers from Paul's team. Do you mind if Daniel takes some notes while we chat?'

Waltraut nodded. She was trying to hide behind glasses that were far too big for her face. She started to pick at a scab on her forehead as she looked over at Daniel, who had already begun to scribble things down.

Clare stood up and went round next to Waltraut. She placed a copy of the last stock report on the table in front of her and pointed at a number in the centre of the second page.

'What's this?' she asked quizzically, leaning forward as she stared Waltraut in the eye.

Waltraut hesitated, looked at the report and then looked up at Clare like a rabbit facing headlights. She looked down at the report again, her face a blank.

She obviously has no idea, thought Clare, pausing for a few agonising seconds.

In order to effect maximum intimidation, Clare raised her

right forefinger to her bottom lip. She continued to point at the number in question with her left, all the time maintaining eye contact.

'It seems to be linked to the damaged goods percentage, but Paul thought it looked high,' said Clare, without so much as a blink.

'I... er... well... Stefan gave me that. I'll just ask him.'

'He's not in the office at the moment. Surely you know how the forward stock calculator should be working?' she went on, tightening the screws further still.

Waltraut shook her head.

'Something doesn't look right with the gross margin for the Ukrainian handbags either,' said Clare, placing a different report onto the table in front of her, leaning in so closely that she was almost nose-to-blackhead with Waltraut's oily skin.

'What's this?' she asked, pointing to a number at the bottom of the page.

Waltraut stared at it.

'It's based on... based on... the figure that we... Stefan normally does this... I think it's... I don't know,' she finally admitted. Deflated and defeated, she was beginning to fear the worst.

Waltraut's face crumpled.

'Waltraut, I'm afraid we're going to have to let you go,' said Clare firmly, stepping back from the table. 'Today. It's just not working out and we think, in the fullness of time, you'll be happier too. The good news is though, the business will be moving forwards and we have someone lined up to take over from you... immediately. So what that means for you is, you don't even need to worry about working your notice. Isn't that great?'

Waltraut let out a howl as tears starting streaming down her face.

Clare almost had an orgasm. She did love power. It was the next best thing to sex. Seeing as she wasn't getting any sex, she figured she'd better make the most of the situation.

Clare then put her hands gently on Waltraut's shoulders.

'There, there, let it all go. It's for the best,' she soothed, slowly withdrawing the dagger that she had thrust into Waltraut only seconds ago.

At that precise moment Antje appeared in the doorway with a tray carrying coffee, peppermint tea and some biscuits.

'Ah, Antje, come in. We're just wrapping up in here,' said Daniel as he finished jotting down notes of the proceedings.

Antje put the tray down on the table. As she did, Waltraut got up and ran from the room, crying hysterically.

'What's wrong with Waltraut?' asked Antje, open-mouthed.

'She'll be leaving us, today,' replied Clare crisply. 'There's no need to worry - it's got nothing to do with you. Daniel, I don't know about yours, but my kebab is a bit dry. Antje, could you pop outside and see if you can find any garlic sauce for us?'

Antje stared at Clare in disbelief, but didn't dare say anything.

'What? Yes, I'll see what I can do,' she muttered, backing out of the room.

Daniel and Clare began to pack up their papers.

'That went quite well, didn't it?' she said. 'Of course we'll have to pay her for her notice period at least. Once she's composed herself she'll be taking advice and she'll be sure to make a case for unfair dismissal. You should probably talk to her tomorrow and offer her a compromise agreement – Grace said twelve months pay max.'

'I'll call her tomorrow afternoon when we're back in London.'

'Thanks. Oh, can you excuse me a moment?' said Clare, remembering that she wanted to call Rachel. She dug around in her handbag and found her phone.

'Rachel! Hi, it's me, Clare. Are you still OK for drinks later on? Oh good. I'll just need to check into the hotel first and freshen up and then I can meet you. Where did you say? Oh yes, I know where it is. Lovely, see you there about six.'

Clare was really looking forward to having a shower and then chilling out with her friend – not to mention finding out about what on earth Rachel had been getting up to, and what this secret affair was all about.

Chapter 13

Jack was actually looking forward to going into work. Paulo would be in today. He'd just had a coffee and read his usual morning paper in a café close to Seven Dials. The sun was peeping through the gaps between the buildings as he strolled through Covent Garden on his way to the office, and the flower seller on Neal Street had said good morning to him as he passed by. He had quite a spring in his step. Even Samantha seemed happy for a change and was singing along to the radio as Jack walked through reception.

'Lisa won't be coming in today,' she said to him. 'Something about a constricted larynx, a rash and diarrhoea.'

'Lovely,' he replied making a face. 'Hope that one's not contagious.'

'Are you in charge of finance if she's not here?' asked Samantha dimly.

'That's right. Just put any urgent calls through to me,' he said, walking over towards his desk.

Gloria had obviously heard the news about Lisa's unfortunate predicament and was enjoying a large chocolate brownie while leafing through a fashion magazine. She hadn't even turned her computer on yet.

'Apparently she can't speak or breathe without triggering a bowel movement,' she sniggered without any sympathy at all. 'Couldn't have happened to a nicer person,' she added, remembering the royalty schedule incident and the subsequent public chastisement. 'Looks like those double-gusseted bloomers of hers will finally come into their own.'

'Don't be so mean,' he said, though he couldn't help laughing himself, picturing Lisa in what clearly sounded like an unpleasant and compromised state.

Jack raced through the two hundred and twenty emails that had miraculously appeared since the close of business yesterday. One of them caught his eye, standing out like a flashing beacon. It was from Paolo. Jack couldn't click on it fast enough.

'I'm going to be at the Pitstop again tonight from about 8 o'clock to check out another band called Breakaway. I've put your name on the guest list. If you're free why not come along?'

Jack was beside himself and he told Gloria straight away that he had a date. She wasn't as convinced as he was.

'He's probably sent dozens of people a similar email. The band will play better if the place is full.'

'Did he send you one?'

'Well, no, but…'

'Don't be such a killjoy. I'm sure he's gathered that I fancy him, but neither of us can say anything. It's awkward, you know, with work.'

'If you say so, but if was me, I'd have made a clear pass at him by now.'

'Yes, well it's not you, is it, so I'll keep you informed. There will be a right time to make a move, I know it.'

Jack remembered that Paolo's expenses were still in his in-tray and that he'd promised to pay them this week. Retrieving the papers he quickly approved them in Lisa's absence and handed them over to Gloria.

'Can you pay these by electronic transfer this afternoon, by any chance?' he asked. Vince will be in to authorise the payments. Vince was the Chief Executive.

'No worries,' said Gloria, taking the expense claims from him. '£800 for drinks? Lisa will flip. What was he entertaining, an army?'

'I know, but there were quite a lot of agents and promoters

there. He thinks we'll sign the band, so hopefully it was worth it.'

'But still, that's one hell of an expensive party.'

'Speaking of parties, you've not forgotten about the one I'm having a week on Saturday, have you?'

Jack was having a party for Clare's thirty-fifth birthday at his place.

'Will there be any straight men there?' she joked.

'But of course, my friend Brian's bringing some of his mates from Hackney.

'Then I'll be there. Do you want me to bring anything?'

'It's any time from five, and just bring a bottle of wine or something. Brian's already spoken for, by the way,' he added, guessing that Brian would probably want to ask Jessica - if she turned up to the exhibition on Saturday, that is.

'Well that hasn't stopped me before.'

'You can take that wicked grin off your face and keep those talons of yours off him.'

The rest of the day sped by. Jack had to finish off some reports for Lisa and couldn't sit day-dreaming about Paolo and the evening ahead. Before he knew it he had been home, showered and changed and was now sitting in the Dog and Duck in Camden having a glass of wine for Dutch courage. After polishing off two he took a quick raincheck in the mirror in the gents. He'd spiked his hair again, but had decided against ripping his clothes this time, and was wearing his favourite Diesel jeans and a green shirt.

It was only a short walk to the Pitstop, and he was able to jump the queue, being on the guest-list. Jack made his way over to the bar after handing his jacket in at the cloakroom. He couldn't see Paolo anywhere. He looked around at the groups of young people that had started to gather in front of the stage, but still couldn't see him.

'Jack, my friend!' boomed Paolo from behind, slapping him on the shoulder.

'Hey, Paolo! How's it going?' said Jack, turning around, trying to remain as cool as he possibly could.

'The band will be on in about twenty minutes. Come over here and meet some of the guys and have a drink,' said Paolo, already steering Jack towards a table against a wall beside the stage. 'Everyone, this is Jack from Spring. Be nice to him - he's paying for the drinks,' he joked as he introduced Jack to Bobby, Sean, Wayne and Anita from Talk Talk Productions.

Next to them was a bottle in an ice bucket along with a tray of shots. Paolo handed Jack a glass of champagne.

'There you go, my friend.'

Paolo was dressed very casually, in white tracksuit bottoms and a blue vest. Jack loved his three-day beard. It really complemented his short black hair and long eyelashes.

'Cheers, guys,' said Paolo, holding up his glass to the group. 'Here's to Breakaway! They are fucking amazing.'

They all chinked glasses and then went back to their conversations. It was very loud in the club and almost impossible to have a round-table group chat.

'Jack, did you have the time to pay the expenses I gave you last week?'

'They should go through tomorrow. I signed them off today.'

'You are a star! Here - have one of these,' said Paolo, grabbing two of the shot glasses. 'Anita, can you order another round?'

Jack didn't usually mix wine with champagne *and* shots but what the hell, he was with Paolo.

'Bottoms up, or what is it you say?' grinned Paolo, downing his shot in one.

'That's right, bottoms up,' smiled Jack, knocking his back too.

The band had just come on stage and the club was now packed. The crowd applauded and cheered and Paolo seemed to be very excited as he took his seat next to Jack. The band played for about an hour and much better than the last one he had seen here. The effects of three more bottles of champagne and countless rounds of shots were beginning to show. Jack, Paolo and Sean were on their feet, dancing and singing along, Anita was eating the face off Wayne, and Bobby had put his hand under the mini-skirt of a girl who had been sitting on the next table, but was now on his knee, giggling hysterically.

The band finished their second encore to thunderous applause.

'We want more! We want more!' shouted the crowd, but the band didn't come back out for a third time.

Jack was out of breath from jumping up and down.

'Whew! That was great, no?' said Paolo, panting.

'I haven't had so much fun in ages,' said Jack.

'I need some air,' said Paolo, 'let's go outside.'

Paolo grabbed his shirt from behind a chair and started to push through the crowds towards the exit.

The cold air hit them as they stepped out of the door and Jack breathed in deeply, enjoying the refreshing impact. His ears were ringing.

'That's nice, isn't?' said Paolo, breathing in too as he fastened his shirt. 'Come on, let's go for a walk down here and chill out for a bit.'

They walked along the canal past the narrowboats and under the bridge. It was eerily quiet. The streetlights only went as far as the footpath that led back to the main road towards Chalk Farm. They continued to walk further along the canal. It was almost pitch black. Only the light from the moon's reflection on the water stopped them from falling into it. They stumbled across a bench.

'Here is good to sit, no?' said Paolo.

'Great, yes,' said Jack, sitting down next to him.

Paolo took a joint out from his pocket and lit it, the acrid smoke filling the air. After taking a couple of deep tokes he handed the joint to Jack.

'You smoke this shit?' he asked. Jack took the joint and

put it to his lips. He didn't normally smoke grass, but this evening was turning out to be anything other than normal.

'Thanks,' said Jack, inhaling.

He looked up at the starry sky. It was beautiful. He took another toke before handing the joint back to Paolo. They sat like that for a few minutes, in silence, side by side, smoking and staring at the sky. There was nobody around. They were alone.

Then Jack felt Paolo's warm hand wrap around his. His heart started pounding in his chest. This was it! Paolo lifted Jack's hand and put it where he could feel his cock pushing up through the thin material of his tracksuit bottoms. Jack rubbed harder, his confidence growing as Paolo stretched out his legs on the footpath. Jack slipped his hand under the waistband and grabbed Paolo's cock, squeezing it tightly.

'Oh yeah, that feels good,' groaned Paolo.

Jack went down on his knees between Paolo's legs and slowly peeled down his tracksuit bottoms.

'Fuck, that's it, yeah,' grunted Paolo, pulling Jack's head towards him as he took him in his mouth, moving quickly.

'Oh man, that's great, don't stop, I'm gonna cum soon.'

Jack felt Paolo's whole body contract. He leant back, finishing him off with his hand.

'Fuck, that was good,' sighed Paolo, his breathing fast.

'You're not kidding,' gasped Jack, sitting back down on the bench.

Jack was now horny as hell. He started to unbutton his own jeans.

'What are you doing?' asked Paolo, standing up suddenly.

'What do you think?' said Jack, confused.

'I'm not like you,' said Paolo, 'I'm not queer. I have a girlfriend. Don't you say a fucking word about this to anyone in the office, got it? See you around.'

And just like that he walked off into the night leaving Jack frustrated and angry, alone on the bench.

'What the fuck was that all about?' he shouted after him. But there was no reply. Paolo just kept on walking.

Chapter 14

Rachel had finished interpreting for the day and was really enjoying the buzz of being part of the fashion show. She had had to learn a lot of new vocabulary in a short space of time, but it was worth it. The assignment had got her two weeks in Berlin again and the pay was good too. She had arranged to meet Clare in a café called Prinz on Bergmanstrasse, close to where she was working. There was still a little time to kill so she went for a stroll to check out some of the shops. It was a beautiful, warm evening and she felt happy and in love. She'd decided to tell Clare all about it.

The tables outside the many cafés had already started to fill up and the chatter of voices filled the air as Rachel ambled slowly along. She paused outside a small antique shop on a side street and admired a rustic-looking table. She considered briefly how it might look in her hallway at home, before dismissing the thought. It was much more likely that her furniture would be coming out of the house as opposed to more of it going in. She had made up her mind to formally break up with Edward.

Clare was sitting at a table outside Prinz. She had changed into her jeans and was wearing a loose-fitting blouse. Rachel saw her as soon as she came back onto the main road. She was just visible through a cloud of smoke, and was reading a book.

'Clare,' she shouted, running over.

Clare stood up and put her arms out. 'It's so good to see you, Rachel. You look fantastic.'

'Thanks! So do you.'

They hugged each other and Clare stepped back.

'No, really, you look absolutely amazing. What have you done? Been to a health spa, had a chemical peel, what?'

'Nothing - I haven't done anything. It must be the Berlin weather,' smiled Rachel.

'It must be your affair, more like. I presume you're having sex twice a day,' said Clare, never one to beat around the bush. 'Sorry, ignore me. I'm just jealous. I wish I was getting laid more.'

'Only once a day, actually,' laughed Rachel, flicking back her hair, 'and that's exhausting enough, believe me.'

'So go on then, who is he?'

'Let's have a drink first. Have you ordered?'

'No, not yet. I was waiting for you.'

'I could murder a gin and tonic, actually,' said Rachel, holding her hand up to catch the waiter's attention.

'Mmmm… that sounds just like what I need as well.'

Rachel ordered the drinks.

'We really must see more of each other in London. It's coming to something if we have to meet up in Berlin rather than at home, isn't it? I've just been so busy lately.'

'Me too. I seem to be travelling around all over the place and doing two people's jobs. How's the fashion show?'

'It's brilliant. The atmosphere is electric - that more than makes up for the long hours that I have to work. I got to go to one of the after-parties last night - that was great fun. Is work still really tough, then?'

'It's crazy, but it does seem that at last we might get the Japanese deal over the finishing line, though we've a few more meetings to plough through before we get that far. My boss, Grace, is driving me nuts. I could just scream at her sometimes,' she said, lighting another cigarette.

Rachel eyed the cigarette with disapproval.

Clare followed Rachel's gaze to her cigarette.

'Not you too,' she sighed. 'Is this a three-line whip? Brian's been on at me as well. I'm planning on stopping after my birthday party next weekend, which I hope you will be back in time for. But today I'm smoking, OK?' she said, defiantly blowing a plume of smoke into Rachel's face, causing her to cough.

'Ugghh! Stop it, I'll have to wash my hair now. I should be back in London then and I'm really looking forward to your party. It was nice to see Jack and Brian last week, though your party will be the first time that the four of us have got together for ages.'

The waiter brought their drinks to the table.

'Cheers Rachel, good to see you again.'

'Cheers, good to see you too.'

'I had to sack someone today.'

'Oh no, that must have been awful for you.'

'Actually, I quite enjoyed sacking Waltraut. I think I did it quite well.'

'Clare Houghton, you know you don't mean that. You're not that much of a heartless cow,' said Rachel, taking a sip of her drink.

'Thanks. Good to see that my boss is successfully turning me into a superbitch too.'

'Well really, how can you enjoy sacking somebody? The poor woman will have bills to pay and food to buy. Was she expecting it?'

'I don't think so. Judging by the hysterical tears I should think that's highly unlikely. Seriously though, Waltraut was an idle moose. She was hopeless at her job and should never have been given it in the first place.

'But still. Well, let's hope at least *you* will be able to sleep tonight then.'

'I'll try.'

'How are the boys?' asked Rachel.

Clare updated Rachel on Jack being in lust and Brian being in love.

'Goodness - I'm away for a week and look what happens!

Now we're all at it, aren't we - even Brian? Oh, sorry Clare. I forgot about you.'

Clare didn't welcome Rachel's reminder of her singleness, but put on a brave face nevertheless, not really wanting to be drawn into a discussion about it.

'Anyway, enough of all this. What's going on with you?' she snapped.

'Well, like I said, I'm really enjoying this job in Berlin. I'll be here until next Friday. Tongue Twisters have really got me some good assignments recently.'

'That's enough! Just tell me about your bloody affair!'

'I think you'll be surprised,' said Rachel, enjoying winding Clare up – she didn't get the chance very often. 'I hope you don't hate me after I tell you.'

'Oh don't be ridiculous,' snorted Clare, wafting cigarette smoke away. 'Why on earth would I hate you? Unless of course you're sleeping with my ex-boyfriend Richard, and then I'll kill you! Or worse still, sleeping with my non-boyfriend Luke, and then I'll torture you first and then kill you!'

'Oh, you're so funny,' tittered Rachel.

Clare just looked at her – she had meant every word.

'It's neither Richard nor Luke, so relax. Anyway, I've never even met Luke. Have you still not heard anything from him?'

'Not a peep,' said Clare with a scowl. 'I was so upset in Osaka and for a few days afterwards, but I'm over him now. It's his loss.'

Clare's valiant attempt at indifference convinced neither of them.

'Anyway, for the last time, who are you sleeping with?' she demanded. 'And if you change the subject once more I'll pour the rest of my gin and tonic over your head and then you really will have to wash your hair!'

'All right, then. It all started a couple of months ago. As you know I was over here quite a lot, doing some work helping to translate the memoirs of a deceased actress. Things had got even tougher than ever with Edward and I really didn't know what I should do anymore. I know I've talked about it with you, but I was still loathe to give up on my marriage completely.'

'You should have left him years ago, I've told you that a dozen times. Anyway, go on.'

'Yes, I know you have. I suppose I was still clinging to the past, hoping things would get better. I should have known that it was already over. You do, don't you, deep down?'

'Hmmm,' grunted Clare. 'And?'

'Petra, who was working with me on the book, invited me to a housewarming party here in Kreuzberg. I had already planned not to fly back to London that weekend and thought, why not, do something different? I've been to Berlin so many times and I still hardly know anyone.'

Clare lit another cigarette. The suspense was getting too much. If Rachel didn't spill the beans soon she was going to strangle her.

'So I went to the party with Petra on the Saturday night. It was lovely, so relaxed. Everyone had brought some home-made food and made me feel really welcome. After a few glasses of wine, people circulated a bit more to chat. There was even some dancing. That's when I met Heike.'

'You've met a German guy? Wow, I once had a pen-friend called Heiko. How old is he? What does he do? Has he got a good body? I want all the details,' said Clare.

'*Her* name is Heike,' corrected Rachel, 'and yes, *she's* German.'

Chapter 15

'But I don't understand,' said Clare, flustered.

'Neither do I really. It's mad, isn't it?'

'You like men, don't you?'

'Yes, usually,' replied Rachel, looking into her drink for help.

'So why the sudden change of gender?'

'It just happened. I can't really explain it. It was quite late on and we were talking and having a laugh. Then Heike suddenly kissed me, softly, on the lips.'

'And that didn't bother you? Well, clearly it didn't,' huffed Clare.

'I quite liked it. Then she wrapped her arms around me and kissed me again, stroking the back of my neck with her hands. This time I kissed her back. My skin was tingling. Clare, it was amazing.'

'Was it really?' said Clare lighting yet another cigarette.

'Nothing else happened that night,' continued Rachel, ignoring Clare's cool reaction, 'but Heike asked me if I wanted to meet up the following Tuesday, and we did. I felt more loved and understood in that one evening than I had done in the last two years. And that's when it did happen. Clare, I can't tell you how erotic and sensual it was. You're shocked aren't you?'

'Me? Don't be silly. Of course I'm not shocked. Why should I be shocked? It's your life and if you want to tongue twist at work and at play then that's up to you.'

'Very funny. Well, if you just want to make jokes about it I won't bother…'

'OK then, YES, I'm shocked. Have you always found other women attractive?' asked Clare, fastening one of the buttons on her blouse.

'Not in that way, not really. Well, apart from Wendy Skiffington at school when we were nine. She had everything. I wanted to be just like her.'

'I think that's probably different,' said Clare. 'It's just, how can you go to a party and let a woman, who you don't even know, saunter over and stick her tongue down your throat?'

'Must you be so crude? You sound like Jack. This isn't exactly easy for me either - and it wasn't quite like that.'

'Sorry.'

'The party was women only. Petra's gay and she told me that when she invited me.'

'Right, now I see. So you decided just like that to put yourself out onto the lesbian party circuit! I need another,' she said, draining her gin and tonic and then catching the waiter's attention, holding up her empty glass.

'Make that two. So I went to a lesbian party: big deal. We go out with Jack to gay bars all the time.'

Ignoring Rachel's rationale, Clare continued.

'So, when Heike started kissing you, you just thought, what the hell?'

'I was surprised, yes, but for some reason my reaction wasn't to push her away.'

'And you've never fancied other women before, apart from Wendy Skiffington?'

'Not consciously, and no Clare, don't worry. I don't fancy you, if that's what you're getting at.'

'I wasn't thinking any such thing,' said Clare, not sure if Rachel's swift dismissal made her feel better or worse.

'Have you told Edward?'

'About Heike? No, and I'm not planning to either. He wouldn't understand. I will be splitting up with him, though it's not because of her. Look, Clare, I don't know how long this will last with Heike, but I really do like her. I don't fancy any other women and I think I still fancy men. Just not at the moment. Please, can you be happy for me?'

Clare put her hands across the table to take hold of Rachel's.

'Rachel, we've been close friends for years. Of course I'm happy for you. It's just such a surprise. You have to grant me that.'

'I know it is, and thanks.'

Sitting back in their chairs for a moment they both watched a young teenage couple walking past their table, holding hands and laughing. The boy put his arm around the girl and held her closely as he whispered something in her ear. Whatever he said pleased her and made her blush. She smiled as she hit him playfully on the arm before taking hold of his hand again.

'Life's an adventure, isn't it?' said Rachel. 'There's a beginning and an end and the bit in the middle is up to you. We've only got one and it's all there for the taking if you're prepared to take some risks and do something a bit different. You just have to jump - the net will catch you.'

'I suppose so. Maybe I am just a bit too caught up in convention. I work like a slave, never get laid and don't always have the time or patience to see things from different perspectives. Perhaps I can learn something from you.'

'Well, Petra is having another ladies' night in a couple of weeks if you want me to put your name down,' teased Rachel, lightening up a bit now that the bombshell had been dropped.

'Thanks,' said Clare, 'but I think I'll pass. I'm definitely a guy-girl and have no intention of experimenting with lesbians. But I am going to be more proactive about managing my currently non-existent sex life,' she finished, taking inspiration from her gin. 'I take it you haven't told Jack or Brian yet?'

'No. You have the honour of being first.'

'I'm flattered. So what's your communication plan then?'

'I don't know. How do you think they'll react?'

'It depends on what the message is. Are you saying that you're now a committed full-time dyke, or just enjoying a bit of the other in between men? Jack probably won't mind either way, but will no doubt have a few jokes at your expense.'

'Yes, I'm sure he will,' laughed Rachel imagining what some of his comments might be.

'Brian will probably be more philosophical and regard it as a turn-on, assuming that you'll be back to men soon, in all probability in a fantasy threesome. I have never understood why men, straight ones at least, almost always seem to dream about sleeping with two lesbians,' snorted Clare.

'I know,' said Rachel, 'I don't get that either. I'll give them a call and tell them.'

'Why not wait until you come to Jack's place for my party next weekend? I want to see the look on their faces when you tell them your scoop.'

'Actually, I was hoping to bring Heike with me.'

There was a pause.

'Are you sure? I mean I thought you didn't want to tell Edward?'

'I'm not telling him. We'll stay in a hotel for the weekend. You haven't invited him, have you?'

'Of course we haven't invited him. And yes, it would be nice to meet Heike,' said Clare reluctantly, hoping that her birthday celebrations weren't going to be eclipsed by Rachel's (temporary or permanent) coming out.

'What's she like, then?' asked Clare.

'Caring, thoughtful, understanding… in fact, you can see for yourself. She's coming down the street now to join us for a drink. I wasn't sure how you'd react so I booked the cavalry just in case. It's OK, isn't it?'

Great, thought Clare, quickly racking her brain for an excuse to leave soon. This was getting to be a bit too much for one evening. Hearing about Rachel's new-found interests was one thing. Watching them together so soon after finding out about it would be quite another.

'Of course it's OK, silly, but I can't stay much longer. I have to have dinner with a work colleague back at the hotel,' she lied, her eyes darting around to see if she could spot Heike, even though she had no idea who she was looking for.

A slim woman with short, dark blonde hair stopped at their table and leant over to kiss Rachel. She was wearing a pair of old trousers and a dirty yellow vest. Clare guessed that she was probably in her late twenties and rightly assumed that she was Heike.

'*Na,*' she said in German to Rachel, before turning to Clare. 'Hi, I am Heike,' she said in English, holding out her hand. 'You must be Clare.'

Clare stared at it. Both the hand and the fingernails were filthy. Heike looked as if she had just returned from a Bader-Meinhof mission. Little tufts of hair protruded from her armpits in traditional European style and Clare could see that she wasn't wearing a bra.

'A pleasure to meet you,' said Clare, gingerly shaking it.

'Just look at your hands! Heike's a mechanic,' explained Rachel, catching a face from Clare.

'I just finished work and our water is turned off, sorry,' said Heike, wiping her hands with a tissue that Rachel had held out for her.

It'll take more than a tissue, thought Clare. She needed a good scrub in a bath.

'I'm sweating like a *Schwein*,' complained Heike, wiping her brow with the oil-stained tissue, making more of a mess. 'The *U-Bahn* was packed full. I'll just go to the toilet and have a wash,' she said.

'So, what do you think?' asked Rachel after she'd gone.

'Does she always look that?'

'Of course not,' laughed Rachel. 'Like she said, she's just finished work.'

'She seems friendly enough, I suppose - a bit grumpy though.'

'I think she was just nervous about meeting you. She was worried that you wouldn't understand.'

'Well she's got that one right.'

'Oh come on, Clare. She thought that you'd try and talk me out of it and persuade me to go back to Edward or something. Put yourself in her shoes. Can't you at least try?'

'I am trying! Look, if it's what you want, then go for it. I'm not going to attempt to talk you out of anything. Just be vigilant that's all.'

'Vigilant?'

'She might have an angry ex-girlfriend out there that she hasn't told you about yet, waiting to pounce on you. You remember Jack telling us about the fights that went on in that lesbian bar in Stoke Newington, don't you?'

'Oh, stop it,' said Rachel.

'I was only joking.'

'I know,' said Rachel with a smile. You will like her when you get to know her. Meeting Heike is the best thing that's happened to me for ages. I feel all warm and loved up when she's around. She really listens to me. It just feels right. And honestly Clare, the sex is amazing. When she touched me down there, I couldn't believe it, it was absolutely… '

'I'm sure it is. Now if you don't mind,' cut in Clare, not really wanting to know. Despite having polished off two large gin and tonics she didn't want to hear all the details about Rachel's vibrant sex-life. Her mind, nevertheless, wandered to thoughts about what Rachel and Heike were getting up to in their intimate moments. Judging by her armpits Clare suspected that pubic maintenance wasn't high on Heike's list of priorities. She contemplated her own neatly-trimmed triangle, untouched for almost four years. What was the point of spending hundreds of pounds on expensive personal hygiene products if no one ever noticed? She may as well just use some cheap oatmeal scrub.

'I'm going to have to make a move,' said Clare standing up with a sigh. 'Say goodbye to Heike for me, won't you? It was nice to meet her.'

'If you say so, but I don't really believe you.'

'Well it was. I just need some time to get used to the idea, that's all.'

'It is what I want, for now at least.'

'I know. I can see that. Just promise me one thing.'

'What is it?'

'Remember, I'll always be there for you. You can tell me anything - well, almost anything,' said Clare with a grin. 'See you at the party next week,' she said, kissing Rachel goodbye.

Chapter 16

'How can this tiny table be so fucking heavy?' complained Jack as he struggled with Brian up the steps to the entrance of the exhibition venue in Hoxton. They were carrying a few choice pieces of Brian's handcrafted furniture from his van to display on his stand.

'Stop moaning like a constipated bull and get a move on will you? We open soon,' said Brian, walking backwards up the steps.

'And thanks Jack, for getting up at the crack of dawn on a Saturday morning to help me to carry all my crap,' said Jack, stopping in his tracks.

'Oh come on, I've already said thanks about five times. I'll buy you a pint later.'

Jack put his half of the table down on the steps and folded his arms.

'OK - a pint and a meal out at the Chinese.'

Jack looked up at the sky.

'And a week for two in the bloody Canaries then. Now, is there anything else or can we get on?'

'You're so sexy when you're angry,' teased Jack. 'A pint will be just fine.'

After a couple of trips they were done and Brian set about arranging the furniture on his stand. Doris Elliot, for whom he had made (and shared) a bed a few weeks ago, was hosting the event and had managed to get him a stand for free. The leaflets, hot off the press ready to hand out to potential new clients, looked great. Jack laid them out on a small counter.

'I think that's about it,' sighed Brian with relief, glancing at his watch. It was almost a quarter to eleven.

'It looks fabulous,' said Jack, standing back to admire their work. 'How much did you say it cost you to be here?'

'Er, nothing. Doris got it for me for free.'

'Really? I wonder why! Remember, there is no such thing as a free lunch. Hope you're not going to be popping off into dark corners to return the favour.'

'I wasn't planning on it,' said Brian dryly. 'Donald had better bring Jessica. I can't wait to see her again. If she does come I'm going to ask her out on a proper date. She's gorgeous, isn't she?'

'Yes, very nice. I'm sure you'll make a lovely couple. Now, to change the subject for just a minute, do you remember I was telling you about that bloke I fancy?'

'Oh yeah, the one from work?'

'That's the one. Well, you'll never guess what happened the other night. We'd been watching this band at... '

'Will all exhibitors please make their way to the Henry Granger Hall,' boomed a loud voice through the speakers dotted around the main hall.

'I'll tell you the rest in the pub tonight,' said Jack eagerly as Brian got up to go.

Everyone charged towards the hall like a herd of wildebeest. They were excited about the event and the prospective contacts that they might make. The décor inside the hall was ostentatious, but Jack quite liked it. The crystal chandeliers sparkled like diamonds and complemented perfectly the enormous, lush, chintz curtains framing the double-fronted bay windows.

The exhibitors had to take the standing room behind the VIP guests, who were now all seated at the tables in front of the stage. A man in a grey suit that was much too tight came onto the stage and started tapping the microphone – as one does – to make sure that it was working. It was.

'Ladies and Gentlemen, welcome to the private view of the

fifteenth Annual London Design Exhibition. As in previous years, today is also the regional heat for local artists to be nominated for the grand final of the National Designer of the Year Award. Please put your hands together for your hostess, Miss Doris Elliott!'

The audience burst into thunderous applause as the man turned, clapping his hands towards the side of the stage. Doris strode confidently out from the wings, illuminated by a moving spotlight. She was wearing a long silver dress with matching elbow-length gloves and a pair of black stilettos. Her face was made-up like a porcelain doll and her hair had been scraped back into a tight bun, held together with a ruby-studded pin.

'Thank you, thank you,' she crooned into the microphone. 'Please be seated.'

'That's never the woman who you made the bed for?' asked Jack incredulously, looking at Brian.

'She looks old enough to be Joan Rivers' big sister.'

'Fuck off! She's not that old. She looks younger without all the stage make-up and lights.'

'You mean in the dark?'

'Come off it, she told me she was only in her mid forties.'

'Maybe she was,' said Jack, 'in the 1980s. That one's had more lifts than the weights I use in my gym.'

Brian elbowed him in the ribs.

'Ouch, that hurt!'

'It gives me great pleasure and it is indeed a tremendous honour,' continued Doris, 'to once again host this wonderful event, here in the heart of Hoxton. Following the drinks reception you will be able to explore and marvel at the work of our talented artists from across London,' she said, gesturing to the back of the hall and pausing.

Everyone turned around and clapped again.

'You'll have them all to yourselves until the doors are opened to the general public this afternoon. Please don't forget to vote for your favourite piece before you leave. The voting forms are in your welcome packs on the tables in front of you and the voting boxes for your completed forms are located at the desk just by the main entrance. As Timothy was saying earlier, all the votes will count towards selecting the top three artists and craftspeople to be put forward to the national final in August in Manchester. Enjoy!'

Doris had barely put the microphone back into its stand before the room was filled with chatter, everybody on their feet. Waiters and waitresses filed in carrying trays filled with drinks to get the party started and the cheque books for commissions opened.

'Have you seen Donald or Jessica yet? Maybe they couldn't come after all,' said Brian.

'Stop fretting - your luck's in. Here they come now.'

'There you are!' cried Donald. 'We've been looking everywhere for you boys, haven't we dear?'

'Hi, guys,' said Jessica, 'what a great venue! I can't wait to see the exhibition.'

'Thanks for coming,' said Brian, looking Jessica up and down, admiring her short black mini-dress and retro sixties platform boots that came to just below her knees. He thought she looked knock-out, and noticed a lot of other men staring at her too. Donald seemed to have an outfit for all occasions and today was looking almost paternal in a dark suit brightened up by an orange bow tie. While the group were chatting Doris came over to join them. At such close proximity Jack decided she actually looked old enough to be Joan Rivers' mother. He gave Brian a 'how-could-you?' look as he shook his head.

'Hello again, Brian,' drooled Doris. 'I just wanted to stop by to wish you luck in the competition. Isn't the turnout fantastic?'

Doris' face didn't – and indeed couldn't – convey much emotion. In fact, apart from the central part of her lips, it didn't move at all, frozen into a wide-eyed glaze.

'Cheers, Doris. You did a great opening.'

'Do you think so? I'm probably a little overdressed for

eleven o'clock in the morning, but at least people will remember me,' she jested, raising an elegantly gloved arm.

'Hi Doris,' said Jessica putting out her hand. 'I'm Jessica Dupont. We met last year when you did some work for my PR company.'

'Of course we did! I knew I recognised you from somewhere.'

'This is my father, Donald.'

'*Enchanté*,' said Donald, with a broad beam, pleased that he had abstained from both Botox and cosmetic surgery and could still smile properly.

The only giveaway that Doris was attempting, and failing, to smile back was a slight twitch in her ears as her skin tautened.

'And I'm Jack, a friend of Brian's.'

'How do you do,' she replied, nodding her head. 'Well, it's been lovely chatting to you all, but I'm afraid I need to circulate and do the rounds, you know. Enjoy the exhibition. Brian, I'm sure you'll do very well,' she purred.

Doris turned to Donald and whispered,

'He's done some work for me and I can't recommend him highly enough. He's marvellous.'

Brian blushed slightly and Jack shook his head again.

Nothing was lost on Donald. 'Isn't he just?' he said. 'He's designed a wardrobe for me and is making it as we speak, aren't you Brian dear?' As he spoke he slanted his eyes ever so slightly, giving Doris a look that he hoped would convey, 'you filthy mare.'

Doris, despite being unable to blink, let alone to voluntarily slant her eyes any more than they already were, still managed to communicate a look to Donald that she hoped suggested, 'you've no chance bitch, so don't even try it.'

'Is he really?' she said, turning to go. 'You'll love it, I'm sure.'

'Well, looks like you'd better make something for me next, Brian,' joined in Jessica with a laugh. 'I wouldn't want to miss out on anything.'

'Whatever you need, I'll make it,' said Brian, as he pulled her away to one side. 'Listen, Jessica, I've been wanting to ask you... if you... if you would like to come out for a drink with me sometime.'

'I'd really love to, and thanks for the offer,' she replied, 'but I don't think my boyfriend would be very pleased if I went out on a date with another man. I am flattered though. Thanks,' she said, with a smile.

Brian felt as though he were suddenly wearing a giant church bell on his head that muted everything around him except the word '*Boyfriend, Boyfriend, Boyfriend*', that rang repeatedly through his ears.

He was devastated.

'I didn't realise you had a boyfriend,' he croaked in disbelief.

'Neither did I,' butted in Donald sternly, overhearing their conversation.

'How were you to know? And Dad, I was going to mention it to you, but it's only been going on for a few weeks, so it's early days yet.'

'Right. Well, we'd better get back to your stand, hadn't we?' said Jack, wanting to rescue Brian from the situation, now that he'd opened his heart up to her and had it ripped to shreds.

'He's a lucky fella,' said Brian to Jessica. 'If you ever change your mind you know where I am.'

'I'll remember that,' said Jessica, giving Brian a kiss on his cheek. 'Thanks again.'

Donald gave Brian a look that said, 'I'm so sorry, dear. I wished I'd known and could have warned you'.

'See you guys later in the exhibition room, then,' said Brian. He managed to sound cheerful, but Jack knew that he was choked.

'Come on, mate,' he said, patting Brian's shoulder. 'Just think about that pint tonight.'

Chapter 17

'A bloody boyfriend! How bad is that?' said Brian, knocking back another neat scotch as a chaser for his pint of bitter. 'I haven't wanted a girl that much for ages.'

'Well, I know you probably can't see it right now, but the situation is actually better than you think,' said Jack, trying to cheer him up.

'And how do you work that one out? I've just been given the elbow!'

'For now, yes, but if you look on the bright side, a) she's only been seeing someone else for a few weeks so it's very early days and b) she didn't say no because she didn't fancy you, she had a good excuse. She was definitely flirting with you AND she gave you a kiss.'

Brian reflected on these points and took a mouthful of beer. They had been drinking for about two hours in the Plough & Pheasant, Brian's local pub in Hackney. The rest of the day at the exhibition had actually been quite successful. Brian had had a lot of interest in his work and his stand had been buzzing. He'd even secured a firm order for two chests of drawers from a couple that lived in Brighton.

But Brian wasn't in the mood for celebrating.

'No, there's no bright side to it. It's shit,' decided Brian, after he'd thought about what Jack had said. 'She could have just said yes to me and dumped the other guy without ever telling me about him, if she'd really fancied me.'

'Hmm, that would have been far too simple. Women's minds are different to men's. Don't you know that by now?'

'What are you on about?'

'You have to prove yourself more. Fight for her. Bring her back the scalp of her boyfriend, or something.'

'Oh no, I can't be bothered with all that 'reading between the lines' crap. She either wants to go out with me or she doesn't. It's as simple as that. I'm not being the other man.'

Speaking of being the other man, Jack wanted to tell Brian about his encounter with Paolo.

'You dirty bastard!' he said after Jack had reeled off the tale.

'But it was so exciting, and totally unexpected. Well, not totally. I'd been hoping for ages that something would happen between us, though that caught me by surprise. It did leave me feeling pissed off though, when he didn't, you know.'

'I bet it did - fuck. Do you believe him about being straight? I mean, I can't imagine just having a quickie with another bloke and then going back to my girlfriend. It's not normal.'

'You'd be surprised. You don't have to look very far. In fact you only have to look as far as Donald.'

'That's true,' said Brian, remembering. He ordered two more whiskies. 'It takes all sorts, I guess. So what happens next?'

'Well, I don't know if there will be a next. It's not exactly what I'm looking for, to say the least. I'd like to have a partner again. However, if the opportunity were to present itself, I couldn't say that I wouldn't,' he chuckled.

'So that's a yes then?'

'I suppose so, yes. Guys like him rarely leave their girlfriends, so I'd have no illusions on that score. But he's so hot, if I get the chance again I'll make him rip my trousers down and then really show him what's what,' he joked.

'Too much information,' said Brian with a grin. 'Really, the things people like you get up to.'

'Hey Brian, Jack, how are you doing? Mind if we join you?'

Brian looked up.

It was Declan and his brother Toby.

'Hi, guys,' said Jack.

'Hello. Good to see you, lads - grab a stool,' said Brian, straightening up.

'How was the market this morning?' asked Jack.

Declan had a fruit and vegetable stall on Dalston market. Toby was a fishmonger and owned the stall next to Declan's.

'It was very busy,' said Toby nodding. 'I saved you a nice piece of tuna, but you didn't come today, man - what's up?'

Jack tried to do most of his shopping from the market and usually went every Saturday. He loved the hustle and bustle and the incredibly wide range of food and other things on offer there. Toby had once told him that if you can't buy it on Dalston market, then you probably can't buy it anywhere else in the world.

'Oh, sorry Toby, cheers anyway. I've been helping Brian with his exhibition. Let me get you a pint.'

Jack got up to order another round of drinks, and Brian told them all about his day. He even told them about how much he fancied Jessica and how frustrated he was after she'd turned him down.

'Forget about her, man,' said Declan. 'There are loads of women out there just waiting for a guy. I met a new girl last night,' he boasted. 'We went back to her place and we were still going strong this morning, know what I'm saying?'

'Well, that sounds like you're very compatible. She'll be the one for you then, and you'll be off the market?' joked Jack, putting the drinks down on the table.

'No way! I'm happy coasting along, and there are lots of fish still out in the sea,' he laughed. 'Our Toby's been getting serious with a girl, though.'

'Don't you go exaggerating; it's only been three weeks.'

'Practically married then,' said Jack.

At that moment, a plain-looking woman with a bony ass protruding from black leggings walked past them. Declan, Toby, and even Brian all stared after her, simultaneously and automatically.

Jack laughed. What was it about groups of straight men? There seemed to be an unspoken requirement to stare after anyone at all who is female and then debate whether they would or wouldn't 'give her one' before deciding on where she was on the 'gagging for it scale'. It happened all the time, everywhere.

'So, boys, who would give her one and how badly was she gagging for it?' he asked.

'I wouldn't touch her with yours,' said Toby. 'She'd be all right for our Dec, though.'

Declan hit Toby on the shoulder.

'Yeah right, brother.'

Brian laughed. 'OK, who's up for going for a curry?'

Toby and Declan both said yes and that they were starving.

Jack wanted to go home and watch a movie. 'Not for me. I'm exhausted. You go and do your ogling over a madras and pilau rice,' he said, putting on his jacket. 'Oh, I almost forgot. I'm having a party next Saturday. It's our friend Clare's birthday. You're both very welcome to come.'

'That would be great, eh Dec?' said Toby.

Declan didn't reply. Jack looked over to Declan to see what was up and then shook his head hopelessly. Of course! It was Bony Ass making her way back to her table, followed by six eyes and three hanging tongues.

Chapter 18

It was Sunday evening and Clare was slumped in an armchair in her dressing gown with a towel wrapped around her hair. She'd had a long, hot soak in the bath and was now polishing off a large tub of triple chocolate swirl ice cream that had been begging her to eat it all day. She was licking the spoon when the phone rang.

'I've just had a mad call from Rachel followed by one from Brian. Can you believe it? I had no idea! Our Rachel - tipping the old velvet!'

Clare looked at her spoon and stopped licking it. She put it down and lit a cigarette instead.

'Do you have to be so explicit?' she asked.

'What's wrong with velvet?'

Clare didn't bother rising to the bait.

'I know. She told me while I was in Berlin, but I wanted you to hear it from the horse's mouth. It makes no sense to me at all. I can only guess that it's some sort of escapism to do with things going wrong with Edward. She says it's not, but surely she must be on some sort of rebound,' said Clare, taking a deep drag. 'What do you think?'

'Well, jokes aside - good for her, I suppose. She said that this Heidi makes her feel very special and that she's happy just going with the flow. If it's something she wants to try then let her get on with it. I think it's great.'

'It's Heike, not Heidi. I might have known you'd think it was wonderful. What did Brian have to say about it then?'

'He thinks it's probably just a phase. He seemed quite relaxed about it. But I can bet you that's just because she's a

121

woman. If it had been his mate Declan having an affair with another man then it would be a different kettle of fish altogether.'

'I'm afraid the difference there is completely lost on me. I simply can't understand how she can change, just like that,' she said.

'Oh come on, she's only having a little affair with another woman. It's not like she's changed into a werewolf,' joked Jack.

'Anyway, Rachel's invited Heike to the party next weekend, so you'll get to meet her then.'

'I know, she said. I can't wait. She sounds lovely.'

'Well, she was covered in oil when I met her, so I'd wear gloves if I were you. So what are you doing at home on a Sunday night?' she asked, wanting to change the subject.

'I'm knackered. It's been a busy week.'

Jack told her all about the exhibition, Jessica's unavailable status for Brian and, of course, Paolo.

'That's a shame. For a moment there I thought Brian was going to have the relationship of the year. Still, at least now he finally gets to experience rejection like the rest of us.'

'Don't be so mean. He's really down about it. What's wrong with you today anyway? You sound like a bear with piles.'

'Thanks. I've just eaten the biggest tub of ice cream you can imagine and do actually feel the size of a bear. And I'll also be middle-aged by next weekend: correction, single and middle-aged. Is that a good enough reason?'

'Don't be ridiculous. Forty is the new twenty. Things have changed,' said Jack as he too lit a cigarette.

'I won't be forty,' screamed Clare down the phone, 'just thirty-five!'

'Really? Well there you go then, you must feel better already. I'm only teasing. Come on, lighten up.'

'Oh it's all right for you three. Brian can mope about Jessica – *and* he can get any girl he wants anyway. Rachel has just found out that she can bat for both teams and knock the ball for six, and you've got Paolo.'

'I haven't *got* Paolo. I told you, he's got a girlfriend.'

'You see, there's that too. Paolo's got a girlfriend and takes blowjobs from you. Rachel's married and then suddenly decides at a party that she prefers pussy. Since when did everything become a fucking free for all?'

'Look, I'm not exactly delighted with the Paolo situation, but don't you think it's a good thing when people feel brave and relaxed enough to try out the things they want to? I do.'

'You know what Jack, you're right. Rachel pretty much said the same to me in Berlin. So guess what, I've been toying with the idea of having a fling with my next-door neighbours. I'm fairly sure they're swingers, given all the comings and goings I've seen. She's just had an enormous boob job and I think he's recently had his ass lifted, which should be interesting. It's been on my mind for some time. Yes, I think I'll do it. I might fit into our little group a bit better then.'

'Now there's an idea,' laughed Jack. 'I can just see you getting down with Torpedo Tits while hubby watches and waits for his turn.'

Clare finally laughed too.

'OK, perhaps not,' she said, imagining herself being suffocated between two globes of silicone.

'That's better. You've got loads of time to find the right man.'

'Oh come on, now that is just rubbish. And I've tried everything. When I went speed dating all the best men sped away. When I went online they all went offline. When I actually proposition the men I like face-to-face they say they have to go home to wash their hair even if they're bald. I mean, what's wrong with me?'

'Nothing's wrong with you, you're gorgeous!'

'Flattery will get you everywhere, but really, it must be something. My looks, my shape, my opening lines?'

'What are your opening lines?' asked Jack curiously.

'Nothing much, something like, "Hi, my name's Clare, I'm an accountant and looking for someone to have a serious, monogamous relationship with." I always smile while I'm saying it too. What do you think?'

Jack grimaced, pleased that Clare couldn't see him at the other end of the phone.

'Hello? Are you still there?' she asked after a few painful seconds had passed by with no response from Jack.

'Me? Yes, of course I am. It's… fine, it's honest and er… straightforward.'

It was no good. He had to say something to her. It was awful.

'Look, why don't you try leaving off the bit about looking for a serious, monogamous relationship when you first talk to someone,' he suggested tentatively. 'You might want to leave out the accountant bit too.'

'But I am looking for that.'

'Yes, *we* know that and it can be our little secret. But to be honest, baby, any guy will probably think that you have a pair of handcuffs and a male chastity belt in your handbag and will want to run a mile if you tell it like you just told me.'

'So if I say I'm just after a quickie, then I'll score?' scoffed Clare. 'I want more than that!'

'And you'll get it. Just keep your ball and chain hidden for a while. Play hard to get, like you don't care, and you won't be able to keep them away.'

Clare thought about this rationally. Maybe Jack did have a point.

'Well, we'll see. I'm not sure I like the loose approach, but I am determined to be more adventurous and will try to get out more. I'm just so busy at work. I can't seem to find any time for dating - I mean pulling,' she laughed.

'That's better. How's Japan coming along by the way?'

'It seems to be progressing well at long last. Mrs Suzuki's party are coming over in a couple of weeks to hopefully sign the blasted contract. There's still a lot to do though, and I'm always bringing work home. Grace has got me looking at new markets already as well as four hundred other special projects to keep me busy just in case I manage to find an hour free for myself and switch off.'

'I don't know how you do it.'

'Don't get me wrong. I will be absolutely delighted if we close the Japanese deal - and I'll get my bonus!'

'Money isn't everything, though, is it?' said Jack.

'If I'm going to be single then I want to at least be rich and single. Only kidding, you've made your point. Anyway how are things looking for the party on Saturday? Thanks so much for organising it.'

'It's all under control. There should be about twenty people if they all show up. I've booked the caterers.'

'Jack, you're a star. I'm really looking forward to letting my hair down and having some fun,' she said, sounding excited. 'Oh yes, there's another thing,' she continued, 'it'll be the last party that I will be smoking at, too. I'm giving up the week afterwards. My sister Jo has recommended a book to help. She says it's great and makes it easy to quit.'

'How can you stop smoking right now with all your work stress and everything?'

'But that's just it. Jo says it doesn't matter. The stress is just an excuse.'

'I'm not convinced. It can't be that simple.'

'Well, she swears by it. I am so sick of smoking,' Clare continued, lighting another cigarette.

'Me too,' admitted Jack, lighting one as well, 'I hate being a social pariah.'

'Then why not read it with me and give it a go?'

'But what will life be like without cigarettes? Will there even be a life? I don't think I can do it.'

'Please! Come on, let's try it together and surprise everyone,' she begged.

'Oh all right, go on then, but on one condition.'

'Name it.'

'You'll do whatever I tell you to do regarding your quest for a man – no ifs and no buts.'

Clare wasn't sure she liked the sound of that, but in the spirit of being more adventurous, she agreed.

'OK. It's a deal. See you on Saturday.'

Chapter 19

'What do you think went through her mind when she decided to put that on this morning?' Gloria asked Jack, nibbling a pretzel. She was referring to the orange woollen dress that Lisa was wearing from chin to toe. Apart from her head, hands and flat, lace-up shoes the dress covered her entire body.

'Do you think she thought, "Today I want to look like a sack of potatoes" or "I made it myself so I'll fucking wear it"?'

'Don't be so horrible,' said Jack. 'The poor thing's been ill. She probably didn't have the energy to do any washing or ironing. Maybe that's all she had left in the wardrobe. We can't all be as fashion conscious as you, you know.'

It was true. Gloria did spend most of her money on clothes.

'She's got six of those sacks in different colours – I've seen them all, so don't give me that. And I'm not buying the 'poor thing' routine either. She will be over here like a bat out of hell the minute she can find something to criticise me for, voice or no voice.'

'Did you have a good weekend?' asked Jack.

'Not bad. I bought these. What do you think?' she replied standing up, giving him a quick twirl to show off her new skin-tight white hot-pants.

'Wow, they're fantastic!'

'Aren't they? They're so tight I almost had to stitch them on.'

Gloria caught Lisa scowling at her through her office window and sat down again.

'Did you see that?'

'What?'

'That look she just gave me.'

'What about it?'

'That 'you look like a whore' look.'

'Lisa's probably just a bit jealous of your figure. You're lucky; you could wear a plastic bag and still make it look sexy.'

'Thanks, but luck has got nothing to do with it. It's about how much food you put through your face and how much exercise you do. Lisa should stop eating all those pies at lunchtime and go for a run instead, if she's not happy. No one's force-feeding her.'

Jack wasn't listening any more. Paolo had just come in.

'Hey! How are you two today?'

'Good morning, Paolo,' flirted Gloria, flashing her satin-clad thighs and fluttering her eyelashes.

'Hi! How was your weekend?' said Jack, surprised by Paolo's coolness.

'It was just great, Jack my friend. A bit of walking in the country during the day, a couple of gigs in the evenings with friends, you know.'

'Sounds good,' said Jack airily.

'I'll catch you guys later,' said Paolo, striding over towards the stationery supplies room.

Gloria whistled.

He turned around.

'Jack, stop that! Gloria will be getting the wrong idea,' he laughed, stroking his hair.

'It *was* me actually,' she said, annoyed that he hadn't noticed.

'Why would I be whistling?' asked Jack.

'Well, you know, I thought you…'

'Yeah, well, I don't,' said Jack, not wanting to give him the satisfaction just yet.

'Well, he definitely doesn't seem to be interested in me

then, said Gloria with a pout after Paolo had walked off. 'If these hot-pants don't get him going, then nothing will. He's not my type anyway.'

'No, he's definitely not your type,' said Jack.

He still hadn't told her about what had happened with Paolo down by the canal, honouring the request not to tell anyone at work.

'Have you made a move on him yet?' she asked.

'Me? Oh, he told me he's straight, so that's probably that, something about a girlfriend too. How could I compete?'

'You seem to be taking it very well. Last week it was all Paolo this and Paolo that. Now you're all blasé about it.'

'Don't look at me like that. You can't put a square peg in a round hole, can you?'

'You could try,' laughed Gloria.

'Well you would, I'm sure, but some of us have some dignity and know when to stop.'

'You cheeky bastard! You're getting as bad as Lisa!'

On his way back Paolo stopped by at their desks again.

'Hey, guys, I can't find the big brown envelopes. Do you know where they are, Jack?'

Jack was on his feet quicker than a flash.

'Sure, I think I know. Let's go and have a look.'

As they walked past reception towards the supplies room Samantha shouted something.

'I really enjoyed that band we saw on Saturday, it was great fun.'

Paolo didn't say anything and just smiled back at her.

Jack followed him into the stationery room. As he turned to close the door, Paolo put his arms around him from behind, pulling him close. Jack shivered as he felt Paolo's lips burning on his neck.

'That was great the other night. I'm sorry I ran off like that,' whispered Paolo, pressing hard against him, pushing his hand down the front of Jack's jeans. 'Next time it will be different,' he said, before standing back. Jack was taken completely off guard again, and his face flushed. His skin was tingling. He knew this was crazy, but he couldn't stop himself.

'I'm having a party on Saturday. Why don't you come?'

'Maybe I can pop in for a while, smiled Paolo. 'Email me.'

Samantha was beaming at Paolo as they went past reception. Wait a minute, thought Jack - what was that she had said a few moments ago?

'Samantha isn't your girlfriend, is she?' he asked quietly, in disbelief. This could all get very complicated if she was.

'Ssshhh, I have to get back to work now. See you later.'

They got back to Jack's desk and Paolo gave him a sly wink, a wink that obliterated any doubts that Samantha might have caused him to have.

'So you couldn't find them then?' asked Gloria.

They both looked at her, wondering what she was going on about.

'The envelopes. They're right in front of the door as you go in. I'm surprised you missed them.'

Chapter 20

Brian was late. He'd promised Donald that he would be at his house before ten-thirty and it was now eleven o'clock. It had taken him the best part of a week to make the wardrobe and he had worked long hours every day. It had helped to take his mind off Jessica. He had hoped she might have had a change of heart and got in touch, but he hadn't heard anything. The ball was in her court and she wasn't serving. Maybe he'd just have to write it off after all.

'There you are!' exclaimed Donald, greeting him at the house, looking at his watch. 'I was beginning to think something had happened to you. Isn't it a lovely day?'

'Yeah, sorry I'm a bit late. There was a diversion on Balls Pond Road and I got trapped driving through Islington.'

'What a shame! Would you like a glass of iced tea?'

'Cheers, yes please. I'll just start bringing in the wardrobe.'

The wardrobe was in flat sections of timber in the back of Brian's van.

'Shall I ask Tom to help you carry it up the stairs? It must be terribly heavy.'

'That would be great, if he doesn't mind.'

'Of course he won't mind. I'd help you myself, dear, but my back has been giving me grief again and I can hardly bend down today. I'll just go and get him.'

Donald wandered back into the house while Brian started to get some tools out of his van.

'All right, mate?' shouted Tom, emerging through the garden gate to the side of the house. Tom was shirtless and wearing a pair of faded blue army trousers. 'Donald says you want some help.'

'That's brilliant thanks ever so much.'

It was hard work even with two of them, but after four trips up and down the stairs all the wardrobe parts and Brian's tools were in the bedroom.

'Goodness,' said Donald, surprised. 'And you can make a beautiful wardrobe just like your design out of all those pieces?'

'I certainly hope so. Thanks for helping, Tom.'

'You're welcome, anytime. No Jack today then?'

'Jack? He wouldn't be any use. He couldn't even fit his foot into a work boot, never mind help fit a wardrobe.'

They all laughed.

'Oh Brian, you are awful,' said Donald.

Tom went back to mowing the lawns. Donald decided to leave Brian to get on with it and went off to make a few phone calls.

Alone upstairs, Brian went back out onto the landing and stood in front of the photograph of Jessica and her mother. It was no good. He was crazy about her. He knew that it didn't really make a lot of sense, considering he'd only seen her twice, but it just felt so right. He had to get her to want him too - but how?

After a few hours of hammering, sawing, drilling and polishing, the wardrobe was finished. Brian vacuumed up the sawdust and packed his tools away in their cases before giving Donald a shout.

'Are you finished already, dear? My word, that was quick,' said Donald, sweeping into the room.

He stood in front of the wardrobe and gazed at it in awe.

'I love it. It's wonderful. And the finish - how on earth did you get it so shiny?' Donald opened the doors and looked inside the drawers, running a finger across the smooth shelving. 'What a clever boy you are! I can't thank you enough - it's splendid.'

'Cheers, Donald. Glad you like it. I enjoyed making it for you.'

Despite the friendly banter, Donald noticed the tinge of sadness in Brian's eyes. He could guess why.

'Jessica's a fool,' he said, perching on the edge of the bed. 'I told her that you would be perfect for her and that I was already looking forward to having you as a son-in-law,' he said, hoping to get a smile from Brian. 'But she's so hotheaded. Once she's made her mind up, that's it. Just like her mother.'

'Do you think I should call her and try again?'

'No, not yet, dear. Don't chase her. Leave it for a while. You'll have to be patient, I'm afraid. Play the long game. She knows you like her and I think she likes you too.'

'But if she likes me, what's she doing going out with some other bloke? I don't get it,' said Brian, sitting down next to Donald.

'Sometimes we have to wait for what we want. Sometimes we get it in the end and sometimes we don't,' said Donald sagely, patting Brian's knee.

Brian sighed.

'All right, then. You know her best. I'll cool it for a bit, if that's what you think.'

'I do, dear. Did I tell you that Jessica will be staying with me for the next month or so? She's having her loft converted into a studio and doesn't want to be surrounded by noise and mess. I'm sure you can find a reason to pop over every now and then. You could bring me some designs for a new garden shed, for example.'

Brian perked up at the news and the shed idea.

'Donald, I haven't known you for long, but you're a good friend. Jack's having a party for our friend Clare's birthday on Saturday. It would be great if you could come.'

'That's terribly sweet of you for asking, but I'm afraid I have plans already. I hope you all have a wonderful time. Come on, let's go downstairs and have a drink of tea.'

After two cups of tea and three chocolate biscuits Brian packed his stuff back into the van and climbed in. He was closing the rear doors when Tom came running over.

'You off, then?' he asked Brian.

'All done, and thanks again for helping.'

'Listen, if you ever need help with anything else, give me a ring. Here's my number,' said Tom handing Brian a piece of paper. 'I do all sorts of odd jobs as well as a bit of gardening.'

'Oh right, cheers,' said Brian, folding it up to put in his pocket. 'I'll do that. See you, mate.'

'Tara. Say hello to Jack for me, won't you? Tell him I was asking about him.'

Chapter 21

'It all looks lovely,' cooed Clare, admiring the decorations that Jack and Brian had dressed the living room with for her birthday party. 'You shouldn't have gone to all this trouble.'

Clare had asked Jack to tell everyone not to send or bring any cards or gifts, but she really did like the balloons and banners.

'Glad you like - it was no trouble at all,' said Brian. 'Happy birthday!'

One of the caterers stepped out of the kitchen with a silver tray filled with bubbling glasses.

'Madam,' he said, bowing as he offered her champagne.

'Thank you,' she said, taking a glass and then a sip. 'Mmmm, that's lovely and cold. Where's Jack?'

'He's just upstairs getting ready. He's been charging around all morning sorting everything out.'

'I really am grateful. I should be thirty-five every day,' she laughed, enjoying the attention. 'But I still can't believe I'm thirty-five already.'

'It's no age.'

'Well, it's not for you and Jack. You're both only thirty-two. And Rachel's barely thirty-one. Oh, sod it. Cheers,' she sang, holding up her glass.

Brian chinked with her.

'So what do you make of all this with Rachel?' he asked, grinning. 'She said she's bringing Heike along today.'

'I know. It's odd, isn't it? I was a bit funny about it when she told me, but I'm slowly coming around to the idea. I mean, it doesn't make any difference to me who she sleeps with. It was just so unexpected.'

'You're telling me.'

Brian gazed out onto the terrace and sighed.

'What's the matter?' asked Clare.

'I've been knocked back by that girl I really liked. I can't seem to get her out of my head. Women!'

'Yes, I know. I was sorry to hear about that. Jack told me,' she said, resting a hand on his forearm. 'She's Donald's daughter, isn't she? I wish I could say something to help. She doesn't know what she's missing.'

'Thanks, Clare. I'm fine. I might have lost the battle, but I can still win the war. I'll think of something.'

'Is Donald coming to the party? I'd love to meet him. He sounds like good fun from what I've heard.'

'Yes, he is,' agreed Brian. 'Good fun, that is. He can't make it to the party though.'

'Who can't make it?' shouted Jack, bounding down the stairs and into the living room.

'Hi, Clare. Happy birthday! Are you excited about your party?'

'Of course I am. It all looks great. Thanks, Jack.'

'Donald can't. He sends his regards though and Tom said to say hello to you too,' said Brian, walking over to the kitchen to get another glass of champagne and watch the caterers prepare the canopies.

'Who?' asked Jack, fluffing up the cushions on the sofa.

'Tom. You remember - the gardener.'

'Oh yes, Donald's hired help - the randy old goat.'

'He gave me his number in case I wanted any help with other work, after he gave me a hand carrying the wardrobe parts up the stairs. I think you might have got him all wrong. Bet you'd have thought he looked sexy mowing the lawn with his top off, if you'd seen him. I know you,' said Brian, raising his eyebrows.

'Yes, well, whatever, you have him then. Listen, I've asked

Paolo to come. He only said he *might* be able to and even then it would only be for a little while. If you talk to him, you mustn't say I've told you anything about you-know-what.'

'You-know-what?' asked Clare blankly, turning to Brian. 'Who's Paolo?' she asked, pretending to be clueless.

'You know, the straight guy that likes to have blowjobs from blokes down by canals,' chipped in Brian helpfully.

'Will you be quiet about that?' muttered Jack, flapping his arms. 'The caterers might hear you!'

'Well it's hardly a state secret, is it?' laughed Clare. 'What do the caterers care?'

Jack glared at them both.

'If you say anything at all you'll mess it up for me.'

'I'm sure you can do that all by yourself,' said Brian. 'It sounds a mess to me already. But don't worry, our lips are sealed.'

'Which is more than can be said for yours that night,' joked Clare.

'Very funny, I'm pleased to see that you're back on form.'

'So, who else have you invited to celebrate my birthday with me then?' she asked.

'Of those you don't know, let me see... Brian's mates, Declan and Toby. Toby might bring his new girlfriend, who I haven't met yet. I've asked Gloria from work and of course Paolo. Then there's... '

Jack was interrupted by the doorbell.

'I'll get it,' said Brian, grabbing the intercom and pressing the door entry button.

'It's Rachel and Heike,' he said, putting down the receiver.

'This is it, then,' said Jack excitedly. 'I can't wait.'

'Just stop it. Try to act normally, as if nothing's happened,' said Brian.

Clare, Jack and Brian were all standing in a line when Rachel and Heike came in.

'What's this, a firing squad?' said Rachel, putting her bag down on a chair before walking over to Clare. 'Happy birthday,' she said, giving her a kiss. 'Come here, you,' she said to Brian, giving him a hug. 'You look well, Jack,' she said, hugging him too. 'Heike, these are my very good friends Brian and Jack. You remember Clare, I'm sure. Boys, this is Heike.'

'Hi,' said Heike,' with a smile. 'Nice to meet you both.'

'Hello,' said Jack, shaking her hand. 'Welcome to London,' he grinned.

'Well, hello,' said Brian, shaking her hand as well, admiring Rachel's taste.

'Hello again, Clare. How are you? I hope you enjoyed your time in Berlin.'

Clare was speechless. She couldn't believe the transformation. Gone were the dirty vest and oil-stained trousers and gone were the filthy hands and nails. In their place Heike was wearing a thin white shirt that didn't leave much to the imagination and a pair of hip-hugging bleached jeans. She had eyes the colour of a deep blue ocean on a sunny day, which Clare hadn't even noticed when they'd first met, and her hands looked as if she'd just had a manicure.

'Clare? Is something wrong?' asked Rachel, wondering what the matter was with Clare's ability to speak.

'No, of course not. Sorry,' answered Clare, coming to. 'Hello Heike! Good to see you again too, and thanks for coming. It's just that you look so… different. What a lovely outfit!'

'Thanks - I do manage to get out from under a car sometimes,' she laughed, remembering her last appearance.

'Heike's a mechanic,' Rachel reminded Jack and Brian, taking hold of Heike's hand.

'You're still glowing and looking very… relaxed Rachel,' said Clare, enviously. 'Are those new earrings?'

'Yes, Heike bought them for me. Aren't they lovely?'

Their chatter was interrupted by first the caterers coming round with more drinks and then the doorbell again. Brian did the honours and pressed the door release button.

'Time to party!' cried Jack, turning the music up before going out onto the terrace for a smoke. He was quickly joined by Clare.

'Well, she seems very nice,' said Jack, lighting their cigarettes.

'I never said she wasn't,' huffed Clare, 'but I'm still not sure it's the right thing for Rachel. I hope she knows what she's doing.'

'Just leave her to it and be happy for her. She's a big girl now and can make up her own mind what she wants to do.'

'You know what the funny thing is? Just before Rachel told me, when we were in Berlin, I told a male colleague of mine not to be a prude.'

'Not to be a prude about what?'

'Two men were kissing at the table next to us in a café. My colleague seemed shocked and I told him not to be a prude. A few hours later Rachel's telling me all about her love life and I'm the one behaving like the prude. It does seem to make a difference, when it's one of your closest friends, someone you really care about. Not to mention being jealous about all the sex she's getting,' she laughed.

They heard the front door slamming and then deep voices followed by clanking bottles. Jack looked inside to see what all the commotion was. It was Declan and Toby.

'Brian, mate, we've brought some drinks,' said Declan, holding up two bags filled with beer bottles.

Toby was already taking a glass of champagne from a caterer.

'Come on,' said Brian, 'let's go outside.'

'Wow, nice pad man,' said Declan, having a good look around as they went through and out onto the sunny terrace. 'You've got a great location - and look at that view, you lucky bastard!'

'I know I am - glad you like it,' said Jack with a smile.

The doorbell rang again. This time it was Gloria and her best friend Annette from back home in Australia. They were followed up the stairs by a few friends of Clare's from Richmond and her sister, Jo. The party was really starting to get going and the caterers were now offering the guests canopies as well as more drinks.

'This is the life,' said Gloria to Jack as they leaned against the railings with their drinks. Gloria was wearing a very tiny pair of purple shorts that resembled a serviette and an almost non-existent, low-cut cream top.

'Cheers, girls. Thanks for coming,' said Jack.

'Cheers, and thanks for inviting us. I love parties. Who are those three tasty specimens of manhood?' asked Gloria, indicating to her side.

'The white guy is my best friend Brian and the black guys are his mates Declan and Toby. Declan's the one in the middle. They're brothers.'

'And who are the dykes?' she asked, nodding over to where Heike was straddling Rachel on a sun lounger.

Jack laughed. 'The one underneath is my friend Rachel, who strictly speaking is straight, or was, and the one on top is her girlfriend.'

'Very cosy.'

'It's a long story, but apparently it's love. I'll tell you another time. I am so glad you could come. Lisa's running a bit late though.'

Gloria almost dropped her drink.

'What did you say?'

'Only pulling your leg, but Paolo said he might pop by.'

'Did he now? Paolo's this Portuguese guy from work who Jack's got the hots for,' she said to Annette. 'But he is so into me, and I'm just not interested.'

Jack smiled at Gloria's injured pride. Difficult though it had been he had still not told her all about his escapades with Paolo, though he suspected she knew something.

'Excuse me, girls, I have to mingle.'

Jack found Clare with her sister Jo, feasting on miniature sausage rolls in the lounge.

'Jack, this is Jo. Jo, this is Jack.'

After they had kissed the air three times each, Jo said to Clare,

'I brought you the books. Two copies, right? They're in my bag. Make sure I don't forget to give them to you. I am so glad you're doing this, Clare. Mum will be too. She's worried about your health.'

Jack groaned.

'So we're really going to go through with it then?'

'Yes, we are, next week,' said Clare. 'We'll pick a few nights that are good for both of us and read the book together and then stop smoking.'

Jack didn't want to think about it today. Brian came over and started chatting to Jo, which gave Jack the opportunity to pull Clare to one side.

'So are you enjoying yourself?'

'It's a great party – thank you so much again. I've had far too many of these,' she said, holding up her glass.

'That's what birthdays are all about. Now, seeing as it *is* your birthday, how about making a pass at someone with a new opening line?'

'Who shall I make at a pass at? My sister? Heike?'

'Don't be silly. I was thinking maybe about Declan. He's a bit of a lad and you almost certainly won't coax him into a serious relationship, but you could try your luck and just see what happens.'

'He is quite sexy,' said Clare, thinking about Declan's tight buns as she grabbed another glass from one caterer and a satay chicken skewer from another. 'You're right. Why not? What have I got to lose?'

'That's the spirit. I think he's outside with Toby.'

Clare guzzled down the rest of her champagne.

'Right - here goes,' she said, striding outside.

She could see Declan behind the sun-lounger where Heike was now lying on top of Rachel in a full-on kiss. No more inhibitions there, then, she thought. But was it absolutely necessary to do it at a party? Unfortunately, Clare didn't quite make it over to Declan. Gloria had appeared from nowhere and had made a beeline for him. There she was, already laughing, flicking back her long, blonde hair and most definitely flirting. He seemed to be enjoying himself, judging by his wandering hands – as was his brother, Toby, who was receiving the same strategic treatment from Annette.

Clare retreated indoors like a beaten warrior.

'What happened?' asked Jack. 'You've only been gone for about four seconds.'

'Your Gloria has already snared him,' she snapped. 'Why on earth did you bring her along if you wanted to set me up with someone? Happy fucking birthday to you too!'

'Oh no, sorry, I didn't think. Gloria has been known to move very quickly. At least you had the courage to go over,' he said, trying to pacify her. 'It's a start, isn't it?'

The doorbell rang again.

Although Brian was in the kitchen close by, Jack went over to press the button this time, and held the door open. Paolo came bounding up the stairs. Jack couldn't believe his luck.

'Hiya! You made it then? Come in and I'll get you some champagne.'

'Hey, Jack, sorry we are late,' he said, patting Jack on the shoulder. 'I'm afraid we can't stay long, but I thought we could have a quick drink with you.'

Jack's heart sank as he registered the three *'wes'* in the last sentence and realised that Paolo had brought a female companion with him, who he could hear coming up the stairs behind him.

It sank further still when he saw who the other half of *'we'* was as she reached the doorway.

It was Jessica.

Chapter 22

Although it was actually only a few seconds, the excruciating silence seemed to last for minutes for Jack, Brian and Jessica as they looked at each other and tried to figure out what on earth was going on.

Jack was thinking, 'Who the fuck does Paolo think he is, bringing his girlfriend to my party? Is he rubbing my nose in it, or is he a sadistic psychopath? Was he hoping for a quick one upstairs in the bathroom while she drinks champagne down here? Is he scared of being found out? Or does he get off on the risk of being found out? Maybe he wants to be found out? How did Jessica get to be Paolo's girlfriend anyway? Poor Brian, what's he thinking? But if Jessica's his girlfriend, what was going on in the office with Samantha? Is Paolo sleeping with anyone and everyone? How many more? Maybe he's just misguided and really needs me - and this is his way of getting close.'

Brian was thinking, 'Who the fuck invited Jessica and her boyfriend? Is someone trying to rub my nose in it? What is Jessica doing going out with one of Jack's friends anyway? Did he know about this all along? But isn't Jack's friend the guy who likes blowjobs on the canal towpath? Does Jessica know about what he gets up to when he's not with her? Maybe this is my big chance.'

Jessica was thinking, 'How the fuck did I end up at Brian's party? He must think I'm a bitch from hell, trying to rub his nose in it, turning up with Paolo like this. How does Paolo know these guys anyway? Jack seems very pleased to see him

- how do they know each other? Brian looks great in those jeans.'

Paolo, being completely oblivious to these new complications, was the only one who could speak. He started the introductions.

'Hi, guys! This is my girlfriend, Jessica, and Jessica, this is my work colleague, Jack.'

Jack decided there was probably no point in pretending they didn't know Jessica.

'Hello again, Jessica,' he stammered. 'Do come in. I'll get you both some champagne.'

'*Again?*' Now it was Paolo's turn to look confused.

'You two know each other?'

'Yes, we met recently at my father's,' explained Jessica calmly. 'Jack's friend here, Brian, was doing some work for him. He loves the wardrobe, by the way.'

Brian gave her a look that he hoped said, 'I love you.'

Jessica gave him a look that she hoped said, 'I'm so sorry about this, I had no idea.'

'Small world, huh?' said Paolo, his eyes flitting nervously from person to person. He didn't want to run the risk of any in-depth discussions between Jack and Jessica, so quickly added, 'Well, let's have that quick drink, then we'll have to be on our way to another engagement.'

'Come in, come in,' said Jack. 'I'll introduce you to Clare – the birthday girl.'

Paolo was in no mood for either further introductions or celebrations, but Jack had other ideas. He would make him sweat while he was here, as a punishment.

'Clare!' he shouted enthusiastically through to the lounge. 'Come and meet Paolo, and Donald's daughter, Jessica!'

They stood uncomfortably drinking champagne for a few moments while Clare made her way over. Brian wanted to say something to Jessica, to spill the beans about Paolo's extra-curricular activities, but thought he'd better try to get his head around the situation before jumping in with any bombshells.

'Hello. I'm Clare.'

'Happy birthday,' said Jessica and Paolo, their faces glum.

'Jessica, how lovely to meet you, and thank you for coming – I've heard so much about your father,' said Clare, giving Brian a quizzical look that she hoped said, 'what the fuck is going on – I thought it was all off between you two?'

'And you too, Paolo,' continued Clare, extending a hand. 'Jack's told me all about you. You're even better looking than he said,' she added, doing her best to keep the words 'canal' and 'blowjob' out of the conversation.

Clare hadn't twigged that Paolo and Jessica hadn't just arrived together by chance, but had arrived together as an item.

'Let's go out onto the terrace. I'll introduce you to some more people,' said Jack, wanting to inflict more discomfort on Paolo.

'No, really, we have to get going, don't we darling?' said Paolo gruffly.

'I'm sorry, yes we do. It was nice seeing you both again, and good to meet you, Clare. Enjoy your party.'

'Right then, see you at work next week,' said Jack crisply as they started to make their way through the door and down the stairs.

'Bye, Jessica!' shouted Brian after them. 'Hope to see you again soon.'

Clare didn't get it.

'Can one of you please explain to me what was going on there?'

'Jack, be my guest,' said Brian. 'I'd love to know.'

'How the hell should I know? I asked Paolo to come to the party. I didn't know he was seeing Jessica!'

'And does she know that you're seeing him?' asked Brian.

'Why are you asking me? I very much doubt it, though.'

'You see, if she knows he likes boys like you then maybe she'll see things a bit differently - and prefer a straight man, like me.' said Brian.

'No, that's a bad idea. If you tell Jessica, she'll tell Paolo and then he'll feel that I've betrayed him and it will all be off,' said Jack, not wanting to throw in the towel completely, despite everything. 'I don't see what you've got to gain. She obviously doesn't fancy you that much or she would have left him by now,' said Jack defensively.

'That's crap. Come on, Jack, you know he won't keep you happy for long. But I could make Jessica happier than he can. Please?'

Jack thought about it and sighed. He supposed Brian was right. Paolo was never going to be a full-time partner for him, exciting though their moments together had been. And if Paolo was sleeping with all and sundry then how long would it continue anyway?

'I'm with Brian on this. If my boyfriend was sleeping with you, Jack, then I'd definitely want to know. He's a swine.'

'I think you're getting my relationship with Paolo slightly out of hand. It's not even a relationship - just a bit of fun.'

'He's using you, Jack, can't you see? You're better than that. There are loads of other guys out there,' said Clare.

Jack knew deep down that Clare was right. He also knew that it could only get less satisfying as time went on and the complications and risks increased. Where next in the office after the stationery room? Under Lisa's desk while she was having a meeting? In Jessica's jeep while she was walking the dogs? It would all end in tears.

'OK,' he said to Brian, giving in. 'You win. I like you a lot more than Paolo. So what happens now?'

Brian gave Jack a hug.

'Cheers, mate. I won't forget it.'

'Damned right you won't! I'd play it carefully, though. She won't thank you for it. No one likes to be the last to know. Right, I need a drink. Where are those waiters when you want them?'

The rest of the party was oblivious to the revelations that had just taken place and everyone seemed to be getting on and having fun. Gloria was draped over Declan, glued to him like a second skin. Toby was dancing with Annette, her hands clasped behind his neck and his hands on her butt. And Brian had joined a group of Clare's friends, who had started to play a drinking game on the terrace.

Jack and Clare sat down on the sofa.

'You really will be better off without him,' said Clare.

'I know, and like I said, it was just some fun. I'm not hurt, but I am a bit angry that he just turned up with Jessica like that. I do live in the real world, so let's see if Brian can salvage anything from the situation.'

Jack had had enough. He didn't want to discuss the topic any further. 'To you, my birthday girl,' he said, raising his glass.

'Cheers,' said Clare, looking outside.

She couldn't help being envious of Gloria's figure and the way she could carry off such a tiny skirt so well. The skirt seemed to get shorter every time she looked at it.

'What chance have I got of attracting Declan with competition like that,' she moaned, trying to pull her own skirt down a bit more to cover her thighs.

Jack followed Clare's gaze over to Gloria's petite ass.

'Don't keep putting yourself down. Yes, you're not a size eight... '

'And the rest,' interrupted Clare, helping herself to a passing profiterole.

'But you have brains, a career, a sense of humour *and* good looks.'

'In that order? Do you know when I last had sex with a man?'

'June 12th 1998.'

'It's not funny. It was four years ago.'

'I know, you told me already. But fear not, because I have worked out a plan.'

'If you say go and make a pass at Toby instead, I swear I will stuff this profiterole up... '

'No, it's not that.'

'What is it then?'

'I'm going to keep you in suspense. I will tell you tomorrow when you're sober.'

'I can't wait,' said Clare, already fearing the worst.

'Have you seen Rachel and Heike?' he asked, looking around. 'Don't say they left without saying goodbye. I've hardly spoken to them.'

'Don't worry. Rachel will be fine. She'll be relieved that she's got the introductions over with and had her semi-coming out, or whatever it is. Oh look, they're coming down the stairs now.'

'They'd better not have been on my bed. I only changed the sheets for you this morning. You're still planning to stay the night, aren't you?'

'Lovely! I can't wait to nestle down in a bed where Rachel and Heike have just shared a mutual orgasm. It'll be nice and warm.'

Clare suddenly realised that the music had been turned down and that everyone had started gathering around the sofa where she and Jack were sitting. The dreaded, inevitable moment had arrived. Jo was coming towards them carrying a chocolate cake, ablaze with flickering candles. Thirty-five candles, to be precise.

'Happy birthday to you,' they began, 'happy birthday to you, happy birthday dear Clare-air... happy birthday to you,' they finished, almost in tune, complete with vocal harmonies from Gloria and Annette.

Everyone clapped as Clare was forced to ceremoniously blow the candles out and cut the cake into twenty miniscule pieces. Once the cake had been devoured everyone returned to their drinks and conversations. The music was turned back up and the dancing continued.

It was about midnight before people started to leave. Rachel and Heike shared a cab with Gloria and Declan, and Brian got a lift home with Jo, who had to drive through Hackney on her way back to Plaistow.

After they had all gone, Clare thought she would treat herself to a crème de menthe nightcap. She knew that Jack had a bottle in his drinks cabinet. After she had poured herself a glass she sank down into an armchair with it. The caterers were tidying up and Jack was chatting to Toby. Nursing her drink, she began to feel alone - and very sorry for herself. She even shed a few tears. Why had Luke never called her? She'd really liked him. Why couldn't she meet 'The One'? Why couldn't... she'd nodded off with a snore and an open mouth.

Chapter 23

'I'm so glad you had a good time,' said Jack into the telephone. 'Yes, I think she managed to enjoy it, despite one thing or another. She's just taken her hangover into the bath. I agree. Yes that's exactly what she needs, a man and a good fuck. I know. I've got it all worked out. No, I think she's getting used to the idea of Heike. It's not that. It was lovely to meet her by the way - you make a striking couple. I think Clare's just a bit jealous because she thinks that everyone else has got something exciting going on in their lives, except her.'

'Yes, well, I hope you're right. Heike still thinks that Clare doesn't like her and that she blames her for what's happened, despite the compliments yesterday. Clare just walked off without saying goodbye properly after meeting her in Berlin, and hardly spoke to us at the party. It's not fair on Heike.'

'She'll be fine, trust me. You and Heike were quite… preoccupied at the party, you have to admit, and I don't blame you. Go for it. Have you told Edward yet?'

There was a pause.

'I'm telling him today. We're flying back to Berlin tonight.'

'Right. How do you think he'll take it?'

'I'm not telling him about Heike, but I will be saying that I want us to split up. I'll keep you posted. I'm going to be staying in Berlin a little while longer. Tongue Twisters are happy with me doing more work for them remotely: modern technology is wonderful.'

'I admire your bravery,' he said, 'and you're welcome to stay here any time - both of you,' he added. 'Oh, Clare's just coming down the stairs. Shall I put her on?'

Clare padded over towards the sofa, resembling a polar bear, wrapped in Jack's white bathrobe with matching slippers and hair towel.

'No? Yes, I understand, you're probably right. I'll tell her you'll be in touch. Good luck with everything. Ciao, Rachel.'

'Was that Rachel?' asked Clare, wondering why she hadn't wanted to speak to her.

'Yes, she's, er, a bit busy at the moment, and had to go. She's going to tell Edward it's all over and then hide away in Berlin for a while in her lovenest with Heike.'

'Well, she can't hide away over there forever,' scoffed Clare. 'At some point she will need to take a view on whether Heike really is the be-all-and-end-all.'

'You're going to have be careful, Clare, otherwise you'll end up hurting Rachel, or, even worse, falling out with her properly,' said Jack sternly. 'She thinks you don't like Heike and that you blame her for turning Rachel into a lesbian.'

'Oh, don't be ridiculous, of course I don't think that, or hate Heike, for that matter. I'll call her later and sort it out. Now can you please leave the lecture? My head is throbbing like mad. Where are your aspirins?'

'I'll get some for you,' he said, standing up to go over to the kitchen. 'Today is going to be the first day of the rest of your life.'

'Isn't it always?' said Clare, swallowing the tablets.

'I'm thinking more laterally than that.'

Clare could barely think at all at the moment.

'If you say so.'

'I do. Now have some coffee and go and get dressed. And sort out your face.'

'What's wrong with my face?'

'It doesn't look like yours, somehow. Go and have a look upstairs and you'll see what I mean. When you're ready we'll get some nice fresh air in Russell Square, and then have lunch in Amici's.'

Clare made a face at the thought of solids.

'Don't give me that. In a couple of hours you'll be wolfing down *tiramisu* and washing it down with a bottle of wine.

Clare heaved at the thought, but managed to stagger up the stairs and do as she was told. It was like being four years old again.

Jack was right. A walk round Russell Square did do her the world of good. It was a sunny, breezy morning and the leaves were rustling in the trees. An hour and a half and ten slow laps later they were sitting at Jack's favourite table in the restaurant.

'How's the head?' he asked.

'I feel much better, thanks.'

'Hair of the dog it is then,' he said, ordering some wine.

'I'm not sure that's such a good idea,' protested Clare.

'Nonsense, it's exactly what you need.'

'Right, now that I'm sort of feeling - and hopefully looking – a bit more like myself, what's this secret master plan of yours?'

Jack got out this month's copy of 'Boys for Girls' and put it discreetly on the table.

'I'm guessing that's not a new Sunday paper supplement,' said Clare, looking down at the photographs of men in various stages of nakedness. 'So is that it? You think that the situation is now *so* grave that I should pay for it? Well, you can think again, I'm not that desperate!'

'Calm down and have a drink. This has got nothing to do with being desperate. It's the twenty-first century and a socially acceptable activity. It's no different to getting your hair done or having a facial.'

'Well, it might be all right for you, but I'm afraid it's not socially acceptable in my circle of friends,' she snapped. Can you imagine me at work?

"Did you have a good weekend, Clare? Yes, it was marvellous. I bought a new dress, had dinner with friends and got laid by a rent boy on Sunday afternoon! Did you? That sounds nice."

I mean really!'

'Just hear me out,' said Jack. 'You have to look at it as an investment.'

'An investment? You mean they'll pay me some dividends from their pensions?'

'Not an investment in them, in *you*.'

'Oh, come on, Jack, how is an afternoon with a... with a...' Clare had started to flick through the magazine,' ...with a gorgeous guy, going to get me a boyfriend?'

'You need to take the edge off your emotions. You need to get laid and have a good time. Forget about planning opening lines and asking what his favourite book is, just have a good....'

'Yes, I get the picture, thanks. And then what?'

'You will then be rid of your pent up sexual frustration so that when you do meet other guys you won't put them off straight away. You won't come across like a giant hormonal tarantula any more.'

'You think I am that bad?' asked Clare, distressed at the comparison.

Jack shrugged, leaving her to draw her own conclusions.

Clare agreed that Jack might have a point.

'I'd be so nervous, though. What would I say?'

'Just treat it kind of like a date, bearing in mind that it's actually a cool business transaction. He'll know what he's doing and will take the lead.'

She cast her mind back to the drinks she shared for that mad hour with Marleen in Osaka. Marleen certainly knew what she was doing and had seemed very well organised about conducting her business transactions.

'But isn't it dangerous?' she quizzed.

'Don't worry, with this agency there's a thorough vetting process and an audit trail of numbers, contact details and references,' answered Jack, wanting to appeal to Clare's rational mind.

Clare seemed to be coming around to the idea and was now pouring over the pictures in the magazine.

'He looks nice,' she said, pointing to Sven, a Danish hunk

who promised never to disappoint. 'Look at that body!'

When Clare had got to the end of the magazine, and her wine, she nervously agreed to go ahead. She was thankful that she had kept up her intimate grooming sessions after all.

'OK, let's do it,' she gasped. 'What happens next?'

'Nothing. You just go back to my place and freshen up. He'll be ringing the bell in about an hour.'

'What?'

'I knew you'd see sense so I booked and paid for Sven while you were still unconscious this morning. Call it my little birthday treat. I knew you'd pick him too, and he sounded very pleasant on the phone. I promised Brian I'd go with him to see Jessica and be the star witness in the case against Paolo, so you'll have the place to yourselves. And don't worry - I won't breathe a word about this to Brian. I'll be back about six. Have fun!'

'You bastard!' said Clare, though she was secretly pleased that Jack cared so much about her, even if he did show it in strange ways sometimes. 'Hang on a minute. What would you have done if I'd have said no?'

'Gone home and hopefully got my money's worth,' grinned Jack.

Chapter 24

'Are you sure this is a good idea?' asked Jack, as the van sped up Rosslyn Hill.

'It is, yes. I've thought about nothing else since I got home last night. This is my chance to put the record straight and win her over.'

Brian had been up early (for a Sunday morning) and had showered and shaved, styled and sprayed, all before ten o'clock. He had called Donald to make sure that Jessica would be at home in the afternoon, and Donald had promised not to tell her that he was coming over. He had then called Jack to see if he would accompany him on his quest.

'Thanks for coming with me. I owe you one.'

'You owe me more than one! You've asked me to forsake my lust interest in Paolo so you can pursue your love interest with Jessica. What do I get out of it?'

'The pleasure of seeing me happy. And I'll be helping to free you up so you can go after someone decent who deserves you.'

'How touching!' said Jack, flicking Brian's ear.

'Ouch, that hurt! What was that for?'

'The pleasure of seeing *me* happy,' laughed Jack.

Donald let them in through the gates and they drove up to the house. The dogs were barking and Donald was polishing Jessica's car when they pulled up.

'Hello, boys! How nice to see you again. Brian, I haven't told Jessica you're coming so if you want to pretend you're here to discuss making me a Lazy Susan or something, I'll go along with that. Though I must warn you, she's in a foul mood. Goodness knows what she got up to last night. That boyfriend of hers dropped her off about midnight and they were screaming at each other like a pair of wild beasts,' said Donald. 'Rags! Muffin! Stop that infernal barking at once, do you hear?'

Brian perked up at the news that there had been a row.

'Were they really? Anyway, there's no need for any white lies today. I've come to see Jessica because I need to tell her something.'

'I thought we agreed that you would hold back for a bit. I'm sure it's for the best.'

'Yes, but there's some new information that I think will change things. Do you mind giving her a shout?' asked Brian, eager to get on with it.

'Wouldn't you like a drink of tea or some fruit juice first? What's the rush?'

'Brian needs to get something off his chest,' said Jack.

'Very well. You'd better come in, but don't you go upsetting her any more than she is already,' warned Donald, leading them through to the lounge. 'Wait here.'

Donald went off to call Jessica, and then let the dogs out into the garden.

'When they come back, you take Donald into the kitchen. I don't want a big audience,' whispered Brian.

'Hello, Brian. This is a surprise' said Jessica, coming into the room. 'Jack, I didn't realise you were here as well.'

'Hi, Jessica,' said Jack. 'Donald, how about that tea you were just offering? I'm parched.'

'I have some lovely jasmine and elderflower. It's very refreshing. Come and give me a hand in the kitchen.'

Jessica thought Brian must be angry with her for turning up at the party like that.

'I'm sorry about yesterday. I had no idea that Paolo knew Jack and was going to your friend Clare's birthday party. You must think I'm a real bitch.'

'Not at all, so don't worry about that. How were you to know? Did you get home all right?'

'Yes, thanks, Paolo brought me back here.'

'Jessica, you need to know something about Paolo,' he said, wanting to cut to the chase.

'I do? What do you know about Paolo? He said he'd never met you before.'

'Look, I'm sorry to have to say this, but he's making a fool out of you.'

'Is he really? Well my relationship with Paolo has got nothing to do with you, so just stay out of it. I must have misjudged you after all, coming here to try some cheap trick to split us up.'

'Jessica, I really do like you. Even if you don't want to be with me, I don't want to see you get hurt. Can you understand that?'

'Brian, whatever it is you want to say, just forget it. I'm not in the mood today. Now will you please go?'

'He's been having sex with someone else - another man.'

'Don't be ridiculous! Paolo isn't into men. I can assure you he likes women.'

'Maybe he does, but he also likes men,' shouted Brian, about to play his trump card.

'How the hell would you know? Did he tell you that?'

'No, Jack did.'

'Oh he did, did he? And why would he do that?'

'Ask him yourself. Jack, can you come in here for a minute?' he shouted.

'What on earth is going on in there?' Donald asked Jack, alarmed by the rumpus.

'I'm not sure exactly, but I think we're about to find out,' said Jack, taking his tea through to the lounge.

'Jack, tell Jessica it's true about Paolo.'

'I'm sorry Jessica, it is true,' he said, avoiding eye contact with her.

'What's true?' asked Donald.

'Tell her about what happened on the canal,' said Brian. 'Go on.'

Donald was hooked.

'Haven't you already told her?'

'Will someone please tell me what you are going on about?' snarled Jessica.

Jack suddenly realised that Brian had left him to perform the grand finale all on his own - so he did just that and told her everything.

'I don't believe a word of it,' said Jessica coldly. 'Paolo's told me all about you trying it on with him, though. He told me about how you follow him around, hoping to get a quick peek. He's not gay, so just keep your hands to yourself!'

Now it was Brian's turn to shoot from the hip.

'Actually, it wasn't his hands. It was his mouth.'

Jessica whacked Brian across the face.

Jack flinched.

'How dare you? Get out of this house right now or I'll call the dogs in. You as well!' she shouted at Jack, before stalking out of the room and going upstairs.

'For heaven's sake, what is all this about?' asked Donald, still not fully registering.

Jack filled Donald in with the parts of the story he didn't know already.

Donald was aghast. 'My goodness, what a mess.'

'Do you think she'll end it with Paolo now?' asked Brian hopefully.

'Well, dear, I know I haven't even met him, but he does sound like bad news, so I'll certainly be encouraging her to do so. But she can be as stubborn as a mule sometimes.'

'There you go,' said Brian with a grin to Jack as they were driving back to Bloomsbury. 'It's in the bag.'

Chapter 25

By the time Jack got home Clare had turned into Cleopatra and was lying on the sofa, munching her way through a box of chocolates. Her face was bright and rosy, matching her new and improved mood.

'Hi, Jack! Welcome home.'

'No need for me to ask whether or not you went through with it, then,' he said, throwing his jacket on the armchair next to the sofa. 'You look ten years younger than you did this morning.'

Clare sat up and offered Jack a chocolate.

'To tell you the truth I wasn't really sure I'd be able to do it, but I did,' she squealed.

'Well, how was it? What was he like?'

'Amazing. He was wonderful, and a real gentleman. The sex was just fantastic. I feel like I'm floating on a cloud.'

'Tell me everything!' he said, sitting down next to her.

'He arrived, I fixed him a drink and we chatted for a bit,' she said casually.

'Chatted? What about?'

'About me mainly. He asked me about my job and didn't seem at all phased or bored when I told him I'm an accountant. It was so refreshing to finally talk to a man who was actually interested in what I do for a living.'

Jack thought Sven was probably more interested in how much money Clare earned than how she earned it, but said nothing.

'So how did you make the transition from having a cosy chat to having wild sex?'

'If you would keep quiet for just a minute and stop asking me questions, I'll tell you!'

Jack fell silent.

'He was even better-looking than the photograph in the magazine, and probably about my age, maybe a bit younger. He was a bit taller than me, quite thick-set, and not lacking in the downstairs department - if you get my drift.'

'You mean he had an enormous cock?'

'If you insist on me spelling it out for you, then yes, huge. Not that that's so important.'

'Go on.'

'He just sat down next to me, took my drink from my hand and stroked my cheek. He said 'you really are beautiful' and then kissed me. Jack, I swear, I've never felt so turned on as I did at that moment. Everything else just happened so quickly. I kissed him and then he started taking my clothes off. Within seconds we were naked, a condom was on and we were having mad, passionate sex here on the sofa.'

'On my sofa?' asked Jack warily, checking the upholstery.

'For a while. Then we went into the kitchen and I leaned over the breakfast bar for round two. It was amazing. He found places I didn't even realise I had.'

'I hope you moved the chopping boards before writhing around,' said Jack, not fancying 'toast plus' for breakfast.

'I had two orgasms. Do you know when the last time was that I managed that with a man? He was so attentive! I really think he fancied me. My nipples are as hard as bullets again just talking about it! My God it was awesome!'

Jack rolled his eyes.

'Clare, that just proves how good he is at his job. He made you feel special, attractive, like a woman.'

'I already felt like a woman,' said Clare indignantly. 'No, it was more than that. You wouldn't understand. I know he wanted me.'

'He'd probably taken two Viagra pills before he arrived.

What he wanted was for you to enjoy yourself so much that you would book him again. But remember - next time you're paying.'

Clare was not happy that her blissful bubble was slowly being popped as Jack brought home the harsh realities of the transaction. She did hope, though, that Sven hadn't needed pharmaceutical supplements to perform, and that he had enjoyed himself too.

'Did you have to remind me that it was business so quickly?'

'I'm only saying it because you're my friend. I don't want you getting hurt or flying off with the fairies, hoping for a white wedding in Scandinavia. What did we agree on today? It's not always about falling in love – and don't tell me that you weren't thinking about it.'

Clare made a 'so what if I was?' face and shrugged her left shoulder.

'It was about you taking control and getting what *you* want from a man for a change. And it sounds like you did. Promise me you won't call him again and that you'll destroy the card he gave you with his number on it,' demanded Jack.

Clare's hand shot defensively to cover the dressing gown pocket where she'd put the card earlier, a little piece of Sven to remind her of the afternoon. How had Jack guessed?

'I knew it! Come on! Give it to me. I'll rip it up for you.'

'But it's not a business card! It's his personal number,' she protested.

'That's just so he doesn't have to pay a commission to the agency next time.'

'Look Clare, you've had a great afternoon, and it's human nature to think that you like Sven. But let it go. It was just business for him and a bit of fun for you. Take your new-found confidence and move on. That's what you did it for.'

Clare knew he was right and sighed, though she didn't want to have to go back to Big Ben now that she'd had Big Sven.

'Thanks for arranging it all,' she said after a while. 'I'd never have done it if it had been left up to me.'

'That's better. It was my pleasure. You really do look different, honestly.'

'I feel it. Oh, and I gave Rachel a ring. I just caught her at the airport before they boarded the plane back to Berlin.'

'Oh yeah,' said Jack.

'Yes. It's all sorted out. I apologised for being a bit cool towards Heike yesterday. I also admitted to being jealous about her sense of adventure. I even told her about what happened here today.'

'You didn't?' said Jack. 'What did she say?'

'She said 'good for you and about time'. I suppose I wanted to prove something to her, that I could be daring and spontaneous too.'

'Good, I'm glad you called her. It will mean a lot. Did she say anything about Edward?' he asked.

'Only that she'd told him it was all over between them. Apparently he'd been expecting it, so it wasn't an almighty shock. They've decided to wait a while before discussing what to do next. I mean, they'll have to get divorced and sort out all their finances and everything.'

'I really do think she's doing the right thing,' said Jack. 'She obviously wasn't happy and now she's doing something about it.'

'Yes, you're right. Anyway, how did you two get on at Donald's?'

'Jessica went ballistic when we told her about Paolo and shared the details of his 'moment of madness' with me. She's got one hell of a temper, that girl.'

'Oh dear! So it didn't go down too well then?'

'It most certainly didn't. She didn't believe him – or me. Paolo had already told her that I'd been making passes at him, but that he'd laughed it off, not wanting to appear homophobic. That was magnanimous of him, wasn't it?'

'Well, you have been making passes at him, haven't you?'

'Er, yes, but he has also been making passes at me. Of course, he conveniently left that part out of it, so now it looks like I'm his stalker. I am so not looking forward to going into work tomorrow. He's going to be furious.'

Chapter 26

Jack didn't normally wear a shirt and tie for work, but today he'd decided to dress smartly. He didn't know whether or not Paolo would be in the office, but for some reason he felt safer behind a tie. Clare had treated herself to a taxi home after her evening of passion, and Jack had slept like a log. It had been such an exhausting weekend.

'Are you going for an interview? You scrub up quite well, don't you?' said Gloria.

'And what are you trying to say?'

'Only teasing. So what's the occasion, then?'

'I just felt like a change, that's all,' said Jack. 'Did you enjoy the party? You seemed to be getting on well with Declan - and your leaving with him did not go unnoticed.'

'Who? Oh, him,' she said airily. 'He was all right, but I don't think I'll be seeing him again. Annette quite liked Toby, though. I think they're going out again this week sometime, after he's finished things with the other girl he's been seeing.'

'That's nice. It's good to see love blossoming out of my party,' said Jack sarcastically, sifting through his in-tray. In it he found some cash reports from the stores, a pile of supplier invoices and some staff expense claims. Paolo had submitted three more claims, each for over £1,000 for client entertainment. He'd never seen anyone else claim so much for just a few people. He thought back to the night in Camden and remembered that there had only been six of them. It can't have cost that much for a few bottles of house champagne and one or two rounds of shots, can it? Something wasn't quite right, but he didn't want to question Paolo today. He would just think that he was picking at him because of what had happened at the party.

'I need some coffee. Want some too?' he asked Gloria.

She looked into her empty mug.

'Great, thanks,' she replied, holding it up for him to take. 'And if you can find any of those biscuits Lisa hides behind the washing up liquid and cloths in the utility cupboard then please steal me a couple. She stashes them behind there because she doesn't want anyone seeing her scoffing them in her office.'

'I'll do my best,' said Jack getting up to go to the kitchen.

He was on his hands and knees, rooting around in the cupboard in search of biscuits, when Paolo came in and slammed the door behind him.

'What the fuck did you have to tell her for?'

Jack banged his head with a start as he crawled out and stood back up. For once Paolo looked rough. He had bags under his eyes and his skin had a greyish tinge to it. He didn't look like he'd had much sleep since Friday.

'Sorry, but I didn't really have much choice after you brought her to the party! My mate Brian's been working for Jessica's dad and he didn't want to see her get hurt.'

'Why would I hurt my girlfriend?' yelled Paolo. 'I denied it all, of course. I love her.'

The word 'love' felt like a stab in the neck to Jack.

'Do you really? Brian couldn't understand why a straight man such as your good self would want to fool around with other guys like me. He was worried about her, that's all.'

'And just how did he know about what we'd done in the first place? I thought I told you not to tell anyone!' shrieked Paolo, edging closer towards Jack.

'How was I to know you were going to bring Jessica along on Saturday? Did I ask you to bring your girlfriend? No, I asked *you*!' shouted Jack, matching Paolo's ferocity. 'I haven't told anyone at work – that was the deal. I can say what I like to my friends.'

'Yeah?' taunted Paolo.

'Yeah,' said Jack, getting a little worried about Paolo's escalating temper. He didn't want any blood on his new shirt.

'Well, you've fucked it up now. That's it, it's over.'

'What's over, a few quick gropes? Suits me, you closet queen.'

Paolo pushed Jack up against the refrigerator and put his hands around his neck.

'Don't you ever say that to me again or I'll fucking kill you!' he said, breathing heavily on Jack's face as he tightened his grip.

They struggled for a few seconds before Jack managed to prise Paolo's hands from around his neck and push him away.

'All right, calm down,' said Jack. 'And stop shouting or someone will hear you. It never happened, OK? Forget it.'

Jack straightened his tie and tucked his shirt back into his jeans before side-stepping Paolo to make his coffees and catch his breath.

'Don't worry. I'm not going to tell anyone at work.'

'You'd better not, Jack, my friend. You don't want to mess too much with me, understand?'

'Sure, whatever. Now can you get out of the way so I can take these back to my desk?'

Paolo opened the door for him.

'What was all the noise about?' asked Gloria, not being one to miss a trick. 'Lovers' tiff?'

'Not funny,' said Jack. 'Like I said, there's nothing going on between us.'

'Well you were arguing about something. There's something fishy about what you're not telling me.'

'Can you please just leave it? It's nothing. Paolo's girlfriend lost an earring on Saturday and Paolo thought she might have dropped it at the party.'

'So why would he be shouting at you?'

'Because he bought them for her and they cost a fortune. He was just irritated, that's all. I said I'd have a look.'

'Hmm - if you say so. I hope he doesn't think I've got it. I wouldn't want him shouting at me like that.'

Jack started to calm down and sipped his coffee as he worked through the papers on his desk. Before going out for lunch he went over to Lisa's office to drop off the blue folder, labelled 'Lisa to sign', containing a few invoices and Paolo's expense claims.

'Hi, Lisa,' he said chirpily, waving the blue folder. 'Can I just leave these with you?'

'Of course you can, Jack,' she replied, looking up from the file she was reviewing. 'Just leave them on the table. Is there anything urgent in there?'

'No, not really, just a few staff expense claims that we normally pay weekly.'

'Are there any from Paolo Fernandez in there, by any chance?' she asked, nodding towards it.

'One or two, yes. Why, is there a problem?'

'I don't know, you tell me. What did you think when you processed them? I see here that you authorised a payment for £800 while I was off last week with diarr… off ill. Didn't you think that it seemed like a lot of money?'

'Well, it did seem quite high, but then isn't that what A&R is all about? Entertaining and networking?' said Jack, not quite sure where this was going.

'There was no back-up to his last expense claim. Did you ask him where the itemised bill was to support the payment summary, and the signed statement outlining who was being entertained and for what purpose?'

'No, I forgot, sorry,' said Jack, lowering his head, waiting for it to be chopped off.

'It's not the first time that his expenses seemed excessive either. I've been looking at some of these other claims that he got Vince to sign off instead of me,' she sniffed, pointing at the documents on her desk.

Vince was the Chief Executive of Spring Records.

'Please make sure that in future you always get enough back-up for all expense claims. It's the golden rule. You know better than that, Jack. I'd expect Gloria to forget, but not you. What about the claims you have just processed? Is there enough back-up and detail to support those?'

'I think so,' said Jack, gingerly leafing through the folder. 'Actually, no, there isn't. Only the cash receipt totals.'

'All right, just leave them there,' snapped Lisa, not wanting to get too cross with her golden boy. 'And don't forget next time. It's your job to ask and make sure you get answers and…'

'… back-up.'

Lisa smiled.

'Yes, that's right.'

Jack retreated back to his desk to get his jacket before going out for some lunch.

'What's wrong with Droopy Drawers? Did you tell her that her skirt looks like it was made from an old circus tent?'

Jack laughed.

'I forgot to get enough back-up for some of the paperwork, that's all.'

'Now if it had been me who'd forgotten back-up you'd be reading me my last rights by now,' she said, looking at Lisa as she tried to telepathically inflict a migraine on her.

'Right, I'm popping out for some air and a sandwich. Do you want anything?'

'No, thanks, I'm on a diet this week and have my crispbread and dried fruit with me.'

'You can't survive all day on that.'

'I know, but I'm going to have to try. Now go and stuff your face on a chicken and bacon sandwich and don't forget to bring back half a dozen pork pies for Madam over there.'

'Stop it. Lisa will hear you.'

Jack went for a stroll around Covent Garden. It was packed with tourists clamouring to buy useless knickknacks and tacky souvenirs of London, but it took his mind off what had been an emotionally charged morning. He knew that it was definitely finished with Paolo now – whatever 'it' was – but he didn't really care any more. Having seen Paolo in a different and quite violent light, and witnessed his bare-faced arrogance and lies, he'd had enough anyway. He only hoped that Jessica would eventually see sense and bin him. That would certainly make Brian's day.

When he got back to work there was quite a commotion going on in Lisa's office. Paolo was in there with Lisa and Vince and the door was closed.

'What's going on?'

'You've been missing all the fun,' said Gloria excitedly. 'I don't know what it's about but they've been in there for about half an hour, ranting and raving.'

Paolo was now waving his arms around and Vince's face looked like it was about to explode. Lisa kept shaking some papers and was looking angrier than even Gloria had ever seen her look before. Paolo suddenly flung open Lisa's office door and stormed out.

'I don't need all this shit! Fuck the expenses and fuck this job too!'

'Paolo come back here,' shouted Vince. This wasn't the result he'd wanted. Paolo was his best A&R man. But when Lisa had been to see him about the expense claims he hadn't had any choice but to support her questioning him about them. Paolo didn't go back. He didn't say even say goodbye - or look at Jack either - as he left the office.

'Oh my God, did you hear that?' exclaimed Gloria.

'Of course I did, I was sat here with you!'

'What do you think happened?'

'I have no idea, but it couldn't have happened to a nicer guy,' he said, actually feeling quite pleased that Paolo had gone.

Chapter 27

Clare was on her way to work, humming a tune that she had heard on the radio that morning. She was still feeling rejuvenated from the escapades of the weekend, and was in a better mood than she had been in for weeks. Uncharacteristically, she had taken a long lunch break the day before and had popped down to Bond Street to buy herself a new power suit. She was wearing it today, and paused to appraise her reflection in one of the windows on New Oxford Street. She liked the bold red fabric of the skirt and jacket and thought that she looked like she'd actually lost a pound or two. Perhaps it was just the effect of the heels that she was wearing, but today she didn't care.

It was Wednesday morning and Grace had summoned a management team meeting. Clare was the first to arrive in Grace's office, closely followed by Paul (Head of Finance), Sarah (Head of Operations & Merchandising), Daniel (Head of Human Resources) and Simon (Head of Marketing). Karen (Grace's Personal Assistant), was poised to take the minutes of the meeting.

'Good morning, everyone,' said Grace merrily.

'Morning,' murmured the team in unison.

'I'm sure that Karen will have already briefed you,' continued Grace, 'that the reason I wanted to have this meeting was a) to bring you up to speed with the Japanese deal and b) to make sure that we have all bases covered, so that everything goes as well as it possibly can regarding a successful deal closure during their visit here next week. Has everyone brought along their copies of the revised Japanese business plan that Karen distributed last night?'

There was a frantic shuffling of papers.

'Good. Now, as you know, Clare has been a turbo of energy since her last trip to Osaka, and has been working very closely with Just for You's lawyers, Rosenberg & Hoffmann. There have been some... issues that needed to be ironed out, particularly around the minimum order, but they've almost been resolved now, haven't they?' asked Grace.

Clare was gazing out of the window wondering what Sven was doing. She had a fair idea, and couldn't help herself smiling at the thought.

'Clare?' said Grace.

'What? Oh, I am, yes.'

'What are you?'

'I'm sorry, what did you just say?'

Grace batted her eyelashes and gave Clare one of her stares that meant 'pay attention or else'.

'The last few issues in the contract – have they now been resolved with Mrs Suzuki's lawyers?' snapped Grace impatiently, with four additional bats of her eyelashes.

'Yes, Grace, that's right. Lance is fully aware of our position.'

'So, Clare, have Mrs Suzuki and her lawyers now agreed to our terms?'

'I've made our position clear,' said Clare, trying to dodge the question, as Sven was being slowly but surely obliterated from her thoughts.

'But what is *their* position on *our* position? Have they agreed to our terms?'

Grace was like a dog with a bone. She would not give up until she had a clear answer.

Clare had no choice.

'Well, not exactly, but I think that they will eventually agree.'

'Clare,' said Grace, banging a heavily-braceleted wrist

down on the meeting table, 'Mrs Suzuki's party is coming over next Thursday to meet us all, see some stores and, most importantly, hopefully sign the heads of terms. *You* need to make sure that this issue is resolved *before* they arrive. I don't want any last minute hitches. Does that make sense?'

'Yes, Grace.'

'Good. Now, Clare, when do you think you'll be able to confirm to me that you've reached an acceptable consensus with Mrs Suzuki?' asked Grace with an icy stare.

Here we go, thought Clare. There's no escape.

'I'll get on to Lance as soon as we're finished here.'

'Thank you, Clare,' said Grace with a smile. 'Karen, what time will they be arriving?'

Karen opened her diary and quickly flicked through it.

'They get here a week tomorrow, at about two o'clock.'

'And just remind me, who's coming from their side.'

'The President Mrs Suzuki, her lawyer Lance Rubenstein and Kohei Sawayama.'

'Who's Kohei Sawayama?' asked Grace, turning back to Clare.

The name wasn't familiar, so Clare could only assume that it must be the Wizened One who always accompanied Mrs Suzuki in her meetings, but had never been introduced. He's probably some sort of mentor, thought Clare.

'I think he's Mrs Suzuki's special advisor.'

Three bats of the eyelashes.

Clare guessed that 'think' probably wasn't a precise enough answer. Her new expensive power suit didn't seem to be having much impact on Grace. She may as well have worn a floral patterned dress with puffy arms and lace trimmings.

'I'll check with Lance when I speak to him,' said Clare, making a note on her papers.

'When will you be able to let the rest of the team know who… ?'

'Before the end of the day,' groaned Clare.

'Thank you, Clare. Now, where were we?' asked Grace, pretending to have forgotten, as a test for Karen.

Karen sprang back into action and picked up her diary again.

'They arrive at two, and I've ordered a buffet lunch before the meeting at three. I've booked dinner at eight at the teppanyaki restaurant... hang on a second... Samuri, which is just off Piccadilly Circus. On Friday morning Sarah is taking them to see two or three stores followed by lunch before bringing them back here to sign the heads of terms in the afternoon.'

'Thank you Karen, efficient as always,' laughed Grace, before turning to Sarah.

'Sarah, which stores are you planning to showcase to Mrs Suzuki? I know you'll have already given the managers an in-depth briefing, but if you could just give us a flavour of how you are planning to make the most of the visit,' she said, licking her lips, her tongue moving quickly, like a viper poised to attack its prey.

All eyes were on Sarah.

'Er, no, I mean, I haven't made a final decision on which stores yet, it all depends on... '

Four bats.

'I'll let Karen know by five o'clock this afternoon,' trembled Sarah.

Three bats and another quick lick of the lips.

'Two o'clock,' she corrected quickly.

'Thank you, Sarah. Karen, could you put Sarah's detailed synopsis of what outcomes she is looking for from the store visits in with the management team briefing pack that you are planning to distribute ahead of the Suzuki party arrival?'

Sarah hadn't even started to think about the store visits yet, let alone write a synopsis on expected outcomes. She'd been too busy with her team appraisals.

She gritted her teeth as Grace turned back to face her again.

'Sarah, when... '

'I'll fire it over to Karen by tomorrow evening.'

'Thank you, Sarah. Does anyone have any comments on the itinerary?' asked Grace.

The team were silent, heads bowed.

'Let's move on then. Has everyone read through the new business plan?'

The bowed heads nodded reluctantly.

'Initial reactions, thoughts? Let's have a quick trot around the table. Who wants to go first?'

Silence.

'Sssssssssssssss,' started Grace,

Sarah clenched her fists fearfully. She hadn't had a chance to even open the business plan yet, never mind read it.

'Sssssssssssimon, I know you'll probably have most so say from a PR perspective. I'm really excited about hearing your views.'

Sarah heaved a sigh of relief. Now she at least had the opportunity to steal a few glances while Simon was in the hotseat, before it was her turn.

'I think it's really great,' he said hurriedly. 'They get what it is that we are about and have some interesting takes on how we can market and communicate together strategically. What I thought really jumped out of the paper was how clearly their vision chimes with ours and how it firmly underpins our medium-term operational objectives. It's so exciting!'

Grace knew that he hadn't read any of it, but let it go. He'd played a good game.

One bat.

'Thank you, Simon. Daniel, I could see you practically champing at the bit to jump in there with your thoughts, so do you want to go next?'

The only thing Daniel had champed on was his tongue as he worried about what he was gong to say when it was his turn.

'Yes, it looks like a good plan,' he stuttered. 'I started reading through it just before the meeting, but I didn't have time to finish it,' he admitted honestly.

Wrong answer. No points for honesty.

Five bats.

'Well, I think that's about it,' said Grace after Sarah and Clare had offered their contributions, signalling that the session was coming to a close. 'We don't want to spend all our time in meetings, do we now? Oh yes, one last thing, I'd like us to hold a staff conference as soon as possible after the Suzuki party have departed. It will be an ideal opportunity to communicate the news about Japan as well as to give everyone the chance to ask questions about what the deal might mean for them. Now, who would like to lead on that?' she said, her eyes roving around the table to select a victim from the stooped heads.

'Sssssssssssssssssss,' began Grace.

Clare, Paul, and Daniel all exhaled with relief.

Simon and Sarah had turned white with fear, their faces tense. They were unsafe.

'SssssssssssssssssssssDaniel, could you take that on for me?'

Simon and Sarah collapsed in exhausted heaps.

Daniel started to shake and tremble.

'But I've already got three reports to get to you by this afternoon,' he stammered, 'and then there's the feasibility study on compressed hours that you wanted by tomorrow morning. I really don't think I can... '

Ten bats – the maximum anyone had ever seen. Any further attempt at resistance would be futile and result in almost certain death.

'Daniel, when do you think you'll have scoped a timetable and draft agenda for the conference for me to review?'

'Friday afternoon, say, four o'clock?' quaked Daniel obediently, now a defeated, convulsing wreck.

Grace paused.

He still got three bats for admitting earlier to not having read the business plan.

'Friday morning at eleven o'clock,' he mouthed, his words barely audible.

'Thank you, Daniel. Karen will schedule an extra

management team meeting for Friday afternoon for us to discuss your ideas. We shouldn't need more than three hours.'

Everyone groaned.

'Oh, and Daniel?'

'Yes?' he spluttered, fearing the worst.

'Well done in Berlin! I'm so glad that you and Clare were able to… resolve matters. Thank you both so much.'

Daniel sighed with relief before crawling out of Grace's office.

Clare was the last to leave. She'd dropped her pen and had to retrieve it from under the table.

'That's a lovely suit, Clare,' purred Grace. 'I did want to try one on that was almost identical to that, but the shop didn't have it my size! It's almost impossible to find anything suitable to wear for work in anything less than a fourteen these days, don't you think?

Chapter 28

'I could have throttled her!' shouted Clare. 'Just because Grace manages to survive on eating dust and termites she tries to make everyone else feel fat. I thought I looked OK in that new dress but she made me feel like an overweight hog in need of emergency liposuction.'

'I'm sure you looked knock-out in it. Don't let her spoil the new, glowing you,' said Jack, trying to suppress a giggle.

Clare had come straight round to Jack's place after the meeting at work had finally finished at six-thirty. Tonight they would get to the end of their books and then try to stop smoking. True to their word, Jack and Clare had been reading the book together, albeit in separate houses. They had started on Wednesday evening, continued on Thursday and today they wanted to finish it. The book advised them to keep smoking while they were reading it, which seemed like a luxury. Consequently, they both smoked like chimneys during their reading sessions.

Jack had had less faith in their chances of success than Clare and had wanted to buy in wheelbarrows full of nicotine patches, nicotine chewing gum and sleeping tablets to help him get through a life that would almost certainly be a miserable existence without cigarettes. But she had persuaded him not to.

It was nine o'clock and they were up to the last chapter.

'This is it,' said Jack, woefully turning the final page. 'Are we sure about this?' he asked, handing Clare what could be her last ever cigarette.

'I've never been surer about anything,' she said, lighting it. 'I am so sick and tired of being a slave to these things.'

As they got to the last sentence they stubbed out what was left of their cigarettes and hugged each other.

'So what do we do now?' asked Jack, solemnly putting down his book.

'You tell me all about your day and I'll make us a nice cup of tea.'

'But it's a Friday night! I don't want tea.'

'I know, but if you drink gallons of wine then you'll definitely want a cigarette.'

'I knew this was a bad idea. I should never have let you talk me into it,' said Jack, pacing up and down in the lounge. 'I want one already.'

'No, you don't, so stop being silly. Here - drink this.'

Clare handed him a mug of steaming tea.

'I still can't take it all in about you and Paolo and Paolo and Jessica. How bizarre is that?'

'Tell me about it.'

'Have you heard anything else from him?'

'Not since Monday and I told you all about that. It was awful, though not a complete surprise, I suppose,' said Jack, fidgeting with a coaster. 'Jessica had obviously confronted Paolo about what Brian and I had told her about him and me, but of course he'd denied it all to her and she seems to have believed him.'

'The lying, spineless pig,' spat Clare. 'Surely she must suspect something? I mean apart from Brian fancying her, neither of you really has a motive for making it up, do you?'

'I know. Anyway, it's all off between us now. He's gone.'

'Was there an *all*?'

'Not really. But it was quite exciting,' said Jack, reflecting on their few crazy moments together. 'Oh well, time to move on.'

'I think Brian needs to get a grip and move on too,' scoffed Clare, beginning to bite her nails. 'Just leave Paolo and Jessica to it, I say. She doesn't sound like she deserves Brian in any case, from what you've said, the pompous cow.'

'Stop biting your nails – you'll be angry tomorrow when you've chewed them all off.'

'I can't help it,' said Clare, continuing to nibble.

After almost an hour Clare was starting to feel the nicotine withdrawal symptoms and was getting more than a little tetchy as a result.

'I've got to do something to take my mind off smoking and I can't keep eating otherwise I will be the size of a super hog.'

'Here, play with this.'

Jack handed Clare the television remote control.

'Any thoughts yet about what you are going to do to find a decent man?' she asked, trying not to think about inhaling cigarette smoke.

'I've got next week off work, so I'm going to go out a bit more again. But never mind me - what about you? Now that your hormones are more appropriately balanced, do you have any ideas about how and where you will meet Mr Clare?'

'No, not yet. I will make some time soon and get on the case, but the next couple of weeks will be impossible,' she sighed, twizzling the remote.

'Why, what's up?'

'Things are coming to a head with the Japanese deal and I'm up to my eyeballs with it. Mrs Suzuki and her people are coming over next week, but the only thing that I'm looking forward to about the whole thing is the meal we're having on Thursday evening. We're going to Samuri, just off Piccadilly Circus. The food is supposed to be amazing.'

'I've heard of that place too. I think Paolo's been with some of our clients, notching up his expenses.'

They decided to watch a film, and Clare made some hot chocolate. She even found some mini-marshmallows at the back of the cupboard, next to a packet of instant cake mix.

'This has to be the weirdest Friday,' complained Jack. 'I don't think I've ever sat at home drinking hot chocolate.'

'I am dying for a cigarette! Why are you not moaning about wanting a cigarette like I am? Did you secretly buy some patches?' she asked, narrowing her eyes.

'No I didn't, honest, but I don't feel too bad.'

'So, why do I feel like I need to crawl up the walls?' asked Clare, almost breaking the remote in two.

Jack laughed

'Don't destroy that, please. My television needs it!'

'But Jo said it would be easy,' she moaned, scrunching up a cushion. 'I know I won't be able to cope with my work and all those meetings next week feeling like this. It's as if I've had my teeth removed with pliers without an anaesthetic. It'll be unbearable.'

'Now come on, you'll be fine. Give it time,' said Jack, surprised that he was the one giving moral support to Clare. He had been sure that he would have been the first to crack and was amazed that he actually felt all right.

'You'll feel better in the morning.'

Clare couldn't sit still any longer.

'I think I'm going to make a move. I can still get the train if I leave now. The Friday night crowds might help take my mind off smoking. Sorry I'm a bit snappy,' she said putting on her coat. 'I know this was my idea in the first place and I do still want to stop. It's just harder, a damn sight harder, than I thought it would be.'

'It's not even been four hours yet, so go home and have a nice bath.'

Clare was picturing herself in her hot tub with a glass of champagne surrounded by ashtrays and thousands of gorgeous, secret cigarettes, when Jack's phone rang. He leaned over the armchair to answer it.

'Hello,' he said, turning the television volume down with the remote that was thankfully still functioning. 'Hi, Rachel,' he sang down the phone, wondering what she wanted so late on a Friday evening. 'Clare? Yes, she's here. No, I don't mind, I'll hand you over to her.'

'It's Rachel,' he mouthed silently. 'She sounds upset.'

Clare grabbed the phone from him, giving Jack an irritated 'Yes, I fucking know who it is. I heard you say hello to her' look.

'Hello, Rachel,' she said as softly as she could muster under the circumstances. 'Yes, thanks, I'm fine.'

Clare was quiet for a few seconds as Rachel spoke.

Jack looked on as Clare's eyes suddenly widened.

'You're what? But I don't understand!'

Jack stood up with a start.

'Yes, yes, of course. Call me at home tomorrow morning. OK, now go and try and get some sleep. I love you too. It will be all right,' said Clare, hanging up.

'Oh my God! Rachel's pregnant!'

Chapter 29

It was years since Jack had last been to Shepherd's Market in Mayfair. Brian had suggested meeting him there for a few drinks on Saturday afternoon and he was really looking forward to going. The revelations about Rachel had been a real shock, to understate the matter, and not something that any of them had expected, least of all Rachel herself. They had arranged to meet at the Spinners Arms: Jack had decided to walk there from Bloomsbury. The weather was nice and sunny and the streets of Mayfair were bustling with well-heeled shoppers as he made his way towards Berkley Square.

Jack had really surprised himself. He hadn't had a single cigarette since he and Clare had stopped the night before. What was more amazing was that he hadn't actually wanted one. Even seeing other people smoking on the streets didn't seem to affect him. He was looking forward to a drink, though. Clare, unfortunately, wasn't faring quite so well. He had called her before setting out.

'I feel like I am going insane!' she screamed down the phone. 'I've eaten everything in the house that is edible and have now started on things that aren't. I don't know what to do with myself!'

'Go for a walk and get some nice fresh air,' he suggested, looking forward to his stroll across town.

'I don't want any fucking fresh air,' she bellowed. 'I want to smoke twenty cigarettes, one after the other, in a darkened, smoke-filled room!'

She had sounded bad, and Jack was relieved that he wasn't

going through the same cold turkey. Brian was standing outside the pub drinking a pint of bitter when he arrived.

'Hiya,' said Jack, wandering over. 'You've got a nice sunny spot here. Shall we grab that table?'

'Hey, man! You sit down then and I'll get you a drink. What do you want?'

'I'll have a pint of cider if you're sticking with beer, or if you want to switch to wine I'll join you in a bottle,' he answered, sitting down at the table.

It was extraordinary how Shepherd's Market had managed to retain its own identity as a market village within Mayfair, defying time and modernisation. True, an eighteenth century dog kennel would set you back millions of pounds, but apart from that minor factor it was like having a day out in the country, in the very heart of Central London.

Jack was watching an elderly couple kissing across the street standing in front of a cake shop when Brian returned carrying a bottle of wine in a wine cooler and two glasses.

'It's on days like these that I wouldn't want to live anywhere else in the world except London,' said Jack.

'It's gorgeous, isn't it?'

'Just look over there at those two old birds still in love. How long do you think they've been together? Thirty years? Forty?'

'They're lucky, aren't they? Somehow it doesn't seem fair that they can have forty years together and I can't even have one day with the woman I want.'

'I hear what you're saying, but it's not their fault, is it?'

'Oh, I know. I'm sorry, I'm just still pissed off about Jessica.'

'Why, has something else happened?'

'Not really. But I mean, we told her the truth about your Paolo and how does she thank us? She goes bonkers, whacks me across the face as if it's entirely my fault, and then throws us out.'

'He's left work, you know. I think he would probably have

been sacked anyway if he hadn't gone of his own accord, but it was quite a dramatic exit. I haven't a clue why he was claiming all that money. They were crazy amounts.'

Jack told him all about the expense claims and Paolo's aggression in the kitchen.

'I'm starting to get angry just thinking about him,' said Brian, scratching his cheek. 'I hope you're not going to carry on with him in his love triangle.'

'Oh, I doubt very much that it was just the three of us. More like a love octagon, I bet,' joked Jack in an attempt to lighten the mood. 'No, you can count me out now. Good riddance.'

Brian couldn't help smiling at the thought of keeping eight secret affairs going simultaneously. The warm weather, the relaxed atmosphere, the wine and Jack all made him feel a bit better. Jack always made him feel better. He was a great friend.

'That's more like it,' said Jack. 'I just wish Jessica would see sense too.'

'You and me both, mate. I know I hardly know her and I can't really explain why I'm so bothered about it all. It's just that I feel so… I don't know… attracted to her, hypnotised by her.'

The light breeze ruffled Brian's short blond fringe and he squinted in the sunshine.

'Well, it's her loss,' said Jack supportively.

'I called Donald to see what had happened after we left.'

'And?'

'He said she didn't say much, but he regretted to have to tell me that they seemed to be very much still a couple. Apparently they're going to Barcelona for a week's holiday to spend some 'quality time' together.'

'I bet the only quality time that Paolo will be spending will be in the gay bars,' said Jack dryly.

Brian laughed.

'Well, come on! Does Jessica need her head examining? Unless the sex with Paolo is out of this world, how can she be so blinkered about what we've told her?'

Brian stopped laughing. He did not want to picture Paolo and Jessica having 'out of this world' sex.

'Sorry, I didn't mean to… '

'Oh, don't worry, it's me. I'm going to have to get over it,' said Brian, emptying his glass.

'I'll go and get another bottle.'

Brian soon came back with more wine and two packets of crisps.

'Haven't you noticed anything?' asked Jack, pouring the drinks.

'Like what?'

'Something different about me.'

Brian looked Jack up and down.

'Have you had your lips done?'

Jack threw a bag of crisps at Brian.

'No, you've done something to your eyes, haven't you?' he joked, leaning over to get a closer look.

'I'm not smoking! We're sitting here drinking wine and I'm NOT SMOKING. Isn't that brilliant?'

'Congratulations!' said Brian, shaking Jack's hand.

'When did you stop?'

'Last night, with Clare. I can't believe that apart from an odd empty feeling in my stomach I don't actually want one.'

'I'm really pleased you're doing it. You will be too. How's Clare coping?'

'Well,' grimaced Jack, 'my guess is that she'll have scratched off all her wallpaper with her bare hands since last night and will probably now be wandering around Finsbury Park like an axe murderess in search of nicotine.'

'That well huh?' smirked Brian.

'Don't,' laughed Jack. 'It's such a shame for her. She was so enthusiastic about quitting, you wouldn't believe it. I can't understand why I'm doing all right. I guess it affects people differently.'

'I was a bit like Clare for the first few weeks, but then it got easier.'

'Anyway, I've got some much more important really big news for you. If you don't know already, that is,' whispered Jack, putting down his crisps. 'I'm guessing you don't know, otherwise you'd have said something, and I wanted to wait until we'd had a couple of drinks before spilling. This will knock you for six.'

'Why are you whispering and what are you going on about?'

'It's just habit – I feel like I'm gossiping.'

'You are gossiping.'

'Rachel's pregnant!'

'She's what?' spluttered Brian.

'She's preg… '

'Yes, I heard you! But I don't understand. How? I thought she was having a girl phase?'

'None of us understand,' said Jack, taking a mouthful of wine. 'It's crazy. I haven't spoken with her directly, but she called Clare at my place last night, woman to woman, and then they spoke again this morning, and Clare's filled me in. Please don't say anything to Rachel unless she tells you herself. Clare felt bad telling me, but she's not really feeling herself at the moment, you know, with no nails and no wallpaper.'

'I'm not going to say anything, am I?'

'Rachel told Clare it must have been just over two months ago when she was back at home in Blackheath. Edward had been very depressed with work problems and she had felt sorry for him, something about a mercy fuck.'

'Well, that obviously wasn't such a good idea, was it? Is she sure she's pregnant?'

'Clare says so. She's thinking about keeping it and says Heike likes the idea of starting a family together.'

'Wow, hold on there, that sounds a bit mad. I thought the thing with Heike was just a lesbian fling, or whatever the right name is. What about money and her freelance work with Twisted Tongues?'

'Tongue Twisters. I said the same thing and Clare of course

went ballistic. Her nicotine withdrawal symptoms didn't help, though.'

'Well, it's no good shouting at her, I suppose. It's our support that she needs.'

'I guess we'll just have to wait and see what she decides to do. Clare's offered to go over to talk face-to-face, but Rachel said not to for the time being.'

'What a mess.'

'I know. At least she still has a bit of time to think about it properly.'

'I guess so. I've got some news, too,' said Brian. 'Nowhere near as big as Rachel's, but I'm through to the final for the National Designer of the Year Award. They picked my chair.'

'Hey, that's fantastic! Well done! I knew you'd get through.'

They sat chatting for about another hour and finished off the rest of the wine. The sun had started to disappear behind the old houses when Brian got up to leave.

'Sorry, mate, I'm going to shoot off now. I promised Declan and Toby I'd have a quick one in the Plough & Pheasant and then it's an early night for me. I'm off down to Brighton first thing tomorrow to see that couple about those chests of drawers. You remember, from the exhibition?'

'Oh yes. Well, good luck in Brighton then. Tell Declan that Gloria is a good catch for him. He should think twice before doing his usual tricks.'

'I'll tell him. Have a good one.'

Brian ruffled Jack's hair before making his way towards the bus stop for the number thirty-eight back to Hackney.

It was still early and quite warm so Jack decided to have a stroll through St. James's Park on his way home. He crossed over Piccadilly and then ambled slowly along through Green Park and past Buckingham Palace. He loved St James's Park, especially the lake and the cherry trees.

The lake was particularly beautiful this evening and the reflections of the trees shimmered on the water like dancing holograms. He decided to sit down on a bench and watch the world go by for a while. A moorhen was making a terrible racket close to the edge of the water. It seemed to think that an approaching goose was about to storm its nest and was preparing to defend it to the death. Jack thought about the significance of defending a few twigs with all your energy. Would human beings be as committed?

Suddenly, Jack's thoughts were distracted by a skinhead walking past.

Jack's eyes turned to follow him. He was about Jack's age and wearing jeans, trainers and a red polo shirt. Jack was admiring his ass when the skinhead turned round and looked at him. Embarrassed, Jack immediately averted his gaze and tried to focus on the moorhen again. After a few moments of fidgeting he looked up to where the guy had been walking. He was gone. All of a sudden Jack felt an enormous pang for a cigarette. Supposing it had to come sometime, he took a piece of regular chewing gum from his pocket and unwrapped it. The moorhen had secured territorial control over its nest and was now settling down.

'Is anyone sitting here?'

Jack looked up.

It was the skinhead.

'Er, no, go ahead,' Jack said, popping the mint-flavoured strip into his mouth.

'My name's Mark,' said the skinhead boldly in a Geordie accent, revealing a set of uneven white teeth from beneath his grin.

'Hello. I'm Jack.'

'They're my favourites,' said Mark, pointing to a pair of black swans that were swimming towards them.

Jack could see now that Mark's head wasn't completely shaven. His light brown hair was clipped very short all over, less than a number one. Mark stretched out his arms and rested them on the back of the bench, his right hand only a few inches from Jack's shoulder.

'They mate for life, you know, swans.'

'Do they?' said Jack, surprised at the comment.

'Can I buy you a drink?'

Jack liked Mark's confident and uninhibited style, and held his gaze.

'Sure, why not?' he smiled.

Connections in Soho was already busy when they arrived and they had to push their way through to get served. Mark ordered a pint for himself and glass of wine for Jack.

'I like this place,' said Mark, leading the way over to a quieter corner, where he had spotted a couple of empty stools.

They sat down and Jack took a mouthful of wine, his eyes glancing around the bar.

'Busy, isn't it?' he said.

'Have you been here before?' asked Mark, drinking some beer.

'Only once. I think it was comedy night or something.'

Mark then surprised Jack again by leaning over and kissing him, putting his hands around his neck to pull them together. His hands were hot and his lips soft. Jack quickly responded and pushed his tongue into Mark's mouth, running his hands over the back of his head, loving the prickly feeling of the short hair. They stopped for a moment and looked at each other intensely.

Mark broke the silence and grinned at him.

'So are we going back to your place or mine?'

Jack didn't normally jump into bed with guys quite so quickly, but there was something about Mark and his forwardness that he really liked. Besides, he was a free agent.

'I suppose I can always do the cleaning another night,' he said excitedly. 'Come on, let's go to mine.'

Chapter 30

Clare's week had so far been ghastly. Although she hadn't actually consumed a cigarette, she was constantly gasping for one. She found herself staring manically at other smokers as they huddled together in doorways or took shelter from the rain under shop-front canopies. Sometimes she even stood next them to try to breathe in some of their second-hand smoke. This was not how she had imagined stopping smoking was going to be. Instead of being happy and celebrating her new, smoke-free life, she was always in a foul mood, irritable and as cranky as a menstruating sow. She was sure this must be God's way of punishing her for being mean to Waltraut.

How Jack was able to cope so well was a complete mystery. It just wasn't fair. He'd even called to say that he'd met someone new, a guy called Mark. No flies on him, the lucky bastard! She had just about managed to stay calm during another telephone call with Rachel on Tuesday, though it hadn't been easy. Rachel was leaning towards keeping the baby, which Clare thought was a dreadful idea, especially with her separating from Edward. Even though she'd never really liked him, Clare still thought children should have both a mother and a father, at least at birth. She'd advised Rachel to think things over for a few more weeks before making any final choices.

Today was the Big Day. It was Thursday and Mrs Suzuki was coming over to London this afternoon to hopefully put the deal to bed and sign the heads of terms. Clare was feeling very nervous and her whole body tingled. It was day six of nicotine withdrawal and she could have killed for just a single drag on a cigarette.

'Good morning, Candice,' snipped Clare, as she arrived at work, looking like she was chewing a wasp. She was wearing the same red suit she had bought last week, though it had been much more difficult to get on this morning. She had struggled with the skirt zip and had had to lie on her side on the bed to finally zip it up, almost trapping her thumb in the process. Last week's fantasy, in which she had lost a couple of pounds, had obviously been just that. It was much more likely to have been attributable to the residual elation of her Sunday afternoon of raw passion with Sven. She felt like she had put on a stone and a half since stopping smoking at the weekend, and Sven now seemed to belong in another lifetime.

'They're here already, in the boardroom,' said Candice.

'But it's not even nine o'clock!' exclaimed Clare in horror. 'They're not supposed to be here until this afternoon.'

'I know. Grace said to tell you to go straight to her office for a management team briefing when you finally get in.'

Clare couldn't ignore the word 'finally', and was furious. After all the hours that she had worked over the last few months to get this deal to where it was today she wanted to gouge Grace's eyes out for all the 'thanks' she got.

She sat down at reception for a moment and took two large glazed doughnuts out of her bag. Grace would just have to wait. If she couldn't have any nicotine then she at least needed a sugar fix. As she was devouring the second doughnut the double doors to her left were flung open. A wailing Karen flopped out through them, wringing her hands in despair.

'It's not my fault they got confused between Russian time and English time,' she sobbed.

'Russian time?' asked Clare, stuffing the last bit of sweet dough into her mouth.

'They had a stopover meeting in Russia, or something. Grace said I should have confirmed the time as British by email, fax and phone, and that I had proved myself to be incapable of even organising a simple meeting. Please, please, come now!'

'But how does she know I'm even here yet?'

Clare looked at her arms to check whether she had been bugged.

'I don't know! She just does, and if you don't come right away that will be my fault too.   Please!' she begged, her eyes wide with terror.

Clare stood up, brushing off some crumbs, and was promptly escorted by Karen through to Grace's office. Everyone else was already present. All except Daniel, that is, who had been rushed to hospital yesterday with a violent, stress-induced nose-bleed.

'Clare! How kind of you to join us at last. No doubt you've already heard that Karen has totally screwed up the itinerary and that the Suzuki party are assembled in the boardroom as we speak.'

Karen was beside herself with grief, her lower lip trembling, as she perched on the edge of her chair.

'I think you're being a bit hard on her,' began Clare. 'If Mrs Suzuki's people get the times wrong then you can't really blame poor… '

Four bats.

'… Karen, can you?' finished Clare, for once refusing to be cut-off.

Everyone looked at Clare in amazement and awe. She had dared to defy Grace. It was unheard of.

Grace looked at each of them and then glared at Clare.

'I expect my Personal Assistant to be able to co-ordinate a few simple meeting times without causing the kind of confusion and pandemonium that could derail this deal,' said Grace coldly, determined to restore the balance of power.

It must have been the overwhelming, almost irrepressible urge to eat a whole packet of cigarettes that spurred Clare on into unchartered waters.

'Karen is absolutely the best assistant that you could ever

hope to have. She has worked tirelessly on getting everything co-ordinated for this visit, and I for one really appreciate her commitment,' she railed, looking to her colleagues for support for this unprecedented challenge to Grace's authority.

All heads were again stooped and all voices silent. Clare was on her own.

'So what time are you planning on us going into the boardroom, Grace? If we leave them sitting there any longer it will be lunchtime.'

No bats this time, just an acidic smile and a faint twitch of the nose.

'We'll go in now. But before we do, are we and Mrs Suzuki finally on message with the main deal terms?'

'I've done what I can. I couldn't get Lance to confirm anything in writing yet, but he thinks that Mrs Suzuki will agree. And before you say anything, I'm sorry that it's only a 'thinks'. I've worked my butt off too, more than you will ever know,' she finished, reflecting on the unpleasant incident with John Goldschmied in Osaka.

'There's no need to be vulgar, Clare. If you've done your best, then that's all I can hope for. I just didn't think you would be happy with failure. I must have misjudged you. You should have warned me that there may still be some unresolved issues *before* this meeting today with Mrs Suzuki.'

'And I was planning to do just that this morning before they arrived this afternoon! How was I to know they would be trooping in here at the crack of dawn?'

'That's quite enough, Clare, calm down. Let's go in, then,' said Grace, collecting her files and handbag. 'And remember to bow.'

The team made their way over to the boardroom. Daniel had just arrived back from hospital, having been kept in overnight for observation. He was hovering nervously outside the boardroom with what appeared to be two congealed travel tampons stuffed up his nostrils.

'Sorry I'm late,' he said nasally.

Grace glowered at him. There was no way that she was taking him with her into the meeting looking like he had just had open-face surgery.

'Daniel, is there anything particular that you wanted to ask Mrs Suzuki this morning?'

Daniel shook his head, wiggling the tampons.

'Then in that case perhaps you would feel more comfortable joining us tomorrow morning instead?'

'Yes, that's fine by me,' he said, not believing his luck at being let off the hook for the meeting.

'Oh, and Daniel?'

'Yes, Grace?' he snivelled.

'I've had a look at your report on compressed hours this morning. There are some good points, but I think it needs to be more... more cutting edge, if that makes sense to you? I've been reading about a new Korean retail staffing model that I think might help you. It's truly fascinating. I'll get Karen to pop a copy into your pigeon hole. It would be really helpful if you could get an updated report over to me by lunchtime today.'

Daniel's nose had just started bleeding again. He rushed off to the toilets.

Grace turned to the team.

'Under the circumstances we'll have the meeting first and then aim to have the buffet lunch at midday. Karen, have we got tea, coffee and some nibbles for this morning?'

'I've already arranged for them to be taken through,' said Karen hurriedly, fearing more of Grace's wrath.

'Thank you, Karen.'

Grace went in first.

Mrs Suzuki rose from her seat and took a step back from the meeting table. Lance Rubenstein, her lawyer, stood to her right and the Wizened One to her left. The Wizened One, whose real name was Kohei Sawayama, had turned out to be Mrs Suzuki's father. Apparently she rarely conducted any important business without him, or so Lance had told Clare.

'Mrs Suzuki,' grovelled Grace. 'What a pleasure it is

indeed for us to welcome you to our shores and to our humble offices,' she said, splaying her arms. She even gave Mrs Suzuki a bow.

Mrs Suzuki nodded before introducing Lance, but, as usual, she didn't introduce her father. Lance had advised Clare against pressing the issue, and the team had been briefed to avoid asking the man any direct questions unless he spoke first.

Grace went on to introduce her team, accompanied by enthusiastic, if rather stilted, bowing, 'And, of course, Clare Houghton, who you know quite well by now.'

Clare suddenly realised that she hadn't a hope in hell of executing even the slightest of bows for Mrs Suzuki. The zip on her skirt had made that quite clear when she was wrestling with it while getting dressed this morning. By way of formally greeting their honourable guest she dared to opt for a handshake instead.

Mrs Suzuki stared at Clare's outstretched hand. Even Grace looked visibly shocked.

She then surprised everyone by gently shaking it. Clare looked at Mrs Suzuki's diminutive little hand, engulfed by her own, that looked the size of a garden spade in comparison.

'A delight to see you again, Mrs Suzuki,' said Clare. Hello, Lance.'

She turned to the Wizened One and gave him a nod.

'Sorry about the mix up with times. Our mistake,' said Lance.

Grace shot Karen two bats and pursed her lips before ever-so-slightly baring her teeth at her.

'And thanks for the itinerary for today and tomorrow,' he continued, 'that all looks fun. Mrs Suzuki is really excited about visiting some of your stores.'

Mrs Suzuki looked about as excited as an anaesthetised cockatoo.

'Clare and I have been up through the night all week working on the last few bits and pieces, haven't we Clare?'

'Yes, and I'm so pleased that we've managed to finally get agreement on all the main terms,' said Clare, confidently and unperturbed.

Mrs Suzuki got out her cigarettes. They were like a rag to a bull for Clare.

'I'm afraid you can't smoke in here,' she said. 'It's against the… '

'Of course you can smoke, Mrs Suzuki. What's a little cigarette between friends?' interrupted Grace, laughing as she flicked the air conditioning unit on. 'Why don't you have one too, Clare? You can keep Mrs Suzuki company. Karen, could you get Mrs Suzuki an ashtray?'

Karen stood up as if on autopilot. Where the hell was she supposed to find an ashtray? Nobody had ever smoked in the office before.

'I don't smoke any more. I stopped at the weekend,' said Clare proudly, refusing to rise to Grace's jibe.

Mrs Suzuki lit a cigarette and blew a plume of smoke across the table at Clare.

'Oh, go on, Clare, one little ciggie won't hurt, will it?' taunted Grace.

The smell of the grey blue smoke was almost irresistible. Perhaps she could just have the one and then stop again. What would be wrong with that? She could almost feel the nicotine firing round her brain. Resistance was agony.

'No thanks, I'm fine,' she said at last, regaining her resolve. She wouldn't give Grace the satisfaction of watching her crumble. 'Mrs Suzuki, we are really keen to move forward and are very pleased that you agree to our minimum order requirements. We've studied your latest business plan and think you have some great new ideas for the launch. Simon is looking forward to coming over to help you get started on the launch if you want him to, aren't you Simon?'

Everyone looked at Simon.

'Er, yes,' he stuttered, choking on a biscuit.

Three bats.

'We really like your plan to focus your media campaign on exclusivity,' he added hastily.

Karen returned, miraculously armed with an ashtray.

Mrs Suzuki promptly extinguished her half-smoked cigarette in it.

'Clare, Grace,' began Lance, 'Mrs Suzuki is really behind the trading deal for your merchandise and believes that we now have a sound business model that will work well for us in Japan, and of course for you, here in London.'

'That's settled then,' said Grace, standing up, 'Karen - champagne for everyone!'

'Not quite yet, I'm afraid. Mrs Suzuki is still waiting for a call from her Board about the minimum order clause. They should be getting back to her by tonight. It's a really big deal for them, as I'm sure you can appreciate.'

Grace's face froze over.

'Is that tonight British time?' mumbled Karen.

Lance smiled at her and nodded.

'Yes it is, Karen. Now, what time do you want us at the restaurant this evening? Mrs Suzuki has some shopping to do this afternoon, followed by a facial and a seaweed wrap that she has booked in for four o'clock.'

Clare could almost hear Grace's frozen face cracking.

Chapter 31

Jack had already been out to buy some rolls and croissants from the bakery on Store Street and was laying the breakfast table on his terrace. The coffee was brewing and Mark was in the shower. This was the third time Mark had stayed over since they'd met on Saturday evening. It had only taken them about fifteen minutes to get home that night, and they'd barely closed the entrance door to the building before Mark had stripped off to the waist. He'd pushed Jack down on the stairs and then pressed his naked torso against him, kissing him roughly on the mouth and neck, before tugging at Jack's jeans, breathing heavily. Jack hadn't wanted to risk bumping into any neighbours on the communal staircase and had had to prise himself away and run upstairs. Once inside the flat Jack hadn't been able to hold back any longer either, and they'd ripped their clothes off before falling down onto the floor, devouring each other.

'Something smells good,' said Mark, coming down from the bathroom, a towel wrapped around his waist.

'Breakfast for Sir will be served on the terrace in five minutes,' said Jack. He was really enjoying this. It had been a long time since he'd had someone nice to spoil.

'Can you just take the cups out?'

Mark walked over and stood behind him, reaching up to a shelf for two coffee cups. He put the cups down and turned Jack around to kiss him, losing his towel in the process, wearing nothing but a silver chain and crucifix around his neck.

'Not before breakfast. Now take these outside,' joked Jack,

handing the cups to him. 'And put that towel back round you. I don't want Mrs Petrovski falling off her balcony if she sees you strutting around butt naked on my terrace with an erection.'

Mark went straight out onto the terrace and leaned over the railings.

'Good morning, Mrs Petrovski!'

'Come away from there!' cried Jack, running out.

'You'll have to catch me first,' said Mark, dodging behind one of the sun loungers.

'Right, when I get you I'm going to… '

'I certainly hope so!' Mark ran around to the other side of the terrace. As he tried to escape between the parasol and the barbecue he stubbed a toe on a damaged terracotta pot housing a large Yucca plant.

'Aaaaghh!' he screamed, grabbing his foot with both hands and hopping around.

'Stop being such a queen,' laughed Jack.

'I'm serious, it hurts. I think I've torn my big toe nail on that fucking plant pot.'

'Come over here then and let me have a look.'

Mark hopped over and sat down on the side of a sun lounger, holding out the injured limb for Jack to examine.

'That does actually look quite painful,' said Jack, cringing.

'It is fucking painful!'

'It looks like you've got a small piece of plant pot wedged under the nail,' said Jack, inspecting the inflamed toe. 'Just wait here.'

After a few minutes he came back with a pair of secateurs, a screwdriver and a small hammer.

'You can fuck off! Stay away from me!' shouted Mark, putting his hands around his foot.

'You won't feel a thing, I promise,' said Jack, moving closer, the secateurs glinting.

'No, go away,' he said, kicking Jack with his good leg.

'I never thought a tough-looking skinhead could be such a big baby.'

Jack laughed as he put down the tools and got out a small pair of tweezers from the pocket of his shorts.

'Trust me with these?'

Mark slowly extended his bad leg and rested his foot gingerly on Jack's thigh.

'Take a deep breath,' ordered Jack as he positioned the tweezers just next to the toenail.

'Were you teased at school because of your balls?' he asked out of the blue, digging the tweezers under the nail to remove the small, jagged piece of pot.

'What do you mean? Aaaaghh, what are you fucking do…?'

'All finished.'

He held out the foreign body clasped between the tweezers for Mark to see.

'No wonder it hurt - look at it! How would you like that rammed under your toenail? And what's wrong with my balls? Why would I have been teased at school?'

'Nothing's wrong with them. I was just trying to distract you from the pain I was about to inflict. In fact, they're the nicest balls I've seen all month.'

'All month, eh? It's only the fifth of June,' grinned Mark, his crooked teeth gleaming in the sunshine. 'Come here, you,' he said grabbing Jack and pulling him down on top of him.

'I really like you, you know,' said Mark, stroking Jack's unshaven chin before giving him a kiss.

'You're not bad yourself,' said Jack pulling away, 'despite your balls.'

'Fuck off!' shouted Mark, throwing a cushion at Jack as he ran inside, before lying back down to enjoy the sun.

Jack watched him for a few seconds. He really did like him. He was different. The sex was great, and he made him laugh. After a long breakfast outside and a hot session inside, Mark and Jack decided to go into town. They went the scenic route, walking along the Thames before making their way back up Charing Cross Road to have coffee at a bar on Soho Square.

'So what do you do for a living?' Jack asked, pouring some cream into his cup.

Although they'd spent quite a bit of time together this week, most of it had been put to use exploring each others' bodies. Neither of them had yet raised the more mundane question of work, but curiosity eventually got the better of Jack.

'I'm a builder. I'm self-employed as a sub-contractor along with the Polish boys. The work's not always regular but that suits me. I like to travel. What about you?'

'I work for a record label,' said Jack.

'I wanted to be a singer once. What do you do there?'

'I look after the bills, you know, pay the suppliers and pay the staff.'

'You've got the most important job there, then.'

Nobody had ever said that to him before.

'Cheers! So where have you been travelling?'

'Oh, all over the place - Europe, America, the Far East.'

'The building work must pay well, then.'

'It's enough to get by on. I have simple tastes.'

'Well, thanks very much!'

'Not you, you burke.'

Jack grabbed Mark's hands and kissed him.

'Let's go and get drunk. There's nothing more decadent than being sloshed during the day when everyone else has to work. I'm so glad I booked this week off.'

The rest of the afternoon was spent bar-hopping around the streets of Soho. They were having yet another drink, sitting at a table outside a lively bar on Old Compton Street, when they were interrupted.

'Hello, Jack dear! Isn't it a beautiful day?'

Jack would have recognised those tight black leather trousers and that pancake-ass anywhere.

'Hey, Donald! What are you doing down here? This is my friend Mark.'

'Hello Mark, how nice to meet you.'

'Likewise.'

'Do you want to join us?' asked Jack, pulling out a chair.

'I'd love to, dear, but I'm afraid I have a prior engagement with, well, an old acquaintance, shall we say.'

'Next time, then. How's Jessica?'

Donald scowled.

'I'd rather not discuss it now, dear. I can't understand her sometimes. Brian is such a lovely boy. Anyway, I have to dash. Bye, darlings.'

Donald minced off along Frith Street.

'Who was that? And who's Jessica?'

Jack explained briefly how they all knew each other, preferring to omit the Paolo connection.

'So, where to next?' asked Jack, staggering a little as he got up to go.

'Wow, steady on there,' said Mark, supporting him with his arm. 'Looks like I should be taking you home.'

'Nonsense. Let's get the tube from Piccadilly Circus to Vauxhall and make a night of it.'

'You're the boss,' said Mark, slapping Jack's ass. 'Lead the way!'

Chapter 32

Clare looked at her nails – well, if you could still call them nails. They had been bitten almost down to her knuckles. She was desperate for a cigarette after having endured a day from hell in the office. Predictably, Grace had tried to punish Clare for being outspoken and attempting to defend Karen from her vociferous attack. Punishment had, of course, been indirect, in the form of the cigarette taunt and additional workload with impossible deadlines. She'd even requested that Clare dress up as a mystery shopper and visit a shopping centre in North Wales as part of a new market research exercise on Sunday. Clare had actually managed to say 'no.'

'I'm sorry, I didn't catch that. Did you say something Clare?'

'Yes, Grace. I said no.'

'Clare, you're skating on very thin ice.'

'I already have plans for this weekend, so I'm afraid the answer is NO. I really did try to get it all sorted with the deal before today. I've been on the phone to Lance every night this week. But I can't control everything and everyone.'

Grace gave her a look that said, 'Why can't you? I can.'

They were alone in Grace's office, getting ready to drive over to the restaurant to meet up again with the Suzuki party.

'Are we all set for the meal this evening?' asked Grace, flicking open her handbag to refresh her make-up.

'Karen said the car will be here at a quarter to. Simon and Paul will meet us there. Sarah is coming with us.'

'I'll see you downstairs, then,' said Grace. 'Oh, and Clare, best behaviour tonight, understand? No more nonsense.'

After Grace had gone, Karen came out of the kitchen and caught Clare as she was getting ready to leave too.

'Thanks for sticking up for me. It was very kind of you.'

'You're very welcome. It's no more than you deserve, Karen.' Clare smiled at her. She couldn't make up for being more than a little mean to Waltraut in Berlin, but at least she was able to do this for Karen, for what it was worth.

It was only a short cab ride and they arrived at the restaurant bang on eight o'clock. Simon and Paul were having a drink at the bar.

Grace strode over towards Paul.

'Are they not here yet?'

'No, I checked with the head waiter – maybe she had an allergic reaction to her seaweed wrap,' he joked.

'I hope you're not drunk,' snapped Grace. 'This is an extremely important dinner. Now remember, no direct questions to Mrs Suzuki's father, no personal questions to anyone at all and smile to demonstrate that you are enjoying their company and enjoying yourselves.'

'Sarah, can you order us a large bottle of sparkling mineral water? We can sip that here while we're waiting.'

'I'll have a glass of pinot grigio,' said Clare defiantly.

If she didn't get some alcohol into her body soon she did not want to be held responsible for her actions. She had seen a group of young women that had been smoking and laughing just outside the restaurant and had been highly tempted to join them and smoke five cigarettes at once, bound together.

'Are you sure you should be drinking, Clare? You really need to have your wits about you this evening.'

Clare was almost past caring what Grace thought.

'Make it a large one please, Sarah.'

Grace glowered at her.

Sarah was dying for a drink too, but wasn't as brave as Clare.

'Mmmm, that's lovely and refreshing,' said Sarah instead, taking a drink of her water. 'Oh look, I think they're here.'

Everyone turned round to look at the door.

The Suzuki party had arrived and they were all wearing black suits. Mrs Suzuki looked stunning in a new Versace two-piece she had bought that afternoon.

'Mrs Suzuki,' beamed Grace, 'may I say how wonderful you look. Black is most certainly your colour. And what a fabulous stone!' she said, bending down to admire the large diamond pendant that was nestling prominently between Mrs Suzuki's pert breasts.

Grace paused, fiddling with her Chanel neckscarf, expecting a return compliment, but it wasn't forthcoming.

'Can we go to the table now? I want to sit down,' said Mrs Suzuki.

'Me too,' boomed Lance. 'Say, this looks like a neat place.'

The Wizened One said nothing as they made their way through the restaurant, led by the head waiter. Karen had booked the best table. It was next to the window that looked out onto Lower Regent Street, just on the corner of Piccadilly Circus.

'Welcome to Samuri. I hope you enjoy your meal with us this evening,' said the waiter with a deep bow, once they had reached their table. 'Your chef will be with you in a moment. May I take your drinks order?'

'Two large vodka tonics,' said Mrs Suzuki crisply.

'I'll have an iced tea,' said Lance.

'We'll just have another couple of bottles of bubbly,' said Grace on behalf of everyone, pointing at the bottle of sparkling mineral water that was now on the table.

'I'll have another glass of this lovely wine please,' said Clare boldly.

Grace glared at her, but didn't say anything. She didn't want to risk Clare answering her back again and causing a scene in front of Mrs Suzuki.

Simon thought he would order an alcoholic drink too. Why not? Clare was having one.

'Actually, I'd like a glass of … ' he began.

Four bats.

'… still water with a slice of lime,' he finished, defeated.

'Isn't this fun?' exclaimed Grace.

As this was a traditional *teppanyaki* restaurant the table was arranged around a large hotplate on three sides. The chef usually prepared some of the food at the table in front of the guests and typically joked around while he cooked, which usually resulted in bit of light-hearted laughter.

Their chef arrived with the waiter, who was carrying their drinks on a tray.

'Good evening, ladies and gentlemen. *Konbanwa*,' he said, bowing to Mrs Suzuki and the Wizened One before handing around the menus. 'The specials for tonight are as follows:

"Surf and turf" – this is a beautiful combination of Pacific lobster and Scottish prime beef, served with asparagus and peppers

"Soft-shell crab" – this delicious grilled crab is marinated in garlic and soy sauce and served with a ginger dressing on a bed of *shitake* mushrooms and sliced aubergine

"Stir-fried vegetables with tofu, bamboo shoots and water chestnuts" – this is the vegetarian option and served with *udon* noodles in a sweet chilli sauce.'

'Well that all sounds delicious, doesn't it?' said Grace, looking over to Mrs Suzuki, who was sitting opposite her on the other side of the hotplate, next to her father.

Mrs Suzuki was looking at her menu.

'We also have the freshest, finest cuts of *maguro* tuna in the whole of London and a wide selection of *sushi* and *sashimi*.'

'Sounds wonderful,' said Paul, his mouth watering. 'Can I have the… '

Three bats.

'Mrs Suzuki, would you like to order first?' asked Grace.

'We'll have two bowls of *miso* soup and two bowls of boiled rice,' she said quickly, looking at her father.

The Wizened One nodded his agreement.

'And what about for your main courses?' asked Grace.

'That's fine, we ate earlier,' clipped Mrs Suzuki, folding her menu and handing it back to the chef.

Grace almost swallowed her water down the wrong way. This was the best Japanese restaurant in town. It was supposed to be her treat for them, and they'd *eaten earlier*?

'I see,' she said, 'Lance, what would you like from this tantalising menu?'

'Can I just get a steak, well done please?'

'Coming up,' said the chef.

Clare ordered the surf and turf and a plate of assorted *sashimi* – she was starving. Paul and Simon went for the same, without the fish, and Sarah opted for the vegetarian stir fry. Grace reluctantly decided to order the same as Mrs Suzuki, hoping that this appeared suitably frugal and onside with her guests.

'I'd like to propose a toast,' said Clare, raising her glass, feeling much better now that food was on the way.

Everyone raised their glasses, even the Wizened One. Grace was worried about what Clare might say, especially after a couple of glasses of wine.

'Here's to good health and to long and happy lives.'

'To good health,' toasted the group.

Mrs Suzuki drained her vodka noisily through a straw and held up her glass to catch the waiter's attention. Clare marvelled at the speed with which Mrs Suzuki knocked back her drink.

'I think I'll join you in another one, Mrs Suzuki,' she said, casting a look at the mournful, longing faces of her colleagues.

'Ouch! What was that?' cried Clare, looking under the table.

'I'm sorry, did I catch your shin there? I was just rotating my foot - spot of cramp, you know,' said Grace coldly, her patience being tested.

Clare valiantly held up her glass.

The chef had started to chop the food and had begun cooking on the large hotplate. He was extremely dextrous with his knives as he set to work. The steak and lobster were soon sizzling in one corner of the plate and the vegetables were being tossed and turned in another. He flicked a small cube of steak over to Clare.

'He wants you!' said the chef, attempting to raise a laugh.

Clare was just about to the snare the tender morsel between her chopsticks when the chef somehow managed an interception and flicked the chunk of steak back over towards himself. She gave him a wry smile, and Sarah squealed with delight – she didn't get out much.

Desperate for a thaw, Grace started clapping enthusiastically, looking like a deranged seal.

'Wasn't that funny?' she said, looking across to an expressionless Mrs Suzuki.

Paul and Simon feigned laughter. Lance smiled. Mrs Suzuki picked up her refreshed vodka and tonic and took another long slurp through the straw before checking her watch. The chef thought that he was on a roll and so repeated the performance by tossing a small piece of lobster tail over in Mrs Suzuki's direction. She looked at it with the same disdain as if she had been tossed a slug.

'So what new products are you bringing out this year?' asked Lance.

Grace looked at Sarah, who had now been served her stir fry.

Sarah automatically reeled off a spiel about a new boutique range, aimed at the young professional lady, that would be available in time for Christmas and New Year.

'I think it will be really great for the Japanese market too,' she said, struggling with her chopsticks. Grace had insisted that no one use knives and forks. She finally managed to grasp a water chestnut and had almost reached her mouth with it when her thumb twitched and flicked one of the chopsticks. The water chestnut flew through the air across the table and hit Mrs Suzuki's father squarely between the eyes.

Grace's mouth hung open for a second in shock.

'What on earth are you trying to do?' shouted Mrs Suzuki angrily. 'Kill us?'

'I am so sorry,' apologised Sarah, standing up with a napkin.

'Here let me… '

'Don't come anywhere near us,' said Mrs Suzuki, holding up the palm of her left hand.

'Please, just eat your food.'

Grace kicked Sarah savagely under the table, not even bothering to pretend that it was an accident.

Clare was glad it hadn't been her and had had to stifle a snigger when the water chestnut hit the Wizened One. His face was a picture. Clare looked up and noticed that two men were now standing outside the restaurant in front of the window opposite her. One of them had started breathing on the cold glass, causing it to steam up. How childish, thought Clare. Then they were both doing it and she could hear them laughing.

Grace shot her a 'go and do something about it, before Mrs Suzuki sees them' look. Clare excused herself and went back through the bar to go outside.

'Do you have to do that?' she shouted at them. 'We are trying to entertain our… '

'Hi Clare! We just wanted to say helloooooo on our way to the tube station,' slurred Jack drunkenly, before bursting out laughing. 'This is Mark.'

'Jack, will you please just fuck off and stop blowing on the window? I've got Mrs Suzuki in there, remember?'

Jack lifted a hand to cover his mouth.

'Oops!'

'I'll look after him and we won't do it again. Nice to meet you, Clare,' said Mark, looking through the window at Mrs Suzuki, who was now standing in full view to see what all the commotion was.

'Is that her?' he asked.

'Shit!' said Clare, turning round.

Before going back in, Clare said to Mark,

'Please make sure he gets home in one piece. Look at the state of him.'

'Don't worry, he's in good hands,' he grinned.

Clare stared after them. Something about Mark had looked familiar, but she couldn't place it, and she didn't have time to think about it now.

Mark steered Jack off towards the tube station and Clare went back inside.

'What on earth was all that about?' asked Grace. 'Do you know those drunken louts?'

'Er, no. I just asked them to move on, that's all.'

Mrs Suzuki's phone started to vibrate violently on an empty plate beside her. Everyone stopped talking.

'*Moshi moshi*,' she said, quickly answering it. 'Hello?'

It was the call Grace and Clare had been waiting for, the call that would close or reject the deal on the table, the deal that Clare had worked so hard on for so many months.

'*Hai*,' said Mrs Suzuki, hanging up. She whispered something to the Wizened One and then to Lance, before standing up. The Wizened One stood up too.

'I'm afraid Mrs Suzuki has to leave now,' said Lance. 'She wants me to thank you for a lovely dinner and a thoroughly enjoyable evening.'

Clare wondered why Mrs Suzuki couldn't speak for herself. Was she suddenly mute? Mrs Suzuki just stood up, smiled at them and then stalked off out of the restaurant, with the Wizened One in tow.

'I don't understand,' said Clare to Lance. 'I'm guessing that the call wasn't the one from her Board about the contract. Has something else happened?'

'I'm afraid that *was* the Board,' said Lance, putting out his hands. 'They won't agree to the deal unless you strike the minimum order clause. We will be in London for just over another week, flying back to Japan next Saturday. If you change your minds and relax your position about it, give me a call and we will come back and sign the heads of terms. If not, it was nice meeting you guys.'

Clare couldn't believe it. Her heart sank. Not again! She knew she would be blamed for this and would be made to suffer for time immemorial. She quickly moved over to sit where Mrs Suzuki had been sitting, safely out of reach of Grace's foot. What was she going to do?

'You'd better fix this, Clare,' snapped Grace, kicking Paul, who was nearest, instead.

Chapter 33

Rachel was looking radiant and waving a bunch of flowers at him when he came through the arrivals gates at Tegel airport. Brian had been surprised when she had called on Tuesday evening and practically begged him to see if there was any way that he could fly to Berlin as soon as possible. She had told him straight away on the phone that she was pregnant and that she would explain more when he got there, adding that she was desperate to talk to someone face-to-face to make sure that she was making the right decision.

'But why me?' he had asked her.

Rachel had said that she really needed a good friend to talk to but didn't feel that Clare was the right person at the moment. Ever since she had stopped smoking Rachel thought Clare had been reacting like a speared rhinoceros to practically everything and everyone. It would be bad karma for the unborn. She had persuaded him to come over, saying that one of the reasons she really wanted to talk to him was because she believed he would be objective, and not judge her. She wanted someone to bounce her own thoughts off, not someone who would tell her what to do. There were, after all, only two options to decide between.

Brian agreed, and got a flight on Friday morning. As it was to be his first time in Berlin he had planned to stay the night with Rachel and Heike and fly back home on Saturday.

'You look fantastic,' said Brian, giving Rachel a big hug.

She kissed him noisily on both cheeks.

'I can't thank you enough for coming over. Haven't you

got any luggage?' she asked, dismayed, looking at his empty hands.

'Yep - toothbrush and a clean pair of socks and underpants,' he said, patting his jacket pockets.

'You always did know how to travel light. Come on, let's get the bus and then go for a walk. You have to see a couple of sights before I bore you to death with baby talk.'

'Don't be daft! That's why I'm here, isn't it?'

'And I'm truly grateful. But no womb debate until I say so, OK?'

'OK,' said Brian with a chuckle.

They got the bus from the airport to Kufürstendamm.

'This is the heart of what was West Berlin before the wall came down,' said Rachel, giving Brian a guided tour from the bus. 'These boulevards are amazing, aren't they?'

Brian couldn't believe how wide the streets were. Even the pavements were wider than some London roads. Mature oak trees swayed gently in the breeze, offering Berliners and tourists some shade from the midday sun.

'That's the famous Kaiser-Wilhelm Memorial Church that was bombed during the Second World War,' said Rachel, pointing across the road. 'Let's get off here and then we can have a closer look.'

They climbed down from the bus and walked over to Breitscheidplatz. The exterior of the old church had been left pretty much in the same state as it had been in after the bombs had done their damage. Most of its spire was missing, leaving a jagged, incongruous-looking top.

'I cried when I first saw it,' said Rachel, walking over to the church to touch its old stones. 'It was the most humbling experience to see this magnificent structure still standing defiantly, despite its loss.'

'It really is something,' said Brian, staring up into the sky.

'Coffee?' asked Rachel.

'That's a great idea. The coffee on the plane looked and tasted like tar.'

Rachel took Brian to a café a bit further down Kufursten-damm.

'Look at those cakes!' exclaimed Brian, gazing through the window. 'What's that one covered in wasps?'

'*Zwetschenkuchen*. It's a bit of a mouthful to pronounce and means plum tart. It attracts the wasps like crazy, as you can see. No one seems to mind though.'

Brian thought there were more wasps than plums.

'I think I'll give the wasp tart a miss. Just a filter coffee for me, thanks.'

They sat down at a quiet table in the shade and Rachel ordered their coffees.

'You already knew I was pregnant before I told you, didn't you? When did Clare tell you?'

Brian couldn't see the point of pretending.

'It was Jack who told me, actually.'

'Oh, so the whole world's been told then?' asked Rachel indignantly. 'Did she YouTube it and tell everyone on Facebook too? Then again, he was with her when I told her, I suppose.'

'We're your friends, Rachel. We all care,' he said reaching out to hold her hand.

Rachel sighed.

'I'm sorry. I know I'm being a bit hard on Clare, but one minute she's fine with what's going on in my life and the next we're back to square one and she's shouting the odds again. It's as if she has the right to tell me what to do and I need her approval.'

'I'm sure she does care about you and I know it's no excuse, but like you said, the smoking thing isn't helping and Jack says her work is really stressing her out.'

'Yes, well, she needs to get a grip. She's not the only one with stresses and headaches.'

'So, how did it happen?' asked Brian, immediately embarrassed by his own question. 'I mean I know *how* it happened biologically, but, well, you know.'

Rachel smiled as she lifted the cup of coffee that the waitress had just brought over.

'It was a one-off with Edward. About two months ago, just before I met Heike, actually. I can't really explain why I did it. I guess I felt sorry for him. He was so down and miserable about work, so I thought 'one last fuck, for old time's sake'. He used a condom, but it broke. He was sure that he'd got everything out in time. Obviously he was wrong. I missed my period, and the next one, and then finally did a home pregnancy test. Da da!' she said, patting her stomach.

'You're certain that Edward's the father?'

'Yes, of course I am. There haven't been any other men, well, not within the timeframe in question anyway,' said Rachel, looking away sheepishly.

'Oh I see, well, you kept that quiet,' he teased.

'We all have our little secrets, don't we?'

'I'll come back to that another time. Seriously though Rachel, do you want to keep it?'

Rachel paused and stirred her coffee with a spoon.

'I always intended to have kids, though I was planning to leave it a few more years, until my mid-thirties. That was always based on the assumption that Edward would be with me and that we would raise them together. Then I met Heike and that's all changed. Babies have been the last thing on my mind. I've been exploring something different, finding parts of a new me that I hadn't met or discovered before.'

Brian was listening carefully, letting Rachel pour her heart out to him.

'I suppose deep down I already knew I was pregnant as soon as I started missing my period, but I just hoped it was down to stress or excitement. It could have been. After I did the home test I thought I'd better have a proper test too, just to make things irrevocably official. I went to a clinic that some of my friends have been to in St Johns Wood. The doctor was very friendly and helpful and I got the results back later that day. I was as pregnant as I could possibly be. Confirmed!'

'That must have been hard for you.'

'Not really. I flew back to Berlin and told Heike straight away. She was overjoyed, cried and promised to support me and be with me, whatever I decided. She said she loved kids and that maybe it was all meant to be. She really is great, you know.'

'Yes, she seemed very nice at the party. What about Edward? Have you told him?'

'No, not yet.'

'But you are planning to?'

'Yes, once I've got my head around things. Of course he could be part of it all. I think he'll want to be, and I will need his help financially too.'

'You want to keep it, don't you?' said Brian softly. 'You've already decided.'

'That's what I'm strongly leaning towards. OK, the timing's far from perfect, but maybe Heike's right and it is meant to be. I don't think I could have a termination anyway, not now.'

'I've only really got one thing to say,' said Brian, putting down his cup.

'And that is?'

'Make sure you're having it for you and not for anyone else. Not Heike. Not Edward. And definitely not because of what I say. You don't know yet whether Heike will still be around when you have it – and I'm not being mean by saying that, just realistic. Even if she wants to be part of your life with the baby, you might not want her to be. Edward might not be there for you either once he gets filled in on the… the bigger picture.'

'I know, and you're dead right. It has to be for me. And it will be. You've been a great help. Thanks, Brian,' she said, squeezing his arm.

'I've hardly said anything!'

'But you listened, and it's what you said and how you said it. Jessica must be out of her mind not to be snapping you up. Still no change?'

'No. She's on holiday with lover boy at the moment. I'm not really sure what else I can do. Move on, I suppose.'

'You won't have any problem finding someone – but it's finding the right one, isn't it.'

'It sure is. Anyway, I'm not here to talk about that, or me. I'm here to talk about you. Whatever happens, you won't be alone. You know that, don't you? You'll always have us - and by us I mean Jack and Clare too. Give her time and a bit of slack. Packing in smoking is a tough nut to crack. But when she does come around she'll be supporting you one hundred per cent. We all will.'

Rachel beamed.

'I'm so lucky.'

'But I'm afraid I draw the line at changing nappies. You're on your own with that,' he laughed.

Rachel laughed too.

'I can't say I'm particularly looking forward to that aspect of motherhood either, but I'm told that it comes naturally when it's time.'

'If you say so. Rather you than me.'

Rachel took a deep breath before sharing her extra piece of news.

'Well, I certainly hope it does come naturally because there are going to be an awful lot of nappies to change. I had my scans confirmed this week and there's something else I've got to tell you.'

'What's that?'

'I'm expecting identical twin boys!'

Chapter 34

Mark was peeling potatoes in Jack's kitchen. He wasn't a natural cook, but he wanted to show willing and help. Jack had called Clare and Brian on Friday to invite them round for Sunday lunch at his place. He had apologised to Clare on the phone for the restaurant window episode and wanted to make it up to her. He also wanted Brian and Clare to meet Mark properly, so this was his treat. He'd been over to Dalston market early on Saturday morning and had bought a lean beef joint from a new butcher recommended by Toby, and picked up some fresh vegetables from Declan's stall. The joint had been in the oven for a couple of hours and Jack and Mark were preparing the ingredients for the rest of the meal.

'If you peel those potatoes down any more they will look like white peas!' scolded Jack. 'Have you never peeled a potato before?'

'Not recently, no,' said Mark, shaving off yet another perfectly good slice. 'Shall I peel the carrots now?'

'Er, no - that's fine. I was planning on serving nice glazed carrot chunks, but if I let you loose on them we'll end up with threads of carrot floating in honey.'

Mark dipped a finger in the honey jar and walked over to Jack.

'So you don't like my help in the kitchen?' he joked, trying to smear the honey on Jack's face.

'Stop it! Get off, and mind those pans.'

Mark put his finger in his own mouth and sucked off the honey.

'Come here, you,' he said, pulling Jack towards him.

He put his arms around Jack and held him close.

'You look quite sexy in that. Do you always cook with no clothes on?' he whispered, kissing Jack's ear and tugging at the apron strings.

'Not again,' said Jack, pushing him away and tying his apron back up. 'Surely last night and this morning were enough?' he laughed.

Mark smiled and pointed towards his shorts.

'I'm flattered,' said Jack looking down, 'but I'm afraid there's no time for that. You'll have to wait until later. Brian and Clare will be here in an hour and a half and I've still got to do the Yorkshires.'

'I would wait forever for you, just you see.'

Jack was really getting to like Mark. He couldn't believe how lucky he had been meeting him like that. An hour later and the roast potatoes were in the oven, the joint of beef was 'resting' and the vegetables were just about ready to re-heat to be served when the guests wanted to eat. The weather forecast had been for rain, but - as usual - seemed to be completely wrong, and the sun was beating down. Mark had laid the table and was still out on the terrace and Jack was mixing a jug of cocktails in the kitchen when the doorbell rang.

'You're bang on time,' said Jack, opening the door to let Brian in.

'Hi, mate. Mmmm, that smells good. What are we having, fish?'

'Beef actually,' snapped Jack. 'Does it smell like fish?'

'Only kidding. Nothing fishy about your cooking – I've been looking forward to this all morning.'

The doorbell rang again. It was Clare.

After they had all said their hellos and got one of Jack's cocktails in their hands, Jack, Clare and Brian joined Mark on the terrace.

'Hi, I'm Mark,' he said standing up from his chair.

'Nice to meet you, Mark,' said Brian, shaking his hand.

'Hello again,' waved Clare. 'Thanks for getting him home safely last week. You were so drunk!' she said to Jack crossly.

'I know, and I'm sorry,' said Jack, pouring Mark a cocktail from the iced jug. 'We'll eat in about half an hour, if that's OK with everyone?'

'Great,' answered Brian. 'This is delicious,' he said, taking a gulp from his glass. 'What is it?'

'I made it up myself, actually. It's got gin, vermouth, tequila, dark rum, pineapple juice and blueberry juice in it.'

'It's fantastic,' agreed Clare. 'I could just do with a two-foot-long cigarette to go with it, though! I never thought it would be this hard. How are you surviving?'

'I'm doing OK, actually. I can honestly say I don't even want one. Of course it feels a bit odd, but I'm enjoying being a non-smoker. Kissing someone is so much nicer,' he added, casting a glance over to Mark. His grey-blue eyes shone in the sunshine, and Jack just wanted to lean over and kiss him again.

Clare couldn't help but feel just a bit envious of Jack. He seemed to have effortlessly rid himself of all compulsion to smoke. It was also blatantly obvious how much sex he was having. You only had to look at them. They were like two kids in a sweet shop and probably giving Rachel and Heike a run for their money in that department.

'All I can say is that today it was ten o'clock this morning before I started thinking about smoking. Usually I wake up in the night gasping for one. So is that progress? Is that a sign that these hateful pangs will eventually disappear?' she asked no-one in particular.

'It sounds like you're doing really well, from what I've heard,' chipped in Mark supportively. 'I stopped six years ago and it was two years before I stopped wanting one.'

'Oh, great, that's something to look forward to then, isn't it? Two more years of hell!'

Clare was sure she had seen or met Mark somewhere before, but still couldn't place it.

'It's different for everyone, though,' said Brian. 'I was like

Jack. Well, not quite as good. It took me a bit longer to get through it, but I did.'

'How did your meeting go with the Japanese?' asked Jack, changing the subject as he refilled their glasses.

'Awful. It was a complete waste of time. The deal seems to be off.'

'Oh, shit,' said Mark. 'I hope it wasn't anything to do with us blowing on the window.'

'No, don't worry, that wasn't it. Oh well – that's that I suppose. I really don't know what will happen now. I'm at loggerheads with my boss and it's all a bit of a mess.'

'Try and forget about it for a bit and enjoy today,' said Jack.

'You're right. Fuck it. To Sundays,' said Clare, raising her glass, 'and to friends, old and new,' she finished, looking at Mark. Where had she seen him before? It was niggling her.

'How was Berlin?' asked Jack.

'It was good.' said Brian. 'Shame I couldn't stay longer.'

'More to the point, how was Rachel?'

'She's doing OK. She's made up her mind to go ahead with it. She's thought it all through and she wants to be a mother. Heike's keen on the idea too. I think she's really nice, you know, and a lot of fun - not to mention attractive.'

Heike had taken Brian for a few drinks on Friday evening after she'd finished work at the garage. Rachel had wanted them to go out for an hour on their own to give Brian the chance to get to know Heike a bit better while she prepared dinner. They had been to one of Heike's local haunts in Prenzlauer Berg, close to where she lived.

'Well, it won't be much fun when there's a screaming baby around, I can tell you. It won't be quite the same little lovenest when there are three of them in it,' scoffed Clare. 'I really have been trying to support Rachel throughout all this, but she can be a bit 'pie in the sky' sometimes. She doesn't always see the bigger picture.'

'You're being too harsh on her, Clare,' said Brian angrily. 'Come on, give her a break, will you? We all know it wasn't planned, but I really think that Rachel on her own or both Rachel and Heike together would make great parents, and will look after the babies as best they can. And don't forget there's Edward too.'

'*Babies?*' cried Clare. 'Don't tell me Heike's pregnant as well? This is unreal. Sorry, Mark, it's not usually quite this lively.'

'I think I'll just go and check on the vegetables,' said Mark standing up and going inside to the kitchen.

'Isn't he lovely?' said Jack proudly.

'He seems like a nice bloke,' said Brian. 'Don't fuck it up.'

'Me fuck it up? What about you and your track record?' retaliated Jack, knowing that Brian was only teasing.

'When you've both quite finished,' interrupted Clare impatiently. 'You said *babies* a few moments ago.'

'That's right,' said Brian slowly. 'I did.'

'So is Heike pregnant too?' she asked in disbelief.

Brian paused as Clare glared at him. She was jealous that Rachel had chosen to confide in Brian rather than in her.

'No, Heike's not pregnant. Rachel's expecting twins - identical twin boys. There'll be four of them in the nest, not three.'

Jack was speechless, but Clare wasn't.

'She's having *what*? This just gets better and better. What's her masterplan then? Pop one out for herself and another for every German lesbian while she's at it? I can't take any more of this nonsense. How on earth is she going to cope with fucking twins? I am dying for a cigarette. Please Jack; you must have a secret stash?'

Jack shrugged his shoulders and shook his head.

'She'll cope,' said Brian. 'People do – and we will be there to help her, won't we, Clare?'

'Oh no, you can count me out. If you think I'm spending my weekends pushing a customised baby buggy filled with two bawling brats around Regent's Park then you can think again.'

'Now you know you don't mean that,' said Brian. 'When you get chance to talk to Rachel properly I'm sure you'll feel differently. To be honest Clare, the reason she chose me to talk to was because of the mood you've been in ever since you stopped smoking.'

Clare sighed.

'I can't really blame her then, can I? I know I've been hard work since I stopped. I just can't help it at the moment. It's like I've had a mouth transplant, the poison that comes out of it. I'm sorry.'

'Well, I hadn't noticed much difference,' said Jack.

'You cheeky bast… '

Mark was coming back from the kitchen.

'Everything's almost ready,' he said to Jack.

'Welcome to my crazy world!' said Jack, getting up.

'Why, what's happened?'

'I'll tell you tonight.'

Ten minutes later they had all calmed down a little and were sitting at the table on the terrace, heartily tucking into their Sunday roast. The thought, smell and finally the sight of food had worked wonders for Clare's mood. She had even asked Brian if Rachel had started thinking about breastfeeding or not, wanting to show more of an interest.

'I don't think so,' he laughed, enjoying the red wine that Mark had poured him. 'She's only just decided to keep them! Give her a chance. Can you breastfeed two at the same time?'

'I have no idea – maybe Rachel could give them their starters and then Heike can help out with the main course. I'll buy them a couple of breast pumps,' said Clare, finally with a smile.

'Clare Houghton, you are awful,' said Jack.

Brian laughed. 'Does it work like that?'

'Of course it doesn't, Clare's just being Clare again,' said Jack.

'The beef is delicious by the way,' she said, savouring the

tender meat. 'And just look at these little miniature roast potatoes. How cute are they?'

Mark gave Jack an 'I'm sorry' look.

Jack gave Mark an 'I don't care what you do, I'll still like you' look.

The rest of the lunch conversation was much more light-hearted and the four of them ate and drank the afternoon away.

'What do you do for a living Mark?' asked Brian.

'I'm a builder, you know, working on building sites and some private home jobs too.'

'Apparently it pays really well. Mark's always going off travelling, aren't you?' said Jack.

'Well, not always, but I have been around a bit. I just got back from Japan, too,' he said nodding at Clare. 'Jack said that you were there recently.'

'Did you? What did you think?'

Clare was racking her brain about where she had seen Mark's face before.

'It was really good, but a bit too humid at this time of year for my liking.'

'That was a fantastic meal, Jack… and Mark,' said Brian. 'I'll wash up.'

'Don't be silly, you're my guest,' said Jack.

'So what? You two have been slaving over a hot stove all morning for us, haven't they Clare?' said Brian, expecting Clare to offer to help.

Clare didn't hear him. She was too busy studying Mark's face.

'I insist,' said Brian, picking some plates up from the table.

'All right then, thanks. Let's do them together. You can update me on Jessica while we wash and dry.'

'Not much to tell, really,' said Brian as he followed Jack inside to the kitchen, leaving Clare and Mark on the terrace.

'So, where were you in Japan?' asked Clare.

'Osaka mainly, but I spent a couple of nights in Kyoto too.'

'That's where I was - what a coincidence.'

She took a sip of wine from her glass before leaning forwards a little.

'I'm sure I've seen you before. Have we met somewhere?'

'I don't think so,' said Mark, 'I don't normally forget a face.'

'Neither do I,' said Clare, peering closer still.

Suddenly it all clicked into place. But it couldn't be, could it? She knew she'd seen Mark before… and then she recognised the small L-shaped scar just above his left eyebrow. But the last time she'd seen it, it had been on a woman's face.

'You're Marleen, aren't you?'

Chapter 35

Mark looked at Clare, quickly trying to assemble his thoughts. How did she know about Marleen? She didn't look at all familiar, sitting there with him at the table wearing shorts and scandals. This could ruin everything he had going with Jack, and he couldn't let that happen. He was really falling for him.

'You've lost me there! I don't know what you're talking about. Maybe you've had too much red wine?'

'No, I haven't. In fact, I haven't had nearly enough,' she said, pouring herself another glass. 'Marleen, can I refresh yours too? Or shall I go and see if Jack has any absinthe?'

Now Mark was really getting worried. How did she know about Marleen's favourite tipple?

'I'm sorry, love, I haven't got the faintest idea… '

'And your accent's changed a bit too,' said Clare, continuing her assault. Last time we spoke you had a Canadian accent. And your hair was different. Well, that's a huge understatement. You, or rather Marleen, had big red hair. Loads of it! I remember envying your boots.'

Mark was snookered.

'All right, you've got me. But how do you know about Marleen? And please, can you keep your voice down?' he whispered, casting a nervous glance indoors.

'That was going to be my next question. I take it Jack hasn't had the pleasure of meeting Marleen yet?'

'No,' said Mark, all of a sudden looking like a little boy about to cry.

Clare softened her tone, and explained how they had met.

'We had a few drinks together in a downtown bar in Osaka last month. It was before lunchtime. I was alone in the bar drinking *sake*, drowning my sorrows after an awful meeting. You came into the bar shortly afterwards and we got talking. You'd obviously already had more that just a couple of drinks before you got there. You did look quite the part as I recall. Though with hindsight, I'm surprised I never guessed you were a man. It was very dark in the bar, I suppose, and I'd had a lot to drink too.'

Mark looked at Clare more closely. He still didn't recognise her.

'You told me all about your profession and working with elite Japanese businessmen. You even thought I was on the game as well. Of course, I wasn't dressed like this either when we met. I had a suit on – a short skirt and jacket if I recall correctly. I told you all about my meeting with Mrs Suzuki and how badly my morning had gone.'

Mark remembered.

'I called you Candy, didn't I? I still think the name suits you.'

Clare couldn't keep herself from smiling at the thought of telling everyone she had changed her name to 'Candy'.

'What's going on, Mark?' she asked seriously. 'What's with the double life? Are you a cross-dresser, a transvestite, or a transsexual? You're definitely for hire - you told me that much in Osaka.'

'It's not really very complicated. I'm mainly me, Mark,' he said, deciding that there wasn't much point in trying to lie his way out of it.

'I'm all ears,' said Clare, casting a look indoors towards the kitchen, where Brian and Jack were as thick as thieves at the sink.

'I've always enjoyed dressing up a bit, ever since I was a boy, but I don't do it all the time.'

Clare listened as Mark did his best to explain.

'About eight years ago I was doing a job at a woman's

house in Belgravia. Her real name was Doris. She wanted me to touch up some brickwork around an old fireplace and then repair part of the cornicing that had been crumbling for years. After she'd given me my instructions she left me alone to get on with the job. About half an hour later I heard shouting in the next room. I went over to the door, which hadn't been closed properly, and I could see though the gap.'

'What did you see?'

'There was a naked guy on his hands and knees cleaning the floor with a small brush and sponge. Doris had got changed and was all dressed up in a tight blue latex outfit and high-heeled ankle boots. She was holding a cane in her right hand and her hair was scraped back into a bun.'

'Then what happened?' asked Clare, almost spilling her wine with curiosity.

'She came back into the room I was working in. She knew that I'd seen the guy next door and said it was all right and that I needn't worry about the noise. She said that he comes around once a week to do some cleaning for her with no clothes on. Apparently that was his thing. I made a joke about her at least getting the house cleaned for free. She threw back her head, laughed, and said,

'For free? Don't be ridiculous. He pays me £300 an hour to clean my floors. All I have to do is shout at him, tell him what a bad job he's doing followed by some light to moderate caning on the buttocks. Then I bend down and warn him that it'll hurt a lot more than that if he doesn't put more effort into the cleaning. That usually does the trick.'

'No way!' said Clare, in disbelief.

'I know! That's what I thought… at first. But I couldn't stop thinking about it, and after a few weeks I went around to see her to ask if she needed an apprentice. After all, I liked dressing up and I thought it looked like easy money. She earned more in an hour than I did in a week.'

'I assume she agreed to take you under her wing then?'

'Well, yes. Marleen was born shortly afterwards. There

was a bit more to it than I expected. It was a whole new ball game.'

'I'm sure,' said Clare, imagining whipping a naked Grace as she cleaned Clare's office on her hands and knees.

'After a while I built up my own client base, found a specialist international agency, and the rest is history. Now I only work in the field for a few weeks a year. I'm good at my job and it pays a fortune.'

'I don't quite know what to say,' said Clare, for once lost for words. This had to be the maddest, most insane day of her life. First it was Rachel, Heike and twins. Now it was Mark aka Marleen catering for the global fetish scene. And all set against the backdrop of a traditional Sunday roast.

'You'll have to tell Jack,' she said eventually. 'He's my closest friend and I can't sit by and watch him get hurt. Don't get me wrong, I've nothing against your industry. I actually know a few people, who have... er... sampled purchased goods,' she added coyly.

'Who's hurting him? I'm certainly not,' cried Mark. 'I lov... I'm really fond of him.'

'How can you say that? You've lied to him about your job and your life and you're having sex with all kinds of strangers behind his back.'

'Hang on a minute,' said Mark. 'I haven't lied about my job. I do still do some building work. All right, I haven't told him about Marleen or that side of things yet. But let me make one thing very clear. I have *never* had sex with any of my clients. That's not what it's about. They pay me for certain services, yes, but never for sex.'

'Well, that's all very well, but if you won't tell him then I'm afraid I will. I'm sorry, Mark. Why should it be kept a secret from him?'

'Please don't tell him. Not yet. I've only known him for a week or so and he's the best thing that's ever happened to me. If I tell him right now then I might lose him. He doesn't know me well enough yet to understand.'

'You've got that one right.'

'Clare, I'm begging you.'

Clare was fidgeting with her napkin when Jack suddenly reappeared.

'Are you two all right out here? I'll crack open another bottle of wine for you, shall I? We won't be long - just having a man-to man chat about Brian and Jessica.'

'Yes, please,' said Mark, still managing to give Jack a lopsided grin despite his current very uncomfortable predicament.

'Why shouldn't I tell him just because you don't want me to?' challenged Clare after Jack had gone back inside.

'Because I'm good for Jack and we're good together. Please don't spoil it for us.'

'But I just don't think it's fair to keep such big secrets. Yes, you seem like a nice guy, but I don't really know that much about you, or about Marleen, for that matter.'

Mark grunted.

'Well, you do actually know quite a lot about me already. Much more than most people I know.'

'You're asking too much from me.'

Mark sat back in his chair and folded his arms.

Clare put her sunglasses back on, sat back and folded her arms too.

They were locked in stalemate for a few minutes before Mark jolted forwards.

'I think I might be able to help you too.'

Clare took off her sunglasses.

'Oh, I doubt that very much.

'That was your Mrs Suzuki the other night at the restaurant, wasn't it? The one that Jack said won't sign a contract or something? I recognised her when I saw her looking at us through the window.'

'So?'

'I'm breaking a code of practice here – but needs must.'

'What are you going on about?'

'I know her. Well, I don't exactly know her, but I have seen her before, a few times.'

'Maybe you have. She's a successful entrepreneur who travels the world, not a recluse,' snapped Clare.

'No, I've seen her on the circuit.'

'What circuit?'

'The fetish circuit.'

Clare laughed.

'You're making this up now, aren't you?'

'No, really, I've seen her at private clubs in Japan and one in London. It's important for me to go to them – call it market research, to keep up with the trends. Do you know how long she's staying in London?'

'Until next Saturday. But I don't see what any of this… '

'That's it then. She'll be going to an exclusive fetish night at a club near London Bridge on Wednesday. It's only on twice a year. She's timed her visit to tie meeting you in with the date of the club night. I'd bet thousands on it. She's been before.'

'Look, please stop this rubbish. There is no way that Mrs Suzuki will be going to a fetish club. I suppose you think she'll be taking her lawyer and father along too - a family outing perhaps?'

'I suppose it does all sound a bit weird. How can I prove it to you?'

'You don't have to. I really don't care what they all get up to.'

'Look, we don't have time to talk about this now. Jack will be back in a minute. I've got an idea to help you. Please hear me out – can you come and meet me tomorrow morning?'

'I really don't see the point. Just tell Jack about your double life as Marleen and then we can all get on with whatever we need to get on with.'

'Honestly, Clare, please come tomorrow – I think it will be worth your while, but you have to trust me for a few days and promise not to tell Jack yet.'

Clare stared directly into Mark's eyes. There was something very truthful about them.

'If you're winding me up… ' she warned, shaking her head.

'Thanks,' said Mark, sighing with relief. 'Here's my number. Give me a call later.'

'You've got until the end of tomorrow before I tell him, unless you can persuade me otherwise with whatever your plan is.'

Brian and Jack were making their way back to the table. Brian was carrying a tray of glasses and a bottle of port and Jack was holding a generously stocked cheeseboard.

'Here we come!' shouted Jack. 'I hope you've got room for this.'

'I could still eat a horse,' Clare shouted over to the patio doors, where Jack and Brian had stopped to examine a geranium, for some reason or other.

She leaned over to whisper something to Mark.

'He thinks his world is crazy! Wait until he finds out about yours.'

Chapter 36

The weather forecast had been almost right - just a day late. It was Monday morning and pouring down with rain. Before going to the office Jack stopped by at the dry cleaners to drop off some shirts. He'd got a bit behind with his laundry over the last couple of weeks, and decided that he would treat himself to the service. Washing and ironing had been the last things on his mind. He'd spent almost every day and night of his week off work with Mark and it had been wonderful. He couldn't get enough of being with him. In fact, the only day that Jack hadn't spent with Mark had been Thursday, when he had had to go off on a building job. They'd still managed to meet up again that night though, and, for a change, Jack had stayed over at Mark's place in Tufnell Park. His flat was small, but cosy, and they'd enjoyed a takeaway and watched movies curled up on the sofa.

Jack was pleased that the Sunday lunch had, for the most part, gone well, and that Brian and Clare had both seemed to like Mark.

'Good morning, Samantha,' he said cheerfully, going into the office, pausing at reception to check his pigeon hole. He'd only been off a week but it was still crammed full of envelopes and papers.

Samantha barely looked up from her screen as she muttered something back.

'Did you have a good weekend?' asked Jack, sorting through his post, dropping the unwanted junk mail into the recycling bin.

'No, I didn't, actually. Do you want to know why not?'

Jack didn't really.

'Of course.' he said. 'What's wrong?'

'I found out my boyfriend was seeing someone else,' she said, her face crumpling.

'Don't cry. Come on. He's not worth it.'

'I feel so ashamed. I had no idea,' wailed Samantha.

'I'm sure you've nothing to be ashamed about. He's the one that appears to be in the wrong,' said Jack, choosing his words carefully. 'Here, have a tissue.'

'Thanks,' said Samantha, taking it from him and loudly blowing her nose with it.

Jack remembered how Paolo and Samantha had given him the impression that something was going on between them, on the day that he and Paolo had been in the stationery cupboard together. Perhaps they really had - and now Samantha had found out about Jessica, or maybe some other woman - or man. Who knows? What a selfish pig Paolo was!

'How was your week off?' asked Samantha quietly, throwing the soggy tissue into her waste paper basket.

Jack didn't think it appropriate to tell her that he had had the best week off ever, and was falling very much for a handsome young skinhead, who worked as a builder, was fantastic in bed, loads of fun to be with and just generally a nice, uncomplicated guy.

'It was all right, but a bit quiet,' he lied instead. 'I'm glad to be back at work actually.'

'Oh dear, never mind,' said Samantha, cheering up a bit on hearing that someone else hadn't had a great time either.

'I'd better get on,' said Jack, wanting to break away to go and tell Gloria how happy he was feeling, 'You *will* get over it,' he soothed. 'Just don't try and rush it.'

Lisa was hovering above Gloria like a kestrel over a field mouse when Jack arrived at his desk.

'Good morning,' he said to them both.

Gloria looked stressed and just nodded. Lisa looked up.

'Good morning, Jack, and welcome back. It feels like you've been off for a month, doesn't it, Gloria?'

Gloria thought it felt more like a year. She was gritting her teeth and clenching her fists. Every day last week Lisa had given her a hard time. She somehow expected Gloria to do both her own work and Jack's too, while he was off. Lisa, of course, had never been happy with anything that Gloria produced, and had complained about this and moaned about that. Gloria hated her with a vengeance. She wanted to slowly pull off her eyelids with a pair of rusty pliers while simultaneously biting off her nose.

'Uh huh, yes it does,' she said, flashing him a maniacal smile.

'Jack, after you've checked your emails I'd be really grateful if you could have a look at these reports that Gloria has tried to do in advance of quarter-end,' said Lisa, waving a handful of papers. 'They're sort of there in places, aren't they, Gloria? But I think she would be grateful if you could go over them thoroughly with her. Wouldn't you, Gloria?'

'Yes, Miss,' said Gloria, under her breath.

'I beg your pardon?'

'I said I've missed him. Yes, I really would appreciate Jack's help because I'm just a dumb bush pig, that can't add up or type properly.'

'Now that's not what I said. But it's this sort of childish attitude that is affecting your concentration and your work. If you could just apply half the time to your reports as you do to your make-up, then I think we'd be almost there.'

Lisa strode across to the water cooler to fill her glass before returning to her office and closing the door.

'I can't stand her any more,' screamed Gloria, her jaws shaking. 'Aaagggghhh!'

'Sounds like you had a good week.'

'It was bloody awful. I'm seriously thinking about looking for another job - or maybe even just resigning. Every time I see her I want to turn her face inside out.'

Jack tried to imagine what an 'inside out face' might look like, but failed.

'Sorry, you can't leave, because I would miss you too much.'

'Well, you'll have to come with me then,' said Gloria, tearing up a letter she'd just written, having spotted a couple of typos.

Gloria was often like this on a Monday morning, so Jack wasn't overly worried. He wanted to do something to diffuse the situation a little.

'Why don't you come out with me today for some lunch? You might feel a bit better after you've had some air.'

'I don't need any air! What I need is for Lisa's tongue to be stretched as far as possible out of her mouth and then for someone to use it to strangle her with.'

'Is this before or after her face has been turned inside out?'

Gloria laughed.

'Preferably after. I really don't know what I'd do without you here, you know. You wouldn't believe the times I've thought about just getting on a plane and going back home to Australia.'

Jack frowned.

'You want to go home to Wollongong?'

'I didn't mean *home* quite so literally. It would have to be Sydney or Melbourne. I think Sydney.'

'Maybe you just need a holiday.'

'Yes, I do, away from HER.'

'So will you come out with me at lunchtime?'

'Oh, all right, I suppose I could pass on my diet for one day.'

The rest of the morning passed without any further clashes between Gloria and Lisa and before long Jack and Gloria were walking over towards Leicester Square. He knew a good Spanish restaurant that did quick lunch specials. The weather had brightened up a bit so they picked a table outside next to a fake hedge. The waiter brought them their menus.

'Shall we have a glass of wine?' asked Jack.

He didn't usually drink at lunchtime on a work day, but he thought it might help today.

'Oh, sod it,' said Gloria, folding her menu. 'Let's have a bottle.'

They ordered their food - seafood paella - and a bottle of Rioja.

'To us,' said Jack, raising his glass.

'Cheers! Isn't this outrageous for a Monday?'

'I feel like I'm still off on holiday.'

'So how was it, your holiday?' asked Gloria, relaxing a little.

'I have had the best week! I didn't want to say earlier because you were having a hard time, but I've met this guy called Mark and it's going so well. I can't believe it.'

'You're over Paolo, then?' said Gloria with a snort. She'd finally managed to wheedle the truth out of him after Paolo resigned. It hadn't surprised her.

'That was just a mad crush. This is different and I think he feels the same way. Everything's good – the sex, the chat, the just being together. I'm really happy.'

'Well, good for you, you deserve it. What does he do, Mark?'

'He's a builder. He's such a nice guy. I think you'll like him. Anyway, what about you? How was your weekend?'

Gloria poured them both another glass of wine.

'It was all right, actually. I saw Declan again on Saturday. We went out for drinks to a new bar on Broadway Market with his brother Toby and my friend Annette. They've been seeing a lot of each other. She says she wants to give up hairdressing and go and work with Toby on the market. Somehow I can't see her gutting fish instead of weaving hair extensions, but there you go.'

'It sounds like the four of you could work together on the market. I always buy my fruit and vegetables from Declan. At least that way I would still get to see you if you left here.'

Gloria put her hands down on the table in front of Jack.

'Do these expensively-manicured nails look like they would be happy scraping dirt off potatoes and turnips? I don't think so. Besides, I'm not quite as enthusiastic about playing happy families as Annette is.'

'Why not? I thought you two were doing OK. Look, if you've seen Declan more than once, that constitutes a serious relationship for him.'

'Ha ha! Don't get me wrong, he's not bad at all. And he's wild in bed. We were at it like koala bears on Saturday night,' boasted Gloria. 'He really knows what he's doing, which is a nice change. It's not all about him as it is with some guys, know what I mean?'

Jack could guess.

'So what's the problem then?'

'I just don't think I want to tie myself down, especially if I might be going back to Australia.'

The waiter arrived with their food.

'Black pepper?' he asked, holding out a large pepper grinder. They both nodded.

'You're not seriously thinking about going back, are you?'

'Maybe. The exchange rate is good. I could afford a deposit on a flat somewhere in Sydney. If I stay here I'll be renting forever.'

'But what about your friends? What about me?'

'You'll be able to come and visit and have holidays in Australia. Don't look at me like that. I haven't decided anything definite just yet. Anyway, why don't we order another bottle and not go back to work today,' she suggested daringly.

'What do you mean, not go back?'

Gloria got out her phone and started to stab at it.

'Hello, Samantha, it's me, Gloria. Listen, Jack and I have got food poisoning from our lunch and won't be able to come back to the office this afternoon. Yes. No. Awful! The stomach ache is agony and the runs are... OK sorry. Is that too much information? Right. No, I didn't realise you were eating pea and ham soup. Look, I've got to go again. I don't want to have an accident. Would you mind telling Lisa for us? I really don't think I can hang on until you put me through to her. You're a star, thanks. Hopefully see you tomorrow.'

Jack looked at Gloria, impressed with her spontaneous performance.

'Forget about weighing vegetables in Hackney or moving to Sydney - you're destined for the West End stage. That was quite something!'

'Did you think so?' said Gloria, feeling much better and already imagining what she might say, collecting her first Oscar.

'Well, I didn't think we'd be doing this when I got up this morning,' said Jack, topping up their drinks. 'It feels so... naughty.'

'I know,' said Gloria. 'Isn't it wonderful? Life's too short as it is. You've got to grab it while you can.'

Chapter 37

Mark had asked Clare to come round to his place on Monday morning. As agreed, she had called him on Sunday evening and made the arrangements to go and listen to his idea in person. Clare still thought it was a waste of time, but had given him the benefit of the doubt. She had to do something to try and rescue the deal with Mrs Suzuki and didn't currently have anything else to go with. She really had wanted to persuade Mark to tell Jack all about Marleen, or simply to tell him herself. Now she felt a bit uncomfortable about not having done it. It seemed disloyal to be holding out with information until she could see whether or not Mark could somehow be of help to her, but she was desperate.

Clare had called the office on her way over to Mark's to let them know she would be working from home today. She knew Grace would probably be furious about it and that she would still be hopping mad from last week. She would have to speak to her later.

The trains were chaotic as usual, but she eventually arrived at Mark's flat at eleven-fifteen.

'Just through the door and down the stairs,' said Mark through the intercom.

Clare felt even more uncomfortable about this whole thing now that she was actually at Mark's flat. What would Jack think about her if he knew she was meeting Mark secretly?

'Mark, listen,' she said, after she had descended to the lower ground floor and gone inside.

'This isn't a good idea at all. I feel awful sneaking around in secret like some sort of spy. I'll go,' she said turning around.

'Just come and sit down and don't be silly. Nobody's sneaking around and you're not behaving like a spy. Well, not yet you aren't.'

'What do you mean, not yet?'

'I'll tell you in a minute. Do you want milk or sugar in your coffee?'

'Just black, thanks,' she answered, reluctantly slipping off her jacket, wondering what Mark's plan could possibly be.

She walked around the room while Mark was in the kitchen. There was a picture of Mark with his arm around an older woman in a brushed steel frame on the mantelpiece.

'That's my mum,' said Mark proudly, coming back with their coffees.

'She looks kind.'

'She's the best.'

'Right- I'm all ears,' said Clare, sitting down.

Mark began to tell Clare about his plan to encourage Mrs Suzuki to sign Clare's contract.

'It's not that complicated. She will be going to SMelt on Wednesday night.'

'SMelt?'

'Yes, it's an exclusive international fetish party near London Bridge. She will be there. All we have to do is get some photographs of Mrs Suzuki at play and then you can re-negotiate with her.'

'Are you crazy? You want me to blackmail her?'

'Isn't she blackmailing you?'

Clare thought about this for a second. It was true that unless Clare's company backed down, there would be no deal.

'No. I couldn't possibly do that,' said Clare, standing up. 'Who would I show the photographs to anyway? For all I know her husband goes with her to the fetish nights.'

'I've only ever seen her with another woman, a large woman. They make a remarkable looking pair.'

'So now you're telling me that Mrs Suzuki is not only a fetish freak, she is also a lesbian fetish freak?'

'That's not what I said, and like I told you before, it's not always about sex. It's highly probable that Mrs Suzuki isn't into women in that way. She will just be having some fun at the clubs, living out some fantasies and fetish desires. So, if there's a husband, then you could say that you might have to show the photographs to him if she doesn't cooperate.'

'Threaten her, you mean?'

'Threaten is such an ugly word. Persuade is a much better one.'

'I couldn't. It wouldn't be right.'

'Business is business. She's doing the same thing to you, just in a different way. You're not hurting anyone, are you? Besides, have you got any better ideas before they fly back at the weekend?'

Clare thought about this. She hadn't. Grace wouldn't relax the deal terms any further. It just wouldn't be financially viable, so it would all be off if Mrs Suzuki and Lance didn't turn out to be calling their bluff with a stalling tactic. The deal wouldn't be the only thing that would be off either. So would her head.

'But what if it goes wrong?' she asked, daring to consider the idea for a moment. 'What if she doesn't care about the photographs?'

'You just said she has a husband. I think you can safely gamble on guessing that he doesn't know about her pastimes and neither will her company.'

'I suppose you've got a point. But who will you ask to take the photographs?'

'Ah,' he replied. 'That's where you come in. It could get complicated if we involve anyone else.'

Clare threw back her head and laughed like a madwoman.

'I see. So I just walk into a fetish club and go straight over to Mrs Suzuki and ask her if she wouldn't mind posing for a few snaps so that I can blackmail her the following day? Sounds like a plan Mark! Why didn't I think of that?'

'We both need to be there. I can make sure no one's watching you and you can take the pictures – with a secret camera.'

'Don't you think I'd stand out like a sore thumb wearing these to a fetish club?' cried Clare, pointing at her skirt and blouse.

'Of course you would. That's why we'll have to get you something else to wear.'

Clare looked at him, shaking her head.

'This just gets more fun by the second.'

'What have you got to lose?'

'My job, my self-respect, my freedom if I go to jail?'

'Now you're being daft. All you have to do is put on a little outfit, have a few drinks with me and take a few photographs. Who knows? - you might even enjoy it, and we might have a laugh too.'

'Why would you do all this for me? Are you really that scared of telling Jack about Marleen?'

'Of course I'm not. But I want to tell him myself and *I* want to choose when I tell him. I promise I'll do it soon and I promise not to hurt him. And Clare, believe it or not, I actually like you and I want to help you. Is that so hard to believe?'

Clare hadn't looked at Mark's offer of help from that angle before.

'I suppose I should say thank you, then,' she said quietly. 'Do you really think it could work?'

'Marleen doesn't like to fail - and I don't think Clare does either.'

'Oh, what the hell. Promise me you'll visit me in prison?'

'I promise – but only if I can come as Marleen. I think she would like the bars, chains and keys,' he laughed.

'Right - now we need to find you something nice to wear,' said Mark, going over to a cupboard in the corner.

He took out a catalogue and sat down again, this time next to Clare.

'By the time I've finished with you you'll look and feel like a different person.'

Right at this moment Clare did indeed want desperately to feel like a different person - and be somebody else. Anybody else. She was exhausted, and still sometimes gasped for cigarettes. Thankfully the little gremlin that had haunted her night and day had started to move away from dangling in front of her eyes *always* shouting 'give me nicotine' to somewhere in the side of her head *sometimes* shouting 'give me nicotine.' This was one of those moments.

'What about this?' asked Mark, pointing to picture of a woman wearing a pink basque and a pair of black, crotchless latex shorts.

'Perhaps something with less ventilation.'

Mark turned the page.

'Now this would suit you,' he said, pointing at a maid's outfit made from red leather.

'I think it would have to be something I could hide behind, something less flesh-baring.'

'OK,' said Mark, turning another couple of pages.

'This is it! What do you think?'

Clare didn't really want to approve anything from the sordid catalogue.

'It would certainly cover me up,' she said, looking at the black rubber catsuit that Mark had selected.

'How do I know what size I need?' she asked solemnly.

'Stand up,' he said, pulling open a drawer to find a tape measure.

'Is this absolutely necessary?' she complained as Mark measured her inside leg.

'Of course it is. It has to be skin tight. You want to look the part don't you?'

Clare didn't, not at all, but she had now taken her first nervous steps towards fetish-hood and she felt that she had no other choice but to take the next one.

'I'll get the catsuit for you. Do you have any black boots?'

'I do as it happens. They have heels and are about knee-high.'

'Perfect. Now we need something for your face. Maybe a hood?'

Clare looked at the hoods in the catalogue.

'I don't think I could breathe in one of those,' she said, grimacing.

'You're not always supposed to,' he grinned. 'How about a gas mask?'

'Definitely not.'

'We could just go for a simple mask for your eyes and brow – that would be in keeping with the catsuit. As long as you do something with your hair as well nobody will be able to recognise you.'

Just the thought of somebody recognising her gave Clare palpitations.

'I don't know how we go about getting a secret camera, though,' Mark sighed, closing the catalogue. 'We're going to have to sort that out quickly.'

Oh well, in for a penny, in for a pound, thought Clare.

'Leave that one to me.'

Clare had once engaged the services of a private detective. She hadn't trusted her last boyfriend, Richard. During the last six months that they were together they had hardly seen each other, except on Sundays. There was always something else more important that he had to do. Clare didn't believe him, and was convinced that he was having an affair. Eventually, she couldn't stand the not knowing any longer, and she had hired a detective. She was sure the agency would be able to help her with a camera.

'Really?'

'You're not the only one with secrets,' said Clare peering at him, though she decided against sharing hers with Mark for the time being.

'Right, then. We're all set. Let's meet here on Wednesday evening at seven o'clock. Then we can get ready, have a drink or two and get a cab over to London Bridge. Don't eat much before you come otherwise we'll never fit you into your catsuit.'

Clare couldn't believe what she was getting into. If someone had told her last week that she would be planning to go to a fetish club to secretly photograph a Japanese businesswoman in order to secure a contract, she would have had them sectioned on the grounds of insanity. Even if everything that Mark had told her was true, what were the chances of them pulling this stunt off? There was only one way to find out.

Chapter 38

Although Brian had wanted to call Donald practically every day to ask him about Jessica, he hadn't. As it turned out it was Donald who called Brian.

'Brian, darling, thank goodness I've caught you. I've had a bit of an accident. I was standing on a stool, you see, to get a box down from a shelf in the kitchen. As I was lifting the box I somehow managed to knock a cookery book from the shelf below. The blasted book fell off and has cracked the small window, you know, the one next to the kettle.'

Brian remembered the window.

'Are you hurt?'

'No, dear, I'm fine thank you - but I am a bit worried about leaving it like that, and Tom's not here today.'

'I can pop over and fix it later this morning if you like? I can pick up some glass on the way.'

'Could you really? That would be splendid.'

'You'll need to measure the window for me.'

'Yes, of course, dear. Just a moment.'

Donald went off to measure the window and then gave Brian the dimensions over the phone.

It was about eleven o'clock by the time Brian arrived at Donald's. He'd stopped off near Dalston market for the glass and had grabbed a late breakfast in the café with Toby and Declan. They'd been talking about how often Toby was seeing Annette and how Declan was repeat-dating Gloria.

'She's smouldering,' said Declan tearing into his bacon and sausage sandwich. 'Know what I'm saying?'

'Not as sizzling as my Annette,' said Toby, with a beam.

Seeing his friends happy with their girlfriends had made Brian feel very single. He hadn't been out with anybody else since meeting Jessica. He still wanted her, but he couldn't have her. He had to do something to try and win her over. He could understand why she'd been angry about what he and Jack had told her about Paolo and why she had wanted to lash out. But surely she must know that they couldn't have made it all up?

Donald was wearing a pair of yellow washing up gloves when he opened the door to let him in. Brian was almost knocked over by Rags and Muffin as they bounded through it, barking like wolves, but reassuringly wagging their tails.

'Hello Donald, hello dogs,' said Brian, stroking their heads. He was getting to quite like them.

'It's so good of you to come over in my hour of need. I can't thank you enough.'

'I haven't done anything yet,' grinned Brian, going inside. 'So where's Tom today?'

'Oh, he doesn't come every day. I could never afford it. He was here at the weekend and did the lawns and planted a few busy lizzies along the side of the garden. Aren't they lovely?' he said, gazing outside. 'He's such a dear, isn't he?'

'Er, yes,' said Brian, not quite sure of what an appropriate response might be.

'I do worry about him though. He's seemed a bit down recently and he doesn't say much at the best of times. I can tell that something's bothering him. I've asked him if he wants to talk, but he just said that it's not going too well with his girlfriend and carried on with his weeding. He's only twenty-four, bless him, and he's such a nice boy.'

'I might give him a call, you know. I could so with some help with a new commission for two chests of drawers that I got from a couple in Brighton. They came to the exhibition. He might be able to give me a hand with some of the sanding.'

'I'm sure he would do a marvellous job. Now, come and

sit down. I have something to tell you that I think may be of interest,' said Donald, walking out onto the patio. 'I spoke to Jessica a few days ago and the poor thing was in bits. Her holiday with that Paolo one hasn't been much fun. In fact she said it had been ghastly.'

Donald offered Brian an olive from a bowl on the table.

'Oh, really?' asked Brian, taking one and popping it into his mouth.

'It seems they had a huge row and the whole thing is off,' said Donald with a smile.

'Well, that's brilliant news! It's a shame she's upset and all that, but he is such a tosser, and this means I can have a chance. That is, if you will allow me to court your daughter,' he finished, bowing down on one knee.

Donald laughed.

'Get up, get up. Nothing would please me more. But I really think that you need to wait a while.'

'Come on, Donald, I've been waiting for weeks and weeks! Surely I can see her when she comes back and tell her that I'm really keen on going out with her, if she's interested, and when she's ready.'

'Well, yes, you could. The thing is, she's not planning on coming back for a while.'

'What do you mean?'

'She told me she needs to have some time to think, and wants to be on her own. She can't go back to her own house because of the building work so she's rented an apartment in Barcelona. She said something about doing some remote work on her mail, but it didn't really make any sense.'

'Maybe she said she can work remotely and communicate by email.'

'Yes, dear, that sounds about right.'

The doorbell rang.

'Excuse me a moment,' said Donald, wafting back inside to open the door.

Brian's head was spinning. Of course he was pleased that

everything seemed to be off between Paolo and Jessica. The problem was that he wanted to drive to the airport right now, get on a plane and arrive in Barcelona today to rescue her and tell her that everything was going to be all right. But he couldn't. Or so Donald said. But what if she met someone else before coming back? What if she never came back? He knew the last option was probably unlikely, but he just wanted to *do* something now rather than just sit waiting in hope.

'Brian, this is Lucille. Lucille grooms the dogs once a month. She's marvellous. Lucille, this is Brian. He's an amazing furniture maker. He made me a new wardrobe to replace the one that... well, you know, don't you?'

'Hi,' said Brian with a wave.

'Hello! So where are my babies?'

'They're just having a run in the garden. Shall I call them in?'

'No, that's fine. We'll do it outside today, while it's nice.'

Lucille picked up her bags and went outside to the garden, calling to the dogs.

'She really is terribly good. She brings everything with her. Biscuits and treats to keep the dogs still while she works, countless clippers and brushes and a little hand-held vacuum cleaner to tidy up when she's finished. You'd never know she'd even been - that is, until you see the dogs looking like they've spent the afternoon at Vidal Sassoon,' he chuckled.

Brian started knocking out the damaged glass in the small kitchen window.

'How long will Jessica be staying away, then?'

'I'm afraid she didn't say. I don't even think she knows. A couple of weeks, maybe even a couple of months.'

'A couple of months?' shouted Brian, angrily bashing out the last bit of broken glass. 'But anything could happen in that time. Are you sure I shouldn't just fly over to Barcelona to at least say hello and show my face?'

'No, dear. Not yet. I already offered to go over but she

wants to be alone. Trust me, I know her. If you go over now you won't be doing yourself any favours.'

Brian sighed. He felt very frustrated with the situation. What could possibly be wrong with saying hello? He didn't get it.

'You're so clever,' said Donald, as Brian sealed the replacement glass.

'No worries. That was easy. If only everything was as straightforward.'

Brian cleaned the new window and then looked through it onto the garden.

'What the hell is Lucille doing with your dogs?'

Lucille was on her back on the grass with one of the dogs standing above her, sort of head to toe. She was working meticulously with a small instrument and it looked most undignified for both parties.

Donald came over to see and stood next to him.

'Oh, she's just cleaning up all the pesky little residual clumps. I don't know how she does it, but they're as clean as whistles by the time she's finished.'

Brian made a face.

'How does she get them to stand still while she prods and pokes?'

'I don't ask, dear. Maybe she puts Class A drugs in their doggie biscuits. Look Brian, I hate to see my daughter upset and of course it's good news for you if she's single again. But she's not a parcel waiting to be passed around from pillar to post. She needs time. If you want to stand any chance at all you'll give her that time. What's the rush anyway? You're both young and beautiful. You should be happy! Enjoy *life*.'

Brian didn't know what to say any more. There was no point. He couldn't just turn up in Barcelona on the hoof with no address or telephone number and he didn't think that Donald would give it to him. Not just yet anyway.

'Right, you're all done,' he said, packing away his tools. 'If you need anything else, just give me a shout.'

'That's splendid. Thank you, dear, and please be patient. Actually, I don't suppose you could give me a lift down to Charlotte Street, could you? I have an appointment and I'm running just a tad late.'

'Sure, I'm going that way.'

'Wonderful. I'll just get my hat and coat.'

'Lucille,' he shouted, 'can you let yourself out and leave the dogs outside as usual. I have to leave now.'

The phone rang.

'Donald Dupont,' he answered, picking up the receiver.

'Jessica, my dear! Are you feeling any better today?'

Brian looked up. Jessica was on the phone in this very room - so close and yet so far.

Donald listened for a few minutes.

'The dogs are fine. Lucille is just working her magic on them as we speak. Brian's here too,' he added, tentatively. 'I am so grateful that he came over to help me today after an accident I had with a window earlier. Yes, dear, I'm fine, no need to worry. Are you sure that's such a good idea? Very well, if that's what you want. I'll tell him,' he finished, laying the receiver back into its cradle.

'What?' asked Brian, 'what did she say?'

'I am sorry, but she said to tell you you were right about Paolo and that she was glad she heard it from you first. She said you and Jack must be feeling very pleased with yourselves for making her look a complete fool.'

'But why is it my fault?' stuttered Brian. 'I only told her what Jack told me. She had a right to know, don't you think?'

'She doesn't mean it. She's hurt,' said Donald softly, patting Brian's arm. 'You'll get your chance, trust me.'

Chapter 39

Clare would have eaten her way through an iron crate if there had been any chance of finding a cigarette hidden in it. Her chest felt empty - she was desperate for a smoke. Grace had interrogated her during the morning to see what the next steps were regarding discussions with the Suzuki party. Clare had, understandably, refrained from describing any plots involving fetish clubs. Instead, she had tried to fob Grace off with a plan to talk to Lance about a possible compromise between the two positions. Grace had wanted details, but Clare had just about managed to bide some time.

She'd hardly eaten anything all day, as Mark had advised, but it hadn't been easy. She was used to a hearty sandwich as a bare minimum for lunch and the miserable little fruit tub from the supermarket had not hit the spot.

After having had second, third and fourth thoughts about Mark's plan for the evening, Clare resigned herself to the fact that she would be going along with it. She had called Mark a number of times on Tuesday with a whole list of questions, ifs and buts. Finding the camera had been the easiest part. The private detective from the agency had, as always, been very helpful – but it had cost a small fortune. They had decided on a tiny lens resembling a black button. This could be attached to the mask she would be wearing and controlled from a small, wireless hand-held device about the size of a flash memory stick. The pictures would be stored on the stick and could be printed off from a computer later. Clare had fixed the lens to a pair of sunglasses and then played with the focus dial on the memory stick, snapping away by pressing a small button.

She had practiced for hours, both in the shop and at home, and was quite surprised with the quality of the results. The detective had explained that the only problem with this model was the fact that there was no flash, and had pointed out that it was therefore important to try and operate with as much external light as possible.

It was bang on seven when Clare arrived at Mark's flat. She was so nervous. Her heart was beating like a jungle drum and her face felt hot and flustered. She pushed open the buzzing door to the house and went down the stairs. Clare's eyes widened and she held a hand to her mouth in surprise.

'Oh my God, Marleen! I wasn't expecting... I mean, wow, you look amazing!'

There stood Mark, or rather Marleen, complete with the same red mane that Clare had last seen in Japan. He was wearing red leather, thigh-high boots and a matching mini-skirt, complemented by a black basque.

'Thanks, Candy – are you happy with Candy for the evening? Can I fix you an absinthe?' he asked, in the same Canadian accent that she had heard in Osaka.

'Candy? Oh, yes, fine. Er, no thanks to the absinthe, Marleen. Do you have any white wine, by any chance?'

'Yes I do, oh, and just call me Mark when we're on our own.'

Clare watched Mark clip into the kitchen. He was very dextrous on his heels, but didn't look quite as feminine this time, dressed up to the nines in his very bright flat.

'There you go,' he said, handing Clare a glass of wine and carrying the bottle.

She gulped it down in about three mouthfuls.

'That's nice,' she said, holding out her glass for a refill. 'I don't mean to be rude but I'm nervous as hell.'

'That's OK,' he said, doing the honours. 'It's your first time.'

'And last! I can't believe we're doing it. Anyway, I got the camera and it works a treat.'

Clare took the tiny device out of her bag and placed it on the coffee table. She explained to Mark how it worked and the detective's idea about attaching the lens to the mask.

'Perfect. That's good to know about the lighting, too. Now, let's turn Clare into Candy.'

He reached behind an armchair and produced a large carrier bag.

'You will just love this,' he said, taking out the black rubber catsuit.

Clare looked at it disapprovingly.

'Do I have to?' she asked, knowing the answer already.

'Just keep an open mind,' laughed Mark, holding it up.

'Are you sure you got the right measurements? It doesn't look big enough for a pygmy.'

'It's fine. Right, come on, you need to take those clothes off. All of them.'

'I'm not taking my knickers and bra off,' she shouted at him, horrified at the prospect. She hadn't been expecting that.

'You'll have to take them off otherwise you'll be all lumpy and bumpy. It needs to be skin tight.'

Clare reluctantly did as she was told and undressed, hesitating at the knickers. Of course she knew that Mark was gay - that wasn't it. She just wasn't comfortable standing naked in front of anyone. Cellulite was best kept under wraps. Even with Sven she'd managed to keep her stockings on as a distraction.

'Don't mind me. I've seen it all before, trust me. Here, we need to put a bit of talcum powder on the inside of your new suit. It acts as a lubricant with the rubber and stops it from sticking.'

'You're well-informed.'

'You don't know the half of it. Now, come on, get those off. I'll turn round and you can put your hands over your bush.'

Clare felt like a prisoner about to be examined, but nevertheless she gingerly slid out of her silk panties and put them into her bag.

'Are you ready?'

Clare sighed.

'I suppose so.'

'Right, now you have to put your feet in here first. It's an all-in-one catsuit so it can be a bit tricky to get on, but don't worry, we'll get you into it.'

Once her feet were through, Mark started to tug the suit up, stretching the thin rubber over her legs.

'Can you pull the front part while I see to the back?' The suit had snagged around Clare's thighs.

'After we get it over your ass it'll be plain sailing.'

This was easier said than done. They both wrestled with the garment, but couldn't get it to stretch over her hips. Clare was panting with all the effort and had started to sweat.

'I've got an idea. Lie on your back on the coffee table and then I can support my foot against the door and really put some weight behind it.'

Clare lay down on the table, feeling like a harpooned whale being squeezed into a condom. Hopefully there were no hidden cameras filming *this* escapade. Eventually it worked and Mark was able to zip up the top half of the suit behind her neck.

'At last,' he said. 'Now we need some shine. Close your eyes.'

Mark began to spray silicon over the suit to give it the right finish.

'How does it feel?' he asked, standing back to admire his work.

'Do you really want me to answer that? It's so tight it feels as if the fat in my buttocks has been squelched up to my chin. How many chins have I got now - five?'

Mark smiled at her. At least she wasn't screaming for the suit to be taken off.

'Just the one. It really looks good on you, you know. Come and have a look in the mirror.'

Clare padded over to the hall mirror, her rubber squeaking.

'Oh my God! That's awful! Are we going deep-sea diving?'

'You'll need a few minutes to feel right and get into role. Just wait until we're finished.'

'How am I going to get all this off and on again when I want to go to the toilet? It'll be impossible,' she complained.

'Don't worry, you don't need to. There's a zip here.'

Clare looked down and noticed the tiny zip that ran from her crotch all the way down the gusset to just below her lower back.

'Are you serious? I just unzip and squat?'

'Be careful with your bits and pieces while zipping, though. I've heard of some terrible mishaps.'

Clare winced.

'Did you bring your boots?'

'Yes, I did,' she said, taking the boots out of her bag.

Slowly but surely Clare was being transformed into Candy. First the boots, then the make-up, followed by the hair up in a bun and finally the little mask. Clare looked in the mirror and was practically speechless. She didn't recognise herself.

'I look like a cross between Dracula's Daughter and the Bride of Zorro.'

'You look awesome!' said Mark, with a shake of red hair. 'Here - take this.'

Clare looked at the whip that Mark was holding out for her.

'I'm not whipping anybody.'

'It'll look good. You don't have to use it if you don't want to. You can just hook it onto your left hip… that's it. You'll be the most popular domina there. They'll be all over you! Are you sure you haven't done this before?'

Clare was now strutting up and down the living room in her shiny catsuit, slowly gaining confidence, safe in the knowledge that if she couldn't recognise herself then nobody else would.

'I'm the daddy,' she said gruffly, gently cracking the whip.

'Well you go girl, work that catsuit,' he cheered. 'You really are a natural. Seriously, if you do ever need another job I'm sure I can… '

'No, thank you, this is for one night only. Can you help me with this lens?'

Mark fiddled with the lens and then pinned it to the mask, just above her right eye. It was barely visible. By lowering the mask slightly she was able to look through the lens.

'Does it work?' asked Mark, taking a sip of his absinthe.

'It's fine. I can see you in the frame and then snap and freeze it. Hang on - got you. I'll just have to hold this little stick in my hand. Are you sure you can't see the lens?'

'No, the layers of the mask, your mascara and eye make-up all create an effective camouflage. There should be a tiny pocket just big enough for some money and a finger on the right hand side of your suit. You can pop the stick in there if you need to.'

'Oh yes, so there is,' she said, locating it.

'Well, can you do it? The cab will be here soon but you can still change your mind.'

Clare looked Mark straight in the eye and then raised her glass. She was actually getting quite excited now and into the spirit of things.

'Let's go and get her,' she said, polishing off her drink.

Chapter 40

Brian was at Jack's flat. They were eating pizza when Jack's phone rang.

'Hey Mark, how are you?' asked Jack, getting up from his stool.

'I'm just having a quiet one tonight. Brian's stopped by with some pizza so we're eating that and having a few drinks. When are you back in London? Friday? OK, sounds good. I miss you too. Sleep well.'

'That was Mark,' he said, hanging up. 'He's working away for a couple of days.'

'He seems like a nice guy - you picked a good one there,' said Brian, stuffing another piece of pepperoni pizza into his mouth and standing up. 'Have you got any more beer?'

'Cheers - I think so too. Help yourself to beer, it's in the fridge. I'll have one as well.'

Brian walked over to the fridge. He was still in his work clothes and wearing a pair of light blue jeans that had seen better days. Both of the back pockets were hanging off and there was a hole on the right knee.

'That's a great ass, you know, Brian,' teased Jack. 'Jessica must be mad not to want a piece of it.'

'Fuck off,' said Brian, handing Jack a beer.

'Still no change, then?'

'There is, actually. The good news is that Jessica has thrown Paolo out of their little holiday home. From what Donald said it sounds like she believes us after all - and now she's ditched him.'

'Well that's brilliant! Now's your big chance then!'

'That's what I thought, but Donald is still telling me to cool it, which is driving me nuts. If I cool it any more I'll freeze.'

'So what are you going to do?'

'Donald says I should wait until Jessica gets back from Barcelona, but I don't want to. The thing that bugs me the most is that I'm not even sure that she knows I'm waiting for her. Me, Brian! When have I ever waited for a girl? She doesn't know how mad I am about her.'

'Trust me, she knows,' said Jack sagely.

'And how do you work that one out?'

'Women do. She won't have forgotten what you said to her at the exhibition and she most certainly won't have forgotten how your tongue hung down to the floor on the two occasions that you saw her.'

'Well, maybe you're right, but I've got to do something else to give it a real try. I have my needs too, you know!' said Brian, offering Jack another slice of pizza.

'I'm sure you do,' said Jack, taking it. 'I can lend you some gay porn if that's any help.'

'I'll let you know if it comes to that,' laughed Brian, lightening up as he threw a bit of pizza crust at Jack.

'Hey, watch it! I don't have a cleaner like Clare. I'll probably find that down the side of the sofa next Christmas.'

'Is that the next time you're cleaning?'

Jack couldn't be bothered with the wind-up.

'So, if Jessica is saying that we were right about Paolo, then that must mean she knows that he's partial to a bit of cock too.'

'I suppose so,' said Brian. 'And?'

'Well, if that's the case, then either he decided to come out and told her himself or she must have caught him at it with someone. I can't actually see the slimeball ever being straight with her, so to speak, so she must have caught him out.'

'Probably,' said Brian. 'She must have been devastated. Still, all for the best, eh?' he grinned.

They finished off the pizza and drank their beers.

'Rachel called me yesterday,' said Brian.

'Oh yeah? How are they all doing?'

'Everything sounds fine. She said that she feels much better now about the baby, or rather babies.'

'I can't believe she's having identical twin boys. What are the odds on that?'

'About three in every thousand.'

'How did you know that?' asked Jack in disbelief.

'Rachel told me, you idiot. Do you think I know all about birthing statistics?'

'You might! How do I know what websites you look at when you're at home all alone?'

'Not that kind, that's for sure.'

Jack smiled. 'Has she told Edward yet?'

'She didn't say. It was only a quick call to let me know she was OK.'

'I wonder if she'll stay with Heike, or whether it is just a phase,' said Jack, emptying his can.

'Can't answer that one, mate, I guess we'll just have to see. It's certainly cheered her up though, and that's got to be a good thing.'

'Do you want another?' asked Jack getting up.

'Go on then, twist my arm. I'll have one for the road and then I'll get my bus. I have to go down to Brighton tomorrow and I'm picking Tom up at six-thirty.'

'Tom?'

'How many more times? Tom, Donald's gardener.'

'Ah yes, Donald's fit bit of rough.'

'I think you've got him all wrong, you know. Donald said Tom was having girlfriend troubles.'

'Who knows what they all get up to? Anyway, why are you picking him up?' asked Jack.

'He's been helping me make a couple of chests of drawers and is coming with me to fit them in Brighton. He's a good worker and it's been great to be able to give someone a few of the easier jobs to do so that I can get on with other stuff. I might use him again.'

'Oh, you're probably right about him,' said Jack. 'What do I know?'

'Where did you say Mark is?'

'He's working in Hastings for a couple of days. I think he said it was a kitchen extension or something.'

'How's it going between you two?' asked Brian, cracking open his can.

'It's great. But I don't really like going on about it, you know, with you being down about Jessica.'

'Don't be daft. I'm a big boy. I can handle it.'

'She really doesn't know what she's missing, does she?'

'Get stuffed,' laughed Brian.

'Seriously, Mark's an all right guy. We're having a lot of fun. I feel like we've known each other for ages. I love being with him.'

'You're really lucky. It's good to see you so happy.'

Brian held up his can.

'To you and Mark.'

'Cheers,' said Jack, pleased that he had such good friends like Brian, Clare and Rachel - as well as a nice boyfriend.

Brian was scratching his chin, looking deep in thought.

'You know what? I'm going to go to Barcelona, regardless of what Donald thinks,' he said decisively, looking up. 'It was Rachel's tip, actually. She said earlier just to do it, and she's right. So if Jessica's not back in London in two weeks time, then fuck it, I'm going over there. What have I got to lose?'

Chapter 41

Mark and Clare, about to take on the world dressed as Marleen and Candy, were sitting in the back of their cab. They were driving southbound over a foggy Tower Bridge and Mark was looking out at the Tower of London.

'It's so eerie, isn't it? Just thinking about Mary Queen of Scots being brought here along the murky Thames in the dead of night still gives me the creeps,' he said.

'I know. There must have been some strange things that went on in there.'

'Not half as strange as some of things you might see later,' he said with a chortle.

'How much further is it? If I don't stand up soon I don't think I'll ever be able to again. This suit is so tight I can hardly move.'

'Feels good though, doesn't it?'

'It certainly feels different. I'm not sure about good,' said Clare, trying to stretch a leg.

'We should be there in a few minutes.'

'If you just take a left here, and then right at the lights and then first left again,' said Mark to the driver.

The driver didn't seem to be at all phased by having a woman in black rubber and a man dressed as a woman in red leather as his passengers in the back seat. But then again, this was London - where anything and everything is possible.

'Right you are, Guv'nor,' he said to Mark, looking into his mirror.

'Are you getting excited?' Mark asked Clare.

'I am absolutely petrified and I'm dying for a wee.'

'You'll be fine, I'll take you to the toilets when we get in.'

'If I can last that long,' she said, trying to cross her legs.

After a few more minutes they had reached their destination.

'That's great. Just here's fine.'

The driver pulled up outside a crumbling, old warehouse. The street was badly lit and full of potholes, as Clare discovered, when, after prising herself out of the car, she landed in a puddle.

'Shit,' she said, wiping the mud off her boots with a tissue that had been on the seat of the cab. 'Oh my God,' she gasped, standing up straight, staring at the building in front of her. 'It looks like something out of a horror movie.'

'Looks can be deceptive. Come on - let's not hang about out here.'

Mark steered Clare around to the back of the building where there was a large double-fronted door. On it was pinned a small piece of paper that simply said,

'SMelt'

'Is this it?' asked Clare with both surprise and dread.

'What were you expecting? A red carpet, like they have for the big film premieres in Leicester Square?'

'Well no, but some sign of life would be reassuring.'

'Right, before we go in I'll give you a few ground rules.

1. Try not to stare at intimate-looking situations unless you are invited to, but feel free to have a good look around.
2. If someone approaches you and you're not interested, say 'no' firmly. If they try and touch you, just lift their hand off.
3. If you do want to go off with anyone or get involved with a group you must find me first and let me know.
4. Keep your drink with you at all times and don't let anyone else buy you one unless you can see it being served by the bar staff. Is that all clear?'

'Have you quite finished? I have absolutely no intention of joining in any orgies or anything else for that matter. This isn't a fucking social outing. We're here for a purpose. God, I'm gasping for a cigarette. Now, what do we need to discuss to figure out exactly how we are going to get these pictures?'

'We'll have to see once we're inside. First we'll need to make sure that she's here, then watch her movements. As soon as we think we can get a good shot of her somewhere there's enough light, and when nobody is watching you, you'll be able to get snapping away with that gizmo of yours. That's about it, really. Make sure you get as many as possible to increase the chances of getting a few decent shots.'

'I need a wee, a drink and another drink, in that order,' said Clare, suddenly feeling very exposed, convinced that everyone would see she was a fake.

'In we go then,' said Mark, pushing open the heavy door.

Inside the dank hallway was an iron staircase that led down into the basement.

As they walked over towards the staircase Clare caught her heel on a stray bottle and almost tripped.

'Why is it so quiet? Are you sure this is it?' she asked, sweeping away a cobweb with her hand.

'Fear not,' said Mark, as he descended the ominous-looking stairs, turning slightly to the side to maintain a good balance in his heels.

At the foot of the staircase was another large door. This one was locked. Mark knocked four times, paused and then knocked a further three times. The heavy door clicked and groaned and then slowly swung open. They were greeted by a plump woman with spiky black hair, wearing a white latex mini-dress.

'Marleen!' she cried, throwing her arms around Mark as if he was a long lost sister.

She closed and locked the door behind her.

'Denise,' cooed Mark, with a shake of red plumage. 'It's been too long.'

'I know! We missed you at the Milan party at Easter.'

'I heard it was the best one you've ever thrown. I was so sorry I couldn't make it.'

'Nonsense - this will be the best party. And you must be Candy,' said Denise, checking her guest list.

'That's me. Hello,' said Clare, waving the handle of her whip.

'Marleen said this is your first time with us. You look great! Welcome to SMelt, Candy - enjoy!'

'Thanks, Denise, catch you later,' said Mark, leading Clare down another dark corridor.

'Don't we need to pay?'

'There's no cash here. We pay by direct debit. See this ring I'm wearing?'

Clare looked at the ring.

'They scan it at the bar and the drinks get charged to my account. Isn't that neat?'

Mark's Canadian accent was back.

'Why are there all these doors?'

'This is a very exclusive, expensive and private club. The members and their guests want to be amongst private, like-minded people. There are no security cameras inside the inner chambers. What happens in there stays in there.'

'Except when you're about to be caught on candid camera,' said Clare.

'I know - and if anyone notices you taking holiday snaps then I'll be thrown out with a lifetime ban of global proportions, so be very careful. Denise isn't alone upstairs, either. She has four very big guys in a separate office next to where she is sitting. She can see who is coming into the building through a hidden CCTV system outside, and she'd call out the boys if there was an uninvited intruder. They would also be down here like a shot if anyone saw you taking photographs.'

'How would she know if someone wasn't a member?' asked Clare.

'Oh, she knows. She knows all her members, every single one. Right,' he said, 'this really is it. This is the door to the coveted inner chambers.'

The thick steel door in front of them was already unlocked. Mark pushed it open and they walked through. He took hold of Clare's moist hand. They could hear muffled voices as the door closed behind them. It locked automatically.

Clare couldn't believe her eyes as the final door in front of them slid open. There must have been hundreds of people inside the dimly-lit cavern. There was a large, circular bar in the middle and the barmen were wearing blue rubber shorts. It was the normality of the room that surprised Clare the most. People were chatting in clusters, laughing and joking and generally behaving as they would in any other bar or club. Of course the clothing and outfits were different and some of the accessories like nothing she'd ever seen before. A hairy man near the entrance was wearing a very realistic mask of a pig's head complete with black boots, a leather jockstrap and a curly tail.

'Well, this all looks very nice,' she said to Mark sarcastically, looking around to see if she could spot Mrs Suzuki.

'This is the central social chamber. As you can see it's pretty tame and normal-looking. The music is simple and hypnotic and the bar boys are cute. Check him out over there.'

Clare followed Mark's gaze over to where a chunky young barman was shaking a cocktail shaker in time with the music.

'You're with Jack, remember. My God, he would die if he knew where I... where we were. Where did you tell him you are tonight? I said I have to work late all week, which is true enough.'

'I had to say I was out of town on a building job, otherwise he wouldn't have understood why we couldn't meet up later. I didn't want to run the risk of him just turning up at home to surprise me. Anyway, I thought your bladder was on the brink of exploding. I'll show you where the loos are.'

Mark made his way across the floor. Clare followed.

'*Bonsoir,* Marleen!' shouted a woman with short brown hair. She was dressed in a black harness, pink tights, black platform boots, and nothing else.

'*Bonsoir,* Eve! How nice to see you again,' cried Mark. 'Is Henri not with you tonight?'

'Henri is… a bit tied up at the moment in the wax chamber. Who is your little friend?' asked Eve, her French accent thick and husky.

'Hi, I'm… Candy,' said Clare, who warmed to most people who referred to her as anything less than 'large'.

'The pleasure is all mine,' said Eve. 'You keep her on a tight leash, Marleen. I could be tempted.'

'Who on earth was that?' asked Clare as they continued to cross the floor to the toilets.

'That was Eve Gautier. She's a millionaire. Made her fortune selling sports equipment.'

'What were those things on her nipples? They looked painful,' winced Clare.

'Spiked clamps,' explained Mark. 'You can put little weights on the hooks on the side if you want to. Did you notice them?'

Clare hadn't noticed.

'No, I didn't look that closely actually. But wouldn't they stretch?'

'Like elastic bands.'

'Ouch.'

'Eve seemed to like you. I'm sure she'd let you watch her and Henri - that's her husband - or even join in with them if you wanted to,' teased Mark. 'They're into wax and hot irons. You should see her ass under those tights. It looks like a hundred cigarettes have been stubbed out on it. Mind you, they probably were, before the smoking ban.'

'Did you have to mention cigarettes and remind me? I think I would seriously consider letting someone put one out on my ass if it meant I could smoke it first.'

Mark laughed. 'You're doing really well. The hard bit's over. But if you have even a single drag then you'll be back to square one. It's a bit like playing snakes and ladders. Right, here are the toilets. They're unisex and only have cubicles. I'll wait here for you and ignore the Toilet Bitch.'

'Ignore the what?'

'The Toilet Bitch. There will be a guy inside offering paper towels for after you've washed your hands and some perfume to freshen up. He'll also expect a tip. He has a scanner too with a special code, but I think I pay enough membership fees without having to pay extra to use the loo. You don't have a ring anyway, so just hold up your hands and smile.'

Clare nervously went in and found the Toilet Bitch sitting next to the washbasins.

'Hello,' he said.

She nodded and bolted towards a free cubicle, quickly locking the door. She knew that the Toilet Bitch was out there listening and it was putting her off. Eventually she managed to complete the task in hand and succeeded in carefully zipping back up. After washing her hands she defied the Toilet Bitch by not giving him a tip before leaving to rejoin Mark.

'Well, that was fun,' she said. 'Can we get a drink now?'

'Over here, come on.'

They went to the bar and ordered cocktails.

'You just want to see your sexy barman flexing his thighs in those tight shorts,' said Clare, admiring the barman herself.

Once they'd got their drinks, Mark announced that he was going to have a quick walk around to see if he could find Mrs Suzuki.

'I'll go alone so that I can get a feel for who's here as well, you know. Will you be OK for a few minutes on your own?'

'I'll be fine. Just don't be long!'

Suddenly alone, Clare felt very conspicuous. The suit was hot, and itched between her legs. The bar was filling up even more now. She took a big gulp of her cocktail and stared over at one of the barmen, which seemed the best bet for where to fix her gaze.

'Hi,' boomed a deep voice behind her. 'Can I get you a drink, mistress?'

Clare took another sip of her cocktail, ignoring the voice.

'I said, can I get you a drink?' boomed the voice again, this time from beside her.

Clare hadn't realised that the offer had been directed towards her and was now mortified at the prospect of having to speak to someone.

'No, thank you, I'm all right with this.'

The woman smiled at Clare, revealing a familiar-looking black stub in the centre of her mouth.

'If you say so mistress, you're the boss. Two vodka tonics,' she said to the barman.

Clare would have recognised that tooth anywhere. It was Sumo, the burly customs officer from Kansai airport in Osaka. But what was she doing here?

'You survived, then,' said Mark as he returned.

'Just about. A woman I've seen before in Japan was just here, calling me 'mistress'. How many more people am I going to recognise from that last business trip? This is just so weird,' said Clare, looking around again.

'I suppose it is a bit.'

'A bit? This must be some kind of wind-up. First you, and now Sumo! You're stitching me up, aren't you?'

'Of course I'm not,' laughed Mark. 'It's just one of those things. If you hadn't have come here tonight, then you'd probably never have seen her again.'

'Hmmm. Any sign of Mrs Suzuki?'

'She's here all right. In the wheel chamber. It's her favourite.'

'The wheel chamber?'

'I'll show you. Now, there are lots of specialist chambers that lead off from this central bar. One of them is the wheel chamber. You don't talk in the chambers like you do out here. It's important to keep the right vibe for each chamber. Nobody wants to be asked where they had lunch today while someone else is dripping hot wax onto them - get my drift?'

Clare didn't have a clue what he was talking about.

'Be ready with your camera,' whispered Mark. 'I'll shake my hair as a signal that I think it's a good time to snap. That will mean I don't think anybody is looking at you, got it?'

'Yes, mistress,' joked Clare, pleased that they were finally making progress towards their target - though still very nervous, despite being fuelled with alcohol.

Just before they got to the wheel chamber Mark paused outside a different room.

'Have a quick look in there,' he said, nodding towards the door.

'Why, what's in it?'

'Just have a look.'

Clare stepped cautiously forward. Inside, a man was kneeling on a large table. He was wearing a dog collar and a muzzle. Apart from that he was naked. There was nobody else in the room. Clare came out looking puzzled.

'I don't get it. What's he doing?'

'He's being trained to be a dog. He has to 'stay' until the others come back.'

Clare was shocked.

'I suppose this is what you get up to with your clients, is it?'

'No, it's a lot tamer than this,' he laughed. 'Right, this should be our chance. Ready? And remember, no talking.'

'As I'll ever be,' said Clare, taking as deep a breath as was possible within the tight constraints of the rubber suit.

She followed Mark into the dark chamber and they made their way over towards what was called 'The Wheel'. It was an enormous wooden structure in the centre of the room, mounted on a raised platform that was almost like a stage.

Someone was tied to it, face down, in a spread-eagled star shape. There were quite a few other people in the room watching, so it was obviously a public display.

Suddenly there was a bang followed by flashes of light. The wheel was fitted with strobe lights and it started to creak and groan as it slowly turned. Clare stared at the wheel in astonishment, now realising who it was that was tied to it. It was Sumo. Her huge ballast filled the wheel to capacity and her ass hung towards her head as she was turned upside down. She was wearing leather trousers that were struggling to keep their contents inside them and Clare suspected that they had needed the hide from at least three cows to produce them.

And then there she was. Mrs Suzuki slowly walked out onto the platform holding a cat-o' nine-tails. She was wearing a rubber bra and thong and knee-high tight black boots. Amazingly, she wasn't wearing a mask.

Clare couldn't help but stifle a giggle at the thought of the tiny Mrs Suzuki disciplining the giant Sumo. A lightening whip crack accompanied by a loud scream from Sumo quickly changed Clare's mind.

'You've been a bad bitch!' screeched Mrs Suzuki, as she leant backwards before lashing out at poor Sumo with a ferocity that made Charlton Heston in Ben Hur look like the tooth fairy. Again and again she horsewhipped Sumo to within an inch of her life. The strobe lights had re-started and Mark was shaking his red mane. This was her cue. Clare had been focussing the tiny lens on Mrs Suzuki and then on Sumo and was able to quickly start clicking away on the little control stick that she held in her hand. Click. Click. Click. She managed to take about twenty shots in all before the wheel and strobe lights stopped. Mrs Suzuki coolly left the platform before someone unclamped Sumo, who then crashed to the floor, thrashed to a pulp. Maybe that's what happened to her teeth, thought Clare.

'Well, did you get them?' asked Mark once they were back at the main bar. 'I don't think anyone saw us.'

'I got some great shots. Hopefully the lighting was bright enough. Can we go now?'

'Are you sure you don't want to spend an hour with Eve and Henri? They're the best on the scene.'

'I'll put a cigarette out on your ass if you're not careful.'

'Promises, promises,' joked Mark.

'Come on! I can't wait to get home and see what these look like.'

Chapter 42

It had been a long night and Clare was exhausted, but brimming with excitement. It must have been about eleven when they left the club and then almost one o'clock by the time she finally got home. The minicab had dropped them off first at Mark's place to get changed and pick up her things and had then driven her back home to Finsbury Park. Mark had offered her his sofa to sleep on, but she'd wanted to be in her own bed tonight.

Once home she eagerly switched on her computer and downloaded the camera files. Almost all of the pictures had turned out well, if a little dark, and she smiled gleefully as she looked through the results. The pictures were perfect, showing without a shadow of a doubt Mrs Suzuki dressed in a skimpy outfit cracking a whip to Sumo. Clare was particularly pleased with a close-up shot she'd got of Mrs Suzuki actually spitting on Sumo in a final display of degradation, just before the end of the scene.

For the first time in weeks Clare slept well. She had a nice hot bath and lounged in it for about half an hour before applying the night creams and potions that promised to make her look fifteen years younger by the morning.

Despite the short night Clare was practically skipping down Long Acre on her way work.

'Good morning, Candice!' she sang, as she arrived at reception.

'Oh hello, Clare – watch out, Grace is on the warpath. Is something wrong with your phone? She's been complaining that she's not been able to get hold of you since Tuesday. She said to tell you you're to go straight to her office as soon as you come back to work, if you ever did come back, and interrupt whatever she's doing.'

Clare had switched her phone off for the last two days and had worked from home again yesterday so that she could psyche herself up for the big evening. She knew that Grace would only have been harassing her for news on what was happening with the Suzuki people, and she hadn't had anything new to add – not at that point, in any case. Grace would be climbing the walls with anger by now.

'Thanks for warning me, Candice,' said Clare, less afraid of the pending wrath now that she had her bag full of very helpful glossy prints.

Clare hastily made a beeline for her own office and closed the door behind her. She had to make her all-important call to Lance before Grace got wind that she was here. Flicking through her business cards she quickly found Lance's and picked up the phone.

'Lance? Hello, it's Clare. I'm fine, thank you. How are you? That's great. No, I'm afraid I haven't called to strike the minimum order clause,' she said rolling her eyes. 'Yes, I know you're flying back on Saturday. Lance, I need to meet with Mrs Suzuki as a matter of urgency. Alone, and today please. I'm sure she is very busy, Lance, aren't we all? But trust me; she *will* want to see me. It's private. Can you get her to call me? Suit yourself. Make sure you tell her that I want to talk to her about SMelt. Fine - I'll wait for your call.'

Clare hung up and smiled smugly, wondering what Mrs Suzuki's face might look like when Lance said the word 'SMelt'.

'Where the hell have you been?' screamed Grace, almost battering the door to Clare's office down to the ground.

'Good morning to you too, Grace,' said Clare softly.

'You really are trying my patience, Clare. The Board have been asking about the status of the deal and I can't tell them because I don't know! I can't very well just call Suzuki's lawyers and ask them what you've been negotiating for me, can I?'

Clare stared at her for a moment. This was the first time she had seen Grace looking like something approaching being rattled. She could see that Grace was trying to inflict her most intimidating of bats, but was succeeding only in blinking alternate eyes, which looked like some kind of party trick instead.

Clare's phone rang.

'Will you excuse me a moment? Lance! Thanks for calling back so quickly. She can? Great. Two o'clock in the café of her hotel. I'll be there. You take care now.'

'That was Lan… '

'I heard who it was!' bellowed Grace. 'Now will you tell me what is going on? This sort of behaviour is totally unacceptable.'

Clare shook her head and sighed.

'Grace, will you just chill for one moment?' she dared to say. 'I am meeting Mrs Suzuki this afternoon and am hopeful that I will achieve a breakthrough before they fly back on Saturday.'

Two bats and then a wink because one eye had got stuck and remained closed.

'Just trust me for one more day and I promise I will supply you with all the details you need. If I don't deliver, I'll fall on my sword,' said Clare magnanimously, placing her right palm on her chest.

'That's if I haven't stabbed you with it first,' snapped Grace. 'I expect a full update by tomorrow morning. Nine o'clock at the latest.'

She then leaned in so closely that Clare could smell Grace's favourite blackcurrant tea on her breath, along with something else that was much less pleasant.

'Do I make myself clear?'

'As crystal,' said Clare glibly, edging backwards. 'Is there anything else?'

Grace shot her a final warning look before spinning round to go.

Now I really DO have to pull this turkey off, thought Clare. War had been declared. It was blatantly obvious that she had been too defiant for Grace's liking.

Clare couldn't really concentrate on much else that morning and drank too much coffee. She called Mark to let him know that the pictures had turned out a treat and then decided to take an early lunch and walk over to Mrs Suzuki's hotel rather than take a cab. It was only about thirty minutes away on foot and she wanted some fresh air. She actually felt quite relaxed about what she was about to do. Mark was right. Mrs Suzuki was hardly likely to go to the police. Clare would just deny it anyway. She had worn latex gloves when handling the pictures so as to avoid any irksome fingerprints getting on them.

She looked at her watch as she strode into the hotel foyer. She was bang on time. The garden café was at the back of the hotel. A demure-looking Mrs Suzuki was sitting alone at a table in the corner of the garden.

'Mrs Suzuki, thank you ever so much for agreeing to meet with me at such short notice.'

Mrs Suzuki didn't get up – she didn't even speak. Instead she took a drink from her glass. Clare assumed it was a lunchtime vodka and tonic.

'Before I go any further can I just say how much we really want to do business with your company and how wonderful it would be to… '

'What do you want to talk to me about?' interrupted Mrs Suzuki, lighting a cigarette.

Clare looked at the smoke. It didn't seem to bother her as much today.

'I saw you at the club last night,' said Clare quietly, sitting down opposite Mrs Suzuki. 'A friend of mine thought you might want to have these.'

Clare reached into her bag and produced the incriminating photographs. She put them on the table in front of Mrs Suzuki. Clare watched her closely as she inspected them. There wasn't so much as a twitch on her expressionless face. She was one cool cookie. The only thing that Clare did notice, however, was that Mrs Suzuki was actually smoking a whole cigarette for a change. After a couple of agonisingly slow minutes, Mrs Suzuki looked up.

'What is it you want for these and your word of honour that you will destroy whatever other evidence you have and promise never to speak of it again. Money? How much?'

'I don't want money. Well, not your personal money. But I do want us to agree this deal on our original terms. It really is a good deal, Mrs Suzuki, for your company too. You'll see, once it gets going.'

'Lance and I will be at your office at ten in the morning tomorrow to sign the heads of terms.'

Mrs Suzuki got up to go, leaving Clare alone at the table.

'Yes!' said Clare triumphantly, before calling Grace to give her the good news.

Now all she had to do was decide if she was going to say anything to Jack about Mark, or leave it to Mark. He had been a huge help - he had saved her hide - but Jack was her friend and she didn't want to see him betrayed.

Chapter 43

At last it was Friday. Jack couldn't wait to see Mark again. Two nights and three days apart had seemed like an eternity. Had they really only known each other for two weeks? They had spoken on the phone three times yesterday and Mark had told him that he would be back from Hastings on Friday afternoon. They had arranged to meet for a drink in Connections.

Lisa had been furious with Jack and Gloria for not coming back to work on Monday because of their 'food poisoning'. They had both moaned and groaned all day Tuesday and had rushed to the toilets every now and then to try and convey an image of authenticity, but Jack knew that Lisa was no fool. Still, it had been good fun and had given him and Gloria something to laugh about all week.

Gloria had said that she and Annette were going to meet Declan and Toby at a pub in Lewisham that night. They were turning out to be quite a foursome. Jack was glad to see Gloria happy. For all her tough exterior, she was a soft little kitten underneath, just wanting to find a bit of love and respect. He hoped Declan would be kind to her.

Jack strolled through Leicester Square before heading through Chinatown towards Soho. The air was filled with delicious-smelling aromatic spices and it made him feel hungry. Perhaps he and Mark would eat here later. Connections was empty when he arrived and he ordered a pint of lager and took a seat in a corner. He picked up a couple of the free London magazines to leaf through, while he waited for Mark. He didn't have to wait long.

'Come here, you,' said Mark bounding over with outstretched arms.

Jack stood up and put his arms around him.

'That feels good,' said Jack, squeezing Mark closely before kissing him.

'You've had your hair cut,' noticed Jack, running a hand over Mark's almost shaven head.

'Yeah, I stopped off for a trim on the way,' he grinned. 'I go every two weeks. I'll just get a drink. Do you want anything?'

'I'm fine for now, cheers.'

He watched Mark walk over to the bar and order a pint of bitter. He looked good in his jeans and green polo shirt. Fate is such a funny thing, he thought. If he hadn't gone for a stroll in the park two weeks before none of this would have happened. He'd probably just be out with Clare, giving her a pep talk about how to find a man. Not that he would have minded that, but actually being here with a guy that he fancied so much himself was far preferable.

'How was Hastings? You must be tired after driving back. It's a horrible journey, I've done it before.'

Mark didn't like having to lie.

'It wasn't too bad coming back. The roads were very clear for a change. We finished the kitchen about midday, so we could take our time. Anyway, never mind about that, have you missed me?'

Jack made a face as if he had to think about it and Mark laughed, blowing some froth from his glass into Jack's face.

'Yes, I've missed you,' said Jack, wiping it off with the back of his hand before leaning over to kiss him again. 'I'm really looking forward to this weekend. I thought we could have a barbecue tomorrow. I've invited Brian and Clare. Clare called me today to say that her deal with the Japanese is in the bag, so I thought we could celebrate. Brian has some news too. He's going over to Barcelona next week to find his maiden Jessica and go down on her... I mean to go down on bended knee.'

'That sounds nice,' said Mark slowly. 'I'm pleased it worked out for Clare. But I might not be able to make it tomorrow,' he said, racking his brain for an excuse.

'What do you mean? It'll be great fun, and the weather forecast is good. Why, what are you doing?'

Mark didn't feel up to spending the afternoon with Clare, who knew all about Marleen, not to mention their escapades at SMelt on Wednesday night. What if she said something? He was pleased with the message she had left to say that the pictures were great, but hadn't managed to get hold of her since.

'I have to visit my mum in Newcastle,' was the best he could come up with on the hoof.

'Why, is she ill?' asked Jack, thinking it must be an important reason that necessitated an impromptu visit that would meanly separate them at the weekend.

'Yes. I mean no. She's been feeling lonely.'

'Lonely? Well can't you just talk to her for an hour on the phone or something? If you go to Newcastle you'll be gone all weekend.'

'I know and I'm sorry. I'll try and come back tomorrow evening or early Sunday morning.'

'You've just told me how much you've missed me and practically in the same breath announced that you're off again. I don't get it. Just call her instead.'

'I have missed you. I'm sorry, Jack, she needs me, and I have to go. It's my catholic upbringing.'

'Are you sure nothing else is wrong?'

'No, of course it's not, don't be daft. I just told you what it is.'

'Well, it's weird. I'm getting another drink.'

'Can you get me another one too?' said Mark, trying to kiss him again.

Jack pulled away.

'Sure,' he said, going over to the bar.

Mark knew this was no good. He hated lying to Jack. What

would be achieved by him not going tomorrow anyway? Clare hadn't explicitly said how long she would keep his secret a secret, and he had told her he wanted to tell Jack himself anyway. Clare was a loose cannon and could fire at any time. She was one of Jack's best friends and would eventually tell him everything and all about their night out. It was too bad that she had recognised him in the first place. He knew that if he carried on saying nothing, he was probably in a lose-lose situation. But how would Jack react when he told him? He was very fond of him and didn't want to lose him so soon. They were just getting to know each other.

Jack came back with their drinks.

'You're right,' he said. 'I'm sorry.'

Mark looked up.

'*You're* sorry? What about?'

'I'm being selfish because I really like you and want to spend as much time with you as I can. Your poor mum needs you and I'm whining like a kid whose favourite toy has been taken away. Forget the barbecue. I'll come with you to Newcastle instead.'

Mark was horrified. This was getting worse. He'd no intention of going to Newcastle at the moment.

'No! No, you don't need to do that. You stay here with your friends and enjoy your barbecue. I'll be back before you know it and we can spend Sunday together.'

'Honestly Mark, its fine. I want to come. We can be naughty on the train,' he said, trying to get Mark to laugh.

Mark couldn't laugh. He felt awful. What a mess this was, and how much more of a mess was it going to become! He decided to tell Jack everything, now.

'Jack, come and sit back down,' he started, doing his best to smile.

'I need to tell you something.'

Jack feared the worst. It's over, he thought. He's going to say it's over.

'You have made me the happiest man alive over the last

couple of weeks. Sure, it's only been a short time, but I'm really getting to like you. Getting to like you a lot,' said Mark, taking Jack's hand.

Jack now decided that perhaps it wasn't over after all, and thought Mark might be about to propose a civil partnership.

'Go on, I'm listening.'

'I haven't been to Hastings.'

'What?'

'I had a night out with Clare. I'm sorry I couldn't tell you.'

'I don't understand. Clare didn't say anything. Why would you go out with Clare and say that you were in Hastings?'

'Please Jack, let me tell you. And please don't blame Clare for any of this. She wanted to tell you straight away. It was me that begged her not to.'

'Will you just tell me what the fuck is going on?' shouted Jack angrily, slamming his pint down on the table.

Mark poured it all out. He told Jack about his night out to help Clare. He told him about how Clare had recognised him from the bar in Japan. He tried, as best he could, to tell Jack about how Clare had actually met Marleen in Japan. Finally, he told Jack about Marleen's lucrative sideline. By the time he had finished he felt as if he had bared his soul to Jack. He had never been more truthful with anyone in his whole life.

Jack took a moment or two before he responded. When he did, he burst out laughing.

'This is a joke, isn't it?'

Mark's stomach was in knots as he shook his head.

'It's true - every word of it. But it doesn't affect us. I'm still me, and I still really like you. I just didn't think you'd understand, so I couldn't tell you.'

'Damn right I don't understand!'

A few heads turned towards them to see what was going on.

'What if Clare hadn't recognised you? Would you still have told me?'

Mark hadn't expected that question and was caught off-guard. 'Of course,' he stuttered. 'The timing might have been a bit different.'

'Oh, I bet it would. Like never,' said Jack, standing up.

'Jack, come on. This isn't easy for me either, you know. I'm still the same Mark. We're still the same.'

'Do you think so? Because I don't.'

Mark tried to put his arms around Jack, but was pushed away again.

'Get off. You've spoiled everything.'

'We can still be good together. You just need to see things in a different way.'

'I'm sorry, which way should I be seeing them? My boyfriend turns out to be a tranny prostitute when he's not building kitchens. Have I got any of that wrong?'

More heads turned towards them.

'Can you just keep your voice down a bit?' asked Mark, his eyes darting around.

'Is this embarrassing you? Good, because it's bloody embarrassing me.'

Jack walked out of the bar leaving Mark the subject of shaking heads and wagging tongues.

A few seconds later Mark ran after him.

'Jack, stop! Please will you just hear me out? The dressing up is just a bit of fun and the work is easy money.'

'Don't get me wrong. I've nothing against the transgender community. In fact I know a few transvestites quite well and they're lovely, honest people. But I have got something against a lying boyfriend who's been having sex with other men for money and didn't think to tell me about it!'

'I have *never* had sex with a client, honestly.'

'Whatever. So what happens now? We can hardly just go back to how I thought we were an hour ago, can we?'

'Yes we can, if we try.'

'So you'll give up your little Saturday job then? I take it that's what you're saying?'

Mark looked awkward and shifted his feet.

'I don't believe it. That's not what you're saying, is it?'

'I was hoping you'd get used to it once we'd talked properly about it. It's just work – and easy, well-paid work at that. Please, just listen… '

'No, you listen!' snapped Jack, cutting him off. 'I'm not even sure that I could carry on with this even if you did jack it in. But if you won't even do that, then I'm definitely out of here.'

Jack waited for an answer.

Mark just stood there and looked at him, not knowing what to say.

'So that's it? You'll just let us go, like that? Well fuck you, Mark!'

Jack turned and ran. He didn't stop until he had turned the corner at the end of the road. Mark couldn't see him crying there.

Chapter 44

Jack had been awake since five o'clock on Saturday morning. In fact, he'd hardly slept at all. Everything Mark had said had been whizzing around in his head and he hadn't been able to stop thinking about it. When he finally did drop off he'd had the weirdest, mixed-up dreams. In one of them Mark had been dressed like Tina Turner and had been working in Amsterdam's red light district, prominently displayed in a window. Jack had been standing outside it and Mark had taunted and jeered at him. In another, Clare had been chained naked to the railings outside the south entrance to Russell Square, crying for help. Jack had tried to run over to free her, but his legs wouldn't move. Mark was strutting over towards her, dressed as a cheerleader, brandishing a whip to lash her with.

Eventually he gave up trying to sleep and got up to make an early trip to the market instead. He wasn't really in the mood for a barbecue anymore, but decided to go ahead anyway. He really wanted to see Brian. He also wanted to catch Clare off-guard with his new-found knowledge - that is, unless Mark had got to her first.

'Hey, Jack my friend, how's it going?' said Declan, as Jack walked up to his stall.

'Morning, Dec, I'm fine,' he lied. 'How about you?'

'Couldn't be better, man. I have my market stall, my health and the love of a good woman,' he declared.

Jack presumed the 'good woman' was Gloria, but thought he would just double-check.

'Gloria's a lovely girl, isn't she?'

'That she is. I never met anyone like her before, man. What can I get you this morning?'

Jack bought his vegetables and then moved next door to Toby's stall to buy some fish.

'Hi, Toby! What have you got that's good for a healthy barbecue?'

'All right, Jack? It's a bit early for you, isn't it? I've got some lovely tuna steaks and fresh fillets of sea bream. How about them?'

'Perfect - I'll take four of each.'

As Toby was wrapping the fish, Jack noticed how simple and wholesome everything was on the market. His life had been happy and simple too, or so he had thought, until yesterday evening. He still couldn't get his head round it. What angered him the most was that Mark hadn't even tried to get in touch since their row last night. Had he really meant that little to him?

Back at the flat Jack had just about got everything ready by three o'clock and was waiting for his two guests. He was drinking a glass of wine in his shorts and t-shirt on the terrace when the doorbell rang. Clare was the first to arrive, which was handy. Jack had one or two bones to pick with her.

'Hello, Jack,' said Clare, kissing him on each cheek. 'It is so good to see you. I feel like we haven't caught up properly in ages. I've just been so busy.'

'My poor baby,' he said sardonically. 'Let me get you a drink. I have a nice chenin blanc in the fridge.' How could she be so two-faced?

'That sounds perfect. Isn't it a beautiful day? It's really good of you to throw a little celebration just for me.'

'It's not just for you, it's for Brian too. He's got some news as well,' said Jack, handing her a glass of wine.

'Really? Has something happened with Jessica?'

'Ask him yourself. He'll be here soon.'

'Are you all right, Jack?'

'Fine, why?'

'I don't know. You just seem a bit twitchy.'

'Here's to you, Clare. Here's to your deal.'

'Thanks. I'm sorry you've had to put up with my foul moods over the last few weeks, what with work and stopping smoking. Though I have to say, I'm finally starting to feel a bit better about being smoke-free and life in general.'

'I'm so pleased for you. At least *you* got what you wanted.'

'Jack, what is wrong with you? Have I said something to annoy you?'

'Actually, it's more what you *didn't* say - and what you physically *did* on Wednesday night.'

Clare's face paled as she realised Jack knew something.

'Where's Mark?' she asked nervously. She'd assumed he would be coming and had planned to catch a quiet moment this afternoon to discuss next steps about who would be telling who, what and when. But the cat was clearly already out of the bag. Why hadn't he warned her?

'Mark? How should I know where he is? I'm just the boyfriend to be kept in the dark. No need for me to know where he is. But *you* might know where he is, Candy - so why don't *you* tell *me*?'

Clare's heart sank. She'd feared this might happen.

'Jack, I'm so sorry. I wanted to tell you, but Mark begged me not to, just for a while.'

'Spare me the sympathy, please. It sounds like you've just used the situation to your own advantage without a thought for me.'

'No, honestly, Jack, that's not it. Mark offered to help me and I only agreed to keep quiet about the other until… '

'Until what? Until you got what you wanted out of it first?'

'It wasn't like that. I wanted to tell you because I thought… but he wasn't ready… and then… I'm sorry, Jack, I really am,' she sobbed.

Now it was Jack's turn to feel bad. He hadn't wanted to reduce her to tears.

'It's fine, Clare. No need to cry. Come on. Here, have this,' he said, handing her a tissue. 'I know I can't really blame you.'

'Thanks,' she sniffed, blowing her nose.

Jack poured them both another glass of wine.

'What happened then?' she asked.

Jack told her all about their argument and how he had told Mark he had to choose between him and his work.

'And it looks like he's chosen. I haven't heard a thing from him. I really thought I knew him, and now look!'

'You are *getting* to know him. Maybe you need to give him a bit of space and time to think things through too. I do know that it took a lot of courage for him to tell you. For what it's worth I think he's a really sweet guy. I'm not exactly proud of what we did at the club, but he did it to help me. Have you tried calling him?'

'No I haven't! It should be him calling me.'

'I'm sure he will soon.'

The doorbell rang. Clare answered it. It was Brian.

'Hey, Clare,' he said rushing through the door. 'Are you OK? You look like you've been crying.'

'I'm fine. It's just a bit of hayfever.'

'Hi, Jack. Wow - looks like the barbecue's going to be good,' he said, admiring the fish and salads as he walked past the kitchen. 'Are we sitting inside or out?'

'Let's go and sit on the terrace, shall we? I'll bring some more wine.'

'What's the occasion?' asked Brian, taking his glass from Jack.

'The Japanese have finally signed,' said Clare.

'Hey, that's great.'

'Thanks, Brian. Anyway, I've heard you're celebrating something too?'

Brian looked at Clare and then at Jack.

'Not really, why? Should I be?'

'You might be by this time next week,' said Jack.

'Oh right, well, I bloody hope so. I've finally decided to go over to Barcelona.'

Clare looked at him blankly.

'What, to live?'

Brian laughed and filled Clare in on his plan.

'Well, I'm with Rachel on that. I don't think you've got anything to lose either. If that girl's got an ounce of sense she'll see the error of her ways and beg you to go out with her.'

'I hope she sees things the way you do,' said Brian, getting up to have a walk around. 'Is Mark not coming?'

There was a short, uncomfortable silence.

'No, I don't think so,' said Jack.

'Why not? I thought you two were getting on like two peas in a pod. Is he working today?'

'I don't think he's doing any building work - but he could still be working, couldn't he, Clare?'

Clare had hoped somehow that at least *her* involvement in Mark's affairs, and his in hers, could have been kept under close wraps. It didn't look like that was going to be the case.

'What's going on?'

Jack gave Brian the short version.

'No way!' exclaimed Brian. 'I'd never have guessed.'

'Neither would I, but Clare knew before me, didn't you? Go on, Clare. Tell Brian all about your fun night out, and how you've known Mark for much longer than I have.'

She reluctantly confessed all to Brian – and Jack for that matter. She told them her side of the chain of events, from when she first met Marleen in Japan to the episode with Mrs Suzuki.

'You've got to be kidding me! You've really been running around London in a rubber catsuit with a man in drag taking pictures in a fetish club?'

Clare nodded solemnly.

Brian threw his head back and laughed. Seeing the funny side of what she'd just said, Clare started to giggle too.

'I'm glad you two think it's all hilarious,' said Jack

indignantly. 'This is – or was – my boyfriend we're talking about.'

'Sorry, mate,' said Brian, composing himself. 'Have you tried calling him?'

'Why does everyone think I should call him? He's the one that's got to choose.'

'I can see where you're coming from. I don't think I could handle it either.'

'I'm assuming it's over, unless I hear otherwise very soon.'

'I don't know what to say, mate. I'm sorry.'

'Oh, I'll get over it. Fuck it. Nobody's died, have they? Right, let's have another glass or two of wine and then I'll start the barbecue. I got some lovely tuna steaks this morning from Toby at the market. Has anyone heard anything from Rachel?' he asked.

'I called her this morning to see how she is,' answered Clare, thankful for an opportunity to change the subject. She's almost at the three month stage and she said everything's going great. I've still not quite got used to the idea that she's having twins, though Rachel's sounding really excited about it now.'

'It *is* really exciting, don't you think? It's not often that you get the chance to have identical twins,' said Brian.

Jack seemed to lighten up a bit.

'I think she'll love having two boys. I hope she asks us to be the godparents,' he said.

Clare rolled her eyes.

'Of course it's exciting,' she said, 'I'm just a bit worried about the stability of the other domestic arrangements.'

'You mean Heike?' said Brian.

'Of course I mean Heike, who else?'

'What do you think she's going to do, eat them?' he asked slowly.

Jack and Clare both laughed.

'Don't be silly,' she replied. 'Oh, I don't know. you're right. If it's what Rachel wants then good luck to her. We'll be behind her all the way.'

'At last,' said Brian, patting Clare's leg. 'Good girl.'

Jack stood up to light the coals.

'Guess where I'm going next week,' said Clare suddenly. She had been bursting to tell them since she arrived, but it hadn't seemed appropriate earlier.

'Another bondage party?' joked Brian.

'Very funny. No, I'm going to Tokyo! On Wednesday - and I'm so excited.'

'I didn't know you were going on holiday.' said Jack.

'I'm not. It's a big media launch event for the deal we've just closed. Grace said she can't make it at such short notice, but wants me to go instead. The truth is that she's absolutely petrified of flying and avoids it at all costs whenever she can. Amazingly Mrs Suzuki was fine with me going over to represent my company. The really good news, though, is that Grace was so delighted that the deal has worked out that she said I can take my partner along too. The cow probably knows I don't have one, so - any volunteers?'

'You're asking one of us to come with you?' asked Jack, surprised.

'I am indeed. Any takers for a five-star whistlestop visit to Tokyo? We fly out on Wednesday and get back next Saturday afternoon.'

'It sounds great,' said Brian, 'but I can't. I've got too much work on and I'm behind on making a chair for the final of the design competition.'

'Jack?'

'I'd love to, but it might be difficult for me to get time off right now. I'm not sure I'll make the best company for you at the moment either, you know, with Mark and everything.'

Clare really wanted to do something nice for Jack.

'Nonsense! I think the trip will be just what you need to take your mind off things. Come on, please say yes, please?'

Jack thought about it. Maybe Clare was right. And, wow! - Tokyo!

'I'll ask my boss tomorrow,' he said, getting excited in spite of himself.

'You two will be flying back on the same day that I'm flying out to Barcelona. I've booked for Saturday too.'

'You've actually booked?' asked Jack.

'Yep. If Jessica's not back by next Friday then I'm going over to see her.'

'Do you know where she's staying?' asked Clare.

'Tom managed to get me the address from Donald's.'

'Who's Tom?' asked Clare.

'Donald's gardener. He's been helping me out a bit with my furniture making.'

'It really is time you sorted something out so that I can meet these people properly.'

'Maybe after I've won Jessica over – that'll be a good time. You'd like them.'

'Well, good luck in Spain,' said Jack. 'I really hope it works out, and that she doesn't keep blaming you.'

'I'm quietly confident,' said Brian, with a grin.

'Right, who's for some food?' asked Jack.

'I'm starving!' said Brian. 'But is there any chance that Clare can serve us in her rubber catsuit? I'd love to see it.'

Chapter 45

It was Monday morning and Jack was the first person in the office. He wanted to make sure that he was there before Lisa so as to appear as hard-working as possible before asking for three days off to go with Clare to Tokyo. He'd spent Sunday keeping busy by tidying up after the barbecue and then optimistically packing his clothes for Japan. Clare had said that he should take a suit for the signing ceremony and dinner. Once it got to the evening, though, he couldn't help but start to mull things over again. Why hadn't Mark called him - even if it was just to shout at him and say he never wanted to see him? But nothing at all?

Gloria was next to arrive at work, about half an hour later.

'Oh my God!' she exclaimed, putting her frappé down on her desk. 'This is the first time you've been at work before me in months. What's the occasion?'

'I've just got a lot to do, that's all.'

Gloria could tell something was wrong.

'What's happened?' she asked, turning her computer on.

'What do you mean?'

'Come on, Jack, you've got a face like a slapped possum. Even for a Monday morning that's not like you.'

'Is it that obvious?'

'Taking a wild stab in the dark, I'm guessing it has something to do with Mark? What did he do?'

'It's complicated. You wouldn't understand.' He paused for a moment before continuing. 'Actually, no, it's not that complicated - just weird and selfish, and I don't understand it either!'

Gloria was silent as she digested everything that followed.

'And you really had no idea?' she asked, shocked, when Jack had finished.

'How would I have known? He didn't carry a wig and bondage gear around with him in his rucksack. Well, at least I don't think he did.'

Gloria giggled. 'Sorry, but it is a bit outrageous, isn't it?'

'It's OK. You're right, it is outrageous. Maybe I'm making it worse by telling everyone, but I think it's all over now anyway. He's not prepared to change and I haven't heard a peep out of him since Friday. So that's that.'

'Oh Jack, I don't know what to say.'

'I'm fine,' said Jack bravely, sealing an envelope.

'How was your weekend? I saw Declan on Saturday morning on the market.'

'It was really nice. We went out with Toby and Annette on Friday night to their local and then on Saturday Dec took me to a seedy pub in Greenwich to meet some other friends of his. It was a lot of fun. You know me, I like a bit of a dive sometimes,' she laughed.

'It sounds like all's going well for you two, then.'

'To be honest, I'm surprised myself at how well it's going. When we met each other at your party my first impression of him was that he's most definitely a bit of a lad and probably spends each weekend in a different bed, you know. Well, of course you know, you're the one that told me. But he seems to quite like me.'

'Of course he likes you. You're stunning.'

'You're too kind,' she smiled.

'What about you? How do you feel about him?'

Gloria took a sip of her frappé.

'He's nice. The sex is good, when we go out together I feel safe, and he's a good craic too. I guess I like him. But I still want to go back to Australia.'

'I got the impression that he's ready to get serious with you.'

'What? Did he say that?' fished Gloria.

'I couldn't possibly betray Declan's trust, but suffice it to say that I think he's really into you as well, so don't worry. Why don't you just stop torturing yourself about Australia and enjoy everything that's happening to you here? You could even take a crash course in 'get to know your vegetables' and set up shop with him, like I suggested,' said Jack, managing a smile.

'Maybe you're right. Oh no, here she comes,' groaned Gloria.

Lisa had just come in and was making her way towards them. Something looked different about her today.

'Good morning,' she hissed, without stopping, bolting straight into her office.

Gloria had to put one hand over her mouth to hide her amusement as she pointed at her head with the other.

'Did you see her hair?' she cried, barely able to contain herself. 'What the hell has she done to it? I mean, it was bad enough before - but that!'

Jack couldn't help but snigger too. It was awful.

'Do you think she went to the hairdressers and asked for their worst possible mullet? Or did she just do it herself in front of her bedroom mirror with a pair of garden shears?'

Now Jack was really laughing and Lisa was looking over at them from her office. They knew she couldn't hear exactly what they were saying, but the way she was fidgeting with clumps of hair gave them an indication that she had a fair idea of the subject matter of their conversation. Lisa was clearly displeased with it herself.

'If that had happened to me, I'd have chopped my head off.'

'You're so funny,' he laughed. 'Anyway, there's something else that's happened that's quite nice. I've been invited to Tokyo, on Wednesday. It's just for three days.'

'Wednesday? You never said. That sounds fantastic! Who with?'

'My friend Clare. You met her at the party. It was her birthday.'

'Oh yes, I'm sure she was giving me the evils.'

'She's not like that really. She was just having a bad day - but yes, her. Clare's company is paying for her and her boyfriend to go on a business trip.'

'Her boyfriend? Is there something you're not telling me, Jack?' teased Gloria.

'Oh, you know me - I'm strictly a man's man. But this week I'll be Clare's man too.'

'I hope you have a lovely time. Hang on a minute! That means that you'll be leaving me alone with axe-head in there again.'

'It's only for three days. I've still got to ask Lisa actually. I was only invited on Saturday.'

Gloria looked over at Lisa's office.

'Rather you than me. She looks as if she's just swallowed six bees.'

Jack looked over too.

'Hmm, perhaps you're right. I'll have another coffee first and then ask her. Do you think it would help if I told her how nice her hair looks today?'

Gloria sniggered. 'Not unless you want yours to end up looking the same. If I were you I'd steer clear of the hair subject.'

Jack went to the kitchen to make himself some more coffee. Was it really only a few weeks since he and Paulo had argued in this very room? So much had happened in such a short time. The whole affair with Mark had been and gone.

'I've never been to Japan,' said Gloria as Jack returned. 'It sounds great. Are you going to tell Mark you're going?'

'I think he should be the one calling me, not the other way round.'

'But you're the one going off travelling. You'd only be letting him know where you were.'

'Actually, my phone won't work outside Europe so even if he did try to call me he wouldn't be able to. He could leave a message, though, and that would be on my voicemail when I get back.'

'So if he calls you on Wednesday you won't get the message until Saturday? It wouldn't look like you were very interested, would it, sitting on a message for four days?'

'I don't even know that he will call, and even if he did, what the message might be. It might just be to say, 'fuck you too'.'

'Well, if you're happy to leave things to chance... I know what I would do if I were you,' said Gloria, trying to be supportive. She knew that Jack's pride had been dented.

'All right, I'll call him. In fact, I'll go and do it right now and get it over with.'

'Good for you,' said Gloria, examining a ladder in her white stockings.

'But what will I say? I can't just announce that I'm off to Japan, in case he was thinking of calling me, can I?'

'Of course you can - but how about saying,

'Hi, Mark. I'm sorry I haven't been able to call you since Friday, I've been really busy. We do need to talk, but I'm going to Japan on Wednesday for a few days and my phone won't work over there.'

'Do we need to talk?'

'Of course you do. You'll get to a final 'one way or the other' that's not being said in the heat of the moment. You've both had time to cool off. Or do you just want to walk away without even asking him again?'

Gloria was right. One of them had to make the first move. Jack went back into the kitchen. There was nobody else there so he closed the door behind him.

Gloria was waiting at her desk. He'd been gone for almost ten minutes. What was happening?

'Well, what did he say?' she asked when he came back.

'Nothing. His voicemail was on so I just left a message.'

'And that took ten minutes? I was beside myself with curiosity.'

'It took me a while to actually dial his number. Oh well, like you say, I've given it my last shot. If he doesn't call me before I'm back from Japan then he can forget it - and so will I.'

'Well done. You did the right thing.'

'OK, while I'm on a roll… one down, one to go,' he said, standing up. 'I'd better go and make sure Lisa's OK about me taking another few days off.'

Jack walked over to Lisa's office and knocked gently on the door.

'Come in.'

Lisa's hair looked even more peculiar at close range. There seemed to be a bit missing close to her right ear, and that side looked very different to the clumps on the left.

'Yes, Jack,' she snapped, aware that he was looking at her hair.

'Lisa, I just wanted to ask if it was all right to have a few days off this week. I know we're busy but it's a once in a lifetime opport… '

'No you can't. You've just had a week off and, like you say, we are really busy - even more so since your unfortunate absence with Gloria due to… food poisoning. I'm sorry, Jack, I just can't spare you.'

Jack was taken by surprise. He had expected her to just say 'yes'.

'But Lisa, it's a trip to Japan. It's only for three days. I'll work the weekend after to catch up if you need me to.'

'I don't care if it's a trip to the moon! Which part of NO don't you understand?' she spat, shaking her tortured fringe and banging her fists on her desk.

Jack quickly considered his options.

'I'm sorry, Lisa, I'm taking those days off. I think you're being unreasonable. It's not month-end and there are no other deadlines. Gloria can handle the routine work and I'll put in the extra hours to catch up as soon as I return.

'If you are not in this office all week, don't bother coming back next week,' she said, waving a finger at him and starting to froth at the mouth.

Fuck it.

'Fine, then I quit!'

'Jack, I'm warning you. If you walk out of here now, that really is it,' Lisa said, giving him one last chance to change his mind.

Jack's heart was pounding in his chest.

'Sorry, Lisa, I'm going to Japan. Oh - and Lisa,' he said, just before turning round to walk out, 'I can recommend a really good hairdresser if you need one.'

'Get out!' she screamed, slamming the door behind him.

Gloria watched Jack in awe as he packed his things.

'Have you lost your mind?'

'Actually, I think I've just found it. I'm ready for a change anyway,' he said, taking a deep breath.

'But what are you going to do?'

'I'll go to Japan.'

'I mean after Japan, silly.'

'I have no idea. And you know what? It feels great. It looks like I beat you to it. Paolo started quite a trend, didn't he?'

Gloria was in shock. Talking about resigning was one thing. Doing it was quite another.

'She'll blame me for all this, you know,' she said, already beginning to think about the aftermath. 'My life will be hell on earth, alone here with her.'

'She'll soon get someone else to replace me. You'll be fine. You've been the best colleague in the world, and my going won't affect our friendship, you know.'

Gloria stood up and put her arms around Jack, starting to cry.

'I'll miss you so much.'

'No, you won't. As soon as I'm back from Japan we'll arrange to meet up for lunch. OK?'

'OK. I'm sorry about the tears. It's just that this was all so unexpected.'

'Tell me about it. I can't believe what I've just done.'

'You can still change your mind. She'll have you back in an instant once she's calmed down.'

'Or grown her hair back,' said Jack dryly.

Gloria laughed.

'That's better. Now you look after that Declan of yours. He's a good chap at heart.'

'I will. Listen, Jack, good luck with Mark and have a fantastic trip.'

'Thanks, Gloria. Take care,' he said fondly as he put his jacket on and left the office.

Chapter 46

'You did what?' asked Clare as they were waiting to board the plane at Heathrow on Wednesday morning. The business class lounge was closed so they had had to sit with the general travelling public on the main concourse.

'I walked out, which was the same as resigning.'

'Well, I'm delighted that you're coming with me, but wasn't that a bit extreme? Maybe if you apologise when we return Lisa will give you your job back and forget all about it. You can buy her a *geisha* wig as a present,' she laughed.

'It's fine. Maybe it was just the push that I needed. I don't have a mortgage to pay, and I've got you to look after me and give me my spending money.'

'Yeah, right. I'll pay for your meals-on-wheels for a week and that's it. OK, two weeks because I still feel guilty about not telling you immediately what I knew about Mark.'

'You're all heart. I'm going to take some time out when we get back while I think about what to do next with my life.'

'Sounds like you've thought about it properly after all. You'll be fine. Anyway, change is good for you,' said Clare, rummaging through her handbag. 'Right, now, have we got everything? Tickets, passports, money?'

'I'm really excited about going at such short notice. It's so outrageous!'

'It'll be work for me, of course, but it should be great fun too. I'm a bit nervous about meeting Mrs Suzuki again. She didn't seem to mind when I said I would be coming to sign the contracts instead of Grace, which I found a bit odd. But then again, she could hardly have found any valid grounds to refuse, could she? Not any that she would care to share with anyone, that is.'

'I can't wait to see her. She sounds awesome. Will her sumo sparring partner be there too?'

'I doubt it very much,' Clare laughed. 'But seriously, Jack, you mustn't utter a single word about anything that I told you about what happened that night. I gave her my word of honour that I would never discuss it again. Strangely enough, that meant something to me and I want to stick by it.'

'I'll take it to the grave.'

His phone started to beep and vibrate in his pocket. It was a text message.

'Sorry I've not been in contact,' he read aloud. 'Had some thinking to do. Will be in touch when you're back. Mark.'

He looked up at Clare.

'That sounds promising,' she said, 'doesn't it?'

'What do you think it means?'

'I think it means that he'll be in touch when you get back and that he has had some thinking to do. But perhaps it's a coded message,' she said, reapplying her lipstick.

'Yes, I know that. But *what* has he been thinking about?'

'Jack, relax. I doubt he's been thinking about whether or not to take up a course in Peruvian ceramics. He'll have been thinking about you and him, you idiot,' she said, studying herself critically in the mirror.

'I think I'd prefer it if he had been considering a course in pottery. At least that might mean he's decided on a career change.'

'Well, I think it sounds promising.'

'Should I text him back?'

'Do you want him to contact you when we come back?'

'Yes, of course I do.'

'There you go then. Text him.'

Jack did as he was told.

'What did you write?' asked Clare when he had finished.

'"OK".'

'Is that it? Nothing else? Well, I suppose you kept it brief.'

'Until I know what it is he has to say, I'm not hanging my feelings out on the washing line again.'

Clare giggled.

'What's so funny?'

'Nothing. It's just that I don't think that I've ever heard that saying before,' she replied, applying some rouge.

'I think I just made it up,' said Jack, laughing as well.

'Stop laughing, I'll smudge my make-up.

Jack read the newspaper while Clare finished her face.

'How do I look?' she asked, sealing her travel-sized tubes and jars back into a small, transparent plastic pouch.

'Not bad for six forty-five in the morning.'

Clare took the paper from him, rolled it up and hit him on the head with it.

'I mean, you look stunning. Are you planning on joining the mile-high club?'

'I might. Have you ever, you know?'

'Have I ever what? Had a fuck on a plane? No, I can't think of anywhere worse to have sex than in a tiny unhygienic cubicle with a queue of people listening outside.

Clare made a face.

'Put like that, I think I'll pass too.'

'Shouldn't we be boarding soon?'

'Yes, let's make our way over to the gate. It's number twelve.'

It took them a good fifteen minutes to get there and when they did it was very crowded.

'Looks like the plane will be packed. Let's just sit and wait on the side over there,' said Clare, pointing over to a large window. 'They'll call us to board first anyway. I'm so getting ready for my breakfast now. The food is really good in business class - and we can have champagne!'

'Can you believe that we're actually sitting here without gasping for cigarettes?' said Jack. 'A month ago we would have been scouring the airport for a smoking area.'

'I know. I can't say that I feel completely happy about not smoking, and I do still have pangs, but I'm so glad we did it. Anyway, let's stop talking about it otherwise I'll start thinking about cigarettes again.'

The airline staff had started to assemble at the counter that barred their passage to the plane. As the prospect of getting on it grew, passengers began to stand up and gather together, forming a thronging mass around the counter. Of course this did nothing to speed up the boarding process. After a further fifteen minutes of shuffling papers and drinking tea, the ground staff positioned themselves at the gate.

'Flight 689 to Tokyo is now ready for boarding,' declared a nasal voice through a microphone. 'Business class passengers will board the plane first. Please make sure that you have your boarding cards ready and that all electronic devices and phones are turned off ready for take off.' A loud groan erupted from the masses. They would still have to wait for their Economy call.

'That's us,' said Clare, standing up and smoothing down her dress.

'At last,' said Jack, tucking his shirt back in. 'Japan, here we come!'

Chapter 47

Taking a well-deserved break, Brian was drinking a cup of coffee in his workshop. He'd spent the morning working on his chair for the design competition. He still couldn't believe this was the first time that he had entered a professional contest and that he had won a place in the national final in August in Manchester.

He was all set to go to Barcelona on Saturday morning and was getting very excited. Tom had been brilliant and had managed to find the details in Donald's house of where Jessica was staying. It turned out that Jessica was actually staying in Sitges, about a thirty-minute drive from Barcelona. The address that Tom had given him was for an apartment in the old town. Jack knew Sitges very well and he had given Brian the addresses of some good hotels, just in case, before jetting off to Tokyo with Clare.

What should he say to Jessica when he arrived? He didn't want to call her first in case she refused point blank to meet him. So he'd decided on the relatively high-risk strategy of just turning up at her door. She might still refuse to see him, but she would know he was physically standing outside - so he hoped that, eventually, he would get his chance to say something to her. He was hoping beyond hope that she might even allow him to sleep on her sofa – especially if he told her he had nowhere else to go.

This was the first time in his life that Brian was preparing to go to such extreme lengths for the chance of a date. Was she really worth the effort? Yes, she was. But this would be his last shot at it with her. With Paolo now out of the equation he figured Jessica had had enough time to think things through and get over whatever anguish he had caused her. If she still wasn't interested in him after that, well, there wasn't really much else he could do.

He picked up the phone to call Donald, to check that she hadn't come back already. That would be the nightmare scenario - Brian in Barcelona and Jessica back in London!

'Hi, Donald. It's me, Brian.'

'Brian, darling, what a lovely surprise! What is it, dear?'

Whatever else Donald might mince it was most certainly never his words.

'Is Jessica back yet?' he asked, tentatively.

He heard Donald sighing down the phone.

'I'm afraid not. I don't think she'll be back for a while yet. I spoke to her a couple of days ago and although she does sound much better than she did, she still doesn't sound right. In any case, her building work at home is taking much longer than they thought and you know how tiresome that can be.'

'I've decided to go over there on Saturday,' Brian blurted out spontaneously.

'Go where, dear? To see Jessica's builders? Do you think you'll be able to speed them up?'

'To Barcelona.'

Donald was silent for a moment.

'Well, I think I've already given you my very clear views on the matter, so I won't waste any more of my breath repeating them.'

'Please don't be like that, Donald. I honestly value your opinions, but I just can't hang around any more like a spare part. I'm only human, and I really want to see her, so I've decided to go.'

'Whatever the consequences?'

'Yes, whatever the consequences.'

'When are you going?'

'Saturday morning.'

'So you've already booked a flight?'

'And packed.'

'I see. And are you planning on just aimlessly roaming the streets of Barcelona hoping to bump into her by chance?'

Brian didn't want to drop Tom in it, so thought he was better off at least trying the direct approach with Donald after all.

'Will you give me her address, Donald? Please?'

'On one condition,' said Donald after another pause.

Brian was taken by surprise.

'What's that?'

'If you get there and she still doesn't want to see you, you must promise to leave her alone and catch the next flight back home. I do like you, Brian. Perhaps more than you know. But Jessica has had a nasty shock and I don't want her getting any more distressed or hurt than she needs to be. Is that clear?'

'That's brilliant, Donald - and it's as clear as your new pane of glass. Thanks ever so much.'

'Yes, well, you didn't really leave me much choice, did you?'

Donald gave Brian Jessica's address over the phone.

'It's a quaint little town just outside Barcelona. It used to be a fishing village.'

'Yes, Jack said. And I know what people like you get up to over there,' he joked, trying to lighten things up.

'Really, Brian - people like me? I can assure you, dear, there is nobody like me,' laughed Donald. 'I'm afraid I have to go now and see what's going on outside. Lucille is in the garden doing the dogs and they've just started yelping and barking. What on earth is she doing to them?' he said, peering through the kitchen window.

Brian pictured Lucille lying flat on her back on the grass with either Rags or Muffin straddling her. Perhaps she had made an unfortunate snip with her grooming implements.

'OK,' he said with a wince, wanting to get off before a new dog drama unfolded. 'I'll let you know how I get on. Wish me luck!'

'Have a safe journey, dear. But if she just slams the door in your face, don't say I didn't warn you. You two are worse than a pair of headstrong bulls.'

Brian felt much better now about going out to Spain. He didn't like sneaking around behind Donald's back. He decided to call Tom and let him know the latest.

'Tom? Hi, it's Brian. Yeah, I'm fine. I just wanted to say that Donald has given me Jessica's address in Spain after all, so you don't need to worry about anything. Listen mate, while I'm away you can get on with varnishing the table if you have time? Great. I'll leave the key for the workshop under the broken brick. Can you remember the alarm code? That's right. You can call me if you have any problems. I might be back on Sunday anyway if it all goes tits up. OK, will do. Thanks a million.'

Brian was glad he'd made the call. Tom had sounded very guilty after searching through Donald's drawers and he was a good, honest lad. It was a shame that he seemed to be worried about something. Brian decided to ask him when he got back from Barcelona. Maybe he could help, even if it was just being someone to talk to.

An hour later Brian was sanding down one of the chair's spindles when there was a knock at the door to the workshop. He turned around and walked over towards it to see who it was.

'Mark! What are you doing here?'

This was the first time he had seen Mark since the recent revelations.

'Hello, Brian. You OK?'

'Er, yes, thanks. Jack's not here if you're looking for him. He's gone to Tokyo for a few days with Clare.'

'Yes, I know. Thanks. Actually, it's you I've come to see. Excuse me for just coming round like this. Jack and I walked past here one morning on the way back from the market and he pointed out that it's your workshop.'

'No problem,' said Brian, wondering what it was that Mark wanted.

'Listen, I know that it's a bit out of the blue, but will you come out for a drink with me tomorrow evening?'

Brian didn't want to get involved in Jack's domestic feuds, and politely declined.

'Sorry, mate, I'm already meeting up with a couple of other guys.'

'That's OK - bring them along as well.'

'No, really, we've already arranged to… '

'Brian, I'm sure you know that Jack and I have had serious words. I think you probably know what about, too.'

He nodded, putting a screwdriver back in its case.

'So I've decided to say goodbye.'

'Goodbye? Does Jack know?'

'Not yet. Please, just come for one drink. You're the nearest thing to Jack I've got.'

'But can't you wait until Saturday? He's back then and you can tell him face to face.'

'I know a bit about what you're going through with Jessica. Jack hasn't told me much, but he has told me that once you've made your mind up, that's it, your mind's made up. Is that true?'

'I suppose so, yes.'

'Well, me too. My mind is made up. Come on - a farewell drink tomorrow. It really would mean a lot to me.'

Brian thought about it again. He supposed it couldn't really do any harm. At least Mark will have been able to say goodbye to someone. Maybe he could even get a forwarding address off him for Jack. Should he tell Jack before going along? He could contact the hotel in Tokyo - he had the details. On second thoughts, telling him would definitely ruin his trip. He might as well at least enjoy that and then find out when he gets back home. Mark had clearly already decided what he was going to do anyway.

'All right, then. Where do you want to go?'

'Great stuff. Would you mind meeting up at a gay pub in Camden, the Dog and Duck? I'll be there from about six.'

Brian knew the Dog and Duck. He'd been a few times with Jack and he knew Declan and Toby would be cool, so he agreed.

'That's fine. I'll definitely come for a couple and my mates will probably come too.'

'Thanks, Brian. Jack's right - he is lucky to have a good friend like you.'

'Cheers. I just wish you two could have sorted things out with each other. He really likes you. Just think about that again before you go, will you?'

Chapter 48

It was Thursday morning and Shinjuku station was teeming with busy people as Jack and Clare prised themselves out of the train that had transported them from Narita airport into the heart of modern Tokyo.

'Thank goodness for that,' panted Clare. 'Have you ever seen so many people on one train?'

'What's with all the white face masks?' asked Jack. 'Has there been an outbreak of bird flu or something?'

'You'll get used to them,' laughed Clare. 'The Japanese are very considerate when it comes to colds and flu, so they wear the masks so as not to spread their germs around. Some people even wear them to try to prevent catching colds too. You saw how packed that train was.'

'Still, they are quite severe-looking. Did you see that woman who just walked past us on the escalator? She looked scarier than Anthony Hopkins in Silence of the Lambs.'

'I know, I must admit I can't really see me wearing one out shopping in Harvey Nicks.'

It was bright and sunny when they got outside and only a short walk to the prestigious Plaza Hotel, where they were staying. Mrs Suzuki had booked the best banquet suite for the signing ceremony and dinner on the forty-sixth floor - the top one. She had also reserved the rooms for her guests. Only one room had been booked for them, as Jack was supposed to be Clare's partner. They were actually both looking forward to sharing. It would be just like old times.

'Wow, this place is amazing,' said Jack in awe, looking up at the soaring skyscrapers.

'Isn't it? This is us right here.'

As they were checking in, Clare remembered the last time she had checked into a Japanese hotel in Osaka. She had made such a scene because she wanted – or rather needed – a smoking room.

'A no smoking twin room please,' requested Clare proudly to the girl at the reception desk.

A few minutes later they were in their room.

'Just look at those beds!' exclaimed Jack. 'They're bigger than my queen size at home.'

'Will it do for you, then?' asked Clare, walking over to the window.

'Are you kidding? I could stay here for a month.'

'You'd need to work for a year to pay for it, though. It costs a fortune.'

'What shall we do first, then?' asked Jack, eager to get out and explore Tokyo despite feeling a bit tired after the long flight.

'Well, I'm afraid I have to do a bit of paperwork this afternoon and then I have to courier it over to Mrs Suzuki's office. Why don't you pop out and have a walk round, see some of the sights? Here's my guidebook and that local map that I picked up downstairs.'

'Thanks, that sound's like a plan. What time should I come back?'

'Well, I want to take you for a drink in the bar at the top of the Met, so let's just meet there.'

'Where?'

'The Tokyo Metropolitan Building. It's just around the corner and the views are the best in the city. I should be done by about three-ish. We can decide what to do later while we're having a drink. The festivities tomorrow start in the afternoon at five o'clock sharp and we fly back on Saturday at eleven in the morning.'

After Jack had showered he took the subway over to a part of the city called Shibuya. It was fairly close by and Clare had recommended that he go to see it. Shibuya was the birthplace for practically all Japanese fashions and crazes and unlike anywhere else in the country. High-heeled boots and short skirts were all the rage this season – Mark would have loved them! Jack could see that the neon-lit roundabout just next to the station was the epicentre of activity – similar to Piccadilly Circus in London, but on a much larger and more chaotic scale. Despite the apparent mayhem, most people waited patiently for the 'green man' before crossing the roads. When red turned to green it was like a polite stampede of soldier ants. He was amazed that there didn't seem to be any collisions considering the vast numbers of people crossing in different directions at the same time - scrambled crossing, as it's known in Japan.

Next stop was Kabukicho to explore the seedier part of town. Kabukicho was the red light district and even by day the love hotels and hostess bars seemed to be busy. Jack spotted what he suspected were members of the *yakuza* – the Japanese mafia – arguing outside a sex shop. He recognised the 1970's tight perms from films that he had seen. A short walk away was the gay area, and Jack enjoyed exploring the inviting side streets, crammed full of little restaurants and cafés, tucked away behind secret curtains. Perhaps he and Clare would come out again later on if they had any energy left.

At about two-twenty he made his way back to the Met to meet up with Clare for drinks. He couldn't believe his eyes as he came out of the lift. The room was huge and spanned a full three hundred and sixty degrees. From up here Jack could truly believe that Tokyo was home to twelve million people. Before going over to the bar on the right hand side he paused by a fountain feature next to a different window. There it was - Mount Fuji, mighty and powerful, its snow-capped peak being caressed by the clouds.

'You found it, then,' said Clare from behind him. 'I thought I saw you getting out of the lift. It's quite something isn't it?'

'I've never seen anything like it! It really puts life into perspective. How important is one person within all of this?' he said, gesturing outside.

'I know what you mean. Come on, time for a drink.'

Clare led him over to the bar and they took a table by the window to enjoy even more breathtaking views.

'Let's have some champagne - and I'm paying.'

They were soon sipping their drinks and relaxing in their armchairs.

'This is so nice, just sitting here with you, watching the world go by.'

'It's fabulous. How do you feel about tomorrow? Nervous?'

'To tell you the truth I'm petrified about meeting Mrs Suzuki again. I practically blackmailed her, didn't I? Can that really be a good start to our working relationship?'

'All's fair in love and war, as they say.'

'I guess, but still. Anyway, apart from that minor factor, I am really excited about it. I'm also looking forward to when it's all over with so that I can switch off for a while.'

'So what happens tomorrow then?'

'I think there will be about a hundred and fifty people attending. I have a list back at the hotel. Mrs Suzuki and her husband will obviously be there, along with her lawyer, Lance Rubenstein. Who else? Ah yes, her three sons, the directors of 'Just for You' and a whole host of suppliers and business associates. There are some minor celebrities attending too, for the photo shoot. As for the main event, we'll be starting with a drinks reception, then the signing ceremony, followed by the meal. Remember to wear clean socks as you'll almost certainly have to take your shoes off in the banquet suite. I'm amazed that they've managed to get all this together in just one week.'

'I can hardly wait! It all sounds thrilling.'

'Good. You deserve a break after what you've been through.'

'I wonder what Mark's doing? I have missed him, despite everything,' said Jack.

'I know you have. He's probably planning what to say to you when he sees you. Does he know that we get back on Saturday?'

'Yes, I said all that on the voicemail I left him. Anyway,

we're in Tokyo today and I want to enjoy it. We'll be back in London soon enough and can hopefully sort things out then, one way or the other.'

Jack held up his glass.

'Cheers,' he said with a smile.

Clare smiled back. 'Cheers - and good luck with Mark.'

'Oh, my God,' he said putting down his glass with a start.

'What is it?'

'Rachel.'

'What about her, is she here?' exclaimed Clare.

'No, of course she isn't. But she won't be able to drink any alcohol for months, not until the babies are born! Can you imagine anything worse?'

'Physically having to give birth to twins springs to mind,' laughed Clare. 'What on earth triggered that thought out of the blue?'

'Drinking here with you and watching that pregnant woman behind you, over there.'

Clare turned around and stared at the woman who was so enormous with child that she looked as if she might explode at any moment.

'Yes, I see what you mean. Poor Rachel will probably be huge too by the time she's ready,' she said, making a mental note to buy her an ample supply of stretch mark cream.

'Do you still not want kids, Clare?'

'Not at this precise moment in time, no I don't,' she answered, surprised by the question.

'Not ever?'

'That's not what I said. Maybe, or maybe not. I don't feel a strong maternal instinct, if that's what you mean. And anyway, I'd like a man first. If I've dried up before that ever happens, then that's that,' she said with a giggle. 'How about you? You once said you thought you'd make a good father.'

'I know, but I'm not so sure now. It's one thing thinking about having a baby and quite another looking after it once it's there, isn't it?'

'It is indeed. Well, we'll be able to practice first, won't we?'

'Will we?' asked Jack, horrified.

'Got you there! I mean Rachel and Heike are bound to need babysitters for the twins, aren't they?'

Jack heaved a sigh of relief.

'Yes, I'd like to do that. But if they decide to stay in Berlin we'd have to go over there to help out, wouldn't we?'

'I know. Some might say it's a bit extravagant flying in your babysitters, but if you want the best... ' she joked.

After polishing off two bottles of champagne they decided not to go out anywhere else and just go back to the hotel and have an early night. Jet lag was now kicking in on top of the alcohol, and room service at the hotel sounded like an invitation to heaven. They enjoyed the rest of the evening just pottering around and taking long soaks in their deep Japanese bath.

*

The following morning they awoke early. Jack was first out of bed.

'That toilet seat is unbelievable,' he said, emerging from the bathroom.

The heated toilet seat with its integrated control panel was something Jack had never seen in England before.

'There's a little button you can press to wash your butt,' he said in amazement. 'A nozzle comes out from under the seat and manages to spray at just the right angle. There's even a button for your front too and a built-in drier. I was half expecting it to make me some tea and toast!'

Having enjoyed a light Western-style breakfast they went for a stroll in Shinjuki Central Park before taking the subway over to Ginza, Tokyo's luxury-shopping district. Although they were only going to window shop, Clare couldn't resist buying a new handbag and Jack bought himself a tie to wear later for the meal.

To his surprise Clare had booked massages for them back at the hotel, so by the time they were getting ready to go to the ceremony they were feeling revived and rejuvenated. They made their way up to the top floor just after five o'clock.

'She's over there,' whispered Clare, grabbing a couple of glasses of wine from a passing waiter.

'Who is?'

'Mrs Suzuki.'

Jack looked through the already crowded room over to where Clare's gaze was focussed.

'She's very beautiful,' commented Jack, admiring her outfit.

'I'd better go over and say something to her while she's alone,' said Clare bravely. 'Will you be all right here for a moment?'

'I'll be fine. Good luck,' said Jack, helping himself to another passing drink, thoroughly enjoying himself in spite of Clare's anguish.

'*Konbanwa,* Mrs Suzuki,' said Clare, going down into her bow.

'Hello, Clare. I'm so glad you could make it.'

Clare was taken aback, both by the friendliness and informality.

'You are?' she asked, standing up straight again.

'Yes, I am. Look, this may come as a surprise to you, Clare, but I really do admire you. You've got balls. It's such a pity I didn't recognise you in the club, I would love to have seen you in your outfit,' she said with a smile.

It was the first time Clare had seen any emotion at all on Mrs Suzuki's face, let alone a smile.

'Well, thank you very much,' she said, feeling her face reddening at the unexpected compliment.

She decided to bow again, suddenly overcome with embarrassment and guilt for blackmailing this woman.

'Mrs Suzuki, I'm really sorry for what I did. It's just that I was desperate for you to agree to this deal. I know you won't regret going into business with us, but I feel terrible now about following you like that and taking those photos.'

'Ssshh,' said Mrs Suzuki, holding a finger up to her lips. 'What's done is done. But remember that it must remain our little secret. I'll have to be more careful in future, won't I? See you for the signing photos,' she said, before strutting off to mingle with her guests.

About fifteen minutes later there was a loud gong and the room fell silent. Clare and Mrs Suzuki went up onto the stage and took their places at the main desk. It was overflowing with bouquets of colourful flowers and sample Destiny merchandise. The two women posed with their pens and were almost blinded by the flash photography. Mrs Suzuki said a few words about how delighted she was to be bringing Destiny to Japan and Clare said a few words about how thrilled her company was to be partnering with Just for You.

A second gong signalled the start of dinner and the guests made their way over towards two very long, low tables. The tables gave the impression that you were sitting on the floor on *tatami* mats. In fact, there was a hollow, lower floor section underneath the table for your legs. This meant that it was possible to sit Western-style, as if on a chair, and Clare was relieved at the prospect of not having to kneel.

As expected, the tables had seating plans. It looked like everyone was playing musical chairs as they circled the tables in search of their own names. Jack was seated next to Clare on her right. She didn't recognise the name to her left. Mrs Suzuki's good-looking eldest son Takeshi was sitting next to Jack on his right, and Lance was diagonally across from Clare, next to Mrs Suzuki and her husband. The seat directly opposite her was still empty.

Slowly but surely everyone started to take their allocated seats. A man sat down next Clare and introduced himself.

'Hello, I'm Robert Kaaps,' he said in a South African accent. 'My company is a supplier to Just for You.'

319

'A pleasure to meet you,' said Clare, eyeing him up. 'I'm Clare Houghton.'

'I know, I saw you on the stage. Mrs Suzuki drives a hard bargain, doesn't she? But they're good business partners.'

'You're not kidding. Hello again, Lance,' she said, reaching across the table.

'Hi, Clare. Bet you're glad it's all over with, huh?'

'I'm glad we've finally reached an agreement,' said Clare, ever the professional. 'Thanks for all your help.'

Meanwhile, Jack had introduced himself to Takeshi and they were chatting away when another voice with an American accent boomed into the conversation.

'Hey, Clare! Great to see you again!'

To her horror, she saw that it was John Goldschmied. He was sitting opposite her. She was sure his name hadn't been on the list.

'John,' she said curtly.

'Isn't this great? Lance here managed to get me an invite too. It's been too long since we last saw each other, hasn't it?'

The end of time would have been too soon for Clare. She had had no further contact with John since receiving the flowers after returning to London from her last trip to Osaka. Clare cringed as she reflected on the unpleasant events of the evening they had spent together.

Luckily, the waiters came to her rescue and started serving the food and drinks.

'What do you think?' she asked, turning to Jack.

'It's fantastic. Takeshi was just showing me how to hold these chopsticks properly. I think I've got the hang of it now. I've been doing it wrong for years!'

'Hello again, Takeshi. How are you?' asked Clare, leaning backwards so that she could see him properly.

'Very well, thanks,' he answered with a 'modern bow'. 'Welcome to Japan.'

The 'modern bow' was frequently adopted by the younger generation. It was actually less a bow and more a drop of the shoulders and thrust of the neck, all the time maintaining eye contact. Clare found it quite sexy.

'Is something wrong?' she asked Jack, who was now looking open-mouthed at a small dish that a waitress had just placed before him.

'What's that?'

'I think that it's sea urchin, but check with Takeshi.'

Jack cringed as he studied the contents of the dish. It resembled slimy orange plasticine.

'Don't worry, I'll eat yours if you don't want it,' said Takeshi with a laugh.

Jack heaved a sigh of relief.

'Thanks. Sorry to be unadventurous.'

Course after course was served and Jack found that he did in fact get more adventurous as the *sake* flowed. He tried crab legs, lobster claws, wriggling sea cucumber and even lightly grilled cod testicles. He was surprised at how large the latter were, considering they had originated from a fish.

Clare was tucking into her food too and quite enjoying chatting to Robert Kaaps. It turned out that he supplied Mrs Suzuki's company with lingerie. While she was talking, one of the chefs walked over towards her. He was pushing a load-bearing silver trolley covered with a purple velvet sheet. The chef stopped next to her and then bowed before slowly peeling off the sheet to reveal a fish tank. The tank contained a single, enormous-looking fish. Clare looked at the tank, perplexed, and then looked up at the chef. Everyone had stopped talking and was watching.

'It is fugu – balloon fish,' he said with another deep bow. 'Is very fresh,' he added proudly.

Clare looked into the tank again. Well, obviously it's very fresh, she thought - it's still alive! Clare hadn't encountered this ritual before and didn't quite know what to do. She looked across the table and thought Mrs Suzuki actually winked at her, but could have been mistaken. Surely she wasn't supposed to reach in and try to catch it? Then what? Just take a bite out of it while it was still 'very fresh'? She turned to Jack for help, but he just shrugged a 'don't look at me, I don't know what's going on either' face.

'Oh my God!' she exclaimed, raising a hand to her mouth. This must be a trick, she thought - Mrs Suzuki's revenge. Clare might not have been familiar with the fish tank routine, but she did remember reading somewhere all about the tank's content. One balloon fish contained enough tetrodoxin to poison and kill thirty human beings. If not prepared correctly, with the organs properly removed, one mouthful could prove fatal, resulting first in paralysis and then death.

All eyes, including those of the fish, were looking at her expectantly. Takeshi came to her rescue.

'The chef wants to show you that the fish is fresh before he prepares thinly sliced *fugu sashimi*,' he said quietly, with a smile, seeing Clare's horror. 'You are the guest of honour. That's why he's brought it out for you to inspect.'

Relieved that she wasn't expected to eat it live, Clare thanked Takeshi. She then dutifully leaned in towards the fish tank to get a closer look, her nose almost touching the glass. In panic, the fish suddenly puffed itself out to almost double its size and began flapping its fins, snarling at her through its sharp, pointed teeth.

Clare sat back startled, causing first Jack and then everyone else to laugh. She laughed too, before nodding her approval towards the chef and then turning to face Mrs Suzuki to say thank you. Everyone clapped and then resumed their chatter. A few moments later the chef wheeled the tank away, the fish now relaxed again and blissfully unaware of its impending doom.

'That was one hell of a balloon fish,' guffawed John Goldschmied. 'I once saw someone have a heart attack after eating that in Malaysia.'

A pity it wasn't you, thought Clare. She found him repulsive, and was trying her best to ignore him. Unfortunately she couldn't ignore his shoeless foot under the table that he was now sliding up her leg beneath her skirt. He simultaneously grinned at her in a lecherous manner that made her feel quite ill, almost putting her off her food. Clare leaned forward across the table, considered biting his ear off, but then whispered into it instead.

'If you try that again,' she began slowly, 'I will stand up here and now and tell everybody that will listen about how ridiculous you are underneath those horrid trousers.'

John's smile froze manically as Clare continued.

'I will also tell them that you can't manage even the briefest of performances. You fell asleep on that ghastly night I endured with you, flaccid as a miniature, wiggly worm. I invented our night of passion as a little story just to make you feel better. But seeing as you seem to believe you are Stud of the Year, I really do have to tell you that you're much more like Spud of the Year. Here - have another French fry,' she said, stuffing a couple of the chips he had ordered especially into John's now quivering mouth.

Feeling quite pleased with herself, Clare relaxed and enjoyed chatting and flirting with Robert. Although she thought he was a bit uncouth, she did find him quite attractive. He was also very good company and had her rolling around in stitches at his jokes.

Jack was getting on well with Takeshi too, and, after countless gold leaf *sakes* served in a little wooden box, he decided to confess that he wasn't really Clare's partner at all.

'Yes, I had guessed that,' smiled Takeshi, pressing his thigh against Jack's as he turned away to talk to the woman sitting on the other side of the table.

Clare was starting to feel bolder than she had done for years. She actually made the first move, asking Robert if he wanted to go downstairs to his room. He didn't need asking twice. They agreed that he would leave first so as not to arouse suspicion and that Clare would follow him down after he had gone. Before leaving, Clare said her goodbyes to Mrs Suzuki and Lance and then to Jack and Takeshi, who looked like they were having a lot of fun together.

'Just you be careful what you're doing,' she whispered to Jack. 'You've had loads to drink and you don't want to do anything you might regret in the morning.'

'I can look after myself, thank you very much. And just where do you think you're going anyway?'

Clare glanced at the empty seat beside her and raised her eyebrows.

'You're not going to… ? You are, aren't you?'

'I most certainly am. I intend to enjoy a night of wild, uncomplicated sex with Mr Kaaps.'

Chapter 49

Camden Town was already bustling with eager 'beginning of the weekend' activity even though it was only six o'clock on Friday evening. Many restaurants had tables out onto the pavements to take advantage of the good weather. They were rapidly filling up with drinkers and diners, keen to enjoy a warm al fresco evening after being cooped up all week in their offices. It was on weekends like this that London really did come into its own, transforming itself from an urban metropolis into a glistening Mediterranean jewel.

Brian had met Declan and Toby an hour earlier in the Plough and Pheasant for a quick pint before getting the bus from Hackney over to Camden. Declan and Toby were both wearing black jeans and tight, white t-shirts that hugged their muscles and Brian was wearing his combats and a brown t-shirt. He wanted to look his best for Jessica and had had his hair cut earlier in the afternoon in preparation for his trip to Barcelona.

'Well, gentlemen, this time tomorrow I could be sitting in a bar with Jessica, drinking sangria and feeding her olives,' said Brian as they paused outside the Dog and Duck where two young Latino men were smoking.

'You could,' said Toby. 'Or you could be on your way back to the airport, wearing the sangria jug on your head and the olives stuffed up your nose,' he laughed.

'Fear not, brothers. I know this is my big moment. I've got a very good feeling about it.'

One of the Latinos whistled as the trio passed them to go

into the pub. Declan shook his ass playfully and the guy whistled again.

'That was quick! Looks like you're in there,' said Brian with a smirk.

They were stopped at the door by a female bouncer.

'You know this is a gay bar, don't you boys?'

'I certainly hope so,' said Declan with another wiggle. 'You ever see a straight guy with an ass this good?'

The bouncer grinned and let them through.

'Have a good night.'

'Let's grab that table over there by the window,' said Brian as they went through to the main bar. He threw his jacket on one of the chairs.

'Here, you two sit down and I'll go and get the drinks in. Pints?'

'Yeah, cheers man,' said Toby, sitting down next to Declan.

'So who's this bloke you're meeting?' asked Toby, when Brian returned with the drinks.

'He's sort of Jack's boyfriend. Well, he was. They recently split up and it sounds like he's decided to leave London. We're his goodbye party. I don't really know. It all sounded a bit weird.'

'Well, it's a small party,' said Declan. 'Where's Jack?'

'He gets back from Japan tomorrow. Clare took him with her.'

'The lucky bastard! No woman has ever taken me on a big holiday,' complained Toby, putting his pint down on the table.

'Gloria and Annette are coming along a bit later. We'll probably shoot off once they get here,' said Declan.

'That's fine. I'm not sure how long I'm staying either. It feels a bit strange being here without Jack and meeting his boyfriend, or ex-boyfriend. I have to get up early tomorrow anyway. Did I tell you I'm flying out to Barcelona in the morning?'

'Yes, you did,' groaned Toby and Declan in unison. 'Now can you change the record?'

'Come on - give me a break, will you? How long have I been waiting for this moment?'

'Is this seat free?' asked a voice in a Canadian accent.

Brian, Toby and Declan all looked up.

A formidable-looking redhead in a short gold dress and five-inch purple stilettos had approached their table.

Six bewildered eyes just stared for a moment.

'Well, is it free? Or does a girl have to stand up all night? Have any of you ever tried standing up in heels this size for any length of time?'

'I haven't,' said Declan shaking his head and turning to his brother. 'Tob, how about you, mate?'

Toby threw a beer mat at Declan.

'Er, look, I'm sorry, but we're expecting someone,' said Brian. 'He should be here any minute. I think that table's free over there, though.'

'I prefer it here,' said the redhead, sitting down. 'You boys will just have to throw me out when your friend gets here.'

After a couple of seconds with no one quite sure what to do, the redhead spoke again.

'That shirt really suits you, Brian. It brings out the colour of your eyes beautifully.'

Toby and Declan looked at Brian, waiting for an explanation as to how they knew each other. Brian was about to say something but was beaten to it.

'Come on Brian, you can't have been so drunk that you don't even remember me? We had such a wild night! - and you promised me that you'd ring. I've been waiting all week and heard nothing so I thought I'd come and find you. I knew you'd be here.'

'But I've never met you before! And I haven't been here for… ' stammered Brian, before he was cut off.

'It's alright, honey, I'm not angry with you. Just give me a kiss and we'll take it from there, shall we?'

'Stop it! I've no idea who... '

'If you two lovebirds want a bit of quality time to catch up, Toby and I can make ourselves scarce, can't we bro?'

'No problemo. You must be the famous Jessica. I'm Toby. Brian's told us loads about you. We'll be back in a bit, mate,' he said, turning to Brian, patting him on the shoulder.

'This isn't fucking Jessica!' he spluttered.

'Not so fast, you two. Brian, it's me - Mark.'

'What?'

'Well, at the moment I'm actually Marleen. Would one of you boys please be so kind and get me another drink? Absinthe on the rocks,' said Mark, his Geordie accent returning.

'I was just going to the bar,' said Toby, draining his pint in amazement.

'I'll help you, mate,' said Declan, hastily joining his brother.

'I don't understand. What the fuck is this all about? Why are you dressed up like this? I thought you wanted to come out tonight to say goodbye before you leave London.'

'I am saying goodbye.'

'I don't get it.'

'I'm saying goodbye, but I'm not going anywhere. It's Marleen that's going. I'm saying goodbye to her. This is Marleen's last ever day. I really do care for Jack. Perhaps more than I knew when we argued. He's the best thing that's ever happened to me and the last few weeks have been really brilliant.'

'Marleen has been quite a big part of my life, you know, Brian. And when someone asks me to change something big, I can't just do it like that. But I've been doing a lot of thinking, and now I've made up my mind. Jack means more to me than the money Marleen earns. I'm going to surprise him and meet him at the airport tomorrow afternoon. I'm going to tell him that I've decided to change things and that I love him. I do - I really love him to bits.'

'That was quite a speech,' said Brian when Mark had

finished. 'You know what? I think Jack will be very pleased to see you.'

Declan and Toby returned with the drinks and Brian explained about Mark as best he could. Forty minutes and two more rounds of drinks later and they were all getting along famously.

'So, Toby,' said Mark, running a finger up Toby's arm and over his bicep. 'What sort of girls do you like?'

Toby looked over to his brother, who had started laughing.

'Oh, you know, all kinds really,' he joked, joining in the fun. As a rule, though, I generally prefer girls without cocks. But as they say, when in Rome… '

Mark got up and sat on Toby's knee.

'I can see I'm going to have to keep my eye on you, you naughty boy. If you're not careful you'll get a good spanking.'

Declan was still laughing.

'Brian, your friend is crazy.'

'Tell me about it, and trust me, from what I've heard you definitely do not want to be on the receiving end of any spanking,' said Brian with a wink.

The four of them enjoyed yet another round of drinks. Mark was basking in all the attention. He was draped over Declan, who had his hand on Mark's stockinged leg, when Gloria arrived.

'Well, I'm glad you're missing me.'

Declan leapt up out of his chair, almost knocking Mark over in the process.

'Hey, Gloria! Wow - you look amazing. Doesn't she look great?'

Mark was quite drunk, after having polished off half a dozen absinthes, so he decided to perch on Brian's knee instead.

'So you're the Gloria one that Jack speaks so highly of?'

Gloria looked confused. She gave Mark a slanted stare.

'Excuse me, do I know you?'

'Not yet you don't. I'm Mark, Jack's boyfriend. Don't

worry, I was only having a bit of fun with Declan. He's all yours.'

'You bet he is,' she said, grabbing hold of Declan's arm.

'Come on, you two. It's time to leave this showgirl and let the Aussie girls show you a good time. Annette's waiting for us in the car outside. Nice to see you again, Brian. You'd better make sure Jack's girl here gets home OK later. How many drinks have you all had?' she said, shaking her head.

Brian stood up to say goodbye to his mates and gave Gloria a peck on the cheek.

'Thanks for coming to say goodbye to Marleen with me,' shouted Mark over to Toby and Declan. 'It was a blast.'

'Nice to meet you too,' said Toby awkwardly. 'See you around.'

'You can count on it. Next time I'll come with Jack to the market.'

Toby suddenly looked horrified.

'Don't worry. I won't have a wig on.'

'Oh no, look, our Toby's upset now,' teased Declan. 'I think he was looking forward to introducing you to some of the other stallholders.'

'Can we get going, you two?' said Gloria.

'Hey Brian, good luck in Barcelona tomorrow, mate, get what I mean?' said Declan, with a thrusting hip movement.

Gloria whacked him on the back with her clutch bag.

'Come on, Annette will get clamped at this rate, and then we won't be going anywhere.'

After Declan, Toby and Gloria had left the bar, Brian and Mark decided to have one last drink before going home.

'To Marleen,' said Mark, raising his glass.

'To Marleen,' said Brian, beginning to enjoy the taste of absinthe.

'Right. Come on, gorgeous,' he said after they had finished their drinks. 'I've got an early start tomorrow. I need to see you home too.'

'My, how chivalrous of you, but there's really no need,' said Mark.

'I insist. Come on, we'll get the bus.'

Luckily, the bus to Tufnell Park arrived within a few minutes and there were only a handful of people on it.

'Be honest, Brian,' slurred Mark. 'How do I look? Before I say a final goodbye to Marleen I'd like a truthful opinion. I'll still be dressing up from time to time – maybe I'll be called Sherry, what do you think?'

'You make a very handsome woman.'

'Handsome! Great aunts are handsome!'

'OK, you're one of the most gorgeous looking ladies that I've ever met,' said Brian with a smile.

'That's much better,' said Mark, his grin returning, followed quickly by another pout. 'Only *one of* the most gorgeous?'

Brian laughed.

'All right, *the* most gorgeous. Is that good enough for you?'

Before Brian knew what had happened Mark had leaned over and planted a firm kiss on his lips.

'What was that for?'

'To say thanks. Your Jessica doesn't know what she's missing. I really hope you sort things out with her when you go tomorrow.'

'Cheers,' said Brian, wiping lipstick off his mouth.

It didn't take long for the bus to reach Tufnell Park and they got off close to the corner of Junction Road and Bickerton Road, next to a fish and chip shop. Brian wasn't used to travelling on buses at night with men dressed as women, though nobody had seemed to bat an eyelid. Although Mark did look very much the part, it was still fairly obvious that he was a man, particularly under the harsh lights of the bus. Now that they were walking outside it was much less clear. Mark linked arms with Brian as they staggered along.

'I don't often get escorted home in style like this,' he said, clearly enjoying Brian's consideration.

'We are both smashed and I just want to make sure that you get home safely. I wouldn't want you tripping over in those heels,' he laughed.

'Don't you go worrying about me. I could drink another five absinthes and still tap dance in these shoes! Come on, let's go down here and take a short cut.'

Mark led Brian down a narrow alleyway. The path was badly lit and Brian bumped into a large rubbish bin, banging his knee.

'Ouch, that hurt,' he cried, kicking it.

Mark chuckled.

'I'll kiss it better for you when we get back. It's only another five minutes from here if you can limp for that long?'

'Oh you will, will you?'

As they turned a corner someone jumped out from behind a hedge. It was very dark but Brian could still make out the glint of a knife, a quick flash reflecting the moonlight that briefly shone through the cloudy sky.

'Give me your wallet or the bitch gets it!' shouted the man as he grabbed Mark by the arm. The man pulled Mark around and held him tightly from behind, his forearm almost strangling him. Two other large men appeared from nowhere behind Brian. Brian knew that he'd had far too much to drink and that they were ill-equipped to resist weapons. He could just about see that the first man was now holding the knife up against Mark's throat.

'Just give it to him,' said Mark.

'Slowly,' said the first man as the other two closed in on Brian.

Brian took out his wallet and handed it over.

As the first man was putting Brian's wallet into his own pocket Mark seized the moment of distraction and wrestled himself free. He quickly swung around and kicked his captor firmly between the legs with the pointed toe of his right shoe. The man dropped his knife and reeled over in agony.

'You fucking bitch!' he yelled at Mark. 'I'll fucking fix you for that.'

One of the other two men had now grabbed Brian from behind and held him in a tight grip. The other landed a hefty punch in Brian's stomach.

'Get out of here,' Brian shouted at Mark before he received another punch in his side. 'Go on, run.'

For a split second Mark considered running away. But then instead he charged towards the man holding Brian and thumped him in the eye.

'Fuck you too!' shouted Mark, following the thump up with a sharp kick on the shin of one leg and a stamp with a stiletto heel on the foot of the other. 'Take that, you bastard!'

Brian was able to break free and he tried to hit one of his attackers, but the man dodged him. The man laughed as he took a step back before grabbing and twisting Brian's left leg so viciously that he cried out from the searing pain. The first man had now managed to stand up and he was running over towards Mark.

'You think you can fuck with me, you crazy bitch?' he shouted before landing a brutal punch between Mark's eyes, followed by another on his nose. Mark felt it burst and screamed, pulling his hands up over his face.

'Get off him,' cried Brian as he struggled to escape. A steel boot smashed into his arm and he heard it break. A numb, throbbing pain overtook everything as he fell to the ground like jelly. He couldn't hear Mark screaming any more, and the other voices started to fade too. Another kick landed in his thigh. He couldn't feel the pain this time. He was slipping under. Just before he lost consciousness he heard a splintering crack, like a coconut being smashed against a concrete wall. It was Mark's jaw being crushed beneath his attacker's foot. Brian's eyes started to flicker and close as another kick landed in his kidneys. Just before they closed he heard another sickening crack. This time it was Mark's skull.

Chapter 50

The plane landed with a thud at Heathrow. There had been a lot of turbulence throughout the flight and neither Jack nor Clare had been able to sleep a wink.

'How do I look?' asked Clare with dread, unfastening her seat belt.

'Honestly?'

'Thanks,' she groaned. 'I can't wait to get myself back home and into a nice hot, steaming bath. I am so tired. The trip was a blast, though, wasn't it? I'm really glad you could come. It wouldn't have been half as much fun without you there to play with.'

'You had Robert to play with, you brazen hussy.'

Clare smiled.

'He seemed to quite like me, but you know what? I think I'm going to leave it at that. Of course it's flattering - and God knows it makes a welcome change - but I'm not planning on seeing him again. He said he's in Europe on business quite often, but he's not really my type. Not bad in bed though, and he was very entertaining.'

'So what is your type then? Someone who is boring and crap in bed?'

'Very funny. I had a good night and just did what I wanted. I'm quite pleased with myself actually. I never once mentioned monogamous relationships.'

'You're not still hankering after Luke are you?'

'Of course I'm not, no. He was my type though – the bastard.'

'Well, good for you. I'm proud of you.'

'What did you think of Japan?' asked Clare, eager to get off the Luke subject.

'It was brilliant. Make sure you give Grace a thank you kiss from me.'

'I'd prefer to give her a black eye, but probably won't be brave enough.'

'I'd love to go again one day when I have some more money.'

'You seemed to be getting on well with Mrs Suzuki's son,' said Clare, narrowing her eyes. 'I hope you behaved yourself. And I hope you didn't say anything about his mother. She'll have me minced up like that reconstituted fish we had last night if you did.'

'Of course I didn't say anything – well, at least I don't think I did. Takeshi's a very attractive young man, don't you think? He did say something about maybe coming to London later this year. I was a bit tipsy, so it's all a bit of a blur.'

Clare started laughing.

'What's the matter?'

'I'm sorry, but I was just thinking about John Goldschmied's face when I threatened to expose him,' she said, still laughing. 'He didn't dare to even look at me again after that.'

'I'm not surprised. I almost feel sorry for him.'

'Don't even go there. He was vile - trust me.'

Jack wasn't listening any more. He was thinking about Mark.

'Should I call him or wait until he calls me?'

'I'm guessing you're talking about Mark and not Takeshi?'

'Of course I'm talking about Mark!'

'I know, I'm only teasing you. Does it matter who calls who? Just go for it.'

'I'll see if he calls me today, and if not, I'll call him tomorrow after I've had a good night's sleep.'

'There you go,' she said, handing Jack his bag that she had taken out of the overhead locker.

Thankfully the flight had been quite empty and they were spared the usual jostling throng to disembark. They only had hand luggage, so after their passports had been checked Clare and Jack went straight towards Arrivals.

'Can I just pop to the toilets?' asked Jack.

'Go ahead. I'll wait here,' said Clare, collapsing into a chair.

Jack washed his hands in the washbasin and splashed some cold water onto his face. He looked at his reflection in the mirror and saw dark rings around his eyes from lack of sleep.

'I look absolutely dreadful,' he complained to Clare after coming back out.

'No, you don't. Perhaps not your best, but I've seen you look worse.'

'Great! That's cheered me up!'

'Have you turned your phone back on yet? You might have a message from Mark.'

'No, I haven't. Good point.'

After a few moments Jack's phone beeped. It was a voicemail message.

'This is probably him,' said Jack, nodding at his phone, putting it to his ear.

His face paled as he listened.

'What's wrong?' asked Clare.

Jack said nothing as he heard the rest of the message, holding his hand up over his mouth.

'Jack, what is it?'

'It's from Rachel. She says I've got to call her as soon as we land. Something awful has happened,' he said grabbing hold of Clare's hand.

'You're scaring me, Jack. What is it?'

'It's Brian. He's been attacked. He's in hospital.'

Chapter 51

Rachel was waiting for them at the Royal Free Hospital when Jack and Clare arrived. They had come straight from the airport after they had spoken to her to find out which hospital they were at. The adrenaline from the shock was racing through their veins, keeping them both wide awake.

It had been a passer-by that had discovered the battered and bleeding bodies lying in the alleyway. The police came with the ambulance and they'd found Brian's phone in the dirt. Jack's number was in there as his first emergency contact, but the police had been unable to get through to him. Then they'd tried his second emergency contact, and that was Rachel. She had flown over to London from Berlin on the first flight on Saturday morning.

'Oh, thank God you're here,' croaked Rachel, hugging Clare and then Jack.

'We came as soon as we could,' said Jack. 'How is he?'

'He's still unconscious,' said Rachel, who looked like she hadn't slept for days. 'I've been sitting with him all afternoon, talking to him, but he just won't come around. The doctors said that it happens sometimes after such a brutal attack, but I'm starting to get worried.'

'What the hell happened to him?' asked Clare, her voice trembling.

'The police don't know for sure. Neither of them had any money on them when the police searched them so they think it was a random mugging that somehow went wrong. It probably ended up being more brutal than it was intended to be.'

'What do you mean *them*? Who was Brian with?' asked Jack.

'That's the weird thing. He was found lying next to a transvestite in North London. She was pronounced dead on the scene. It just doesn't make any sense, does it? Why would Brian be walking down a dark alley with a transvestite on a Friday night?'

'What did the police have to say? Do they know who the other person was?' asked Clare.

'No, they don't. There was no purse, no handbag and no phone - nothing. The police have asked me how Brian might have known a transvestite, but I had to say I had no idea. And of course Brian can't help, because he's still unconscious. I should warn you that he looks terrible. They broke both his arms and a leg. He's got a lot of internal bruising too. The doctors say he's lucky to be alive. They think the passer-by that called the ambulance must have disturbed the attackers. She was walking her dogs at the time.'

'This is awful,' said Jack solemnly. 'How will he manage with two broken arms? He was supposed to be going to Barcelona today to find Jessica. What was he doing down an alley in North London?'

'Can we see him?' asked Clare, wringing her hands.

'We should be able to. Come on - let's go over to the ward. Follow me - it's this way.'

The hospital was a bustling hive of activity - not quite what Jack expected for a Saturday night. He wasn't quite sure what he was expecting, but it wasn't this. Scores of people were being wheeled around on trollies and carried on stretchers by tired-looking nurses. It was noisy too, with the patients, doctors and nurses all talking and sometimes shouting in a multitude of languages - even more languages than you would hear on Dalston market on a busy Saturday morning.

'He's down here,' said Rachel, leading Jack and Clare

down a long, soulless corridor, after they had come out of the lift. The entrance to the small ward was guarded by a young nurse.

'Hello again, Magda,' said Rachel, as warmly as she could muster. 'Is it OK to go in and see Brian?'

'Yes it is, but I'm afraid visiting time will finish in twenty minutes,' she answered. 'He woke up forty minutes ago, but he is very tired.'

'He's come around? Oh, thank God!'

There were three beds in the ward on the right hand side of the room before Brian's bed next to the window. Two of the occupants seemed to be asleep and the third was reading a book. He nodded at them as they walked past. The curtain around Brian's bed was drawn and Rachel pulled it back a little so that they could go through.

Brian was lying on his bed with both his arms and his right leg covered with a heavy looking plaster. A drip was inserted into the crook of his right arm and he was wearing an oxygen mask. His eyes were open. He just managed a slight wave with the fingers of his left hand.

'Oh, Brian,' said Rachel, rushing in. 'I am so pleased to see you awake. I was worried that you… well, you know. Look who's here to see you,' she said as Clare and Jack filed in behind her through the gap in the curtains. Jack was horrified by what he saw.

'It must have been awful,' said Clare, sitting down on the edge of the bed, gently stroking Brian's fingers, and giving them a very light squeeze. The plaster came right down to cover most of the palms of his hands, leaving only the fingers exposed.

Jack sat down on a tatty chair next to the bed, taking care not to trip over the tube that was connected to Brian's arm.

'I just can't believe it. Look at you! Who on earth did this?'

'Don't, Jack,' said Clare. 'You heard what the nurse said. Just be glad he's alive and conscious for now.'

Brian wiggled a finger to point towards the oxygen mask. He obviously needed help to take it off.

'Are you sure it's OK to take this off?' asked Rachel cautiously.

Brian nodded, so Rachel carefully lifted the mask up over his nose and unhooked it from behind his ears. He looked across to Jack, but before he could say anything he started to cry.

'I'm so sorry, Jack,' he sobbed, tears flowing down his tired-looking cheeks. 'I couldn't do anything to stop them.'

'Hey, come on, stop it,' said Jack softly. 'What have you got to be sorry about? Just look at you.'

Rachel sat down on the chair next to Jack's.

'There were three of them. It all happened so quickly. If we hadn't drunk so much I would have been quicker. I would have been able to fight back.'

'There, there,' soothed Rachel, leaning over to wipe his tears with a tissue that she had in her pocket. 'Don't tire yourself out.'

'He was doing it for you, Jack. He said he loved you and that you meant the world to him. You have to know that,' said Brian, his voice trembling.

'I don't understand,' said Jack with a frown, looking over at Clare and Rachel.

They just shook their heads blankly and gave him a shrug as if to say that they had no idea what he was talking about either.

'I think we should let him rest,' said Clare. 'He's obviously been through hell and back and is in a lot of pain. He must be exhausted too, and probably isn't thinking straight after being drugged up to the eyeballs. Maybe we should go home now and come back tomorrow morning.'

Brian shook his head.

'He told me he loved you.'

'What do you mean? Who loved me? What are you talking about?'

'Mark. He was saying goodbye so that he could be with you,' said Brian, holding Jack's confused gaze. 'He asked me

340

to go out for some drinks with him. Toby and Declan came too. I was supposed to be making sure he got home safely,' said Brian, his face crumpling again. 'I'm sorry, Jack.'

'What do you keep saying you're sorry for? Has something happened to Mark? Where is he?'

'Oh no, please no,' said Clare, quickly filling in the gaps.

'The police have just been back in to ask me some questions. They told me that Mark didn't make it. It was too late before the ambulance got to us. Mark's dead, Jack. He's dead.'

Jack couldn't take it in. His hands started to shake while his brain was still catching up. Mark was saying goodbye, having a night out with Brian, and is now dead? It was madness.

'But the police said you were found together with a transvestite who was killed at the scene,' said Rachel.

Clare stood up and put her hands gently on Jack's shoulders. She felt a lump growing in her throat and tears began to well up in her eyes.

'You're telling me that it was *Mark* that was dressed up with you last night?' said Jack.

'He said that he wanted to say goodbye to Marleen, to be how you wanted him to be. I thought he was leaving town when he asked me to go for a drink to say goodbye. When he arrived at the pub he was already dressed up, you know, in a wig and that. He said that it was going to be the last time for Marleen and that he loved you. He was going to surprise you and meet you at the airport.'

Brian's eyes had started to flutter and his words were becoming less clear.

'It's all right,' said Rachel, reaching over to put his oxygen mask back on. 'Don't tire yourself out. You've been badly hurt and you need to rest to get better. It wasn't your fault,' she said, gently stroking his forehead.

'Oh Jack, I'm so sorry,' said Clare putting her arms around him, holding him closely.

Jack just sat there, completely numb, as if he wasn't

actually in the same room as the others any more. He couldn't think about Mark lying dead and cold in a dark and dank alleyway. He couldn't think about him lying stiff and white in a hospital drawer. He was thinking about how he had planned to tell Mark that he wanted to accept him as he was and carry on, at least giving it a go. He was thinking about how much he liked him and how much he wanted to hear his laugh again. He was thinking about how he had been looking forward to passionately making love with him and then snuggling up together, in a warm and cosy bed.

Chapter 52

The train from London Kings Cross to Newcastle Central Station was on time and very quiet. Jack had been pleased that Clare had wanted to come with him to the funeral and was able to take the day off work. The morgue had been dreadful. So cold, so unlike any place he'd ever been to. The police had asked him if he could provide a provisional identification of the body. Jack had confirmed that the body was that of Mark Sullivan, aged just twenty-nine. He'd also told the police where Mark lived in Tufnell Park. They had tracked down and contacted his mother in Newcastle, and then broken her heart.

Understandably, the police had wanted to ask Jack some questions, and he had helped them as much as he could. In particular they had asked if Jack knew anyone else connected with Mark who might have wanted to harm him, but Jack hadn't been able to offer anything. Brian had told him that the attackers had definitely wanted to mug them and that it had turned nasty after Mark had bravely fought back. For that reason Jack thought it couldn't have been anything to do with Mark's clientele or other acquaintances. Brian didn't think it was a homophobic attack either. In fact, they probably hadn't even guessed that Mark was actually a man - it had been so dark. They had wanted their money.

Jack had talked all this through with Clare and they'd decided that he shouldn't go into any detail about other aspects of Mark's life with the police. If they already knew something they could follow that up themselves. Jack hadn't wanted to add any further distress or upset to what his family would be already going through. As it turned out, the police were satisfied that the attack probably hadn't been a pre-meditated murder. As far as they had told Jack, they didn't have much to go on in terms of who the attackers were, though they had managed to get some DNA evidence from both Brian's and Mark's bodies.

With the agreement of Mark's mother, they had then released the body for the funeral. In return for his help Jack had asked the police if they would pass on his telephone number to Mark's mother, along with a request for her to call him. He wanted to go to the funeral, but only if she invited him to attend. Jack had been so thankful when she got in touch with the details of when and where the funeral would be. She'd sounded genuinely warm when she asked if he would like to come.

The service and burial were to take place today in a small church in North Shields, just outside Newcastle. Clare and Jack planned to get a taxi from the station to the church, which would be easier than trying to negotiate the buses.

'Is it really only five days since we got back from Japan?' he asked Clare, taking a sip of his steaming coffee. 'It feels more like five years.'

'I know. I can't believe it either. Are you sure you're up to this, Jack?'

'Not really,' he answered, staring out of the window as they passed through the Yorkshire countryside. 'It still hasn't really sunk in that Mark's gone forever. I know we were only together for a short time, but somehow that makes it even worse than if we'd been together for twenty years. We've been robbed of that possibility - the years stolen away from us before we could share them together. I mean, I'm not stupid. We might not have lasted for two months, but now we won't even have the chance to try. We'll never know.'

'It's not fair, is it?' said Clare. 'He was one in a million.'

'He was certainly that all right,' said Jack with a smile. 'The poor sod. He was always so bloody determined. I just can't believe that we were *this* close to getting back together, and that Brian and Mark were *that* close to making it home that night,' he said, his smile vanishing. 'I should be taking him out for lunch or something today, not going to his funeral, seeing him lying in a wooden box. Brian should be in Barcelona talking to Jessica, not lying with broken bones in a hospital.'

'It's all too awful. And I know it's not much comfort to you today, but at least Brian's still alive. We could have lost both of them,' said Clare.

'Of course I'm relieved Brian's alive. Jesus, if he had been killed too, I don't know what I would have done. It doesn't even bear thinking about.'

Clare shook her head and sighed as she drank her coffee, looking out of the window at a flock of sheep looking after their baby lambs in the fields.

'Wasn't it mad though that Brian and Mark were out together like that?' said Jack. 'And I believe Brian when he said that he was trying to make sure that Mark got home safely.'

'What do you mean, you *believe* Brian?' she asked, putting down her plastic cup on the table. 'You don't seriously think there was any other reason for them walking home together, do you? Come on, Jack - this is Brian we're talking about, one of your best friends. Stop being silly.'

'I know it's stupid, but the whole thing is just so bizarre. Why did Mark want to go out with Brian in the first place?'

'Like Brian said, to end that chapter in his life, ready for when you came back,' said Clare, looking closely into Jack's eyes. 'Try and stop raking it all over and just accept what Brian has already told you. Mark wasn't interested in Brian and I'm very sure that Brian wasn't interested in Mark - not in that way. So stop this right now. Trust your friends.'

'I know, you're right. I'm being stupid. I'm just looking for a reason, that's all.'

'You don't need to look any further. Mark loved you, Jack. That's the reason. Brian was trying to help, in the best possible way that a friend could help. How would you have felt if you had found out that Brian had left Mark very drunk and alone and then this had happened? You'd never have forgiven Brian, and he would never have forgiven himself.'

'I'm sorry. I shouldn't have even thought what I just said. I'm just so upset.'

'Come here,' said Clare, drawing Jack's head onto her shoulder as he started to cry. 'There, there. It's been a horrible week and your emotions are all over the place.'

The weather improved as the train headed further north and patches of blue sky started to peek through from behind the clouds as they began to disperse. Rachel hadn't really known Mark, apart from what she had been told by Jack and Clare. She'd decided not to go with them to the funeral and that she would be more use visiting Brian in hospital instead. Heike had been really supportive and Rachel had stayed in London since the attack. She'd also been able to use the time to talk to Edward about her pregnancy and decide what they should do next about their marriage.

'I'm glad Rachel's here to visit Brian,' said Clare. 'I know he's had loads of other visitors, but she's been there practically all the time. It's nice that Heike's been over too. She's been great. He said he really appreciates it.'

'I'll go and visit more after today,' said Jack.

The doctors had said he was healing well, but that they wanted to keep him in for a little while longer to do a few more internal tests.

After arriving in Newcastle the pair continued their journey by taxi to the church in North Shields. Jack was staring out of the taxi window. This was the place where Mark had grown up, and this was the place that he had escaped from, to live freely and be himself. Now he had returned home prematurely. The church was tiny and stood on the outskirts of town. It was built from sandstone and had a small but pretty graveyard to the rear. The graves were beautifully maintained and lovingly adorned with flowers and plants.

It surprised Jack that there were only a handful of people inside the church for the service. They took a place on the right-hand side, a few rows from the front. An elderly woman wearing a black veil was sitting on the front row. Mark had said that his mum had been relatively old when she'd had him so Jack guessed it must be her. He would try and speak with her after the service was over. A thick set, younger man sat next to her on her left and a small girl was sitting on the other side.

The service itself was short, with only two hymns. The vicar did a good job, but obviously didn't actually know Mark, judging by the sometimes impersonal references and remembrances. There were no family tributes, so Jack decided not to get up and say anything out of respect for his mother's feelings. He would say his own personal goodbyes to Mark the next day, in private.

The coffin was laid out at the front of the church, carefully dressed with wreaths of white carnations spelling out the word 'SON'. Jack could hear Mark's mum crying as the service drew to a close, before the vicar gave Mark's soul over to God. He watched in silence as the coffin was carried outside by the undertakers. He and Clare were last to file out into the cemetery and to follow the small troupe towards what would be Mark's final physical resting place.

They stood motionless around the hole that had been freshly dug into the ground.

Jack watched as the coffin was slowly lowered down. He felt deeply sad at the thought of how cold it was going to be, buried deep beneath the earth. He laid the flowers they had brought at the side of the grave and then threw a pinch of soil onto the coffin. It was at that moment that Jack finally came to accept that Mark was gone and that he wasn't coming back. Tears rolled down his cheeks as he said a prayer for him.

Clare squeezed his hand.

'That's it, just let it all out.'

'It's so very sad,' he cried, wiping his eyes.

347

After a while they stepped back from the grave and Jack noticed a woman wearing a black chinchilla coat and matching hat standing a few yards away, next to an oak tree. The woman seemed to sense that someone was looking at her, and her eyes caught Jack's for a moment, before he looked quickly away. She pulled up the collar of her coat and then turned to go.

Mark's mum was now walking over towards them.

'Hello, love. I'm Betty, Mark's mum. You must be Jack.'

'Hello, Mrs Sullivan,' he said, extending a hand. 'This is my friend Clare. She knew Mark too. It was a lovely service.'

'I'm glad you liked it,' said Betty, dabbing her eyes with a handkerchief. 'It's such a tragic waste. He was a good lad.'

'He was the best,' said Jack, patting her arm.

'He was a bit of a troubled soul, our Mark. He was sometimes confused about who he was,' she said, letting out a little laugh.

'He used to borrow my make-up and put on my clothes and never thought I'd noticed, bless him. I still loved him - how couldn't I? He had a heart of gold, he did,' she said. She started to cry. 'He told me he was very fond of you, love. He wanted to bring you up to see me for a Sunday lunch one weekend. I'm glad you were friends,' she said, gently kissing him on the cheek. 'You look like a kind young man.'

Jack's own tears began to well up again as her soft, old skin touched his. It felt as delicate as rice paper and as comforting as only a mother's love can be.

'Thanks, Mrs Sullivan, that means a lot to me.'

'You're both welcome to come back to the house for a drink and a sandwich.'

'That's very nice of you, thanks, but we've got to be heading back down to London,' said Jack, taking hold of both of Betty's hands.

'If you need any help with anything in London, just let me know. You've got my number.'

'Thanks love, but I think we'll be all right. Our Wayne's been down to sort out his things, you know,' said Betty, motioning towards the good-looking fellow who'd been sitting next to her during the service. Wayne was Mark's older brother.

Clare shot Jack a look that said, 'Oh my goodness! What will he make of Mark's accessories?'

'Thanks again for coming. Goodbye, love,' said Betty.

'Goodbye, Mrs Sullivan. It was nice to meet you,' said Clare as they turned to leave.

Their taxi was waiting for them around the corner to take them back to Newcastle to get the train.

'So that's that,' said Jack. 'Four weeks ago I didn't even know Mark and now he's in a box, six feet under.'

'I know it's tough. You need to give yourself some time. One of the hard bits is behind you now.'

'I'll never forget him. Tomorrow I'll go to the park and say my own goodbyes.'

They sat in silence for a while as the train headed south, zipping through towns and villages.

'Did you see that woman with the fur coat and hat?' he asked Clare suddenly.

'Sort of. Why do you ask?'

'I know her from somewhere, but I can't remember where,' he said slowly. 'I'm sure that she's got something to do with Brian.'

'Brian?'

'That's it,' he said with a start. 'She was at the furniture competition in Hoxton that Brian and I went to. Do you remember us telling you about it?'

'Yes, of course I do. How could I forget? But why was she at Mark's funeral?'

It was all coming back to him now, but he was as puzzled as Clare as to why she had been there.

'She's called Doris. Doris Elliott.'

Chapter 53

It was very peaceful in St James's Park. The morning sun was shining and Jack was sitting on the same bench where he and Mark had first met only a few weeks ago. The bench was on the north side of the park, next to the water and close to the café. He just sat there, staring out onto the calm lake. It was glistening with the reflections of the cherry trees. A lone moorhen suddenly squawked, momentarily breaking the tranquillity. Jack looked over towards Horse Guards Parade. How many of the Glorious Dead had been remembered and celebrated there, he wondered. Jack had always loved the skyline behind it, a jigsaw of grey and white turrets and spires from the tops of stone buildings that all came together to resemble a Persian palace. He thought it was beautiful.

A couple of middle-aged men walked past in front of him. They were wearing identical beige riding boots and looked as if they had been together for decades. Would he and Mark have been wearing coordinated clothes if they'd been together for many years? Matching wigs and tutus perhaps, he thought fondly. Two black swans were swimming over towards the edge of the water next to where Jack was sitting. They were Mark's swans, the same pair that they'd seen when they had met. Mark had said that swans mate for life.

A group of tourists had now gathered next to the lake and were feeding the birds. The earlier silence was now completely shattered by hundreds of crying moorhens and wrens, diving and fighting for food, as if they hadn't eaten for weeks. Then, as quickly as it had started, the racket stopped dead. The birds dispersed as the last piece of bread was devoured - the bread of life.

Mark's life had been too short, blown out too soon. Ended before he had had chance to tell Jack that he'd loved him. Brian had told him that Mark had said that. Now they had been cruelly torn apart and he wouldn't have the chance either to tell Mark how he felt about him.

They had laughed and cried and shared a few wonderful weeks together. Mark had lived the life that he had wanted to live, making his own path and finding his own way. Mark had made him feel very special and Jack knew he would never forget him. His short cropped hair and crooked smile, his strong hands and warm heart.

He didn't know quite how long he sat there, just staring at the water. Sometimes he closed his eyes, letting the warm sunshine caress his face. A cavalier King Charles spaniel wandered over and was wagging his tail, sniffing at Jack's feet.

'Hello,' said Jack, stroking his head as the dog looked up at him with big trusting eyes.

'Sam, come on!' shouted the dog's owner, walking ahead.

Sam licked his hand before scampering off.

Jack got up from his bench with a sigh and walked over to the water's edge. The swans had started to swim away.

'Take good care of each other,' he said after them.

'Goodbye, Mark. Sleep well.'

Chapter 54

It was one week later and Brian was still in hospital. The doctors had carried out some more tests to make sure there wasn't any other lasting damage to any of his internal organs in addition to his broken bones and bruises. The nurses had just finished their morning rounds and visiting time was about to start.

'How's the patient this morning?' asked Jack, striding over towards him, putting some fresh grapes into the bowl on his bedside table.

Brian was sitting up in bed with both of his arms in slings and his plastered leg stretched out, resting on a support.

'Feeling like Tutankhamen, but much better thanks.'

Jack smiled.

'I still can't move my arms or right leg, but at least I can breathe now, without it hurting. Are those from the market?' asked Brian, nodding towards the grapes.

'Dalston's finest. Toby and Declan both said to say hello. They will come and visit you tomorrow. Gloria sends her best wishes too. She feels really bad about not staying around in the pub longer that night. She thinks that if she had, then maybe you'd all have stayed together and none of this would have happened.'

'Tell her not to be silly. What's the point in 'ifs and maybes'? If we'd left the pub later then we might have been knocked over by a lorry instead. What's done is done.'

Jack was looking down at his hands.

'Oh I'm sorry, mate. That must have sounded very insensitive.'

'No, it's fine. You're right. We can't turn the clock back. If we could I'd never have gone to Tokyo in the first place and the two of you would never have even been out that night.'

'How are you coping?' asked Brian.

'All right, I suppose. I know I have to move on, and I will, but it's only been a week since the funeral.'

'You're doing really well. Don't rush it.'

'What's the food like?' asked Jack, changing the subject.

'Delicious. The chefs come around every evening and prepare all of our meals individually to order at our bedsides.'

'I bet they do,' said Jack, grinning.

'Can you pour me some orange juice?' asked Brian. 'I'm parched.'

'Is it down here in the cupboard?' asked Jack, bending down.

'Yes. There should be some glasses and straws in that tray next to the door you came in through.'

A few moments later Jack came back with two glasses and a straw. He poured them both some juice and put a straw into one of the glasses.

'I'm sorry it can't be a Bucks Fizz, but you're not allowed to drink until you finish your antibiotics,' said Jack holding the glass up to Brian's mouth so that he could reach the straw.

He took a long slurp.

'Aaaghh,' sighed Brian, 'I needed that. Cheers.'

Jack put the glass down on the bedside table for him.

'The police have been in again to see me. They asked a few more questions,' said Brian.

'Oh yeah? Have they got any ideas yet about who did it?'

'Not really. They don't seem to have any leads to follow up. They wanted to know if I could remember anything else about what happened or give them any sort of descriptions. It was so dark, though, and I could hardly see a thing. I think they were all white and about five foot ten or so, but I can't really be sure.'

'I hope they find the bastards and put them away forever.'

'So do I, but don't count on it. People get away with all sorts these days.'

'Brian, I have to tell you something.'

'What is it?'

'I don't quite know how to say this, but I have to. You're one of my two closest friends and I can't believe that I doubted you for even a second.'

'What are you talking about?'

'For some reason I thought that something was going on with you and Mark and that's why you were walking him home,' muttered Jack, waiting for Brian to explode.

'You thought what? Are you mad?'

'I know and I'm so sorry. It just all sounded so crazy, you know, what you told me about Mark saying goodbye and dressing up as Marleen and then you and the lads out with him for drinks. For a stupid moment I thought that you were both so drunk and that you... well, I don't need to spell it out, do I?'

Brian was shaking his head.

'What are you like?' he said. 'As if I'd do that.'

'I know. I've been on an emotional rollercoaster. You were trying to protect him and I should have been thanking you, not accusing you, especially after all you've been through. There, I've told you now. Do you want me to leave?'

'Of course! Nurse, please can you escort this man off the premises?'

Jack got up to go.

'I'm only joking, stupid. Forget about it. It's easy to get the wrong end of the stick sometimes.'

'Really? You forgive me?'

'I didn't say that,' joked Brian. 'But I'm sure I can think of a suitable penance for you.'

'Hello, Brian darling! Goodness, look at you. What a fright!'

Jack turned around.

It was Donald, closely followed by Tom.

'Hi, Donald,' said Brian. 'Excuse me if I don't get up, won't you?'

'Hello,' said Jack.

'All right, mate,' said Tom first to Brian and then to Jack, giving him a firm handshake. 'Good to see you again,' he said to Jack. 'Sorry to hear about your friend.'

'Thanks, Tom.'

'Those savage brutes want executing when they find them,' said Donald, turning to face Jack with outstretched hands.

Jack took hold of them.

'Thanks, Donald. It's been a tough week, but we're getting there.'

'If there's anything I can do to help, anything at all, just let me know.'

'I will. Thanks.'

'Do you think they have a vase for these flowers?' asked Donald, placing a large bouquet of dahlias on the windowsill.

'There's one on the table behind you. The guy went home this morning and must have forgotten it,' said Brian.

'Splendid! Tom, would you be a dear and just put these flowers into the vase with a drop of water?'

'Sure,' said Tom, taking the flowers.

'Now, I've brought you some home-made beef broth and spinach tartlets to help build your strength back up,' said Donald, reaching into a cotton bag to take out a large flask and a Tupperware box. 'I'm sure the food in here must be horrendous.'

'Cheers, Donald. You're my Florence Nightingale.'

Tom came back with the vase of flowers and put it down on the table next to the bed.

'They're nice, thanks,' said Brian, with a sigh. 'I was supposed to be going to Barcelona to try and speak to your daughter - and now look at me. What a mess.'

'I know, dear. It's a terrible thing. I told her about what happened.'

'You did?' asked Brian.

'I hope you don't mind. I don't want to interfere.'

'No, no, that's great. I mean, I'm just surprised, that's all - because you didn't want me to go over and see her.'

'You're right - I didn't think the timing was the best.'

'What did she say?'

'She said it sounded awful and that she hoped you'll start to feel better soon.'

'That's it?' asked Brian, his disappointment clear.

'Pretty much. Why? What else should she be saying?'

'I don't know. Oh, never mind,' said Brian, thinking that he might as well just give up on the whole stupid idea. It was obviously never going to happen, but he shouldn't be blaming Donald. 'Thanks for letting her know. I appreciate it.'

'How long are they going to keep you in here?' Donald asked.

'Only another couple of days. All the tests were fine, so it's just down to these,' he answered, motioning towards his arms and right leg with his chin. 'The doctors said it will be another four to six weeks before they heal, but that I should make a good recovery and have full use of them, which is great news. I was so worried I might not be able to work properly afterwards.'

'If I can help, just tip me the wink,' said Tom.

'Cheers, mate. Actually, if there's any way you could keep an eye on the workshop for me, I'd be really grateful. There are a couple of small jobs that I was in the middle of that I think you could finish, if you have any spare time.'

'Sorted. I've got the keys. Don't you worry about nothing.'

'But how will you manage at home on your own?' asked Donald, concerned.

'Oh, I'll be fine. The hospital is sorting me out with a couple of care workers.'

'No, they won't,' said Jack.

'What do you mean?'

'You won't need them. You're coming home with me.'

'Don't be daft, Jack. I mean thanks a million, but I can hardly, you know, by myself … ' said Brian, his voice trailing off.

'It's fine, Brian. You're coming home with me and that's final. I'm not working at the moment, so I've got the time. You're my friend and I'm going to look after you for a change.'

Chapter 55

Jack had spent all of Saturday tidying and cleaning his flat in preparation for Brian's arrival. Brian was being released from hospital today. Jack had also been shopping and bought enough food and drinks to feed an army. There was no way he would be able to get Brian up and down the stairs on his own to the second bedroom, so the living room would have to be Brian's home for the next few weeks. Jack had moved the sofa bed over to the corner so that it faced out onto the terrace.

The nurses had shown Jack how to get Brian up out of bed and help him to move from A to B. They had practiced in hospital, but it certainly wasn't going to be easy. Jack had been round to Brian's flat with his spare key to pick up some clothes and other bits and pieces. The hospital had given Jack a commode in case it wasn't possible to negotiate the toilet, but it was old and unsightly and Jack had bought a new one.

'What time did they say they would be bringing him?' asked Clare, folding away one of the Sunday papers she had been reading.

It was raining outside and they were having brunch indoors.

'He should be here any time now,' he answered, looking at his watch. 'I don't know why, but I feel really nervous.'

'It's bound to be a bit strange, for both of you. I'm sure Brian appreciates what you're about to do for him, but it's going to be really hard work for you looking after him. If there's anything I can do, just let me know.'

'Thanks. I know it will be tough, but I want to do it. It'll be fine. Besides, it'll help take my mind off things.'

'More coffee?'

'Yes, please,' she said, following him through to the kitchen. 'Guess who called me?'

'Who?'

'Robert Kaaps, the guy I met at the dinner in Tokyo.'

'You mean the guy you used and abused,' said Jack, pouring her coffee.

'I wasn't that bad,' she laughed, 'but it was such a refreshing change, and very liberating. I think that's the first time I've met somebody half decent and just gone into it for the sex, and enjoyed letting them do the romantic chasing afterwards.'

'You're all woman. So what did he want?'

'Me, of course. He's going to be in London in a couple of months and was hoping we could 'catch up' - but I'm not sure it's a good idea. I'm happy to leave it as just being a wild one-night stand that I will always remember being in control of, physically and emotionally. It was you that said that I shouldn't behave like a hormonal tarantula, wasn't it?'

'Yes, but if the guy is clearly chasing you, and you like him, maybe you should go for it.'

'Hmm - we'll see.'

Jack's doorbell rang.

'That'll be them,' said Jack, jumping up with a start to open the door.

A few moments later two paramedics were carrying Brian upstairs on a stretcher.

'I hope I'm not late for the party,' said Brian. 'I'm gagging for a beer.'

Jack held the door open as wide as he could so that the stretcher could be manoeuvred around the bend.

'Where do you want him?' the younger paramedic asked Jack in a New Zealand accent.

'Let me see now. I'll have him sitting up on the sofa bed,' said Jack suggestively.

The paramedic smiled at him.

'Right you are, fella.'

'If you think you're going to be able to take advantage of me while I'm in this compromised state, you can think again,' joked Brian, relieved to be out of hospital and back home among his friends.

The paramedics put the stretcher down on the floor and pulled Brian up, so that he was sitting with his back against the wall. Jack then had a go at helping Brian to stand up, putting his arms under Brian's and leveraging him into a standing position with Brian pressing down with his left leg. They were a bit wobbly, but somehow managed it.

'Well done!' said Clare, 'I think you've found a new vocation.'

The paramedics clapped and whistled.

Now they had to have a go at sitting Brian back down again.

'Are you ready?' asked Jack.

'As I'll ever be.'

The first time was clumsy, but Brian did end up ensconced on the sofa bed in an upright position with no additional injuries.

'If you need anything or have any questions don't hesitate to give us a call,' said the younger paramedic, extending his hand towards Jack.

'Thanks. I will,' said Jack, grinning at him before shaking his hand.

'Cheers for all your help, guys. Take care,' shouted Brian after them.

'You'll be wanting that beer then?'

'Can't wait,'

'I'll get it,' said Clare. 'Jack, what are you having?'

'White wine for me please.'

Brian soon had his beer on the tray that Clare had put in front of him. He didn't want to try holding a glass yet with just his fingers and he had been told to keep his arms in the slings for as long as possible each day. Jack had popped a straw into his glass and Brian sucked hard on it, almost emptying his glass in one mouthful.

'That tastes so good. You've no idea.'

'It's nice to have you home,' said Jack.

Brian took a moment to look around his new temporary bedroom. Jack had put a small chest of drawers next to the sofa-bed, with a reading lamp on top. Then he noticed an odd looking chair that had been positioned close by, in the corner of the room.

'What's that?'

'That's a commode I bought for you. It's much nicer than the one the hospital gave me. Do you like it?'

'You've got to be kidding.'

'You're right. I knew I should have bought the green one. The pink is a bit much, isn't it? I'll take it back and change it for you tomorrow,' said Jack, trying to suppress a smirk.

'It's not the fucking colour! I've been managing to get to the lav with a bit of help, thank you very much.'

'I know, but it's really narrow in the washroom on this floor and I'm not sure we'll be able to sit you down safely. We don't want any more broken bones, do we now?'

'I want to at least fucking try! And can you drop the 'we' talk. I'm injured, not two years old.'

'My gran had a commode once,' chipped in Clare with a laugh. 'She loved it. It used to be just in front of her bay window. She said she enjoyed catching the sun while she was on it.'

'Well that must have been very nice for her. Why not just put it on the terrace and then all your neighbours can watch?'

'What a good idea,' said Jack, standing up.

'Just you sit down,' said Brian, trying to kick him as Jack dodged his good foot. 'You can get me another beer while you're up, though.'

'The girls got back to Berlin all right,' said Jack, closing the fridge door. 'I spoke to Rachel this morning.'

'Oh, good. It was great having Rachel home again, though,' said Brian. 'She should persuade Heike to move to London.'

'I don't think there's much chance of that happening just yet. She seems to be quite happy over there,' said Clare.

'Maybe once the babies are born she'll feel differently. I still can't quite believe she's having twins, can you?'

'I can,' said Brian. 'She showed me the latest scan yesterday and there are definitely two of them.'

'Oh, it's so sweet,' said Jack. 'Just imagine - two identical baby boys. Clare and I have offered our babysitting services to help out, haven't we Clare?'

'Nappy changers at the ready! I can't wait.'

'I'm looking forward to pushing them around too. Good job they're not here just yet, though,' said Brian, nodding at his arms.

They all laughed.

Jack got them all another drink. 'Guess who we saw at Mark's funeral?' he asked Brian after he'd sat down again. 'You won't be able to, so I'll just tell you. It was your friend Doris.'

'Doris?'

'Yes, Doris Elliott, your exhibition hostess and customer, remember?'

'Right,' said Brian puzzled. 'What was she doing there?'

'That's what I thought. I've absolutely no idea. I don't know if she recognised me or not. I only caught her eye for a split second and then she scuttled off. I wonder how she knew Mark.'

'That's weird, isn't it?' said Brian, noisily finishing off his glass of beer through the straw.

'Hang on a minute,' said Clare. 'Doris, you say her name was? Mark told me about a Doris. I didn't remember on the train coming back from the funeral, but I do now.'

Jack and Brian both stared at her.

'He did?' asked Jack.

'She was a domina. He told me how he met her doing a building job and that he ended up being her apprentice. She taught Mark how to be Marleen.'

'Doris Elliott is a domina?' asked Jack.

'Well, I don't know if she still is or even if it's the same

Doris, but I can't think of any other reason why she would have been there.'

Jack turned to Brian.

'What's your opinion? You slept with her.'

Brian was caught off-guard and coughed.

'It was only a quick one! How would I know?'

'Did she tie you up or beat you with a cane or whip?' laughed Clare.

'No, she did not! What do you think I am?'

'How about drip hot wax onto you or bind you in a latex body wrap with a breathing control mask?' chipped in Jack.

'Very funny. No, sorry to disappoint you. She was as gentle as a kitten.'

'It doesn't really matter any more anyway, does it?' said Jack. 'Good luck to her, I say.'

'To change the subject, now that we've closed the Japanese deal my boss Grace has got me researching a new market. I'm quite excited about it, actually. It's Australia!'

'Australia?' cried Jack. 'You lucky cow! I would love to go there. If you need an assistant I'm free at the moment.'

'Hang on a minute. I won't be going out there just yet, not before I've done a desk-research report for her and that could take a couple of months.'

'Still, that's something to look forward to,' said Brian.

'Anyway boys, I'll have to love you and leave you. I'm seeing some old friends in town,' she said, getting up. 'Have a good night.'

'Thanks for coming to my welcome home party.'

'Yes, well just you take things slowly and don't go overdoing it. I'll pop around one night this week.'

'I'll have to check my diary, but I think I'll probably be at home.'

'See you again soon,' said Clare, kissing them both goodbye before she left.

'She seems a lot more relaxed now,' said Brian after she'd gone.

'Isn't she just? She's like a new woman now that the Japan deal is sorted out. That, and the night she spent with a South African knickers salesman in Tokyo.'

'What's that? Nobody told me about it. Come on, spill the beans.'

'I'll tell you later. Now, what do you want for your tea? There's chicken stew or chicken stew.'

'I think I'll have chicken stew then. But first I'm afraid I need the loo. Can you help me up?'

Jack was better this time at getting Brian into a standing position.

'Commode or toilet?'

'The fucking toilet.'

'Number one or number two?'

'One. God, this is so degrading,' groaned Brian. 'I knew this was a bad idea.'

'Nonsense,' said Jack. 'Here we go?'

The two of them managed to hop into the small toilet and Jack undid Brian's pyjama bottoms.

'Do you want me to hold it for you?'

'No, thanks, you're all right. I can manage.'

'If you lean on the wall with your shoulder you should be able to stand on your own for a moment - or do you want me stay and support you?'

'Fuck off. I'll be all right.'

'Just shout if you need anything. If I hear a crash, I'll just come in anyway, shall I?'

Brian laughed, seeing the funny side of it all.

'Thanks for doing this, Jack. I won't forget it.'

Chapter 56

Brian had been at Jack's for two weeks and they had settled easily into something of a routine. After breakfast Jack would usually go and do any shopping that he needed to do and then go to the gym and work out for an hour or so. Every other day Jack gave Brian a bed bath. Today was bath day. In the evenings they often had friends over for dinner. Brian could sit comfortably at the table now, but was still struggling to eat with a fork, so Jack had to help him. Toby, Declan, Annette and Gloria had been over last night and Brian had enjoyed seeing them again.

Gloria had given Jack all the office gossip and taken great pleasure in telling him that Lisa was off work with stress. Apparently her hair had started to fall out after her last unfortunate visit to the hairdressers. A dermatologist had identified a toxic substance on her scalp that had probably been in the hair dye they had used. Her scalp had at first itched like a baboon's butt and had then turned an angry red colour to match. To make matters worse, a few days later her hair had started to fall out in clumps when she brushed it. Gloria had taken the opportunity to kick whilst down, and had bought her a hat. That had been the straw that broke the camel's back and Lisa had been off work ever since.

Clare had come to visit Brian a few times, as had his parents. Donald had been very busy and hadn't been able to make it, but he had spoken to Brian on the phone.

'Look what I've got you,' said Jack, coming home, taking two cakes out of a plastic bag.

'I am going to be as fat as an ox by the time I'm mended. I'm eating twice as much as I used to and I'm hardly moving either,' complained Brian.

'I'll eat them both then, shall I?'

'No, you're all right. One more won't make any difference.'

'It's lovely outside. Let's have these on the terrace. I'll just pop them on the table and come back for you so you can hop out.'

'Cheers,' said Brian.

They were soon enjoying the sunshine and drinking their iced coffees on the patio chairs. Brian could now balance a glass on one palm, but still preferred to use a straw. Jack was wearing beige shorts and a white vest and Brian just had a pair of blue check boxers on.

'This was Mark's favourite flavour,' said Jack, putting down his banana and caramel frappé. I'm surprised he didn't turn into a banana, the number of these things he used to get through.'

Brian smiled. 'He was a funny guy. Declan was in stitches at the some of things he came out with.'

'He was, wasn't he? I can imagine that he was even funnier, all dressed up, being the centre of attention. Clare gave me a photo that she took just before they went out that night. It's a bit mad, but that's the only one I've got of him.'

'You're not kidding,' said Brian. 'Are you sure you're all right, talking like this?'

'I am, yes. We only have our memories of him now and they should be cherished. I hate it that sometimes when people die they suddenly become paragons of virtue and almost saintly, all of their faults forgotten. That's garbage. I want to tell it as it is. That said, I can't think of a bad word to say about him.'

'You're doing really well.'

'Thanks. I saw Tom this morning. He was just arriving at the workshop when I was passing on the way to the market so I stopped to say hello.'

'Oh, right. I called him yesterday to see if he'd managed to finish the garden bench and he said he was going to go in today.'

'You like him, don't you?' said Jack.

'Course I do. Why shouldn't I? He's a good worker.'

'Did he ever tell you what his problem was?'

'Eh?'

'Ages ago you said that he was feeling down and had some problems with his girlfriend or something.'

'Oh, that. Yes. All sorted out now, I think.'

'Well, what was it?'

'I can't tell you. I'm afraid I'm sworn to secrecy,' said Brian, taking a slurp of coffee.

'Come on, you can tell me, I'm not going to say anything to him, am I?'

'No, I can't,' said Brian, laughing.

'Fine, don't tell me then. But just remember that. Next time you want to go to the toilet I might be busy.'

'All right, all right, but you'd better not say anything. I don't want to see him embarrassed.'

'I won't utter a single word,' promised Jack, waiting with baited breath.

'You remember that he kept scratching when we were over at Donald's?'

'How can I forget? It was delightful.'

'His girlfriend had told him he was scratching because he didn't wash enough.'

Jack made a 'you what?' face.

'It was a ridiculous thing to say, I know. Anyway, he went along with what she said and of course, despite washing and scrubbing three times a day, he was still uncomfortable and scratching. After two more weeks she refused to sleep with him any more so I told him I thought he might have crabs. I also told him that unless he had slept with someone else, he must have caught them from her.'

'The rotten bitch.'

'I know. He's very naïve, but I persuaded him to have it out with her properly. So he did. Turned out she'd been sleeping with one of his mates and she got the crabs from him.'

'Poor guy! So what happened next?'

'He dumped her. He actually seems much happier - and he finally got rid of the little bastards with a good cream I recommended from the pharmacy.'

'Well, at least he's sorted it out,' said Jack.

'Anyway, I also told him you thought he and Donald were always at it in Donald's potting shed.'

Jack was mortified.

'You didn't, did you?' he gasped, spilling some frappé on his shorts.

Brian nodded solemnly.

'I thought he had a right to know.'

'Oh, my God! I won't ever be able to look him in the eye again. What the hell did you have to tell him that for?' cried Jack, standing up.

'Of course I didn't tell him! But it was fun winding you up.'

'Right! Just you wait. I'll get you back for that,' said Jack, flicking Brian's left ear.

'Ouch! Stop that, it hurts.'

'I think it's time for your bath,' announced Jack.

'Not while you're angry. Let's wait a bit, until you've calmed down.'

'No, now's perfect. I'm really in the mood. It's such a sunny day, why don't we do it out here for a change? I'll just go and sort out what we need.'

'Out here?' Brian spluttered.

Jack went inside to get a large tub of warm water, some shower gel, a sponge, a cloth, a towel, a clean pair of boxer shorts and a clean vest.

'Oh come on, Jack,' said Brian. 'Do we have to do it out here? I don't even need a bath. Every three or four days will be fine.'

'It most certainly won't be. That's far too unhygienic,' he said, putting the bathing accessories down onto the terrace floor. 'Look, if I pull this sun lounger over here, none of the neighbours will be able to see us. These potted plants and the geraniums hanging down from the garden boxes will make sure that your naked ass remains completely private.'

Brian reluctantly conceded. Jack helped him to lie flat on his back on the plastic sun lounger.

'Isn't it too hard without the cushion?' asked Jack. 'I didn't want to get it soaking wet.'

'It's fine.'

Jack slowly lifted each arm in turn.

'Does it hurt when I lift?'

'It feels a lot better than last time.'

Jack washed first underneath Brian's arms and then moved on to sponge his chest and torso, wringing the sponge out every now and then in the tub of hot water.

Brian had closed his eyes.

'It's actually quite nice lying here in the sun,' he said. 'I could get used to having a maid. Let's leave the bottom half for today, though. I'm good.'

'It's no trouble at all. I've seen everything before,' said Jack, hooking his fingers into the elastic waist of Brian's boxer shorts and easing them down over the plaster to take them off.

'There you go. That was straightforward enough, wasn't it?'

Brian groaned, opening his eyes, staring at the top of a tree.

'Stop being a big baby.'

He washed Brian's good leg first and then squeezed the sponge over Brian's stomach before gently working with the soapy water.

'Isn't this fun? It certainly beats being in the office. I have no regrets at all about leaving my job. Gloria begged me to consider coming back now that Lisa is out for the picture for a while, but I said no. I'm going to enjoy having a bit of time off, and think properly about what I want to do next.'

'Shit,' said Brian.

He was getting a hard-on.

'I didn't know you cared,' exclaimed Jack.

'I don't fucking care! It's just that it's been so long.'

Brian closed his eyes again, willing it to subside.

'Well, I know I said I've seen it all before, Brian, but frankly I haven't seen that,' he said, as Brian's erection uncontrollably peaked, spurred on by the warm sunshine.

'I'm sorry - I can't help it,' said Brian defencelessly.

'All right, then. If you really want me to, then I suppose as a mission of mercy, I could help.'

'No you won't! Just stop that. Put the fucking sponge down for a minute, will you?'

'I know what we'll do,' said Jack, enjoying Brian's predicament immensely. 'Let's flip you over so we can't see it and then I can get on with your back.'

Brian tried to object, but was at a distinct disadvantage. Doing nothing wasn't really an option either.

'You don't need to be embarrassed about it,' said Jack once he had got Brian face down and spread-eagled on the sun lounger. 'It's a perfectly normal biological reaction to a physical stimulus.'

'Nothing to be embarrassed about? Just look at me!'

'Here, put this under your chin,' said Jack, folding up a small towel.

Jack scrubbed Brian's neck and shoulders, applying a bit more pressure, but being careful not to get the plaster wet.

'I still like your tattoo,' he admired, working the lather down towards Brian's lower back.

'Never mind the tattoo. Just get on with what you're doing, if you must - and do it quickly.'

'Well, thanks very much, Brian. Anyone would think we were doing this for my benefit. How's that?' grinned Jack, washing in a circular motion over Brian's muscular buttocks. 'Not too hot, I hope.'

'Do you mind? I'll need a drink after all this.'

'Almost there. Is it safe to turn you back over yet?'

'Very funny, but yes, I think… ouch! What the fuck are you doing?'

'Sorry - slipped,' laughed Jack.

Jack finished off by washing the back of Brian's good leg and his feet.

While Brian was still lying face down, Jack shouted out loudly and cheerfully,

'Good afternoon, Mrs Petrovski! It's a lovely day for it, isn't it?'

Brian's body stiffened.

'Who the hell is that?' he coughed.

'It's only my neighbour, Mrs Petrovski. She was just pruning the wisteria from her balcony.'

'But I thought you said no-one could see us here.'

'Calm down, I'm only joking,' chuckled Jack. 'She wasn't even on her balcony. That was your payback for winding me up about Tom,' he said, helping Brian to put on the clean pair of boxer shorts that he had brought for him.

'You bastard,' said Brian, through clenched teeth. 'Just wait until my arms are out of this plaster! I'm going to… '

They were interrupted by the doorbell.

Jack went inside to answer it. A few moments later he came back out onto the terrace.

'It's someone to see you.'

'Great. I'm not even dressed. Can you ask them to come back another time?'

'You'll never forgive me if I do that.'

'Why, who is it?' asked Brian, wriggling into the boxer shorts that Jack had just pulled up over his plaster.

'It's Jessica.'

Chapter 51

Jack opened the door and led Jessica out onto the terrace.

'Hello, Brian,' she said.

'Jessica! What a brilliant surprise!' said Brian, wishing he'd had more time to sort himself out and get ready. He was all over the place. What was she doing here? After his attempts to try to see her over the last few months hadn't worked out, he'd practically given up all hope. Now here she was, looking even more stunning than he remembered, her dark hair falling over her bare shoulders.

'I hope you don't mind me coming to visit like this. Dad told me where you were staying.'

'No, no, it's fine. I'm sorry I can't get up,' he smiled.

'Don't even try. I brought you these, and this,' she said, waving a bunch of tulips in one hand and a bottle of champagne in the other.'

'You shouldn't have,' said Brian beaming, 'but thanks.'

'Shall I take those and put them in some water?' asked Jack, taking the flowers.

'Yes, please.'

'Can I get you something to drink, Jessica? I've got a very good white wine that should be nice and chilled by now.'

'That sounds great. Thanks, Jack.'

'Yeah, same for me, mate,' said Brian, still not believing that Jessica was actually standing next to him, here on Jack's terrace.

'Please, sit down,' he said to her, nodding towards one of the chairs.

Jessica pulled up a chair and sat down.

'Nice skirt,' said Brian, admiring her long smooth legs.

'Do you think so? Thanks. I bought it in Spain.'

For a moment they both looked uncomfortable at the mention of Spain, but then Jack came back with the drinks.

'There we are,' he said, setting the tray down on the table. 'This is a lovely wine. I hope you like it.'

Jack had brought out three glasses but only poured wine into two of them, before putting the bottle into a cooler.

'Aren't you having one?' asked Brian.

Jack handed one glass to Jessica and put a straw in the other, before putting it on the small table next to Brian.

'Not just yet. I'm really sorry, but I've just remembered I forgot to buy the fish for tomorrow from the market,' he said, giving Brian a sly wink. 'I'm going to have to go back out and see if Toby still has anything decent.'

'Oh, no. What a shame,' said Brian.

'Jessica, lovely to see you again,' said Jack, getting up to go. 'There's plenty more wine in the fridge. Help yourselves to anything.'

'Thanks, Jack,' said Jessica, taking a sip of wine. 'Mmmm, this is gorgeous.'

'Cheers! See you later, mate,' said Brian.

'So, how are you getting on?' Jessica asked, looking him up and down. 'It must be so awkward with both arms *and* a leg in plaster.'

'It looks worse that it is. Sorry about the lack of clothes. I wasn't expecting visitors.'

'Oh, don't worry about that. You look fine,' said Jessica. 'Are you sure you don't mind me just coming over? I should probably have called first, but I didn't want to talk on the phone so I thought I'd just surprise you.'

'You certainly did that,' said Brian, finishing off his wine. 'I almost fell off my sunlounger when Jack said you were here!'

'Shall I pour you another drink?'

'Yes, please.'

Jessica took the bottle from the cooler and leaned over Brian to reach his glass to refill it. He could smell her perfume, and couldn't resist casting a quick glance at her cleavage only inches away, barely concealed by a delicate-looking white lace top.

'When Dad told me that you were planning to come over to Barcelona I was really pleased. More than that - I was over the moon that you still cared so much.'

'Really?' asked Brian, breaking out into a wide grin. 'Donald didn't tell me that bit.'

'I know. I asked him not to because I wanted to tell you myself. I fancied you too, you know, right from day one. When you asked me out at your exhibition I was so tempted to say yes. But I was with Paolo and things were actually OK with him then.'

'So what happened?'

Jessica poured herself another drink. Her eyes sparkled in the sunshine as she took a sip.

'We were on the beach one afternoon when a guy came over and started making a scene about why Paolo hadn't called him. It was so embarrassing. The beach was packed and everyone could hear. Paolo started shouting at him and yelling at me too, saying that he'd never even seen the guy before.'

Brian just listened.

'That was the last straw. Something inside me changed. Yes, you and Jack had told the truth about him all along. He obviously did seem to have 'flexible interests'. But it wasn't just that. I found out that he had a bit of a cocaine habit too. A big one - and it was costing a fortune. One day I even caught him stealing money from my purse. The drugs were causing horrible mood swings and he had started to get violent sometimes.'

Brian stroked Jessica's arm with his fingertips.

'You don't have to tell me if you don't want to.'

Jessica wiped a tear from her eye.

'After we got back from the beach I told him I wanted to

end it, that it was over. I knew he had nothing left and probably nowhere to go. Everything he owned had gone up his nostrils. But I just couldn't take any more. He swore he didn't know the guy on the beach and begged me not to throw him out. As I was stuffing his clothes into a suitcase he suddenly turned into a monster. It was a compete change. There was no warning. He grabbed me by the hair and smashed my face into the bedroom wall. It broke my nose. Then he punched me in the stomach so hard that I thought I was going to die. I fell to the ground, crying in agony, and he just left me there.'

'I'm so sorry,' said Brian softly, shocked.

'It's all right. I'm angry that I didn't get chance to hit him back because he'd caught me by surprise. I couldn't come back to England because my face was such a mess. I had two black eyes and a broken nose. Dad would have worried himself sick if I had told him, so I decided to stay in Spain until my wounds had healed. I needed time to get my head around everything too.'

'What a bastard! I know it's no consolation, but you look absolutely gorgeous now.'

Jessica lifted her head.

'Do I? I'm sure my nose is still a bit bent,' she said, moving her head.

'No, it's not. It's beautiful. Come here.'

Jessica leant down and kissed him on the mouth, her lips full and soft.

'I've missed you,' said Brian. 'I know we hardly know each other, but I've still missed you. I wanted you from the first time I saw that photograph on Donald's landing. I've thought about no one else since.'

Jessica looked deep into his eyes.

'I'm sorry I was horrible to you. Can we start again and pretend that today's our first day?'

'What did you say your name was?' said Brian, with a smile.

She kissed him again, this time more passionately, her

tongue pushing his lips apart. Brian almost melted away, it felt so good. Jessica put her hands around his neck, gently stroking the back of his head before moving her mouth down to kiss his neck.

'Shit,' said Brian.

'What is it?' asked Jessica sitting up.

She didn't need telling. For the second time that afternoon he'd made a marquee out of his boxers.

'You are pleased to see me, aren't you?'

'I'm sorry. I can't help it. This is so… '

Jessica interrupted him with another hot kiss as she grabbed his cock through the thin cotton. Brian was taken completely off guard and let out a loud groan. She stood up and had another mouthful of wine, before kicking off her shoes.

'I'm not normally this forward on a first date, but I've been dying to do this for weeks.'

Brian stared at her in amazement as she slipped off her briefs and threw them under the table.

'I'm not complaining,' said Brian eagerly, watching her produce a condom from her handbag and lay it on the table next to them. 'Good to see you're well prepared,' he laughed, a little nervously.

'That's me,' she said, pulling up her short skirt and straddling him. She rubbed herself up and down, pressing herself against him.

'Oh, that's fucking fantastic. Don't stop,' he said, reaching under her top to caress her breasts.

She leant down to kiss him again before standing up, her breathing now faster as she took the condom out of its wrapper.

'Ready?' she asked, pulling down his shorts.

'I feel like I'm going to explode.'

'Just hang on for a few more minutes,' she said, unrolling the condom over his cock.

'Oh, yes!' she cried, as she slid down, her hands outstretched behind her on the sun lounger.

Jessica groaned as she moved carefully and expertly, bringing them both closer and closer.

'I'm sorry - I just can't hold off much longer,' gasped Brian.

'That's it - just there,' she cried as her orgasm washed over her in sharp waves, her legs trembling. She held her grip as Brian cried out, joining her in ecstasy.

'That was fucking great,' she said panting, standing up after a few moments and pulling her skirt down.

'You're telling me! Wow, Jessica,' said Brian, completely taken aback by what had just happened.

'I'll just do something with this,' she said, gently taking off the condom and wrapping it in a tissue. 'Any chance I could have a quick shower?'

'Of course, you go ahead. It's upstairs. Jack usually leaves clean towels out. I'd show you myself, but I still can't manage the stairs very well. Actually, if you wouldn't mind just getting me a sponge and a bowl of water first, that'd be great. There are some boxers in the drawer next to the sofa-bed.'

Jessica came back two minutes later.

'You must think I'm a complete slut. I don't know what came over me,' she said as she washed him.

'Not at all! I think you're wonderful. That was worth all the waiting.'

She smiled as she helped him to put on the clean pair of shorts she had found.

'Yes, it was. Right, I'll just run upstairs and sort myself out,' she said, retrieving her briefs.

Brian couldn't believe his luck and was grinning from ear to ear as he lay on the sun lounger. For the first time in months he felt on top of the world. Out of the corner of his eye he noticed something moving across the road. It was Jack's neighbour, Mrs Petrovski. She was now indeed on her balcony, pruning the wisteria. Brian had no idea how long she had been there, but she would have been able to see and probably hear everything. He closed his eyes, feeling like an ostrich that wanted to bury its head, listening to her snipping away with her garden shears.

Twenty minutes later Jessica came back down.

'That's better,' she said, looking at her watch.

'You look lovely.'

'Are you sure you still want to see me again? I'll understand if you don't.'

'Are you kidding? Wild horses wouldn't keep me away.'

'I want to see you again too, soon. Here's my number,' she said, scribbling it down on a piece of paper. 'I've got to dash now. You'll call me?'

'You bet,' he said as she bent down to kiss him goodbye.

Jack came back home soon after Jessica had gone. Brian was still lying out on the terrace in exactly the same place that Jack had left him.

'Well? How did it go? Where is she?' he asked, looking around as he went outside.

'You just missed her. But let's just say I needed another wash.'

'You dirty bastard. I knew it!'

Chapter 58

Jack had been out for lunch with Gloria and was walking through Russell Square on his way back home. Jessica had been round to visit Brian practically every day, so Jack had tried to make him himself scarce to give them some privacy. As he passed the fountain he bumped into Mrs Petrovski. She hadn't been able to resist asking him who the young couple were that had enjoyed sunbathing on his terrace so much the other day. With anyone else Jack would have been embarrassed, but he knew Mrs Petrovski well enough to know that she wouldn't have been in the least offended by Brian and Jessica's public display of affection and lust. He had always thought it odd that older people tended to be treated as if they had never had sex in their lives, and only wanted to talk about the weather and their ailments. Mrs Petrovski certainly didn't.

'I'm back!' shouted Jack as he opened the door.

Jessica was in the kitchen and Brian was sitting on the sofa. He was now much better on his crutches and could even stand up by himself.

'Hiya, Jack!' he shouted. 'How was your lunch?'

'I was just making some tea,' said Jessica. 'Would do you like some?'

Jessica had apologised to Jack for her behaviour towards him after he'd first shared his experiences of Paolo with her two months ago. He'd told her not to give it another moment's thought.

'Tea would be great, thanks. Lunch was more liquid than solid, but it was good to catch up with Gloria again. I'm amazed she's still seeing Declan. This must be a record for him, isn't it?'

Brian laughed.

'You're damned right. It's the longest I've ever known him to be with anyone.'

'Who's Declan?' asked Jessica, putting Brian's mug of tea down on the glass table.

'He's one of my mates - works on the market in Dalston next to my workshop. You'll meet him soon.'

Jessica sat down next to Brian. Although Jack was delighted for him that he had finally got to see Jessica again, things were getting a little crowded in his flat. She was nice enough, and he thoroughly approved of their blossoming romance, but he was beginning to feel a bit like a guest in his own home.

'Jack, I've been doing some thinking, and we've been doing some talking,' said Brian soberly, holding Jessica's hand with his fingertips.

'You're not getting married already, are you?'

'Of course we're not getting married! Whatever gave you that idea?'

'The tone of your voice, and the fact that you're sitting there together like conjoined twins.'

'I think it's time I moved out,' said Brian slowly, keeping his eye on Jack, not wanting to hurt his feelings.

'What? But where will you go?'

'Back home. I can almost manage now and Jessica has said that she'll help. With a bit of luck this plaster will be off in a few weeks and I'll be as right as rain.'

'I see,' said Jack, trying not to sound too pleased with the suggestion.

'You've been so good to me since I came out of hospital. I couldn't have done it on my own, but I don't want to outstay my welcome.'

'It's fine. When are you going, then?' asked Jack folding his arms.

'You don't mind, do you?' said Jessica, feeling a little uncomfortable.

'Oh come on, don't be like that,' said Brian. 'We're best mates, but you need a break and some space too. You've been looking after me round the clock for weeks.'

Figuring he'd seemed hurt enough, and having enjoyed Brian's little guilt trip, Jack straightened his face.

'You're right - and anyway, you two need more time alone together. You have a lot of... catching up to do. By the way, I saw Mrs Petrovski just now. She sends her regards.'

'I was so embarrassed,' said Brian.

'Don't be. She said she wants to borrow your sunscreen, if it has that effect on people.'

They all laughed.

'I'll probably go tomorrow, if that's all right with you. We'll get my things ready tonight.'

'Don't worry, Jack,' said Jessica, 'I'll make sure he's OK.'

'I can't thank you enough, you know,' said Brian.

'Right, that's quite enough of the sentimentalities. I've got one last bottle of champagne left in the fridge, so let's have that to celebrate your new beginning,' said Jack, walking over to the kitchen.

The cork hit the ceiling when he opened the bottle and he had to rush to make sure that most of the champagne went into the glasses and not down the sink.

'To the happy couple,' said Jack, raising his glass.

The three of them were chatting and enjoying their champagne when Brian's phone started to ring.

'Hello. Yes, it is.'

Brian listened for a few minutes, looking agitated.

'And you want me to come to the station now?'

Jack looked at Jessica.

'I'll be there as soon as I can,' he said, hanging up. 'That was the police.'

'I'll get your pullover,' said Jack, 'and come with you.'

'I'll come too,' said Jessica.

It was the first time Brian had been out since arriving at Jack's flat and it took a while to get him down the winding staircase.

'Did they say what they wanted to ask you?' asked Jack, once they were in a taxi on their way to Holborn Police Station.

'Not really. They just said that they had something to show me if I could make it over to the station.'

The police wanted to see Brian alone, so Jack and Jessica had to wait at the front desk.

'Thanks for coming to the station,' said the sergeant, helping Brian to sit down.

'What is it you want me to see?'

The sergeant sat down opposite him.

'We've matched the DNA that we found on you and your friend to a suspect.'

'Really? How did you find him?'

'It was by chance, really. Some photographs were passed on to me recently that another station received a while back. They were of a man involved in a robbery, sent anonymously through the post. The victim of the robbery had reported that she had been mugged in the same alleyway that we'd found you in that night. I thought that was a bit of a coincidence when I saw it, so we ran some DNA tests on the suspect. It was a perfect match. The photographs are very professional,' he said, taking out a brown envelope from the filing cabinet behind him. 'I think we have enough evidence to put him away, but I'd like you to take a look at the photographs before we bring him in. Maybe something will come back to you, and you might recognise him. It would obviously strengthen the case even more if you did. It was definitely the same place. You can even see the lamp-post next to the tree here.'

Brian stared down at the photographs that the sergeant was spreading out on the desk in front of him. He couldn't believe what he was seeing. He did recognise the man, but not from the night of the attack. He recognised the man because he knew him. It was Paolo.

Chapter 59

Clare and Jack were hanging out on Jack's terrace. It was Saturday afternoon and the weather was beautiful. There wasn't a cloud in the sky.

'Isn't this wonderful?' sighed Clare, stretching out her legs, curling her toes with glee. 'You do make a wicked Long Island iced tea,' she said, taking a sip from her cocktail glass.

'It's a bit decadent for a Saturday afternoon, isn't it? But the weather's supposed to break tomorrow, so we have to make the most of it. I need a refill,' he said, taking off his sunglasses before picking up an enormous jug to pour himself another drink.

'Top-up?'

'You don't need to ask,' she smiled. 'Thanks.'

'Your shoulders are looking a bit red. You should put some more sunscreen on. What factor are you using?'

'Fifteen.'

'That's way too low. You should always use at least factor thirty.'

'Thirty? This is London, not Florida. If I use factor thirty I'll probably end up being paler by the end of the afternoon than I was at the beginning of it. We haven't all got time to spend the week sunbathing - some of us have to work. Today's my only chance for some exposure to the sun and I intend to get a bit of colour.'

'You're making me feel *so* guilty,' said Jack, who'd been able to build up a slow tan during the heatwave that London had been blessed with.

'You're so lucky not to have been working, with this great weather,' said Clare enviously.

They lay there basking in the sun for another hour, drifting in and out of a cocktail-induced doze.

'I can't believe it's been almost two months since the trial,' said Jack suddenly.

'Is it really that long already?'

Paolo had been arrested shortly after Brian had been to the police station. The evidence against him had been so compelling that his legal aid had advised him to plead guilty to the charges, which he did. In addition to the DNA evidence and the photographs, Brian had made a statement that a recording of Paolo's voice was the voice of the man that murdered Mark. They never did find out where the photographs of the other mugging had originated from, but that hadn't mattered for the case.

'I still can't believe it. What are the chances of one lover killing another without them even knowing what they had in common? I know Paolo wasn't really a lover in that sense - not like Mark was - but you know what I mean.'

'Me neither. But life is full of coincidences, isn't it? That's what it's made up of. By doing things we make things happen. Actions cause reactions, sparking catalysts for other things to happen. If we all lived cocooned at home and made no contact with anybody else, the only certainty would be this: there would be no coincidences.'

Jack reflected on her wise words. 'Where did you get that from?'

'I just made it up,' she said with a giggle. 'It must be this Long Island iced tea - it's so strong. I'm sorry for laughing,' she added, composing herself.

'It's all right. In a way everything that's happened since has helped with closure. I still miss him, though.'

'I know. Mark was very special.'

'Salmon and cream cheese bagel? I bought them on Brick

Lane this morning,' he said, wanting to talk about something else.

'Mmmm, fantastic. I'm starving,' said Clare, as her stomach reminded her that she'd only eaten an apple and a muesli bar all day.

Jack got up to go to the kitchen and returned with a plateful of fresh bagels.

'These are delicious,' said Clare heartily, ploughing through three of them. 'They're so chewy.'

'They're the best in London, aren't they?'

'Have you decided what to do next about work yet?' she asked, lying back down on the sun lounger, her hunger satiated.

'Not exactly, but I definitely want to do something different - something that's helping people. It sounds really clichéd, but it feels like the right direction.'

'If that's what you want to do, go for it.'

'I kind of liked looking after Brian. I enjoyed helping him, and got a lot of satisfaction from watching him grow stronger again. Maybe I'll re-train as a care worker or a paramedic or something. I'm going to leave it for a few more weeks and then get on with sorting something out in September.'

'Good for you. We're only on this planet once, as far as I know, so we've got to make the most of it.'

'How about you?' he asked, refilling their glasses. 'Did you have a good week?'

'It was all right, actually. Grace has been much better since we sorted out Japan. I'm really proud of myself for standing up to her a bit more. I'm sure it was all down to the sheer power of the nicotine withdrawal pangs I had at the time. They gave me the courage. I think I've gained about an inch more slack on my leash, but that's about it,' she laughed. 'I am so glad we're not sitting here with an ashtray full of cigarette-ends like we used to be. But maybe we could just have one? You must have kept some for posterity.'

'No, we can't and no, I didn't,' Jack replied, rubbing more sunscreen onto his arms.

'I thought as much,' she sighed. 'Anyway, I'm bursting to tell you something.'

'Ok then, burst.'

'I'm going to Australia! Grace has finally put my business plan to the Board and they've agreed to proceed with secondary research. And that means I have to fly out there!'

'You're so lucky! Well done you.'

'Thanks. I'm really pleased about it. I can't wait to go.'

'When are you going? You'll need more than factor thirty over there if it's in the summer.'

'In about eight weeks. It'll be spring, so hopefully not too hot.'

'I can't say I'm not just a bit envious,' admitted Jack. 'I don't suppose I'll ever have a job that pays for me to go to Australia, but then I couldn't put in as much effort as you do. I don't know how you do it sometimes.'

'It is really hard work, but I'm not going to do it forever. It's fine while I'm single, and I love the travel. Who knows? - maybe I'll meet someone over there.'

'You'd better not. You're not moving away from me. Mind you, I could come over and stay for months at a time. I'll help you find a man in Alice Springs.'

'Alice Springs?' she scoffed. 'I'm sticking to the big cities.'

'I'm sure you'll have a blast.'

'Speaking of men, Robert Kaaps called me again yesterday. He's going to be in London next week and wants to meet up.'

'Well, there you go! When are you seeing him?'

'I don't know if I will. It was fun and daring and he was nice enough, despite not being my usual type I suppose, but I'm kind of all right at the moment just being me, being here with you - know what I mean?'

Jack's phone started to vibrate.

'Hey, Brian! How's it all going up there?'

Brian was in Manchester with Jessica for the final of the National Designer of the Year Award. He was back on his feet now and had slowly started to rehabilitate and do some bits and pieces in his workshop. He and Jessica had been practically inseparable since he had moved back home and he looked happier than Jack had ever seen him.

'I'm glad you like Manchester. It's a fantastic city, isn't it? You're in Spinningfields? I know - there are some great restaurants there. Sorry, what did you say? You've what? You've won the competition!' he shouted down the phone, looking at Clare, who was clapping. 'That's brilliant!'

'Congratulations, Brian!' yelled Clare.

'That was Clare. We're so pleased for you! OK - see you in a couple of days.'

'Isn't that great?' said Clare after Jack had hung up. 'He really deserves it.'

'Shall we organise a celebration party for him when he gets back?' suggested Jack.

'Oh yes, that's a lovely idea. Where should we have it?'

'We could go to Spartacus in Soho and I'll ask Donald to come along too. I'm sure he'd want to celebrate Brian's win.'

'So I might finally get to meet him! About bloody time too, considering he's practically Brian's father-in-law. You know that Rachel and Heike will be here for the weekend, don't you?'

'Are they? When are they coming?'

'On Friday - and they're staying with me at my house until Monday.'

'Let's have the party next Saturday, then. I'll check that everyone else can make it. I think that calls for another cocktail, don't you?'

'More cocktails?' she groaned, already feeling sloshed.

Jack stood up and strolled inside to the kitchen.

'Oh, no!' she heard him cry.

'What is it?'

'We're all out of Coke. I don't suppose you fancy some exercise?' he asked, looking pleadingly at Clare.

'Oh, all right - I'll go,' she said, grabbing her handbag to find her purse.

'You're a star,' he said, opening the door for her.

It was boiling hot down at street level. Clare walked over to the local convenience store at the end of the road. On her way back she spotted a young man loitering outside Jack's front door. He seemed to be looking at a map. Suspecting he was just another lost tourist, she decided to offer her assistance.

'Can I help you at all?'

The young man looked up.

'I'm looking for number nineteen.'

'Really? My friend Jack lives there. You're standing right in front of it. I'm just going back in, actually. Who shall I say is looking for him?'

'Tom. Tell him it's Tom.'

Chapter 60

A warm summer breeze was rustling the leaves in the trees as Jack made his way down Shaftsbury Avenue towards Soho to celebrate Brian's victory in the design competition. Everyone could make it except Declan and Toby. They'd already booked to go to Paris that weekend with Gloria and Annette, so instead of going to the party they had clubbed together and given Brian a small present.

It had been a huge surprise for Jack to see Tom when he walked into the flat with Clare the week before. Tom had said that he'd been to the British Museum. As he knew that Jack lived close by he'd called Brian for the address, and decided to come round on the off-chance, to say hello. Jack had asked him if he wanted a drink and he'd ended up staying with them for the rest of the afternoon.

It was the August bank holiday weekend and Old Compton Street was even busier than usual. Jack got a real buzz from just taking in the good mood that everyone seemed to be in.

Donald was already holding court at his favourite table when he arrived at the bar. He was wearing his tight leather trousers again.

'Jack!' he cried, when he saw him coming in. 'There's a seat for you over here, dear. Come on and sit down next to Tom.'

Brian and Jessica were already there too.

'Hello, everyone,' said Jack.

'All right, Jack,' said Tom with a broad smile. 'Thanks again for the drinks last weekend. I really enjoyed myself.'

'Me too,' said Jack, shaking his hand.

'Would you boys like some champagne?' asked Jessica, handing each of them a glass.

'Cheers,' said Tom, looking around sheepishly. It was the first time he'd been in a gay bar.

'Thanks, Jessica. Clare and the girls should be here soon. I spoke to her a couple of minutes ago and they were just coming out of the tube station at Leicester Square.'

'This will be the first time we've all been together,' said Brian.

'I know, isn't it splendid?' said Donald. 'Is Clare the one that's had a sex change and is now expecting triplets?'

Brian and Jack both laughed.

'Don't say that to her when she arrives,' said Brian. 'She'll go bonkers. No, Rachel's the one that's having *twins* and living with another woman at the moment. Her girlfriend's called Heike.'

'That's right, yes, I remember you telling me now, dear. It must be all this champagne.'

'Here they come,' said Jack standing up to greet them.

'Rachel! My God, you're the size of a house already!'

'Lovely to see you too,' she joked, giving him a kiss. 'Hello,' she said to the others. 'I'm Rachel and this is my partner, Heike.'

Heike said hello and everyone started to kiss, shake hands, introduce themselves - or all three. Clare was last to come into the bar.

'Clare, I'd like you to meet Donald,' said Jack.

As Donald was turning around to say hello, Jack was distracted by Heike, who was trying to squeeze round him to grab a chair on the other side of the table.

'Mr Dupont!' exclaimed Clare. '*You're* Donald?'

'Clare Houghton?' he said, equally surprised.

'The very same.'

'Before you sit down would you mind helping me at the bar? I think we need some more champagne and glasses.'

Clare spoke first once they were out of earshot.

'I can't believe you're Brian and Jack's Donald!'

'Well I can assure you I am, dear.'

'But do they know?'

'I don't think so, no. Jessica does, of course, and I suppose she could have mentioned it to Brian, but nobody has said anything to me, so I guess not. They're probably not that interested anyway - but I would prefer not to have a big discussion about it now. I'll tell them another time. Today is Brian's big day.'

Clare had first met Donald just over four years ago. She'd hired him as her private detective to follow her last partner.

'Mr Dupont... '

'Donald, please.'

'Donald, I can't thank you enough for helping me with the camera. It worked a treat.'

'Oh good, I am pleased. Now, let's order that champagne.'

Donald had worked in the field of intelligence for many years. In fact, that was the reason he had gone to India in the first place. After taking early retirement he had started his own private detective business in Fitzrovia. He still enjoyed his work, but only did it part-time now.

It had been relatively easy for Donald to set Paolo up in Sitges, and he had been delighted that it had eventually brought Brian and Jessica together. Donald had secretly been over to Spain to follow Paolo to try and get some evidence that he really was sleeping around with other men, as Jack had said. He thought if he could present Jessica with hard evidence, she would surely see sense - and end the relationship. That would give Brian the second chance he needed. But the only thing he saw, on two occasions, was Paolo going to a park, where he met a man, shook hands and left. This was odd, but of no use to Donald in trying to catch him out. Maybe it had been a one-off with Jack - who knows? So instead, Donald decided to pay someone to make a huge scene on the beach in front of Jessica about how he had felt cheated after having sex with Paolo and then never hearing from him again. That seemed to have done the trick.

Even so, Donald had been curious about what Paolo had been up to in the park, so he had continued following him for a couple of weeks. Jessica had thrown him out and he'd returned to London. It was on the last day of tailing him that Donald had witnessed him mugging an elderly lady in Tufnell Park. There hadn't been any violence and Paolo had run off like a shot, but Donald had managed to take some photographs, even though he'd been some distance away. Once developed, the photographs didn't actually look like conclusive images of a mugging. Some of the snaps even looked as if the two of them were laughing together.

Donald had sent the pictures anonymously to the police anyway, along with details of where the incident had taken place and where they could find Paolo. He'd thought that the photographs might be useful if the woman reported the incident. The sergeant then made the all-important link after Brian was attacked. Jessica had no idea about Donald's role in any of it - and he preferred to keep it that way.

'Here we are,' said Donald, putting two bottles of champagne down on the table. Clare was carrying a tray with another bottle and four more glasses.

'Tom, could you open these and do the honours, please?'

'No probs,' he said, taking hold of a bottle.

Once everyone had a drink in their hand, Donald started to tap a pen on his glass. He stood up.

'May I first say how delightful all of this is? It really is lovely to see those of you I already know again, and also to meet some of their friends, who I have heard so much about.'

'Hear, hear,' said Rachel, putting an arm around Jack.

'I'd like to propose a toast to our master craftsman,' he said looking at Brian, whose face was now turning bright red.

'To the best furniture designer in the country,' continued Donald. 'To Brian.'

'To Brian!' everyone cheered, chinking glasses and looking at him as his face burned.

'And may I also say how pleased I am that Brian is now

392

courting my daughter Jessica? I couldn't have picked a better man for her myself, even if I had tried.'

Tom, Jack, Clare and Heike were all clapping and Rachel was hugging Brian, almost squashing the twins in the process.

'I don't know what to say,' said Brian, after his colour had returned to normal. 'Thanks to you all for coming today. Thanks to Donald for all this champagne. Thanks to Jessica for being my girlfriend. Thanks to Rachel, Clare and Heike for being there when I needed someone the most and thanks to Tom for keeping my business going. Lastly, a huge thanks to you, Jack, for looking after me like you did when I couldn't walk or help myself at all. I couldn't wish for better friends. I feel very lucky.'

Jack felt a lump in his throat.

'I still miss our bathtimes,' he said, giving Jack a wink, which made him laugh.

'Jessica and I are going to New York next week for a short holiday to celebrate. We're going to stay with my brother. So I'd like to propose a toast to everyone here. To friends!'

'To friends!' everyone joined in.

'Now I am jealous,' said Jack to Brian as they sat back down. 'You're going to New York, and you're off to Australia,' he said, turning to Clare.

'I'm sure you'll be going away at some point too, so don't expect me to feel sorry for you. Anyway, I'm going to be working! It's not a holiday.'

'You can come with me to the Lake District in a few weeks, if you want to,' offered Tom cautiously. 'I'm going to visit my auntie.'

Jack thought for a moment and then smiled at Tom as he nodded.

'Thanks. You're on.'

Tom grinned back. 'Nice one.'

'There you go, then,' said Clare, drinking some champagne from her glass that Tom had just refilled.

Her phone started to ring. She groaned when she saw the number.

'It's Grace,' she said to Jack. 'I'd better answer it.'

She got up to go outside and paced up and down Brewer Street as she took the call, listening to her boss. She'd called to say that she was taking Monday off 'due to unforeseen personal circumstances' and that Clare would have to chair a couple of meetings that were in the diary.

'Yes, Grace, I'll take care of it. Of course. Thanks.'

She hung up and started making her way back to the bar.

'I think I owe you three bottles of champagne,' said a voice behind her.

Clare recognised the voice immediately and stopped still in her tracks.

'I think you'll find it's four bottles with interest. Luke!' she cried, turning around eagerly.

'I was just on my way to meet a couple of friends when I saw you talking on the phone. I can't believe it. How are you, Clare?' he asked excitedly.

Her smile suddenly evaporated.

'I tried calling you so many times, but couldn't get through to you. What was wrong with your phone? Why didn't you show up, or at least have the decency to call *me*?'

'I'm so sorry, Clare. I left my rucksack on the subway after we'd been out that night. My phone was in it as well as the business card you gave me. I couldn't remember when you'd said you were coming back to Japan and where I was supposed to meet you and I had no way of contacting you. I thought I'd never see you again. I don't suppose you want to, or have time for, a drink with me now, do you?'

Clare looked at him. She would have forgiven him anything.

'One drink to persuade me you're telling the truth. I'll just say goodbye to my friends and get my things.'

Clare went back into the bar and sat down briefly next to Jack, leaning over to whisper in his ear.

'You'll never guess who I've just bumped into outside. Luke! I'm going for a drink with him now, but I'm not going to make a big announcement about it. You can tell them after I've gone. I'll just sneak off. Tell Rachel I'll call her later. She's got a key. Wish me luck. I can't wait!'

Jack looked outside to where a tall, broad-shouldered man was standing. He was looking over at them.

'Is that him?'

She nodded.

'Very nice! Well, you'd better get going, before someone else makes a move on him out there.'

Once she had left the bar Jack told everyone what had happened.

'No way!' said Brian, standing up to see if he could still see them.

After another round of drinks Jack suggested going to a club for a dance. Brian and Jessica were up for it. So was Tom. Even Rachel and Heike agreed to come along for an hour.

'Donald, are you coming too?' asked Jack, as they started to get up.

'I can hardly move in these trousers, never mind dance in them. No, you young things go ahead and party the night away. I'll just have a nightcap in here.'

'Are you sure?' asked Brian, helping Jessica with her jacket.

'Yes, I'm sure. Now stop making such a fuss and go on.'

'If you say so. See you, Donald - and thanks for everything,' said Brian, shaking his hand.

'Goodnight, Dad,' said Jessica, giving him a peck on the cheek. 'Make sure you get a taxi home.'

'Bye, Donald,' shouted Jack and Tom together after Rachel and Heike had said their goodbyes.

Donald waved after them as they left, leaving him almost alone with the barman. He climbed up onto a barstool and sighed contentedly.

'Same again please, Enrico - there's a dear.'